ARE
MISSING

JAMES PATTERSON is one of the best-known and biggest-selling writers of all time. His books have sold in excess of 325 million copies worldwide. He is the author of some of the most popular series of the past two decades – the Alex Cross, Women's Murder Club, Detective Michael Bennett and Private novels – and he has written many other number one bestsellers including romance novels and stand-alone thrillers.

James is passionate about encouraging children to read. Inspired by his own son who was a reluctant reader, he also writes a range of books for young readers including the Middle School, I Funny, Treasure Hunters, House of Robots, Confessions and Maximum Ride series. James has donated millions in grants to independent bookshops and he has been the most borrowed author in UK libraries for the past ten years in a row. He lives in Florida with his wife and son.

A list of titles by James Patterson is printed
the back of this book

JAMES PATTERSON

THE MOORES ARE MISSING

WITH LOREN D. ESTLEMAN, SAM HAWKEN
AND ED CHATTERTON

arrow books

13 5 7 9 10 8 6 4 2

Arrow Books
20 Vauxhall Bridge Road
London SW1V 2SA

Arrow Books is part of the Penguin Random House group of companies
whose addresses can be found at global.penguinrandomhouse.com.

Penguin
Random House
UK

First published by Arrow Books in 2017

www.penguin.co.uk

A CIP catalogue record for this book is available from the British Library.

ISBN 9781787460065
ISBN 9781787460072 (export edition)

Printed and bound in Great Britain by Clays Ltd, St Ives Plc

CONTENTS

THE MOORES ARE MISSING
James Patterson with Loren D. Estleman   1

THE HOUSEWIFE
James Patterson with Sam Hawken   135

ABSOLUTE ZERO
James Patterson with Ed Chatterton   281

THE MOORES ARE MISSING

JAMES PATTERSON

WITH LOREN D. ESTLEMAN

PART ONE

OFF THE FACE OF THE EARTH

PART ONE

IN THE FACE OF THE ENEMY

CHAPTER 1

FORTY-ONE YEARS OLD.

I was all ready for forty. I'd prepared for it since thirty-nine. Forty-*one* blindsided me. When I blew out the candles last Tuesday, it struck me that time was speeding up, like a recorded tape whirling faster as it approaches its end. Before I know it, I'll be fifty, with hair growing out of my ears. Sixty next, getting around with a walker. Then my threescore and ten, and then death.

Thank God for Kevin; he's three months older and never whines. Like he said at my party: "Look at it this way, old-timer: Would you really want to relive your twenties, have to learn that crap all over again?" His seize-the-day attitude is contagious. He's spread it through his family, which is why I spend so much time at their place. My standing weekly appointment to shoot hoops with Kevin is mainly an excuse to see the Moores.

It's an atypical Pacific Northwest Saturday in early

spring: the sun is coming up, revealing what will be a bright blue sky scraped clean of clouds. There's still a chill in the air left over from the night. We like to get going and play early, before breakfast. Maybe we should be playing golf instead. If we played golf.

I ring the magic bell. Kevin's grin, Margo's quiet smile, will ease my worries. They're aging gracefully, visibly in love with each other and devoted to their kids, who love and respect them (when they're not driving them nuts, like healthy normal teenagers).

No one comes to answer. Margo will be cooking breakfast, the fan in the stove hood whirring loudly. Kevin in the bedroom, tying his sneakers Just Right. Josh and Gabby listening to hip-hop or playing video games in the den or texting, whatever it is young people do for entertainment now.

Ray, you're thinking like an old crank.

I ring again, wait, then reach for the button a third time. On impulse I try the door instead. The knob turns.

I frown. Our side of town has had two break-ins in six months, and less than a week ago a terrifying home invasion in Sackville, minutes from here, that left three people shot to death. We don't leave our doors unlocked anymore.

"Guys? It's Ray. LeBron couldn't make it."

I start to open the door. I don't want to spook them. I push it just enough to stick my face through the gap. "Hel-lo-o-o?"

Is it my imagination, or does my voice echo?

6

I step across the threshold into the house. I raise my voice. "Kevin? Margo?"

Buzz-click! I jump almost out of my shoes. But it's just the sound made by the retro mechanical clock on the fake fireplace mantel changing numerals. The place is that quiet.

"It's me, Ray," I say, cupping my hands around my mouth. I'm an invader now. Well-meaning neighbors have been struck down with baseball bats under similar circumstances. "Ray Gillett, not Freddie Krueger."

The house is done in excellent taste, but no antiseptic showcase. Margo manages a doctor's office, and has decorated with the same attention to detail that she brings to files and scheduling. The open living room, cozy den, spacious kitchen, three bathrooms—one on the ground floor, two on the second—are clean and relatively uncluttered. The bedrooms likewise.

And deserted. Huh. If they were in the backyard, I would have seen them as I walked over.

A side door in the kitchen opens into the attached garage. Margo's red Buick is there. There's an old oil stain on the concrete floor where Kevin parks the Flex he drives to work and uses on family outings. Maybe— but no, why would they go off on a lark when they know I'm coming?

I start to worry. This is not Moore behavior, even on Saturday, the most unpredictable day of the week.

Upstairs, I check drawers and closets. I'm violating my best friends' privacy, pure and simple. If they came home, this would be hard to explain. But I can't leave.

What would I do with the rest of my Saturday, not knowing why I'd been stood up? More important:

"Where are the Moores?" I say it aloud.

Everything's in place, as far as I can tell. All tidy—Josh's and Gabby's things casually if not carelessly kept—with no obvious sign of anything missing. Suitcases and duffels stashed out of the way in all the bedrooms. I lift Kevin and Margo's luggage by the handles. They feel empty.

I sit on the edge of Josh's mattress, feeling out of place. Is there any space more private than someone's bedroom? Or anything ruder than someone outside the family entering it without being invited?

Then I see the cell phone on Josh's dresser.

What college freshman leaves home without a way to text his friends?

I get up and go back over old ground. In Gabby's room I draw a pink sweater off the foot of the bed, revealing her iPhone in a padded pink cover.

Picking up the pace now, to the master bedroom. Kevin's slim gray phone is in a stand on the table on one side of the neatly made bed, Margo's blue case on the matching table on the other side.

I reach for Kevin's, then withdraw my hand. How far is it acceptable for a worried friend to dig into someone's privacy?

Strangers disappear, always for a reason. Not whole families with deep roots in the community. Not the Moores. There's no sign, as they say on TV, of a struggle. Silly even to think in those terms. They went out for pancakes and got caught in traffic on the way back, or simply lost track of time.

Leaving all their cell phones behind.

Worried? I wished I were only that. I don't know a word for the chilled feeling I got. It was like the feeling in a nightmare, when your car flies over a hill and there's nothing on the other side.

There's a landline in the kitchen, a yellow wall unit on an old-fashioned long coiled cord. I unhook the receiver, listen for the dial tone, and peck out 911.

CHAPTER 2

"I WOULDN'T BE TOO concerned, Mr. Gillett. You said the car's gone. Sometimes people just play hooky, without thinking to tell their friends. Maybe to unplug for a while. Kind of inconsiderate; but no reason to issue an AMBER Alert."

The Willow Grove police station wouldn't interest a Hollywood director scouting locations. The chief's office in the one-story brick building could belong to an insurance agent. The walls are painted a cheery apple-green and the framed family photo on the desk looks like a publicity still from *Leave It to Beaver*.

It's my first visit. I know Cam Howard well enough to say hello to, but thank God I've never had any official business with his department. He's middle-aged and solidly built, in an inexpensive blue suit with a tie that I suspect clips on. On him the outfit resembles a uniform. His hair is black and so thick you can see the marks of the comb. Sitting in the swivel behind his plastic woodgrain desk, he gives an impression of coiled strength.

"I thought of the same explanation, and rejected it," I say. "You don't know the Moores as well as I do, Chief. They never just take off. Kevin is the chief financial officer for a solid firm in the city and Margo runs a doctor's office. Their son is studying for a business degree, and their daughter belongs to the honor society at Willow Grove High. They're the most responsible people I've ever met."

Howard smiles tightly. "I know them; Kevin, anyway. He donates generously to the Police Athletic League. We take each other to lunch sometimes."

"He never told me that."

"He wouldn't, in case you asked how we know each other. He's the best kind of philanthropist. He never brags. I think he's a swell guy, and from what I've seen of his wife and kids, it's a Moore family trait. They all put folding green in the collection plate every Sunday."

"You go to the same church?"

"Knowing the community makes my work easier."

"In that case, you better call me Ray."

"Ray, I was a big-city cop for fifteen years, and if nothing else, I learned that people are anything but consistent. It'd be easier for us cops if they were, like on TV when a crook steps out of character and nails himself. That's why I asked you to come down, instead of sending a team to the house." He drops the reassuring smile. "I'm not brushing you off. Let's wait forty-eight hours, like it says in the book. If we don't hear from them by then, I'll turn loose the bloodhounds."

"Anything can happen in forty-eight hours."

"So can nothing. They come home, everybody lives happily ever after, and you're glad we waited. Misplaced good intentions can be as hard on a friendship as betrayal."

I lean forward in my chair, my fists clenching. "Chief. Cam. They all left their cell phones behind. Not just one of them. *All* of them. Who does that?"

"Someone who wants a holiday without any interruptions."

"Their kids are teenagers. You can't pry them away from their cells with a crowbar."

"You can if you have their respect as a parent." His eyes flick toward the family photo, then back to me.

"Cam. Chief. Just whose side are you on?"

"What've you got to make you suspect there *is* a side? You said there were no signs of force. Your friend stood you up for a date. As emergencies go, that rates pretty close to the bottom."

"This is pointless." I scrape back my chair and stand up. "An entire family falls off the face of the earth and all you can say is they're on a picnic."

"I said maybe. It's part of the job. Sit down."

Calm as his tone is, I can't overlook the command in it. I sit.

He shrugs. "Okay, the phone part's unusual. It's still not enough to justify a full-scale missing-persons investigation. I'm not a private detective. I serve the community, not one household, no matter how much they give back to it. The worst deadbeat in town is entitled to the same amount of protection as the pastor at St. Matthew's."

"You're the chief. You're supposed to give the orders, not take them."

"If I were to say that, I'd be out on my can. You should come to a town council meeting and listen to the cranks spout off every time someone in this department makes an honest mistake; you'd think we picked their pockets. How will they react if I put out an APB, get everyone in a lather, and then the Moores come back from the beach at sundown with sand in their shoes?"

"How will they react if the Moores don't come back at all and you did nothing?"

Howard's frown is as tight as his smile. "I'm liking them more and more, the friends they've got. I'll look into it, okay? Make some calls."

"You mean like the highway patrol, the hospitals, the"— I swallow. I can't say *morgue*. "I can do that myself. I need to know you're doing something I can't."

"There's a difference between when it's a civilian calling and when it's a cop. I have personal contacts with the state police. They can act unofficially, circulating descriptions throughout the department, minus the paperwork involved with a formal investigation. That's a thousand pair of trained eyes prowling the state and reporting directly to me. I'll call you if I hear anything." He spreads his hands. "Ray, it's the best I can do."

I press my lips tight, then nod. I give him a card. "I work at home. That number's good night and day. My cell's on the back."

He slips the card into his shirt pocket and holds out his hand. "Kevin's my friend, you're *his* friend. I'd like you to be mine as well."

Chief Cam Howard has a firm, dry grip. I don't find it as comforting as I'd like.

CHAPTER 3

I WORK OUT OF my home full-time. The basement's full of stereo receivers, toy rocket launchers, video-game consoles, and Waterpiks. A Golden Nerd Award stands on my bedroom dresser, presented to me by the National Association of Industrial Artists.

I've found that when an attractive woman in a cocktail bar asks my occupation, "writer" gets better mileage when I leave out the adjective "technical." When I told my barber I'm a writer, my time in his chair went from fifteen minutes to an hour. He's writing a book, just like everyone else; in his case a history of the razor. Like every barber I'd ever had, he can't talk and cut hair at the same time, so he stands in front of me waving a comb in one hand and scissors in the other, describing the development of the steel blade from imperial Rome through fin-de-siècle France with enthusiastic gestures. I resolved to clarify my job description from that day forward.

Specifically, I draft owners' manuals for various

tools and appliances. A degree in Creative Writing doesn't guarantee a living wage, as I found out when I plastered the walls in my old bedroom in my parents' house with rejections. About that same time I figured out how to set the clock on my first VCR—after throwing away the instructions—and it struck me that the people who write them may know how to assemble a complex mechanism, but can't put together a coherent sentence. So I sent letters to the manufacturers of every appliance I could think of, offering to write manuals in return for free use of their products while I figured out how they work.

That led to more rejections; but it only takes one acceptance to get a career started. After a year, Miracle Deck bought my clear and concise instructions regarding the operation of its top-of-the-line pressure-washer. More sales followed.

Give me a doohickey, any sort of doohickey. Don't tell me what it does, hold the corporate instructions, and give me forty-eight hours to figure it out on my own. I'll write you a users' guide any five-year-old could follow.

But not today.

I keep writing and rewriting the same paragraph. When I read it back, it seems like worse gibberish than those manuals translated from Japanese by a Swiss national into English. I push back from the keyboard and reach for the phone for the third time in fifteen minutes. I hit redial, and listen once again to the purring on the Moores' end of the line until the recording comes on asking if I want to leave a message. I don't.

The first time, I cut the connection and got halfway through Kevin's cell number before I remembered it would be ringing in an empty house.

I hang up again, but I let my hand rest on the handset. Is it too early to call Cam Howard? If I make a pest of myself, it might annoy him enough to let the investigation hang for pure spite.

Once can't hurt. He didn't strike me as a soulless bureaucrat—quite the opposite, in fact—and anyway a man should get something from his taxes.

"Ray, I'm glad you called."

My heart does a happy flip. "You've found them?"

"No, but there's a man here who wants to talk to you. Can you come down to the station right away?"

My heart drops back into its hollow recess. "I told you everything I know. How many people do I have to talk to before the system goes into action?"

"This one's got information to trade."

"A witness? He saw something?"

"I'll let him tell you in person."

It's a ten-minute drive downtown. I make it in six. Cam is standing behind the desk when I enter his office for the second time that day. The man in the chair where I sat earlier is even more substantial than the chief, with huge shoulders and a big head. His suit is institutional gray, his hair also, and chopped so close to the scalp I can make out the features of his skull.

"Ray Gillett, this is Dale Mercer. Mercer's a US marshal."

He rises just enough to grasp my hand quickly and let go. Gray eyes take me in from head to toe. "How well do you know Kevin Moore?" His voice is thin, but not weak; a guitar string tightened almost to the breaking point.

"Almost twenty years. I was best man at his wedding."

"Know anything about his business?"

"It provides all the maintenance for the university over in Sackville. He's chief financial officer. But what's that got to do——?"

"Maybe everything. Know who owns it?"

"Some corporation."

"Jeremy Adder's majority stockholder. Ever hear of him?"

"Rings a bell."

"Clear to Las Vegas. He uses his legit operation here to launder cash from gambling, hooking, and drug dealing. The FBI's been trying to get something on him for years."

"You're telling me Kevin works for the mob?"

"He says he didn't know. For now the Bureau's deciding to believe him, but that's not my problem. My problem is keeping him alive long enough to tell a grand jury everything he does know."

"You talked to him? When?"

"Easy, Ray." Cam tilts a palm toward another chair. I hesitate, then take it. He lowers himself into his.

"Mercer heard what I put out on the radio and came in to offer assistance."

"The witness protection program is our baby," Mercer says. "The Marshals'. We've offered Moore, his wife, and their son and daughter relocation and a new identity in return for his testimony."

"This is like something in a movie," I say. "What would Kevin know about gambling and prostitution and dope?"

"The FBI will settle for putting Adder away on those charges. It's his other activities that put us in the picture as babysitters."

"What kind of activities?"

Mercer rolls his big shoulders. "Murder. For starters."

CHAPTER 4

"ADDER'S A THROWBACK TO gangland's golden age,"
Mercer continues. "His first reaction, when he suspects
a leak, is to plug it with a corpse. He's believed to have
ordered at least sixteen hits. If he learns we've made
contact with Kevin Moore, he'll try to make it an even
twenty."

Cam says, "Isn't there some kind of underworld
code about not touching civilians?"

"With all due respect, Chief, your experience is
limited to your garden-variety crook. Whatever ro-
mantic guff you've heard about the Mafia, its mem-
bers are as cavalier about the so-called rules as they
are about the laws of the land. This one wouldn't
take the chance of assuming Kevin hasn't confided in
his family. He won't bother with the tedious business
of obtaining proof."

"This gets more ridiculous by the minute," I say.
"Whatever his boss is up to, Kevin isn't part of it."

Mercer's face draws as tight as his guitar-string

voice. Everything about this man is drawn so thin he could snap at any time.

"Maybe he is and maybe he isn't. But as chief financial officer, he has access to the books, which are what Justice needs to indict Adder. If Moore can't provide the actual records, he can tell what he knows on the stand. What's in his head is US property."

"Mystery solved," says Cam. "I'll cancel the search."

"I wouldn't do that just yet."

We stare at Mercer. The tension in his face—in his whole being—is contagious.

"I cleared this meeting with Washington when we caught the squeal. We hoped to keep this under wraps, but we can't be working at cross purposes with local law enforcement. Whether your friend's an innocent dupe or in it up to his chin, we won't know till we find him and talk to him."

"Hold on!" Cam leans forward, resting his forearms on the desk. "You just said the Marshals' office has re-located the Moores. How could you have lost Kevin?"

"I didn't say that. I said we talked to him. It was in his home, with his family present. Two agents from the Bureau told them everything I just told you, and I assured them of the Marshals' successful track record in protecting citizens from retribution. Since the couple's mothers and fathers are deceased and there are no other close relatives, the provision against maintaining contact wasn't the problem it usually is in these cases. When Mr. or Mrs. Joe Blow turns up sealed in concrete at some construction site, it's usually because they couldn't bear to spend Thanksgiving away from Aunt Tilly."

His bluntness freezes my spine. I don't like Dale Mercer. But I play the game. I need all the experienced help I can get, and so do the Moores.

"They were open to the idea; Kevin seemed genuinely shocked when we trotted out Adder's record, and everyone was nervous, the boy especially. They went into another room for a family meeting. Imagine how surprised we were when they came back in and turned us down flat."

"They must have had a reason," I say. "I've known Kevin longer than Margo. I was with him in the waiting room when their kids were born. He'd do anything to protect his family. So would she."

Cam is more direct. "Did they give an explanation?"

"We asked. The agents threatened to book Kevin as a material witness, but he called their bluff. 'I could tell you everything I know, and you wouldn't be any closer to what you want than you are now. I saw nothing wrong with the figures in the books.' Well, even the FBI can't arrest a man without probable cause. In order to hold him, they'd need the very evidence they hope he can provide."

"I thought you people pushed congress to pass a law to get around that little problem." Cam's tone is bitter.

"RICO: The Racketeer Influenced and Corrupt Organizations Act. The Supreme Court's divided on that point. The justices may look the other way when we swing it against a Don or Hells Angels or a smuggling ring, but one more appeal on behalf of Ozzie and Harriet could strike it down, and we'd lose the only effective weapon we have against organized crime. Their lawyers know the rule of law front to back."

"I've managed to operate inside it."

"Once again, Chief, you haven't had the same disadvantages we have on our level."

I definitely don't like Mercer. "I'm with Kevin. Why should a man agree to uproot his family from their home and everything they know when he has nothing to offer?"

Mercer's face now is as flat as a plank. "Then why did he do it on his own? Generally speaking, when someone refuses witpro, it means they have something to hide."

I look at Cam. "You know Kevin. Talk some sense into this guy, will you?"

"Ray." The chief is sitting back again, forted up behind the desk with his name and title block-lettered on its steel trivet. "You can afford to give your friend the benefit of the doubt. We can't. When I'm in a marked car and I stop at a red light beside a motorist who's putting just a little too much effort into looking innocent, I give him a block, then pull him over. Nine times out of ten he blows over zero-eight-percent on the Breathalyzer or has something interesting in the trunk."

"What are you getting at—*Chief*?" Hard to believe I ever called him by his first name.

"Has it ever struck you the Moores are just a little *too* perfect?"

I spring to my feet, and this time I won't be ordered to sit back down.

"I'm not a cop," I say. "I *can* afford to believe in my friends. If both of you are going to treat them like Public Enemy Number One, it's up to me to rescue them."

And for the first time in my sedate life I slam a door behind me.

CHAPTER 5

ANY SATISFACTION I MIGHT have gotten from that childish gesture doesn't last as far as my car in the municipal lot. I'm as qualified to perform a one-man rescue operation as Mr. Magoo.

Thriller fiction is full of private citizens who go off on personal crusades. They're former employees of the CIA, or play poker with plucky investigative journalists, or their girlfriend's a police stenographer.

I bat zero in all three areas.

But if I've learned anything from watching too many episodes of *Law & Order,* it's that all answers can be found at the scene of the crime.

A local police prowler painted green and white is parked in front of the Steiner house next door. Apart from that, nothing about the neighborhood suggests it's the focus of anything official. Mercer wasn't kidding when he said the Marshals prefer to keep the situation secret.

The Moores' well-kept brick house is free of barricades and yellow police tape. All it lacks from the usual Saturday-afternoon routine is Kevin out front, pruning the hedges with the sample Wonder-Cut electric clippers I gave him last Christmas. Nevertheless I cruise past, park around the corner, and stroll back around to the front door—trying not to look furtively past my shoulder to the Steiners' house, where one of Cam Howard's officers has stopped in his rounds, asking neighbors if they've seen anything unusual. No doubt my elaborate show of normal behavior is just as suspicious as if I were creeping through the hedge in a fedora and trench coat.

I have an excuse, and it may just be boneheaded enough to pass: Margo has given me a key to look after her plants while the family's away. *What, Officer? A geranium doesn't know why it's been left alone. It needs water.*

Which sounds lame even in my head.

The house now feels like a museum exhibit. It's no longer a home.

I walk through it like a stranger, my pulse pounding. This visit is worse than my last, disturbing as that was. This time I'm a housebreaker.

The authorities have been here—something about the atmosphere tells me they have, an antiseptic residue of meticulous search by disinterested parties. Uncaring hands have handled all the trophies and treasures like archaeologists sorting out ancient relics.

I commit my second felony in ten minutes. I swipe a cell phone.

Not Kevin's, or even Margo's; the pros will be sure to miss those first off. No, Gabby's pink phone in its pink case. It will be a while before the investigators discover that loss, and a while more before they eliminate all the many bureaucratic slots into which it may have disappeared. By the time they link it to dull old Ray Gillett, he may just have the case all wrapped up in a pretty pink bow.

Well, that's how it works in thriller fiction.

I'm in a hurry now, with the incriminating evidence on my person. I'm six feet from the front door when a shadow enters the frame of the pebbled glass in its window; a shadow in a peaked cap, the kind police officers wear. A key rattles in the lock.

My heart leaps into my throat; for the first time I realize the meaning of that cliché. I reverse directions, loping first across the carpet away from the front door, then forcing myself to slow down. It may be my imagination, but I can hear the boards creak under the padding.

POLICE SHOOT LOCAL MAN IN BREAK-IN, I think wildly.

The dead bolt makes a grating sound sliding back into its socket. Now I'm taking long steps and landing on my toes like a character in a Bugs Bunny cartoon. A hinge squeaks; it's unlike Kevin to let one go without oil, but I might be imagining that sound as well. I cross the threshold into the den just as the door opens.

It's a pleasant little room where the family often

huddles close on the worn sofa, watching TV. A sliding door opens onto the side deck.

A thumb-latch yields to pressure with a click that seems to me like an explosion. I grasp the handle and tug.

The door doesn't budge.

I definitely hear creaking in the living room; that carpet needs replacing. Breath rasping through my mouth, I look down at a three-foot length of dowel lying in the track. Kevin's too good a family man to trust the safety of the house to a flimsy latch. I reach down, lift out the barricade as noiselessly as possible, and lay it carefully on shag. The door slides open with a horrendous whoosh, but I don't wait to find out if it's overheard. I ease it back the other way, look right and left—the old comic-spy turn—and bound off the deck onto grass, running for the side street as I haven't run since I outgrew playing tag.

CHAPTER 6

ALL THE WAY HOME I divide my attention between the block ahead and the block behind, expecting at any time to see blue and red lights flashing in the rearview mirror or a roadblock cutting off my escape to home and hearth.

Okay, I'm being over-dramatic. But see how you feel when you're guilty of obstructing justice and the evidence is burning a hole in your pocket like a red-hot coal. Or rather a pink one.

I'm not cut out for a life of crime, that's for sure. Even if I'd managed to get away from the Moores' without detection, any rookie officer spotting my posture, crowding the wheel with both hands clenched on it, or my pale glistening face behind the windshield, would pull me over on suspicion of anything.

Everything aches, even the muscles in my jaw. My *hair* is tense. I force myself to relax, but moments later I'm back where I was, straining against the seat belt with my shoulders up around my ears.

Stopping for a signal, I roll down my window to cool my sweaty brow. I beat my palms against the wheel like a tom-tom. *Change!*

The driver behind me taps his horn, sending me through the roof. The light is green. I let out my breath and press the accelerator too hard, chirping my tires.

This is agony. How do professional crooks handle it? Pedestrians seem to stare straight at me. I don't draw another easy breath until I'm in my own living room, with all the doors and windows locked. I'd close the blinds, if it didn't seem like switching on a neon sign spelling out GUILTY.

Not much relief, even under my own roof. I keep going to the front door, certain I heard someone pounding on it with the meaty fist of authority.

I go into the kitchen and pop open one of the beers I keep for company. It tastes as bitter as a sunburned potato and I pour it out into the sink after one sip.

The landline rings in the living room. *This is it!*

It isn't it.

It's someone running for office, promising me in a recording to cut taxes.

This isn't worth it. I'd sneak back into the Moores' house and put the phone back, if I weren't sure I'd be caught this time. Is there a special law against *replacing* evidence?

I am so not prepared to play the role of cyber-sleuth.

The desk in my office is a litter of manufacturers' components, scribbles on yellow sheets, and printouts of my instruction drafts. I have deadlines to meet, and I need the money. The people who pay me couldn't care less how many unexplained disappearances I solve as long as I serve them first.

That's the practical priority. But after how I've spent my day, what's practical have to do with anything?

I shove aside my livelihood and direct my attention to my stolen clue. The Home button brings the screen to life, but—oh, no—password. There's no way she would be as dumb as me, and use her birthday…but I try it anyway. Luckily I remember the date, having been invited to her recent birthday dinner, not to mention her actual birth; and I'm in. *That was almost too easy*.

The battery's charged and I'm getting four bars, but as I try to open apps, nothing comes up. No messages, no voice mails, no stored numbers, no record of recent calls in or out. Just the factory settings.

No teenage girl could resist junking up her phone with apps, or abstain from texting and calls. Certainly not Gabby, who makes it a practice to live up to her nickname.

The memory's been wiped clean.

I can't imagine her doing that, tech-savvy as kids are today. Someone proficient with computers must have performed the vanishing act—on the run, flinging the phone onto the bed when finished. Either Josh or Gabby could have done that, I supposed; teenagers know their phones inside and out, as if by instinct.

If so, Mercer was right, and they'd taken off on their own—making sure to leave behind no trace of their recent contacts, and sabotaging attempts to trace them through their signals.

I don't like that. It helps to confirm the marshal's suspicions about Kevin's guilt.

On the other hand, someone else might have covered their tracks, to make sure no one knew where he was taking them and what he had planned for them. A professional, well-versed in police methods.

And I really, really, *really* don't like that.

CHAPTER 7

ANOTHER THING AMATEUR SLEUTHS always seem to have is a friend who can make a computer sit up and beg for him to hack it.

I do have one of those.

Sharon Kowalski works in the Sackville branch of a small chain of computer sales and service centers, blocks away from the university attended by Josh Moore. I met her when my old computer kept turning itself off. She could have complicated the diagnosis and charged me a bundle, but she said only the switch needed cleaning, a twenty-dollar job. On another occasion, she'd spent an hour helping me work out instructions for how to install programs on a laptop that wasn't on the market until the next year. Her boss was out, she said, and it was a slow day at the shop. She refused payment.

If that weren't enough to make me warm to her, she's also a fox.

I'd tried asking her out for a cup of coffee, but she'd

declined firmly—there was a bad break-up still haunting her. The customer's side of the store is shallow, divided by a black-glass counter from shelves of electronic equipment in varying stages of repair or awaiting pick-up and a long workbench littered with tools and parts and scraps of cable. Sharon is standing in front of it with her back to the door when I come in, bells above the door tinkling.

"Be with you in a sec."

"A sec might as well be a year when I'm waiting for you."

Okay, clumsy line. It sounded like Browning until it got to my mouth.

She smiles over her shoulder—indulgently, I'm afraid. She's wearing a white cotton blouse. Her red hair is short, and her high forehead, slightly turned-up nose, and round chin are tailor-made to be seen in profile. "Hi, Ray. Don't tell me you need a new cartridge already. You're the Stephen King of how-to writers."

"Tell that to my clients. They pay me as if I were Edgar Allan Poe. He went hungry most of the time."

When she finishes what she's doing and turns, wiping her hands on a microfiber cloth, I realize all over again that her profile is only the opener for the main event. On her, the sparkling array of precision screwdrivers, tweezers, and circuit-testers in her plastic pocket protector might as well be precious jewels.

Lest I stare too long where I shouldn't be looking, I fumble out Gabby's phone. "Can you recover data that's been erased from this?"

She takes it, examines both sides. "I think so. I know this model. You know, it doesn't go with what you're wearing."

I've got an excuse ready: *I found it on the street. I want to find out who it belongs to so I can return it.* But for once in Sharon's intoxicating presence, I don't let the thought get as far as the spoken word. That explanation wouldn't cover everything I needed, and she's no dummy. "Is there someplace we can talk in private?"

A thin vertical line spoils the perfect symmetry of her brow. "Ray, if this is a gambit, please forget it. You know my situation."

"I wish it were."

Something in my tone cuts off the question on her tongue. She glances at a digital clock on the wall next to the counter. "Jim's on a service call. We've got maybe twenty minutes."

"I hope that's long enough."

"When it's just one person on duty, we close down for breaks. But it's a little early for mine."

"Please, Sharon. It's important."

She nods, comes out from behind the counter, locks the front door, and turns the OPEN sign around.

I follow her around the counter through a door into an unpainted storeroom cluttered with more electronic components and grimy canvas bags bristling with tools on a bench scarred all over with nicks. She turns and waits, her short-nailed hands folded at her waist.

As briefly as possible I tell her what's happened,

swearing her to secrecy. I don't want to get myself in more trouble than I already am, or jeopardize my friends by spreading the word.

"You're kidding, right?"

"I wish I were. The law's treating the Moores like criminals instead of citizens in danger. I want to find out what's happened before they go public. This guy Adder who's after them…I don't feel good about it."

"I believe you. I know Margo. She calls us when the office equipment needs work. I thought she had the perfect family—" She stops herself. "Twenty minutes. Let me see what I can do." She unlocks a drawer under the counter, takes out a cable and a clear plastic case with various adapters nesting in compartments, uses one to plug the cable into the pink phone, and another to plug the other end into a jack in a laptop that looks like something I thought existed only at NASA. Then she draws a pair of red-framed readers from behind her pocket protector and hooks them over her ears, with the solemn ceremony of a matador dressing for the bullring.

CHAPTER 8

AGAIN I DIVIDE MY concentration, this time between Sharon and my watch. I don't want her getting in trouble with her boss if he gets back and finds the shop closed. That would be yet another person in on the investigation, and more risk for the Moores.

Her fingers dart over the keyboard, but not as fast as the second hand racing around the dial. *We've got maybe twenty minutes,* she'd said. That "maybe" thuds in my ears in time with each tick.

"Something," she says.

I look first at the pink phone lying on the bench. I know nothing about this procedure, apart from what I've seen on crime shows on TV. When I shift my attention to the laptop, I see a column of numbers filling the screen from the top toward the bottom.

"What is it, a code?" I ask.

"No, Mr. Hawking. They're telephone numbers."

"Oh."

"Calls going out. When do these kids stop to eat and

sleep and go to the bathroom? This one"—the nail of her index finger taps a row of digits beginning with the local area code—"see, it comes up five times more often than all the others. Gotta be a BFF, or maybe a boyfriend."

"Are they texts?"

"No. I haven't been able to raise those. Can't even tell you what apps she might've had installed."

"I'm hoping it was one of the Moores. I mean, if it was someone else, wouldn't that person just destroy all their phones?"

"I can't help you there. I'm a techie, not a terrorist." She tapped the screen again. "If the girl called anyone to tell them where she was going, this'd be the one."

"Can you match the number to a name?"

"If it's listed." She looks at me over the top of her glasses. "If I had it for the day, I might get more out of it. I'll make some excuse to Jim."

"Better not. I'm hoping to sneak it back into the house before Mercer and Howard realize it's missing."

"Right." She jerks the cable from the laptop's jack and opens another program.

Someone bangs on the front door.

"Jesus!" My heart smacks my ribs like a handball.

"That must be Jim. He's early. Talk to him, will you? Make something up. I need another five minutes."

I leave the storeroom, composing and discarding excuses on the way. The store's manager has his hands cupped around his eyes, leaning against the glass front door trying to peer inside. He's heavyset and dresses sloppily, with half his shirttail hanging below the hem of a too-tight brown suede jacket, baggy carpenter's jeans with a hammer loop, scuffed black Oxfords, and a grubby ball cap with a pair of gigantic women's breasts in a bikini bra patched on the front. If you had to guess what he did for a living, it would probably involve a grease pit. Sharon told me he graduated from MIT.

I twist the latch, tinkling the bells as I pull open the door.

He frowns. "Schick, right? Roy Schick?"

"Close. Ray Gillett."

"Right. Compaq Q. Dirty power switch. Get yourself a can of compressed air, save us both time and trouble."

"Thanks."

"Where's Sharon? If I knew she was going to lock up I'd have taken along my key." He starts inside.

I move to block him. "Uh, give her a minute, okay?"

He stops, stares at the embarrassment on my face. "Oh, for—what am I running here, a dating service? You run interference while she puts her panties back on?"

"God, no, nothing like that! I brought in a cell belonging to a friend for her to look at."

He isn't buying it. A splayed fingertip thumps my chest. "You need to think about another place to take your shit to. I met that jerk she was with. I threw him out when he came bulling in here to finish a fight he started at home. It was another year before she got up the gumption to walk out on him, and then I had to rag on her to get her to file an injunction to keep him away."

"She told me how good you were throughout that mess."

"She's the best employee I ever had. I wasn't about to waste a year training a replacement if she got so messed up she had to quit."

"Leave him alone, Jim. You can't bar a man from the shop just because he likes me."

I turn. Sharon has come in from the storeroom, carrying Gabby's phone and a piece of paper. "Here's the name and billing address."

I went back to the counter and took both items.

Jim points at the pink cell. "This guy's bad news, Shar. We sell more of that model to high-school cheerleaders than anyone else."

"Get your mind out of the gutter. He's doing a favor for the daughter of a friend."

"Yeah? Do me a favor and don't let any civilians into the back. We don't give tours." He storms around the counter into the storeroom and slams the door.

"I'm sorry, Ray."

"Believe me, you don't have anything to apologize for. Thanks, Sharon."

I pocket the phone on my way out and look at the paper for the first time. The girl's name is Tiffany, and she lives in Willow Grove. We're neighbors.

CHAPTER 9

I PROBABLY DROVE PAST the place a hundred times without noticing it. It's a plain box painted white with gray trim in what architects label American Craftsman, because it doesn't fit into any specific category. Whoever designed the first one was interested only in four walls and a roof.

It's well-kept, though, with a small square lawn that's been cut recently and the flag on the mailbox carved into a wooden woodpecker. Thurgood's the name on the box.

The woman who answers the door is tall and middle-aged, with her hair cut in a bob and graying.

"Mrs. Thurgood?"

"Miss."

Her tone is a rich contralto, deeper than mine. Somewhere back in the house, someone is rattling dishes and singing a tune that was popular when the woman at the door was young. This voice is higher.

"I'm looking for a Miss Tiffany Thurgood. I thought—"

"You assumed Tiffany's my daughter. I'm Tiffany Thurgood."

My confusion causes her expression to relax. "You're not the first," she says. "My mother gave birth in the lobby of the Ritz-Carlton in New York. There was no time to get her to a room. She was staring at the Tiffany chandelier when the hotel doctor performed the delivery. The name was unique until the millennials came along."

"I still came to the wrong place, I'm afraid. The Tiffany I'm looking for is a friend of the teenage daughter of friends of mine."

"That would be Gabby Moore?"

I blink. "You're the girl she called all those times?"

"I'm the *woman* she called. Just what is your business, Mr.——?"

"Excuse my manners. My name is Ray Gillett. Gabby has disappeared and I'm trying to help find her."

Nothing stirs the smooth surface of her features, but she steps back, opening the door wider. "Come in, Mr. Gillett."

The living room is spartan, but not uncomfortable. We sit in chromium-and-black-leather love seats set corner to corner, she with her ankles crossed and her hands folded in her lap. Beyond the open arch to the kitchen, the dishes stop clattering. "Tiff, do we have company?"

"A school matter, Do."

"Whatever can they want with you now?"

"Unfinished business."

"Oh." The noise resumes, only now without musical accompaniment.

"School?" I ask.

"Willow Grove High. I was nurse there for twenty-seven years. I'm retired now, but Gabby and I got to be quite close. We stay in touch."

I say, "Oh. I'm sorry to bother you. I'm just concerned for my friends' daughter."

"Why aren't your friends here instead of you?"

"They're away, and can't be reached."

"Are you sure she isn't with them?"

I consider taking her into my confidence, as I did Sharon Kowalski; but I know Sharon. "I'm sure. She left her phone behind. That's how I found you, from the number of times she called."

"Gabby left her phone behind? Her cell?"

"Yes, ma'am."

"What kind of teenage girl does that?"

This is the woman who'd called out from the kitchen. She stands inside the arch, wiping her hands on a striped towel, in a man's shirt with epaulets, stretch jeans, and loafers. Her short brown hair frames a sweet face, wearing a concerned look.

"You don't need to worry about this, Dorothy."

"You forget I've met Gabby. I like her. I worry about the people I like. I worry about you."

I'm learning a great deal about their relationship. The half that looks the less feminine is the one with the open heart; and the effect of it on the partner is immediate.

"I know." Tiffany's tone is softer.

I said, "You can call Cam Howard if you like. He's the chief of police. I reported to him when I learned th—she was missing." I nearly blew it there.

Tiffany Thurgood unfolds her hands and reaches for a console telephone on a black aluminum table at the end of her love seat. All my muscles clench. *What was I thinking?* If Howard and Marshal Mercer find out I'm really butting in on their investigation, they'll jail me. Good God! I've got a stolen cell—*evidence in a federal case*—in my pocket!

Dorothy steps up behind her companion and rests a hand on her shoulder. Tiffany withdraws her hand from the phone and grasps Dorothy's. Dorothy squeezes.

"Tiff, I think you should tell this man what Gabby told you."

CHAPTER 10

"NOT UNTIL I'M SATISFIED."

Tiffany Thurgood, I see now, has thick eyelids, which when lowered partially give her the appearance of a reptile, cold-blooded and infinitely patient.

I'm no match for that. I'm naturally gregarious, and when there's a lull in the conversation I panic, compelled to fill it. I stall for time to put my thoughts in order.

"What do I need to do to convince you I'm telling the truth?"

"Tell the truth."

I spread my hands. "Gabby's missing. That's it."

"It's not it. It may be part of it, but part of the truth is the same as a lie. I've never met her parents, but from what she's told me—complained to me, sometimes—they're conscientious. So why am I talking to you and not one or both of them?"

"I'm very close to the Moores."

"Not as close as a parent to a child, in a normal family."

"I'm curious as to why a teenage girl—a normal one, to use your word—should spend so much time talking to an older woman."

Sour amusement twists up the corners of her mouth. She isn't fooled. "Did you never have a mentor besides the people who brought you up? That's what I am to Gabby; and for that matter to many of the girls in the freshman class, some of whom, like her, remain in contact. The faculty advisor, Mr. Sweet, is a good man, but a man nonetheless. There are certain subjects in which his gender makes him a better confidant to boys than girls."

Dorothy speaks up. "Now that you know more about Gabby and Tiffany than we know about you, Mr. Gillett, it's time to answer her question. Otherwise you can leave and we'll call Chief Howard and get it from him."

I sit back, placing my palms on my thighs, as much to wick off sweat as to rest them. "I can see I'm outnumbered. But you've convinced me, both of you, that I can trust you to keep what I'm about to say in this room."

Tiffany turns her head away from me for the first time, meeting Dorothy's gaze. The nod they share seems hardly big enough for one; theirs, I realize, is an almost telepathic understanding, the kind I hope someday to have with someone. Sharon Kowalski's face flashes in my mind.

"Proceed, Mr. Gillett," says Tiffany.

Once again I tell it: Arriving at the house for my

weekly date with Kevin and the hoops, finding the place deserted, my meeting with Howard and Mercer, and my Junior G-Man stint at the Moores'. I get some satisfaction from the length of the silence that follows my narrative. I know instinctively this pair doesn't shock easily.

Tiffany speaks first. "I agree with you, and I'm no idealist. Only a psychopath could willingly collaborate with a vicious gangster and pose so successfully as a family man."

"That's what I tried to tell the chief and the marshal."

"I hope they leave us alone." She glances over her shoulder at Dorothy.

I say, "I can't promise you won't have to talk to them. They have access to all the other phones in the house. If any mention of you ever passed between Gabby and her parents by that route, you can expect an official visit, just like all the other people the family had contact with. If you're as honest with them as you've been with me, you shouldn't have anything to worry about." I shut my mouth now and open my face. It's Tiffany's turn.

"It was yesterday, around noon," she says after a pause, "the last time I heard from her. I didn't think anything at the time, except she hung up before I could give her any advice, without saying good-bye. That wasn't like her. But girls her age can be impulsive. She was probably distracted by something."

My impatience must show, because she hurries on.

"It may mean nothing. Spring break's coming, and she often accompanies the family on trips. Young women always want to know what to pack."

I'm sitting straight up. I don't even remember shifting positions. "Trip." There's no tone in my voice.

"She asked what the weather's like this time of year in Saskatchewan."

CHAPTER 11

SASKATCHEWAN: WHERE THE HELL is that, Alaska?

Or someplace equally cold and Jack London-y. Canada? If I hadn't memorized the capitals of all fifty states, I'd have flunked geography in high school.

Has either Kevin or Margo ever mentioned visiting Canada? Florida, once every couple of winters, and Hawaii on their twentieth anniversary. No place, anyway, where you have to pack mukluks.

But traditionally a place where fugitives in the movies talk about running to avoid US law.

Ridiculous to think in those terms. But Canada's handy, driving distance from Willow Grove, and maybe far enough outside the reach of a thug like Jeremy Adder. It also explains why Gabby ended her conversation with Tiffany Thurgood so abruptly and why her phone was wiped clean. If either of her parents happened to overhear, it would be snatched from her and every trace removed.

Do I tell Cam Howard and Dale Mercer, or will

that lead Adder to the Moores? Don't gangsters always have cops on the payroll?

I put off the decision. Gabby's phone is burning a hole in my pocket.

Back on the Moores' block, I circle twice to make sure the coast is clear. The squad car is nowhere in sight, and the house looks the same. There's something about an empty house that advertises itself, even if the grass has been kept up and there's no evidence of deterioration. Of course it's just my imagination, but it gives me the courage to become a repeat offender.

I park around the corner, but I resist the temptation to enter the way I'd left, through the side door. That would be tougher to explain if I bumped into a cop inside than if I went in the front, and doubled the chance of a neighbor seeing me through a window and becoming suspicious enough to report it.

This time I try not to attract attention by looking over my shoulder. Better to behave as if I still have the right I had this morning, to approach the place where friends live without acting like a cartoon burglar in a striped jersey and little black mask. I make a show of knocking, wait a beat, and insert my key in the lock, shielding the action with my body.

If anything, the place seems more deserted than before. It's probably just a case of projection, but I sense a tangible loneliness, as if the house itself feels neglected. The flotsam and jetsam of hurried departure has taken on a kind of permanence.

It's a good sign, though. The fact that nothing's been

moved indicates that no one in authority has gone over the house in detail. Even the sliding door to the deck is still unlocked, the dowel-rod security reinforcement lying outside the track. If the officer who came to the front door while I was inside didn't notice it, he likely hadn't discovered a piece of evidence missing.

Unless he'd noticed and just left everything as he'd found it.

I duck into Gabby's room, hurriedly wipe the phone on my shirt, both sides, as much to remove Sharon's fingerprints as my own. I let it fall to the bed and poke it under the discarded sweater, touching it only with a fingernail.

Now that it's back in place I feel as if a thousand-pound weight's been lifted off my shoulders; but over-confidence is dangerous. I once again let myself out the side door. I slip through the hedge.

Just as a green-and-white police car slides to a stop right in front of me.

A wild sense of panic wells up, but I force it down. The officer may not have seen me coming through the hedge. Even if he did, it didn't automatically mean I'd been inside the house. Trespassing in someone's yard isn't a felony; or is it?

But I can still talk myself out of trouble. *I just came to see if my friends had returned. When no one answered the doorbell, I went around and knocked on the side door. Terribly sorry, Officer. I didn't know it was a violation.*

Which sounds quite plausible until the door opens on the driver's side and Chief Cam Howard steps out, looking more official than ever in his tidy blue suit and clip-on tie.

"It's my second time past in two minutes," he says. "I ran your plate. Routine."

I try to make my voice casual, but it wobbles. "I just came—"

"Later. First, I want to know why you borrowed ten thousand dollars from Kevin Moore and didn't tell me. And why I shouldn't put you at the top of the list of suspects in the family's disappearance."

CHAPTER 12

STANDING WITH HIS HANDS hovering near his belt holster, Howard resembles a western gunman. His black hair, as glossy and grooved as a phonograph record, completes the effect. The slight breeze doesn't stir even a strand. He's plastered it down with mousse or Brylcreem or plain iron will.

"How did you find out about that?" I ask.

"I talked to the manager of the bank where the Moores keep their accounts. He drew up the agreement and notarized it. You're to pay off the loan by October. That's only five months away."

"What are you implying, Chief?"

"You tell me."

"You don't think I did something just to avoid paying him back!"

"People have vanished over sums much smaller."

"My God! This morning, you and I were friends. Now I'm a murder suspect?"

"*You* said murder; I didn't. Let's go inside."

I walk around to the front door, feeling him close behind. On the step I wait for him to open the door.

"Use your key, Houdini. That's another thing you forgot to mention this morning when you and I were friends."

"I didn't think it was important. The door was unlocked when I was here before."

"Which time? We locked up after checking the place out. Then one of the men I sent to talk to the neighbors drops by for a routine check and finds the side door wide open."

"It wasn't—" I stop myself too late.

"Uh-huh. How much did you take?"

"I didn't take anything!"

"Inside. Now." His voice is a thin strip of steel.

It takes three tries to get the key into the hole, and then the tumblers resist. It's as if the house has thrown in with the police against me. Finally the bolt slides back and I fumble the door open.

"After you," he says.

He directs me into the den, where he locks the sliding door and rolls the dowel rod over the lip of the track and in place with a foot, maintaining a distance between us of four feet. He's taking no chances. I must look like I'm desperate enough to try to overpower him.

"Sit."

I lower myself onto the worn sofa. This is the room where the family gathers to watch TV and the kids entertain their friends.

It's also the room where Kevin sat at the desk to make out a check in my name.

Now Cam Howard sits facing me across the orderly desktop. He's a man who turns any room he's in into a place of official business.

"I didn't take anything, Chief." Which is a lie; but not in connection to what's in his mind. To a former big-city cop, a man who'd commit one kind of crime would commit another, and when money was involved he'd plunder the house for more.

I'd decided to come clean and give him the benefit of what I'd learned from Tiffany Thurgood. Now that seems a hundred years ago. Then I was trying to clear the Moores of suspicion. Now I have to clear myself.

He says nothing. Instinctively he knows my central weakness: inability to avoid filling an awkward silence with jabber.

"You and Mercer had your minds made up that Kevin's in cahoots with Adder," I say. "I told you how wrong you were, and that if you weren't going to treat them as victims, I'd look for them myself."

"Why'd you come back twice?"

"I didn't think to look outside the first time. I wanted to check out the grounds, in case one of them dropped something on the way out."

He doesn't buy it. I know, because he doesn't even ask if I found anything.

"Why'd you put the arm on Moore? Gambling debt, drugs, pay back a loan shark?"

"I don't gamble or do drugs, and I wouldn't know

a loan shark if I saw one. If I did, I wouldn't have gone to Kevin. When I bought my house, I signed a fifteen-year-mortgage, with a balloon payment of ten thousand dollars due in year fifteen. It made the rate lower, so it seemed like a good deal. I thought I'd have the money by then. The payment came up last October, and I didn't have it. It was a friendly loan, Chief."

"I might have bought it, if you'd told me before."

"I swear the loan didn't even cross my mind. It has nothing to do with the Moores going missing."

"What happens come this October?"

"I'm taking on extra clients. Today's date with Kevin was the last weekend I don't plan to work straight through. If I don't have the entire amount, he'll probably agree to cut me some slack, but I'm hoping I won't have to ask."

Again he makes no response. Sweat trickles down my spine, finding every nook and cranny on the way.

He stands. "Get up."

I obey.

"Turn around and put your hands behind you." He produces a shiny pair of handcuffs from under his coattail.

"You're *arresting* me?"

"If I don't, Mercer will. The feds get a lot of mileage out of obstruction. Do what I said."

I begin to turn. A ride in the back of a patrol car, my fingerprints taken, a strip-search, an orange jumper—

"Okay, Gillett."

I stop. He puts away the cuffs.

"You mean—?"

"Next time I won't be bluffing. The FBI's got the drag out for the Moores, and Mercer's sitting on his hands until they show and agree to protection. I won't muck up a major assignment with a penny rap. The Sherlock act stops now. Now." A finger thumps my chest hard.

"Yes, sir."

"And since you're such a fan of crime fiction, you know what comes next."

"'Don't leave town'?"

He holds out a hand and snaps his fingers. "The key, Boston Blackie. You've broken into your last crime scene."

CHAPTER 13

I'M NOT SURE WHO Boston Blackie is, but I'm pretty sure I don't qualify.

Not when it comes to being a detective, or even a good citizen. I don't know if I held out on Howard out of fear he'd charge me with something even more serious than interfering in a police investigation, or because I'm angry at him for suggesting I have something to do with this.

Back home, I sit and stare at the mound of work waiting for me. It's as if I'm seated in someone else's office, looking at unfinished projects I know nothing about.

What good would it do to explain to the chief how that loan came to be? He'd just think I was trying to wiggle out from under suspicion.

Coincidentally enough, a similarly dissociative situation had taken place after one of our Saturdays on the basketball court. Kevin had a pass that allowed him and a guest to use the university gym when the team wasn't practicing or no event was scheduled.

It was as if I'd never played before. I couldn't dribble or block. I missed four easy shots and wiped out on the fifth, slipping and landing elbow first on the hardwood floor. My friend helped me into the locker room, where Kevin got some ice that he folded into a towel, wrapped it around my throbbing elbow, and tied it off as neatly as a sports doctor. We sat side by side on a bench, me rocking back and forth until the numbness took over.

"Better?"

I nodded. "Guess I don't make MVP this season."

"Brother, you sucked."

That sped up the cure. He can always surprise a laugh out of me. "Don't hold back on my account. Tell me what you really think."

But his face was troubled. "What is it, buddy? You're no Michael Jordan, but you've usually got your head in the game. You worry me lately, and not just on the court. What is it, work or a woman? Still getting the cold shoulder from Sharon?"

"Who told you I liked Sharon?"

"You did. You're still talking about her six months after she fixed your power button."

That reminded me just how well he knew me. So I told him about the balloon payment.

"Is that all?" he said. "I thought maybe you had a lump in your testicle."

"I'm not sure that's worse. I've got insurance for that."

He said nothing, registering his opinion of that remark. As usual, I can't let a silence go unplugged.

59

"What a bonehead, right? Like I was surprised the fifteen years got used up."

"Everybody's a bonehead sooner or later, and it's usually got to do with money. How much you need?"

"No."

"Hey, what are friends for? If that doesn't work, I've got other clichés."

"Forget it, Kev. I wasn't hinting. I can sell my car, ride my bike."

"When was the last time you pedaled?"

I gaze at the ceiling. "Labor Day, nineteen ninety-seven."

"Did it have training wheels?"

I laughed again and put my arm across his shoulders, forgetting the elbow. It reminded me with a sharp stab.

He said, "You've got to meet clients here; that's a twenty-mile round trip. A sweaty, red-faced tech writer doesn't inspire confidence, and by the time you got back home you'd be too stove up to write for a week. A couple of hours a week on the basketball court doesn't make you Tour de France material. Come on, how much? That bonus I got from Adder's just sitting in the bank."

So we went to his bank and drew up a formal agreement with a specific due date for repayment. I insisted on it, despite his protests that it was a matter between friends and I could pay him back when I could. Kevin's savvy in most things, but even I knew that so casual an arrangement regarding money is a friendship killer.

Killer. What makes me use that word?

That's what I'll be—at least an enabler—if the Moores are truly in danger and I keep my mouth shut about where they may have fled.

If they've fled, and their disappearance wasn't someone else's idea.

I scoop up the phone and call the police department.

The doorbell rings while the line's purring. I cradle the receiver and answer. For all I know it's Howard. He's changed his mind and decided to arrest me anyway. Maybe he's talked it over with Marshal Mercer, who'd push for it.

But the visitor on my doorstep is a stranger, a smallish man in an orange-and-silver jogging suit with chestnut hair falling over one eye, lending him the illusion of youth. But the face, the skin an orangish hue courtesy of a tanning bed, is deeply lined. He's sixty if he's a day, much older than his dazzling set of smiling teeth.

Behind him is a pristine, square cobalt-blue seventies Cadillac with aprons on the fenders; it looks like a pontoon boat beached in my driveway. And although I've never laid eyes on the man before, I know who he is before he introduces himself.

"Ray Gillett? You don't know me, but we've got a mutual friend in Kevin Moore. I'm Jeremy Adder."

CHAPTER 14

MY CHEST CLENCHES. I look at his hands, expecting a pistol. They're empty.

"You ever drive a Caddy?"

I pause, then answer numbly. The question is no more surreal than the prospect of a gangster on my doorstep. "In college. I worked for a limo service part-time."

"Those stretch jobs handle like a truck. You're in for a treat. Let's cruise. You're not busy."

Not a question. I manage indignation. "Actually—"

"You work at home, but you've been spending time with cops. After that, a man has to take a break or he can't concentrate. I know, and I'm more used to the situation." His smile is unnerving. That the teeth are dentures is only partly responsible for this impression. "I know what those bozos have been saying about me. I'm not taking you for a ride."

Wouldn't he say just that, to get me in the car? Then I realize what else he said. "How do you know I've been—?"

"There are no secrets in a small town. I don't live here, but a lot of people I employ do. I'll have you back here in ten minutes. But don't take my word for it. You see that gray Buick parked down the block? See the plate?"

He doesn't turn his head, but I peer past his shoulder. The plate reads US-623.

"Government. I've got two feds on me around the clock. I stop too quick, they step on my heels. That's your tax dollars at work. If I was Jack the Ripper, you think I'd try anything?"

"But why?"

"You and Kevin Moore are tight. Me, too, no matter what they've told you. Can't two guys get together to talk about a friend in trouble without the whole world listening in?"

I look again at the gray Buick. There are two people seated in front. I nod, lock up, and step outside.

The big car is spotless, wearing so many coats of blue finish it makes me dizzy, as if I'm about to fall into a mountain lake a hundred feet deep. The interior is upholstered in tan glove leather, including steering wheel and dash with its confusion of gauges, like the control panel of a commercial jet. The smell belongs to a store that sells expensive luggage.

The key's in the ignition. I turn it and the motor starts with a barely perceptible vibration and no more noise than a sewing machine.

"Go ahead," Adder says, when I hesitate with both

hands on the wheel, "pull out. You'll think it's driving itself."

I grasp the shift lever, move the indicator to Drive, and press the accelerator. We peel away from the curb with a slight chirp of tires. "Sorry."

"Forget it. They're new. Swing around downtown."

In the rearview, the Buick slides into the driving lane three-quarters of a block behind us.

Adder frowns at the mirror on his side. "It's prejudice is what it is, only I can't sue because I don't belong to the right minority. I started out as an electrician. Well, I still am; I keep up my dues for old times' sake. Back then, the maintenance game was as mobbed up as Vegas. You had to cooperate in order to eat. Now just because I worked my way up steady, it means I'm a crook, too. It doesn't matter that I employ almost as many people as the university, pay good wages, and give bonuses. Some no-neck who just happens to work for my company floats up in the river and suddenly I'm Public Enemy Number One. Is that fair?"

It's supposed to be a complaint, but it sounds like a threat. But I say, "I guess not."

"Damn straight. All they're interested in is pinning a bunch of unclaimed stiffs on an easy target and closing another drawer in their files. Scalp-hunters!"

"I guess so."

"Kevin's a good boy in the office. Nice family. I met them all at company picnics. I give him a raise every year because he's so good with the books. But then these bastards come along and start working on him, he spooks and blows. If I could just talk to him the way I'm talking to you, I know I can convince him of the truth."

I say nothing. I can't think of a response that won't include the word *guess*. What will he do when he realizes I'm just humoring him?

"I'd like to set up a meet. Someplace where he'll feel safe. We've always been able to talk. I don't want to have to train someone to take his place. I can't afford to hire a newbie who'll make mistakes while he's learning the ropes; not with these buzzards circling around, waiting for me to slip up."

"I don't know where he is, Mr. Adder."

"You don't?"

I turn my head to look at him, still in profile. "I don't. That's why I reported the family missing."

"So that's why. I thought maybe the feds enlisted you to keep an eye out."

I return my attention to the street. "I never met a federal officer before this morning, when a US marshal showed up at the police station in response to the missing-persons complaint I filed."

In the little silence that follows, I hear the mechanical clock in the dash change numerals. Then:

"I believe you," he says. "But you're tight, like I said. If he gets in touch with you, maybe you can tell him what I told you. Let him decide."

"If he contacts me, I'll have to tell the police."

"I wouldn't."

His tone is so even, I can't tell if this is a threat. I notice the red light at the intersection almost too late. We both lurch forward when I slam on the brakes.

"Relax." Adder glances at the mirror, then turns his head my way, resting an arm along the back of the seat. "I know you don't trust me. I can't blame you, the way cops work. But before you go trusting the locals, you might ask Chief Howard how much he's got invested in Adder Enterprises."

CHAPTER 15

THIS TIME I NOTE the light change just in time to avoid the prod of a horn, but I roll so slowly through the intersection the driver behind me swings into the outside lane and passes.

"Why would a police officer put money into—?"

"Go ahead, say it." Grinning his artificial grin, Adder withdraws his arm from the back of the seat and returns his gaze to the street ahead. "'False front,' my ass. I make more money peddling legitimate maintenance work to the university and a dozen other concerns than Whitey Bulger cleared running drugs, and I use the best materials and the best men in the trade. Whatever I might've done to get along in the past, that's years over. The IRS audits me spring in, spring out, steady as crocus, and I account for every penny, all on the up-and-up. I only plow Howard's dinky little portfolio back into the firm because in my situation it's good business to have friends in law enforcement."

"Why are you telling me this?"

"I'm saying it's not in Howard's best interest to play Kojak down the line. Man in my position, I can always make up for what's lost. Not him. The Moores are his last stand."

"Aren't you contradicting everything you said about being a legitimate businessman?"

"You don't listen. I'm talking about what the *cops* think. It'll set me back a bundle in attorney fees and court costs to get out from under this mess, but I will. Meanwhile the ones the Moores have to worry about are the crooked little fish like Howard, who think the simplest way to cover their ass is to chain Kevin, Margo, and their kids to a Chevy short block and drop them in the city reservoir. Stop sign!"

I brake with the front tires in the middle of the crosswalk. The picture he's drawn is vivid.

"So—"

"So now you know why this little joyride. Anything happens to the family, I wind up paying for it. Even if they don't manage to frame me, they'll squeeze me dry in court and call it a win. You might be the best friend the Moores ever had, but *I'm* their best insurance against the Cam Howards of this world."

"I've only got your word for it that Howard's an investor."

"He put you on his fall-guy list based on the ten grand you owed Kevin. Who do you think told me about that little deal?"

I press the accelerator as gently as if there's an egg under the pedal. If I drive any slower I can get a ticket for holding up traffic.

"For all I know," I say, "you own the bank."

Adder's chuckle resembles a death rattle.

"I could, but I don't. Rotten risk."

"I can't believe he'd slaughter a whole family just to protect his investment."

"But you can believe it of me, the big bad gangster you never heard of before today." He slaps his flat stomach. "That sound like a belly full of linguini and chianti? You think I'm wearing a silk shirt under this running suit? I keep in shape, I top off the tan so the big money men I meet with think my business is running so smoothly I've got the time to work out and bask on the beach."

We've put the gift shops, hardware stores, real estate offices, and mini antiques malls of downtown behind us, and are approaching my neighborhood. I hesitate at my corner, then turn toward home.

"Here we are, safe and sound." Adder strokes the dash, as gently as if it's a woman's thigh. "I can put you onto a classic just like this, on an employees' discount, same rate as that motorized roller skate you still owe nine payments on. My people maintain all the dealerships in the tri-county area. Here's my card." He produces a rectangle of heavy rag-stock bond from a slash pocket; closes his hand around mine as I accept it.

"In return for—?"

"Not a thing; seriously. Just a good turn for a friend of a friend. Kevin calls you, you call me."

On the sidewalk in front of my house, he thrusts his hand at me. I take it. It's like grasping the iron handle of a pump, and just as cold.

CHAPTER 16

"RAY, I DON'T MEAN to be rude, but—"

"It's not a date. I just want to go someplace where we can talk in private."

"Ray, that's a date."

I can't believe how fresh Sharon Kowalski looks, and that only hours have passed since she tapped into Gabby Moore's phone as a favor to me. In that time I've broken the law twice, become a suspect in a criminal investigation, and crossed swords with a reputed crime boss. I must look like something that just crawled out from under a bridge.

Jim's tinkering with something in the back room with the door open, and a paunchy customer in a rumpled suit is staring at the ink-cartridge display in the corner like he's trying to remember the combination to his locker. I brace my hands on the counter and lower my voice.

"I just had a talk with Jeremy Adder. Does that sound like a pick-up line?"

Her eyes widen. She looks at the clock. "Half-hour till closing. Meet me at the Blue Parrot."

It's a brew pub within walking distance, recently moved into a former KFC. The giant plaster parrot perched outside doesn't hide the outline of the colonel's signature red-and-white-striped bucket. But huge turning blades suspended from the ceiling and fan-shaped wicker chairs inside make me feel like Humphrey Bogart. The third time a chirpy young waitress with blue feathers in her hair comes to my booth, I order the day's specialty beer just to get rid of her.

In a little while she brings me something medium bronze and foamy in a frosted mug. "Enjoy."

I nod. Too rich for my taste. I'm not much for beer. I let it sit while the head settles.

Then she breezes in from the street, crisp and pretty, even the way she walks, as if she's known all along right where I'd be sitting and makes a brisk beeline that way. Male heads turn. Female, too.

She plops down in the seat facing me. "What are you drinking?"

"Search me. Haven't taken a sip."

"May I?" She gestures toward the mug.

"Please do."

She raises it to her lips, wipes foam from them with a finger. "Not bad. I prefer it dark and bitter."

The plumed waitress returns to offer her something. Sharon looks at me, cocking an eyebrow; I shrug and open a palm toward the mug. "I'll drink this, thanks," she says.

I say, "I'll have a Coke."

"Pepsi okay?"

"Sure."

"I'm starving." Sharon orders the Reuben without looking at the menu. Plainly she's a regular.

The waitress looks at me. I start to shake my head, then realize I haven't eaten since breakfast. I pick up the menu and ask for cheddar bites.

When we're alone again, Sharon smiles. "Isn't it ridiculous you can't have your choice of soda brands?"

"I'm actually old enough to remember when you could."

And now I've admitted I'm over the hill. The Moore thing's gotten me so snarled up, I've forgotten everything I ever learned about dating.

But I don't want our conversation interrupted, so we make small talk until our meals arrive. I watch her dive into her sandwich while I dip a deep-fried sphere of cheese into a little bowl of white sauce, and bring her up to date, including Saskatchewan and my run-in with Chief Howard and what Jeremy Adder told me about him.

"Wow. You've been busy."

"Have I? It feels like they've been gone a month, and this is all the progress I've made."

"You're not working the case alone, remember. You don't know Adder's telling the truth about Howard. If he's guilty, it'd be one way to throw you off the track."

"What makes me so important? I don't qualify as even an amateur detective."

"Then why would he bother to talk to you at all?"

I shove my plate away, almost knocking the bowl of dip into her lap. "Hell if I know."

She glances around, at heads turned our way; this time aimed at me. "Cool your jets, Ray. Even if it's true, you said Howard seemed surprised when Marshal—what's his name?"

"Mercer. Dale Mercer."

"When Marshal Mercer told him Adder was being investigated. Maybe the chief thought he'd invested in a legitimate company. You can't be a cop all your life, and I doubt Willow Grove provides much of a pension."

"You're right, I suppose. Anything can look suspicious if you look at it with suspicion."

"Eloquently put. And remember, it's not just Jeremy Adder *versus* the Moores and maybe Cam Howard. They've got the federal government on their side."

I retrieve my plate, apologize for my fit of temper, and resume dipping. "I knew there was a reason I came to you."

"Now let's talk about Saskatchewan. Passport in order?" She picks up her sandwich.

CHAPTER 17

"WHATEVER GAVE YOU THE idea I was going there?"

I begin the question with surprise; the notion, I swear, has never entered my head. But I realize it was there all along, fighting its way out of my subconscious through layers of worry, fear, and confusion.

"You. Otherwise, you'd have told Howard about your talk with Tiffany Thurgood, let him take it from there."

"You're giving me credit for determination I never had. I was so busy trying to talk my way out of jail I clean forgot about Saskatchewan."

"Maybe. What were you going to do when you found out Howard's one of Adder's investors?"

"That's why I came to you. I'm too close to this thing to think straight. If I was thinking straight, running off to a foreign country to play Boston Blackie would be out of the question."

"Who's Boston Blackie? Never mind. You could have gone directly to Marshal Mercer."

"I don't like Marshal Mercer."

"When you're clutching at straws, does it matter if you like them?"

"I just never thought about taking it to Canada."

"Then let's think about it now."

"Even if I knew what to do once I got there, I can't. Howard told me not to leave town."

"*You* said that, not him."

"I'll be sure and mention that at my arraignment."

Her face twists. "You've been bending everyone's ear all day about your dear friends the Moores, how no one in authority's doing anything to bring them home safe, so it's up to you. Now that you've got a solid lead, you don't pass it on and you don't follow it up yourself because you're afraid you'll get in trouble. How's that make you better than the people you've been bitching about?"

I don't know if I'm shaken more by being accused of cowardice or by this side of Sharon Kowalski. All the times I've taken advantage of her good nature, putting her job in jeopardy, I've never known her to show even slight annoyance.

"You're right. 'Friend' is an easy word to throw around; it should have ten syllables, to prove you're prepared to work at it. Kevin was there for me. I didn't even have to ask. When the time came to show him I was worth it, all I could think about was myself."

She subsides into her seat, as if something rigid and painful has been keeping her spine straight, and has suddenly collapsed.

"Wow," she says again. "I had a longer speech planned, but you finished it."

"I'm sorry I got you into this. I'll go to Mercer right away. He can decide whether Howard can be trusted. The Moores deserve expert help."

"That's not what I've been saying. Ray." She elbows aside her plate and reaches across the table, taking both my hands in hers. "It's a job to them. It's like a surgeon referring to a patient, a fellow human being, as 'my gallbladder.' Even if they're both as straight, they'll never bring the passion to this case that you can."

"Canada's a big place. I don't know anything about Saskatchewan. What do I do, start knocking on doors asking if they've seen my friends?"

She squeezes, lets go. "This isn't 1860. Somewhere among all those beavers and moose they must have private investigators."

"Then I'll call one, give this to the professionals."

"How can you be sure Adder won't intercept the call, or Howard?"

"You think they've tapped my phone?" I ask incredulously.

"Oh, like cops never do that, especially crooked cops. And if Adder's the twenty-first century's answer to Al Capone, do you think he'd apply for a court order?"

"I can use my cell."

"You don't even need to tap a cell. The signal goes out by radio waves and satellite. Any fourteen-year-old kid with a scanner from Radio Shack can eavesdrop. You forget what business I'm in. If I told you half the ways a private conversation can be overheard, you'd dump all your gadgets and communicate by tin cans. And there's another thing," she adds.

"What other thing can there be?"

"Adder will be back, to pump you for information. What do you think he'll do if you tell him you don't have any? You can't be here."

I feel again the empty horror I felt in the deserted house. "What's to stop them, Howard or Adder, from following me? Or meeting my plane in Canada?"

"Speed. The quicker we act, the less time they have to set up. If you have a passport?"

"I've got one of those enhanced driver's licenses you can use to get into Canada."

"Then we're all set."

"That's the second time you've said 'we.'"

She crosses her forearms on the table, looking conspiratorial. "I've got my passport on me."

"Why?"

She smiles, and leans closer, dropping her voice to a murmur. "I've never left the country, but I got a passport after the break-up. Like to carry it around—if only to remind me that I can pick up and go whenever I like. I've always wanted to see Paris. One day when I decide it's time? Two hours later I'm on my way across the Atlantic, sipping a glass of French champagne."

I sit back, winded. "People have your kind all

wrong. Techno-nerds aren't supposed to be men of action."

"They're not. Women are. At least this woman is. What do you say? Every Sherlock needs his Watson, and my passport's an overage virgin."

CHAPTER 18

SHE HAS THE GOOD grace to blush a little when I stare at her.

"Don't read anything into it," she says. "These days I reserve my passion for travel, or, anyway, the dream of it. Separate rooms, buddy."

"Sharon, I honestly wasn't thinking that." The truth of which surprises me; for months now, my determination to repay my debt to Kevin has run neck and neck with moving my friendship with Sharon to the next level. The events of a single day have turned the world on its ear.

"I believe you," she says. "I keep forgetting there's a gentleman or two left in the world."

I press that advantage. "I can't bring you. This scheme's dangerous."

"Are you saying it's no place for a woman?"

I've blown it. The line between gentleman and male supremacist is thin.

"What I mean is, it's bad enough for one. Two would be pushing luck over the edge. One way, we're a threat to a ruthless gangster; the other, to a corrupt police chief. I'd never forgive myself for hauling someone else into that situation."

"Don't be silly. If that happens, they'll probably kill you. So you won't have to feel bad for long."

"That's not funny."

"I suppose not. It's just so much like a movie I'm having trouble believing it's real." She shakes her head. "Look, if you're going, so am I, and that's that. What do they speak there, French?"

"That's Quebec."

"Too bad. I was hoping to get something back on my investment in Rosetta Stone."

"What about your job?"

"I haven't taken a vacation in two years. Jim can do without me for a week."

"That's a risk."

"Ray, I'm more worried about growing so old I can't take that kind of risk. A job's a job. How often does an adventure like this come along?"

"What we've got isn't even a lead, really. Chances are we'll crap out."

"So we take in a hockey game."

"It's not hockey season."

"Hunt grizzlies, then. Anything that doesn't involve a precision screwdriver is fine with me."

"Sharon, this isn't a lark."

"I know that." She's sober suddenly, and I know that by expressing my own concern I've lost whatever ground I might have gained.

"This could be a wild goose chase." A Canadian wild goose chase; though I don't say it.

"It could be. Either way, it's the finest thing any man ever did for a friend."

I've lost the argument but am feeling more and more invested in the war.

"What can two people do in an amateur investigation that one can't?"

"Take turns driving, for one."

"Drive? If I go at all, I was thinking of flying."

"That's okay, if you want the Mounties to meet the plane when it lands; or worse, a couple of gorillas hired by Adder. It's too easy to monitor airport traffic. You can't fly under a phony name, and if that is where the Moores have gone, you'd be leading the enemy right to them. Not to mention, you can't cross into Canada by air with your enhanced driver's license."

"It would take days. Howard's sure to know I've gone, and then he'll put out a dragnet."

"'Dragnet'; does anybody say that anymore?"

"He does. Crooked or straight, I've got a hunch he's old school. I've seen his tough side." I pick up a ched-dar bite, then put it back. My appetite's gone. "You said take turns driving, for one. What's the other?"

"Sit by the phone waiting for the detective agency to call and pound the pavements like Nancy Drew. One person can't do both."

"I have a cell phone. What do you do, spend all your free time streaming Turner Classics?"

She sticks out her tongue. "A phone you should

be careful about using. Let's see just how far it is to Saskatchewan." She produces her own phone.

"Can I get you anything else?"

I almost knock over my glass of Pepsi at the waitress's sudden reappearance.

"Just the check, please."

Sharon's still deep in research when it comes. She looks up finally, ready to report; but the waitress is there with the check, so I hurriedly hand her my credit card so Sharon can tell me what she's found.

At least I got to be the one who paid. I'd been afraid Sharon would insist on splitting it on principle.

"Good news and bad news," she announces. "I was afraid it was one of those western territories bordering on the Arctic. It's just across the Montana border. We can cross it in a couple of days."

"What's the bad news?"

She looks up from the screen. "The province is about the size of New Zealand."

PART TWO

THE ENDS OF THE EARTH

CHAPTER 19

THE TREK ACROSS THE northwestern corner of Montana—through the rural stretches, anyway—blurs together into a collage of roadside stands, arrowhead emporia, historic stagecoach stops, cowboy hats, tight Wranglers, poly-blend shirts, and straight Buck Owens on the radio. Colorfully named cities abound—Superior, Poison, Cut Bank, Chinook—but like any other town, they are ringed with Wendy's, Best Buys, PetSmarts, and auto dealerships, nary a pair of steer horns in sight.

We overnight at a Ramada the first night, occupying separate rooms, but the next we're turned away from all the chain places because of a fly fishermen's convention. We end up just outside a dusty town called Chester, at a cluster of bungalows with faux barn siding, the knotholes painted on.

In cabin six of the Wickiup Motor Lodge, the head- and footboards of the twin beds are shaped like wagon wheels, the base of the lamp on the table between is a ceramic saddle, and cowboy and Indian toddlers cavort on the curtains.

"This is howdy hell," I say.

"What?" Sharon calls from the bathroom, where she's changing into her pajamas.

I raise my voice to be heard through the closed door. "I expect Wyatt Earp to come in anytime, to check the red-eye in the minibar."

"There's a minibar?"

"What do fishermen have to convene about, anyway? I thought the whole point was to wade out into the middle of an icy stream, cast for trout, and revel in the peace and solitude."

"'Revel,' really?"

"Well, whatever they call it. For what we're paying for this dump, we could stay a night in a Hilton, with room service and satellite."

"It's not so bad when you split the cost."

We're dividing everything equally, including gas and Big Macs.

"Ray?"

"Yes?"

"You're not going to be one of *those* travelers, are you?"

"Okay, I'll stop."

"I'm coming out."

Which is my signal to switch off the lamp. She hurries to her bed and dives under the covers.

"Are we having an adventure yet?" I ask in the dark.

"Who said nothing's an adventure when you're living through it?"

"Indiana Jones."

And for some reason we start giggling and don't stop until we're both too exhausted to stay awake.

The border crossing the next morning is uneventful. A very polite Canadian customs guard with an American accent looks at my license and Sharon's passport, asks the reason for our visit ("Pleasure," we answer simultaneously), and waves us across. "Enjoy your stay."

"No stamp." Sharon pouts.

"I'm just happy he didn't call his boss. For a couple of hundred miles I've half-expected a state trooper to pull us over on orders from Chief Howard."

"Or Marshal Mercer. Don't forget the feds."

"Thanks. I feel much better now."

"Relax. We're not breaking any laws. Even if Howard had told you to stay put, he doesn't have the authority to enforce it. It's still America."

"No, it isn't. Canadians don't even call themselves Americans."

"I don't know why. So far I haven't seen anything to convince me we're not still back home."

Which is true. Despite my worries about the Moores, I'd been looking forward to great stretches of tall pines, a glimpse of a bear or a moose. Miles past the border, we're rolling along a four-lane highway, passing and being passed by ordinary passenger vehicles and Bekins moving vans, looking at Golden Arches, Chase Manhattan banks, and Holiday Inns, on our way to Regina. Next door to Moose Jaw, with its echoes of the Yukon gold rush, Regina is the provincial capital and the likeliest place to find a detective agency with all the bells and whistles required to track down our friends.

"I'm starting to miss the Wickiup," I say. "At least that place made an effort not to look exactly like downtown Spokane."

"It's also hot. What's that say, seventy-five?" She's looking at the digital thermometer above the rearview.

"At least Gabby knew enough to ask Tiffany Thurgood what to pack. I should've left the flannel behind and packed shorts."

"In two miles, turn right onto Queen's Highway One East."

The shockingly loud, robotic female voice makes me swerve over the dividing line. "What the hell is that?"

"GPS." Sharon gestures with her phone. "Of course, if you prefer, we can always stop and ask Paul Bunyan for directions."

"Sharon!"

"What, I can't make a jo—" She looks up from the screen, sees me staring at the rearview mirror. She turns to look out the back window, at the cobalt-blue Cadillac three car lengths behind us.

CHAPTER 20

"IS THAT HIM?" SHE asks. "Adder? But, how—"

"He must have followed me all the way from my house." I look beyond the big car. "I don't see the federal car. He must have shaken them."

"Can you shake *him*?"

"I'm not an Indy driver. *He's closing the distance!*"

"Speed up!"

But the Cadillac accelerates faster than my compact. It seems as if the square radiator grille might fill the mirror. Then—

It pulls out to pass.

I see now there's someone seated on the passenger's side. I duck. "Head down!"

But instead of a gun poking through the window, I see a head of white hair pulled into a bun, and behind the wheel a man twenty years older than Adder, wearing a plaid hat with a feather in the band. The car slides past us and drifts back into our lane.

I sit back, drenched. "False alarm. It's just an old couple out for a drive."

"Next time it might not be."

I'm keyed up. My neck is sore and my eyes are watering from scanning the landscape for classic blue Cadillacs, of which Canada seems to be in good supply. And who's to say he hasn't changed wheels? I can't scour every vehicle on the road for a glimpse of a man I've seen only once. I need the security of four walls and a roof.

"Why don't you look up our hotel?" I ask Sharon.

"Right now I'm researching detective agencies, looking at reviews." She taps a finger toward the screen, not quite touching it. "The Crane Organisation seems to be the General Motors of the sleuthing industry. Organisation's spelled with an *s*."

"We won't hold that against them. Are they in town?"

"Their headquarters is in Saskatoon. That's another 120 miles."

"Oh."

"But wait, they've got a branch here: Sixth Avenue North."

"That's encouraging. A place with branches must be doing something right. Right?"

"I'm seeing lots of positives on their site."

"Where's our hotel?"

"In Regina," she informs Siri. "The York Windsor." A chime sounds. She looks up, grinning. "Fourth Avenue. North."

"Let's go to Sixth first."

"I felt sure you'd say that."

We pass Fourth. The next avenue is First.

"What am I missing?" I say. "Do numbers up here run another direction?"

"You wanted different."

"I did. Be careful what you wish for."

Here's Sixth, out of order and so unexpected I almost pass it. My tires squeal as I make the adjustment.

The Crane Organisation identifies itself with a square sign slowly revolving on a post in the grass strip between the sidewalk and a modern low-slung building with a beveled roof, like a strip mall. The sign's design is reassuring. I park between a nondescript station wagon and a sleek Econoline van, which my imagination packs with state-of-the-art surveillance equipment; of course, it may belong to a soccer mom.

"What's the matter?" Sharon pauses, hand on her door handle, to look at me sitting motionless with my hands still gripping the wheel.

"What do we know about those positive reviews?" I say. "Maybe Crane's own people posted them. This is like shopping the Yellow Pages for a brain surgeon."

"Ray." She releases her grip on the handle and reaches across to grasp my arm. "We're here. We might as well go in. I'll signal if my instincts jibe with yours."

"What's the signal?"

She grins again and pats me on the arm. "You look across, I'm not still sitting next to you? That's it."

CHAPTER 21

THE RECEPTION AREA IS set up like a doctor's waiting room, with a tiny short-haired receptionist seated at a waist-high counter separated from visitors by a sliding Plexiglas panel; a glorified kitchen pass-through. Her smile belongs in a toothpaste commercial.

"Have you an appointment?" Her accent is flat, Midwestern; another thing about Canada that hasn't lived up to my preconceived notions.

"No."

She looks up above my head, as if for spiritual guidance. I assume there's a clock mounted on her side of the partition. "I'll see if I can get you in. Name?"

"Ray Gillett. This is Sharon Kowalski."

She shifts her attention to Sharon, the smile broadening. "Ah! Polski!" A stream of language follows. Sharon's answer is monosyllabic.

We turn toward a row of plastic scoop chairs bisected by a composition table scattered with American magazines. "What did she say?"

"Her people came from Cracow. Either that, or she's related to the dead Pope. All I know of the lingo I got from my dad when he called his cousins. I can't believe I finally put my passport into play just to visit Wisconsin."

We sit forty-five minutes, Sharon flipping through a health magazine, while I glance around nervously. In that time, two people enter from outside—a comfortable-looking couple in their fifties, who speak quietly with the receptionist and are shooed into the back—and one person leaves—a pudgy young man in a sport coat and tan Dockers, moving with the assurance of someone who spends a lot of time there. No sign of a trench coat. I scoop up a magazine at random and open it. It's for kids.

The receptionist cradles a phone and slides open her window. "Randy will see you now."

I look up from a third-graders' quiz about trampoline safety. "Randy?"

"End of the hall, last door on the left."

Randy.

I surrender the last of my illusions, so I'm not disappointed when we pass through a wide-open door into an antiseptic office decorated in pastels, with a small chipboard desk, fabric-paneled walls, a couple of low-slung chairs for visitors, and not a blackjack or a bottle of Old Grand-Dad in sight. All it needs is a plastic model of a human eyeball on the desk to complete the resemblance to an ophthalmologist's consultation room.

"Hi! Randy MacBride."

The man who rises from behind the desk, hand out-stretched, belongs to the same generation as the guy who went out minutes before, with red hair badly in need of brushing and a band of freckles bisecting his moon face. He, too, wears a sport coat, green plaid over an oyster-colored polo shirt buttoned to the neck. His grip, at least, is solid, and from appearances he doesn't hold back when shaking Sharon's hand. His gap-toothed smile reminds me of Dave Letterman, only without the smarm.

I introduce us both. "Thanks for seeing us."

"I should be thanking you, by golly. I hate these slow days."

By golly.

He asks us to sit, seats himself, and offers refreshment; elaborate politeness is one Canadian stereotype that seems to hold true. He inquires as to how far we've come—I guess he's detective enough to guess we're Yanks—and how we like his country. We make the expected replies. Then he shifts positions behind the desk, and I sense a sort of shield sliding down between his amiable expression and the brain behind it. "Now, what can Crane do for you?"

We've had ample opportunity to work on our story: the truth, basically, but with certain omissions.

Our friends the Moores are missing, apparently in haste and leaving behind their cell phones; the daughter had asked about Saskatchewan in the last call she made; and although the local police have issued a missing-persons alert, we decided to take some time off and follow the Canadian lead on our own.

"'Lead.'" Randy MacBride permits himself a slight smile, but makes no further comment. "When did you say they disappeared?"

"Saturday," I say.

He glances at a mechanical date calendar on the desk. "Two days ago."

"If today's Monday." I've lost track of the days.

"It is." And the sudden lack of the folksy accent in his tone is joined by yet another shield sliding down behind the first, this one solid steel. "The truth now, if you please, Mr. Gillett, Miss Kowalski. All of it this time, complete and unabridged. Except, of course, for the obvious lies, eh?"

CHAPTER 22

MY FIRST INSTINCT IS to play dumb. Sharon's first instinct is better. She touches my hand.

"Where'd we go wrong?" I ask.

"Apart from the obvious indicators, you mean?"

"I should tell you that before I joined Crane, I designed a program to streamline communications between all the authorities in this hemisphere for RCMP headquarters in Ottawa."

"You were a Mountie?" Sharon asks.

He wrinkles his nose. "I never cared for the nickname; but yes, in an administrative capacity. Anyway, the American authorities usually make contact with all the investigative agencies up here when there's an international connection. I'm surprised we weren't included in the alert. Unless your local law wasn't informed of the Canadian connection," he adds. "That would explain everything."

I open my mouth to fess up—only to snap it shut when Sharon lays her hand on mine and squeezes the bones tight enough to hurt.

"There's a reason for that," she says. "You see, I'm Gabby's godmother; she confides in me, things she'd hesitate to tell her parents. She was suddenly pushing for a family vacation to Saskatchewan, and I could tell it was about school. I pressed her and got the feeling that one of her teachers had done something inappropriate to her…but he's got her scared out of her mind to tell anyone."

"Any report she made should have been to the police. They know how to handle these things." MacBride's tone is as blue-edged as ever. He's not buying it.

"That's what *I* said. She turned white as a sheet and wouldn't tell me anything more. He's got her so frightened that if she says anything, he'll say she came on to him for a grade; she even thinks her parents might accept his side of the story. She's just fourteen, Mr. MacBride. I told Ray, who went to the house to talk with her parents. But they were gone. So I asked him to come with me, find the family, and bring it all out into the open. I'm sure Kevin and Margo can make her see the sense of putting it in official hands."

"You still should have reported it to the police."

Is it my imagination, or has an element of self-doubt crept into his tone?

"Maybe so, but I felt I'd be betraying Gabby's confidence. She'd never trust me again."

He turns his face on me. How did I ever think that moon-shaped countenance was gentle? "I get one story from you, another from her. Which one of you is lying?"

This time I plunge in before Sharon can say anything. "She's telling you the truth. It was my idea to make up that other story. She didn't have much faith in it, but I thought—"

"You should have let her do the thinking." He shook his head. "I'm not sure we can do business. Telling lies is part of the work, but I don't appreciate it from the people I'm trying to serve."

The phone on his desk rings just as Sharon's grip tightens again, the two things acting in concert to keep me from digging our hole deeper with a foolish remark. I can make nothing from the conversation, just some meaningless figures he repeats and scribbles onto a yellow legal pad. "Okie-dokie."

He cradles the receiver and returns his gaze to us. It seems less steely, but every bit as keen. "We charge forty-two dollars an hour American, plus expenses, which in this case will be mostly international calls; the first eight hours up front. We report daily, so you can decide whether to proceed."

Three hundred thirty-six dollars a day. I hesitate; Sharon doesn't. She draws a checkbook from her pocket. "Halfsies," she says to me, and I produce mine.

He glances at the checks, puts them in a drawer. "Pictures?"

I give him one from my wallet, taken last summer of Kevin, Margo, Josh, Gabby, and me at a backyard barbecue.

"Attractive family. Heights and weights?"

I provide as accurate a set of descriptions as I can manage; Sharon gently corrects me on Margo's weight.

"Any identifying marks? Scars, moles, tattoos?"

"Not—" I begin.

Sharon interrupts. "Margo has a vaccination mark on her right upper arm."

"Right." MacBride taps his pad with his mechanical pencil. "Where can we get in touch?"

We answer in unison. "The York Windsor."

"I thought you Yanks preferred the Hilton."

Sharon says, "You shouldn't generalize."

CHAPTER 23

SHARON TAKES THE WHEEL for the trip to the hotel. She notices I'm staring at her. "What?"

"How did you ever come up with a story like that right out of the blue?"

She colors slightly. "The Lifetime channel. Only there it was Nebraska, not Saskatchewan."

"How did you know he'd buy it?"

"I didn't. I had to come up with something fast, and that was the first thing that popped into my mind. It was just sordid enough to be believed."

"What if he checks the story?"

"I'm sure he will. I also think he'll be discreet about it. That much of an impression I got of the way he works. Meanwhile he'll put people on the case. With any luck he'll find the Moores before he finds out what a big fat liar I am."

"You're not big or fat."

She laughs.

The York Windsor is almost refreshingly Old

World: slightly seedy, with a foot-traffic pattern in the carpet in the cramped lobby, and a well-fed sixtyish woman behind the desk wearing a stretched-out cable-knit sweater, her silver hair in waves as permanent as a flash-frozen sea. She wears jet buttons in her ears and silver-framed glasses with a chain attached to the side-bows.

"Right," she says, consulting the anachronistic computer screen on the desk. "Gillett, double room."

"No, we asked for two rooms. Adjoining, if possible."

"I'm sorry, but there's only the one available. Most of our residents are permanent, and we've reserved a block of rooms for—"

"Don't tell me," I say. "A convention. What is it, fly-fishing or bear-hunting?"

"A family reunion. The Parkinsons, from Chicago."

"But we reserved two rooms."

"The other girl must have been on duty. She works hard, but she isn't much of a listener. Will you take it or not?" There's something about Canadians that makes an impatient question sound like a warm reception.

"Ray, we've shared a room before," Sharon says.

"Are there two beds?" I ask.

"No. It's what you Americans call a queen."

I'm about to suggest we try another place when Sharon says, "Two keys, please."

The elevator is about the size of an ancient steamer trunk and smells as musty. With the pair of us and our bags aboard, there's not enough room to turn around.

Sharon says, "We told Randy MacBride to contact us here. We've already had one miscommunication, with 'the girl.'" She squeaks the words like a teeny-bopper. "I don't want to take any more chances, do you?"

"You can have the bed. I'll sleep in the tub."

But instead of the claw-footed antique the rest of the place has prepared me to expect, our bathroom, just slightly larger than the elevator, contains only a tiled shower in addition to a three-cornered sink and a toilet with a tank mounted high on the wall and a chain flush. The bedroom is a shoebox, with a doorless closet and barely space to walk around the bed.

I stare at the bed, piled with pillows and tasseled cushions six deep, my cheeks getting hot.

Sharon laughs.

I join her in a full-out, window-shaking gut-buster.

She recovers first, gasping. "I'm not even sure there's room for us to wear pajamas."

I think she's joking. Right?

"You won't hurt me."

I'm in bed already; under the sheet, in my sleep shorts. The lamp is off, but the light outside leaks around the edges of the curtains on the window, illuminating her long T-shirt, silhouetting the curvature of her body.

You won't hurt me; a statement, not a question. Just where in this crazy, ridiculous, ill-advised journey she decided she could trust me, I'll never know.

I shake my head. I'm not even sure if she can see the movement, but it makes the pillowcase rustle and

I know she can hear that; the silence is like a third oc-
cupant of the room. There is a pause, then, moving
swiftly, as if to prevent a change of mind, she pulls aside
the sheet and slides in next to me. I reach for her ten-
tatively, and in that moment of hesitation she slides up
onto one hip, crosses her arms, gripping the T-shirt by
the hem, and slips it up and over her head.

Our arms wind around each other. Her skin is cool,
then warm, then hot, her lips hotter still. I slide a thigh
between hers, and—

And the telephone rings. It's Randy MacBride, asking me if I'm up for a drive.

CHAPTER 24

"BUFFALO RUN, WHERE'S THAT?" I ask.

"About eighty kilometers. Back when you Yanks finished slaughtering the big shaggies below the border, the hunters pitched camp there and brought the hides and carcasses by wagon to Regina, or 'Pile O' Bones,' as it was called back then, from debris left over from the skinning and butchering. I don't suppose you were aware of that."

"I wasn't aware of Regina until I made this trip," I say.

I'm riding next to the detective in a late-model Chevy. Five minutes have passed since he picked us up at the hotel. The city's well-lit streets slide past at the legal speed limit. No one in this country seems to make so much as a token attempt at even bending the rules.

"Anyway"—with a frown at my ignorance regarding his country—"it was a thriving camp in 1870, but now it's just a sleepy resort town. The lake was fished out decades ago, so it's populated only about three months of the year. I use the term 'town' advisedly; the community never got around to incorporating itself."

Sharon leans forward from the backseat, gripping the back of mine. "You're sure the Moores are staying there?"

"Positive. The Mounties always get their man." He smiles briefly at the windshield. "One of our operatives stopped in at their regional headquarters with a copy of the photo you gave us, and the post commander checked with the troopers assigned to routine patrol. Your friend Kevin had asked one of them for directions to the Bison Inn, a lodge in Buffalo Run. The trooper recognized him from the flyer. He was driving a blue Chrysler minivan with a rental plate, and there were a woman and two grown youngsters in the other seats. Our man went there and saw a vehicle answering that description outside the Bison."

"Did he talk to them?"

"No, but he got the number of their bungalow. He's waiting for us in the parking lot. I didn't want to risk frightening them into flight and the chance of losing them in transit. Confronting them with a pair of friendly and familiar faces instead of strangers is the safer way to go."

Sharon asks, "What sort of place is it?"

"Rustic: No cable or air-conditioning. The tourist season's just under way, but there are only three bungalows hired out of eight. Most Americans prefer the more modern facilities; the ones that provide all the things they piled into the car to get away from."

"Not us, Mr. MacBride," I say in defense of Yanks.

His smile this time lasts longer. "Please call me Randy."

After an hour we enter the Moose Jaw city limits. For me the name evokes a place built of logs with the bark still on, but by now I've learned to expect the usual chain restaurants and big-box stores.

We stop for a light. "Please don't think I'm being patronizing, Randy, but I'd give just about anything for a glimpse of just one prospector. A lumberjack would do."

"Actually, if you go deep enough into the territories, you might see one or two diehards looking for places overlooked during the Rush, although they're more likely to be on ATVs over donkeys. The First Nations people who hunt and trap in British Columbia maintain many of the old ways, though. Some of those rivers are navigable only by dugout and birch-bark canoe."

I glance back at Sharon. "We should go up there sometime." I'm counting on the darkness inside the car to mask any expression of desperate hope.

She smiles in the glow of a passing streetlight. "When we're not on a rescue mission."

"Just don't venture too far off the beaten path."

"Indians?" I ask.

"Drug dealers. The less-populated places are ideal for growing marijuana and cocaine and cooking meth. The men you're likely to encounter are more apt to welcome you with Uzis than western hospitality." He looks at me out of the corner of his eye, the dash lights glittering off the iris. "You wanted primitive."

We resume moving. In a little while we leave Moose Jaw, pass through some open country—seeming more sinister after Randy's warning—negotiate a roundabout, and run out of pavement after a quarter-mile; but the rural roads here are better maintained than those back home. We roll smoothly over packed limestone, and abruptly a huge shaggy beast leaps into the headlights looking like something from the Book of Job. I stifle a gasp. It's a tree stump some six feet tall and carved by an artist with a chainsaw.

"Welcome to Buffalo Run," Randy says. "Bison Inn next stop."

And if there's any mercy in the world, the Moores at last.

CHAPTER 25

THE BISON INN IS two stories of curved cedar siding stained dark honey with four-paned windows and its name burned into a lintel above the front door. With four miniature one-story replicas lined up on either side, the place looks like a midcentury architect's idea of a settler's log cabin that's given birth to a litter. A sign mounted under the lintel reads OFFICE in orange-pink neon.

"Wait here." Randy, who's parked on the edge of a lot containing a scatter of cars and pickup trucks, gets out and walks past the office to a Chevy, identical to his except in a different color, at the lot's far edge. I see no sign of the Chrysler minivan the Moores were supposedly spotted in.

After a minute bent to the driver's side window, Randy comes back. Behind him the other car's motor starts and the car backs around and follows the driveway to the road. Under the security light I recognize the young man in Dockers from the Crane reception room.

"Stevens is our most patient op," Randy says, climbing back under the wheel. "He's been here three hours, and he actually looked disappointed when I said I'd spell him."

"Did he see anything new?" I ask.

"Josh, the boy, went to the lodge for ice about eight-thirty. He was back in number three in five minutes. Nothing since."

I look at the clock on the dash. Almost eleven. "Which one's three?"

He points at a bungalow two doors down from the lodge. There's no light in the windows.

Sharon asks, "What now?"

"As I said, I don't want to alarm them with a strange face in the middle of the night. I'll wait here while you knock on the door."

"Which one of us?" I ask.

"Both. They might not recognize you from the window, and most people are less threatened by a visit from a couple." His teeth catch the glow from a security light mounted high on a pole. "You've got a mobile?"

Sharon passes her phone across the seat. Randy takes it and adds a contact. "I just took over the top of your favorites list. If you have doubts, ring me and I'll come running." He returns the device, then reaches past me, pops open the glove compartment, and removes something in a holster.

"Do you really need that?" My voice is a whisper, although no one can overhear us from outside the car.

His laugh is a surprised cough. "I've found it comes in handy when someone calls me."

I see then that the object is a phone in a protective case with a belt clip.

"You were expecting a gun? Even lecherous high school teachers don't usually come heeled."

I can't make out his expression in the gloom, whether it's as guileless as his words or whether he's giving me the opportunity to come clean.

"I suppose you're right," I say.

Sharon and I get out, she carrying her phone.

The night is crisp, smelling of pine. We walk with our hips nearly touching, our footsteps audible on the packed earth. The traffic from the Queen's Highway, a mile or two distant, seems almost as close as if we're standing on its apron.

"Do you think we should have told him the truth?" Sharon whispers.

I whisper back.

"Our story got us this far." I express confidence I don't feel.

"You mean *my* story."

"We're in this together."

In response she winds an arm inside mine.

The numeral three is fashioned of twisted twine, fixed to the door with square horseshoe-type nails. There's no peephole. Behind us something thumps, probably a guest in one of the other occupied bungalows stepping outside for ice or fresh air. I feel exposed then; but my fist is already raised. I tap my knuckles three times rapidly before I can change my mind.

No response. No sound from inside.

"Try again," she says.

Still nothing. I look again at the dark windows, feeling a sinking disappointment in my stomach. "They're gone. What now?"

"Randy will know what to do." She steers me away from bungalow number three, and we walk back toward the car.

Ten feet from the car I freeze, throwing out my arm to stop her.

"No, he won't."

The overhead light glitters on a kaleidoscope of fissured glass in the window on the driver's side, pushed into a bulge by the impact of Randy's head.

CHAPTER 26

"HOW DO YOU *KNOW* he's dead?" Sharon's voice has returned to level, but with a thread of panic running through it. We're hanging in the shadows at the edge of the light.

I maintain my whisper, hoping she'll take the hint. "I doubt he slammed his head into the window on a whim."

"But you don't *know!*" Not quite a whisper, she can't manage anything quieter than a hoarse shriek.

"You're right." Concern for Randy throbs beneath fears for us both.

So I creep into the light, feeling exposed, looking around me as I go around to the passenger's side door. I pull it open, not overlooking the perfectly round hole in that window, striated only slightly by the swift cold path of the bullet. It passed through the window directly into—

Into Randy's head.

Randy's dead. The purplish hole in the right temple

is the period to a life I know nothing about; wife, children, friends?

In the glow of the security light, Sharon reads the answer on my face.

"What now?" She mouths the words without tonal inflection.

"The bungalow."

We run. I've never run faster, not on the basketball court, and certainly not hauling another human being along with me. And now, she's hauling me along with her, and we both stumble, but run into the stumble. *If we fall, we die.* The refrain repeats itself constantly in my head, and I break all my own records.

Fast as we cross it, the distance from Randy's car is a marathon run, every enveloping shadow populated by an assassin.

Wham! Wham! Wham! Gunshots!

No, just my heart pounding in my temples. I leap up the step to the door of bungalow number three, hauling Sharon along by the wrist. I grasp the knob and yank. It's locked.

There's no time for doubts about my ability to break down a door. I let go of Sharon, step back, raise a foot to kick.

Something clicks and the door swings inward.

My forward momentum almost pitches me onto my face. Instinctively I grab Sharon's wrist and we plunge through the opening and tumble inside.

A hand—Kevin's!—seizes my shoulder and jerks us free of the door so he can swing it shut.

I pause to catch my breath; not that it comes. It's as if I've had the wind knocked out of me by a violent fall. The room is dark, but as my eyes adjust I make out Kevin, Margo, Josh, and Gabby, crowded into a lump, horror stamped on every face.

"Ray." This is Margo, whose eyes are more accustomed to the gloom. She turns her head Sharon's way, and in her silence is a bewildered question.

"It's Sharon," Sharon says. "Sharon Kowalski. From the computer store?"

"Oh, yes! But—"

"Randy's dead!" I blurt out.

"Randy? Who's Randy?"

"The detec—" I start.

Sharon picks it up. "The man who helped us find you. Someone killed him in his car."

She might have screamed the information into a vacuum. All the Moores are in action now: Margo, bundling her children toward the back of a small room with two beds, Kevin making a beeline in Margo's direction. Before us is a sliding glass door, beyond which is blackness. Kevin fumbles with its latch, hurls it aside with a whoosh and a thud, spilling more light from the room onto a wooden deck with a gas grill under a vinyl cover and a quartet of Adirondack chairs.

The only view I see is more blackness beyond the cedar planks, dimly lit by some outside lamp, moths swarming in its glow.

"As we rehearsed." Suddenly Kevin's voice is calm,

with an edge. He claps his hands three times fast. "Go-go-go!"

Unrehearsed as we are, Sharon and I go, inches behind the Moores, who are all moving as one body toward the blackness beyond the deck.

Bundling us all, in one body, into the solid barrier of Cam Howard, chief of the Willow Grove Police, an investor in Jeremy Adder's racket, who has a gun gripped firmly in both hands.

CHAPTER 27

WE SCREAM, ALL OF us; I as shrilly as any.

The sheer volume of sound seems to smack Howard in the face. His eyes, squinted in concentration, open wide, his arms falter.

He lowers the revolver.

"You folks all right?"

Sharon is in motion. She's still holding her phone. She hurls it overhand, snapping her arm as it leaves her fingers. It strikes Howard square on the bridge of his nose. He staggers backward, almost losing his grip on his weapon. He keeps it, and prevents himself from falling by bracing a heel behind him.

My reflexes are slower, but I rush him, both hands straight out in front of me, hoping to shove him off his feet before he can raise his hands and fire.

"Ray, stop!"

It's Sharon, her voice so loud it halts me in my tracks. Howard, holding the gun now in one hand, has the other to his forehead. His eyes are out of focus.

"*What* did you say?" Sharon asks Howard.

He recovers by the millisecond, taking his hand away, looking at the blood on it, and squaring his shoulders, the revolver dangling at his side. A purplish bump shows between his eyebrows with a small diagonal cut in the center.

"I asked if you folks were all right. I guess I got my answer. Don't go out that door!" The gun springs up, pointing past me. I turn just as Kevin and Margo are moving toward the front door. They stop, arrested by his harsh rasp.

"Why?" I ask, just as harshly. "So you can kill us where we stand?"

For answer he crosses the room in four strides, turns, and inserts himself between us and the front door, gesturing with the gun. "Move away from there, you two; if I can see you, so can he."

He?

I have an arm around Sharon's shoulders. We step away from the open back door.

"He," I say. "So you've got an accomplice. All the better to murder seven people." I don't care what his response will be to that. Every second of delay I can buy is precious.

"What are you—wait, seven?" He sounds confused.

"The six of us and Randy MacBride, in his car outside."

"Who's Randy MacBride?"

"The detective we hired to find the Moores. You really are cold-blooded. You don't even bother to find out who it is you're killing."

"That must have been the noise I heard. I was watching the bungalow from the back, with it between me and the parking lot. I thought it was a door slamming. He must be using a suppressor." He shakes his head. "Well, now we know for sure what he's got in mind. Not that I expected anything else."

Kevin speaks up for the first time since Howard's entrance. In the dimness I can see him standing in front of his family, creating a shield. "Are you with him?"

"With who?" I ask. "Is Adder here?"

"Shut up, Gillett." The tone Howard used when he caught me leaving the Moores' house; was it really only two days ago? "No, Mr. Moore—Kevin—I'm not with him. I'm doing my job."

"What job's that?" Sharon says. "Protecting your investment?" But she sounds unsure.

He looks at her. "Who are you?"

"She's with me," I say. "Without her, I never would have found the Moores."

"You mean her and that phone she brained me with. Without it, they wouldn't be in the trouble they're in and your man MacBride would still be breathing. Now I know how he made it this far without taking a single wrong turn."

Now I'm confused. "Who, Adder?"

"No, you idiot. Dale Mercer. You've been leaving a trail of electronic bread crumbs all the way from Willow Grove. He's been tracking your signal. That speech you made back at the office must have convinced him you knew something we didn't."

"But I didn't. Not then, anyway."

"Call it cop's instinct. You led him straight here."

A noise from Kevin draws my attention. In the dim light his face looks incredulous. He starts to speak, but is interrupted by a shout from outside.

"In the cabin! This is United States Marshal Dale Mercer! You can come out now! I've got your back!"

"Thank God!" I turn toward the door.

Howard's free hand clamps tight on my arm. "Stay put, damnit! It's a trick!"

Releasing me with a shove, he turns toward Kevin. "You may as well tell him what's going on. We're not going anywhere fast, and we need everyone on the same page if we're going to get out of here alive. I'll keep watch on the window."

"Josh, tell him, son."

A young throat clears. The boy is standing in shadow, but I can make out part of his face, pale in the reflected light.

"Mercer works for Jeremy Adder," he says, his voice shaking. "*He's* the one after us."

CHAPTER 28

THIS TIME I'M THE one who breaks the silence.

"Last week I'd barely heard of Adder. Now I find out he owns a federal lawman as well as the chief of police."

"Who told you he owns me?" Howard snaps.

"You own stock in Adder's firm."

"Who told you that?"

My face grows hot. The blood has come back into it in a rush of humiliation. Quietly: "Adder."

"And why do you think he told you that, Mr. Amateur Detective?"

Sharon breaks in. "You made your point, Chief. Of course he wanted to throw suspicion off his man."

"All my money's tied up in my mortgage." He turns his attention from me and softens his tone. "Go on, Josh."

"I work part-time at the Rathskeller in Sackville. Thursday before last, the headwaiter sent me into a private room to fill the water glasses. I've seen Mr.

Adder at company picnics, but I doubt he remembers me. Anyway I didn't want to interrupt his conversation by introducing myself, and he never looked up at me. Neither of them did."

I'm holding my breath. I guess what's coming.

Howard already has. "Was there anyone else at the table besides Adder and Mercer?"

"No, sir."

"Did you hear what they were saying?

"I can't remember. I'd never seen Mercer before. But they seemed to be pretty friendly.

"I recognized him the minute he walked into our living room the next day." He starts to go on, but falters.

His father's hand grips Josh's shoulder, as if to help him stay upright. "He told us about it when we went into the den to talk over the witness protection offer. That's when we decided to turn it down. It wasn't hard for me to make a show of disbelief. I was telling the truth about never suspecting anything. If it weren't for what Josh told us, I'd have been certain that some mistake had been made. That dinner between Mercer and Adder convinced me more than any evidence he could have showed me."

"So you fled," Howard says, "instead of calling the police."

"We couldn't risk it. If Adder had a US marshal in his pocket, why not the local law?"

Margo speaks up. "We had no one to trust but each other."

He looks at Sharon. "I'm guessing you came up with Saskatchewan. Your boyfriend's not that smart."

"He was smart enough to succeed where you failed," she says, bristling.

"This is my fault."

Another new voice: Gabby's, sounding almost little-girlish. Her shadow stirs at her mother's side. "I called Miss Thurgood, asking her about Saskatchewan. Dad overheard me."

He says, "I erased everything from the phone, left it behind with all the others so we couldn't—couldn't be traced."

"How did *you* find this place?" I ask Howard.

"The old-fashioned way. I followed Mercer. We don't have the equipment to run an electronic tail. We need the state police for that, and they'd insist on a court order. Mercer didn't bother, having access to the equipment himself. When I called Mercer's office for an update, they told me he'd taken a leave of absence—in the middle of an important investigation. I got suspicious. I went to his home in Sackville, and saw him pull out in his car half a block before I got there."

He shakes his head. "I was disappointed. Feds of all people should be more wary. Anyway, I was glad I decided to take my personal car. He didn't try to shake me. That's when I made up my mind he's dirty. When a cop gets to where he thinks the law's his personal tool, he assumes he's bulletproof."

I say, "Let's hope he keeps being overconfident."

"Let's not. That would be overconfidence on our part."

"So, what now?" asks Kevin.

"I think our best bet is to stay put and call for backup."

Kevin goes for the phone on the nightstand between the beds. "Dead. He must have cut the lines."

"I left my cell in the car, behind the bungalow," Howard says, for the first time sounding sheepish. "When I saw movement here, I came barreling out."

"*Now* who's not so smart? You—" Sharon's face changes suddenly. She makes a beeline for the back door.

"I said keep away from there!"

She's already there, scooping up her phone. Backing into gloom, she looks at the screen. "Broken."

"He's only one man," I say. "Can't we—?"

"Quiet!" says Howard.

The angle of his face draws my gaze to the window at his left. In the edge of the pool of illumination shed by the security light, a hunched figure scuttles through the space between bungalows. It wears a hip-length coat and carries something with a long tube; a shotgun. On its head is an ear-flapped cap.

Sharon says, "There's your lumberjack."

CHAPTER 29

"WHAT'S GOING ON IN there?" Mercer shouts. "I brought help. You're all safe. Come on out!"

"That was no *deputy* we saw," I say.

"The system isn't that twisted," Howard says. "I hope. Mercer must've made a call. Somebody this side of the border, probably, though most likely not a native. Someone like him would keep tabs on handy international fugitives."

"Do you think this man killed MacBride?" I ask.

"Not unless he has a lighter piece. Nobody would mistake a shotgun blast for a slamming door. My money's still on Mercer."

Sharon asks, "Are there more?"

"I sure hope not, because if I'm wrong, what I've got in mind doesn't stand a chance." To Kevin: "Where are you parked?"

"In front of the bungalow."

"Why not put out a welcome mat with your name on it?"

"It's not the Flex. I put it in storage and rented another car before we crossed the border, to keep our license plate from being reported."

Howard does a slow pirouette. My eyes adjusted to the minimal light, and I see what he sees: the usual furnishings, wall art, bathroom door ajar, a squat refrigerator with a small microwave on top. "What did you pack?"

"We left in too much of a hurry, but we picked up some things along the way: changes of clothes, toilet articles—"

"Shaving things?"

Kevin nods. "Of course."

"There a flashlight in here?"

"My phone—oops. Forgot." Sharon flips her broken phone onto the bed.

"I do." Margo steps away from Gabby to rummage in a shiny handbag, extracts something that jingles, hands the chief a key ring with a tiny flash attached.

He snaps it on. The tiny bulb illuminates little more than itself. Kevin produces a cheap vinyl case. Holstering his gun, Howard unzips the case, dumps its contents onto the near bed, and sorts through them rapidly in the light of the flash. He holds up a small tube and curses. "Gel, this is what you use?"

"Josh?"

Without awaiting instructions, the youth produces a red-and-white-striped aerosol can.

The chief takes it, examines it. "Perfect."

The rest of us wait in silence.

"Get ready to run," he says. "If Mercer goes according to standard cop procedure, he's expecting us to make a break out the back. That's why he stationed the shotgunner there."

And whoever else he might have recruited, I think; but I say nothing.

"Mercer will be watching the front, from a little distance so he has a broader field of fire. His plan will be to pin us down long enough to identify his targets and take them out in order: Kevin first, because he's the one Adder's worried about, then Josh."

"But he didn't see me in the restaurant," Josh says.

"He's had time enough to wonder how he tipped his hand, and to find out where you work. Gillett, you're next. After that, he'll count on the female survivors being paralyzed by shock so he can pick them off like tin ducks." In a band of pale light, his smile is tight-lipped and humorless. "Forgive me, ladies. Some cops have spent the last thirty years in hibernation. I'm betting he's one."

"The bastard." says Sharon.

"You took the words out of my mouth." says Margo.

Howard holds up the can of shaving cream. "Kevin, unlock and unchain the door and keep your hand on the knob. The rest of you stay close, but leave space for the door to open. When what happens happens, all of you rush for the car. Is it locked?"

Kevin says, "I'm afraid so."

"Keyless remote?"

He takes something from a pocket and holds it up.

"Wait for the noise, then hit the button twice, unlocking all the doors. Pile in, start it up, and peel rubber. Don't stop this side of the border. Understood?"

A collective "Yes."

"If anyone else has a better plan, I'd sure like to hear it. I don't place a whole lot of faith in this one, but it's better than sitting here and waiting for Mercer to lose patience and rush us from all sides."

Silence.

"Okay, then." He shakes the can. The contents make a noise like surging surf.

"What about you?" I ask. "What will you be doing while we're making a break for it?"

His smile broadens, but is no less grim. "I call shotgun."

The fear is palpable. But so is the resolve. Kevin releases the chain from its slot, snaps open the latch, grasps the knob, turns it, and pauses.

Margo, Josh, Gabby, Sharon, and I gather just beyond the door's sweep.

"Wait for it." Chief Cam Howard tugs open the door of the microwave, puts the aerosol can inside, swings the door shut, uses Margo's flashlight to find the start button, and presses it. The interior lights up behind the thick glass and the mechanism whirs. In no time at all the object inside begins to rattle, its metal base vibrating against the floor of the oven, faster and faster as the pressure builds.

CHAPTER 30

I NOW KNOW THE longest unit of time. It's not an hour, a day, a week, or a year; it's not twenty, it's not half a century. This unit can't be measured on a clock or a calendar, only on a small cheap microwave oven in a cramped bungalow in the Canadian wilderness.

The can of shaving cream is fully animated, its bottom clattering against the molded plastic floor, the whole thing revolving like a spool of thread spinning on top of a sewing machine—but no; not like anything mechanical, more like a living, writhing creature, a small feral beast working itself up into a violent frenzy of self-defense. The whirring of the built-in cooling fan climbs to a whine. Rattle, rattle, spin, shriiiiieeeeek—

Whoom!

The heavy glass in the door bursts outward, driven by a volume of flame, throwing shards the size of cake knives and shreds of red-and-white-striped aluminum in a spray perpendicular to where we're standing, the Moores, Sharon, and I at one end of the room, Chief

Howard at the other, the revolver in his hand now, pointing toward the back door. The flames outdistance the projectiles, far enough to scorch the knotty pine panels on the opposite wall.

All of which is a psychedelic flash of images, impressing themselves on our minds as Kevin tears open the door, thumbing the key tab with his other hand, and we pile through. Behind us, a sharp crackling, the fire gnawing at pine and fabric; and above that another explosion, loud enough to deaden the report that comes square on its heels; or did the lighter bang come first? One is the deep bellow of a large-bore shotgun, the other the sharper sound of a revolver; the lumberjack's big-game weapon versus Cam Howard's sidearm, an uneven match if ever I heard one.

Not over yet.

Something snaps in the open air, sounding like a cap pistol in the echo of the descending three notes of the initial blast, the roar, and the bang; but something buzzes past my right ear and *thunks* the curved cedar siding next to the door we've just come through, Sharon and I gripping each other's arms like lifelines. Before me, a door is slid partially open, belonging to a minivan parked in front of the bungalow. The Moores are already inside. I reach for the door.

"Where's the fire?"

We turn in unison. In the glow from the burning building, Dale Mercer's blocky, gray-clad form stands beside the van, a living barricade. At hip level he holds a shiny pistol with a barrel extension—Howard called it a suppressor—pointed straight at us. Reflected flame seems to dance in both eyes.

Someone cries out, using my voice. In the same instant, I hit his arm as hard as I can, and he drops the gun with a clank. Mercer stumbles backward, fumbling his weapon.

Sharon and I pile on top of others in the back, but before I can sort out who the bodies belong to, the door closes on the calf of my leg, bouncing off as the car lurches across the lot. A blur of gray sweeps past the corner of my eye; Mercer, scrambling out of the way. I don't feel the pain in my leg until we plow over a speed bump—if that's what it is—and careen into tar-blackness. Ahead is the rural road, walled in and canopied by trees blocking out light from all sides and above.

Crack!

Something strikes the back window, where the receding light from the inn glitters on a crystalline web; a bullet has struck it at an angle, glancing off without puncturing.

We're a country block away before the four of us in the back begin to untangle our limbs and find the floor with our feet. The dome light springs on, blinding us.

"Is anybody hurt?" Kevin, anxious, dividing his concentration between the back and the road ahead. Margo's face is a mask of anxiety over the back of the passenger's seat.

Cartoonishly, Josh, Gabby, Sharon, and I pat ourselves all over, searching for holes. We look from one face to another, and despite the tragedy and horror of the night, we burst into hysterical laughter.

By pure chance, scrambling in panic, the Moores and their guests have managed to come to rest in the classic position of a family and friends bound on a weekend outing: Dad behind the wheel, Mom beside him, the kids crowded in with the couple they've invited along.

CHAPTER 31

TWO MONTHS LATER, THE governor makes a special trip to Willow Grove to present Police Chief Cameron Howard with a medal of valor for his actions in Saskatchewan. Commander Lewis of the State Police wheels the guest of honor across the stage of Gabby Moore's high school to accept the decoration. Howard's face, burned in the bungalow fire, is still partially bandaged, and he's had hip surgery after taking a blast from a shotgun fired by one Emmanuel Flood, a known dealer in meth and harder drugs on both sides of the border, and a former resident, now deceased, of Calgary, Alberta. The chief appears self-conscious in his dress uniform, dark brown with brass snaps and the inevitable clip-on necktie. But he can't hide his relief that he's finally out of the hospital.

In his speech introducing the governor, Commander Lewis announces that former United States Marshal Dale Edward Mercer has been apprehended in Toronto, Ontario, while attempting to board a plane for Central America. Canadian authorities report that he's agreed not to fight extradition if the American prosecutor lets him plead to a lesser charge of first-degree manslaughter, and to testify against Jeremy Adder.

"He's getting off easy," Sharon whispers.

"Maybe not," I murmur back, "if what Cam says is true about what happens to cops in prison."

At the reception in the multipurpose room, Kevin excuses himself to shake hands with Tiffany Thurgood and her partner, Dorothy, who played such an important role in finding the Moores. Howard, looking embarrassed, sits in the center of a shifting knot of well-wishers; the only constants are his diminutive blond wife and their preteen twin boys. Kevin returns, and Sharon and I wait with him and Margo for the crowd to thin out before adding our congratulations. Josh and Gabby are chattering away with fellow teenagers by the refreshment table.

"To friends." Kevin raises a plastic glass filled with something nonalcoholic, as per school rules.

Sharon and I lift ours more reluctantly. "You more than us," I say. "We brought the wolf to your door."

"And an end to our flight," Margo adds, sipping. "If you hadn't, we'd still be running."

"I'm glad for that," says Sharon. "I can't stop thinking about poor Randy MacBride. If we'd told him the truth—"

Kevin interrupts. "You didn't know who you could trust. This way, you flushed Mercer out into the open.

None of us knew he was there, except Cam, and he was on his own. We might all have been slaughtered."

"Enough of that." Margo beams at Sharon. "Where are you making this character take you on your honeymoon?"

"British Columbia, can you believe it?"

Kevin's brow wrinkles. "Prospecting for gold?"

"No need. I already hit pay dirt." I wind my arm around Sharon's waist.

He smiles. "Still feeling the years, old-timer?"

I return the expression. "Who you calling old?" Then the smile fades. "I'm taking on extra work, by the way. I intend to pay back that loan on time."

His face doesn't change. "No hurry. Adder will never miss it."

And he winks.

THE
HOUSEWIFE

JAMES PATTERSON
WITH SAM HAWKEN

PROLOGUE

SHE'D DONE IT BEFORE, but every time it was different enough that it thrilled all over again.

For the night her name was Mari. Not like *Mary,* because Mary was dull. No, it was a drawn-out *ah* and felt like a warm breath. The man she was supposed to meet tonight had asked for someone special, and of the options he chose Mari. Mari with the mystery name. He had to know it was a lie, but there was the barest possibility it might be true, and that was part of the game.

In the back of the limousine Mari heard nothing but the low tone of the engine. The city streets, the lights, and people of the midweek night, were locked out behind smoky glass and she was hidden from them in turn. She was alone with her thoughts of what came next. Even the partition between the driver and passenger compartment was firmly closed.

Mari made herself a drink. It was her third so far. She didn't need it, but she liked the sensation of pushing the edge of too much, as if she were floating past those muted lights and people. She relaxed and put her feet up on the long rear seat, looking down at her bare legs, bed-tanned against the dark upholstery.

The dress she wore was a black, silk-lined J. Mendel, the skirt cut above the knees. Dark eyelet lace made subtle floral patterns around her shoulders and formed delicate sleeves. The dress cost two thousand dollars, and she would make half that tonight alone. Her closets at home were full of dresses like this, in white and cerulean blue and more. She had auburn hair that cast down to the lace of her dress in sculpted ringlets, and she chose the colors that made her hair catch fire to the eye. She was a striking woman, but she wasn't as young as she used to be and her hair was all the more important now.

Her phone trilled. Mari opened her tiny clutch purse to find it. She put it to her ear.

"Are you almost there?" the man on the line asked before she said a thing.

"Yes."

"Good, then you're still on time. He said he wouldn't wait. One minute too long, and that's it."

Mari kicked off her shoes and drew her feet up underneath her. Her skin was tingling. It was the drink and anticipation mixing in her veins. "You think he'd be angry if I was a *little* late?"

"You want to test him?"

"Maybe."

"If you disappoint him..." the man on the line said.

Mari smiled and let the teasing into her voice. "Then *you'll* be angry."

"Is that what you want?"

The limousine slowed. Mari saw the familiar windows of the restaurant by the hotel. Her heartbeat picked up and her throat tightened. "Yes," she said quietly.

"Then I'll be very angry."

She flushed. The limousine stopped. "I have to go."

Mari ended the call without letting him say goodbye. She gathered up her shoes quickly and got them on by the time the driver had her door open. She slid over and out, holding down the short hem of the dress to keep the doorman from seeing more than he should. It was brilliant here at the entrance to the Ambassador Hotel, all lights and brass. She flicked a lock of hair away from her face and went in without looking left or right.

The man at the desk knew her by sight and didn't stop her as she crossed the heavy rugs that lined the marble lobby. Mari went straight to the elevator and pressed the button for the tenth floor. When it stopped it made a gentle chime. She stepped out into an empty hallway lined with dark wood. The sound of her heels were absorbed by the carpeting.

She found the room. She stood in front of it, seeing herself reflected in the brass number plate. When she breathed, she felt light-headed. The rest of her was warm and fluid, as if she were infused with something intoxicating. She knocked.

The door came open. A man a little older than her husband stood revealed on the other side. His dark hair was streaked heavily with gray. His tie was undone, but still around his neck. He had his shoes off. Mari saw the amber drink in his hand, and the single, glossy cube of ice soaking.

Nothing was said. He looked at her and she shivered. "Am I…late?" she asked.

"No. Come in."

The room was large, richly appointed, and had a broad window open to a view of the electric city. The man passed a small table by the door and gestured with his drink. Mari saw the plain envelope left there on the polished cherry.

He walked to the window, drank the last of his drink, and put the tumbler down. His gaze was flat. He had a sharp jawline and a swimmer's body. Mari approached him. The heat in her body had risen to her head and she floated across the carpet. She reached up to put her arms around his neck. He caught her by the wrists, tightly enough that she gasped out loud.

When they kissed, it was with urgency. He forced her arms to her sides before he let her go, drawing her by the waist against him. Mari felt the hunger coming away from him in surges. Then he was pushing her until the backs of her knees hit the bed and she sat sharply.

His hands lifted her skirt to her waist. She was bare underneath, and the cool air of the room played over naked skin. He wanted her back to him and she obeyed. His pants hit the floor, the buckle thumping.

She heard him breathing as her hair fell around her face. He held on to her, and she gripped the bed as breathing turned to gasps and then it was done.

He stepped back and let her sit on the bed. She saw his face had gone pink, and a sheen of sweat showed on his forehead, pasting stray hairs to the skin. He breathed through his mouth.

"Is that all you want?"

The man straightened. He pushed his hair back into place. "No," he told her.

He undressed himself and then she helped him undress her. They crawled onto the bedspread. He had his tie in his fist. They kissed and she let him put her hands above her head. The tie slipped between the wooden slats of the headboard, then into place around her wrists before going taut. Their bodies were pressed together.

"Is that all you want?" Mari whispered in his ear.

"No," the man said, and then they went on.

CHAPTER 1

ON THE MORNING MAGGIE Denning saw Holly Gibbs for the first and last time, she dressed her one-year-old twins, Lana and Becky, for the unseasonably cool May morning air. She strapped the girls into the seats of the double stroller, made sure a warm blanket draped over both children's legs and feet, then put on her own jacket to go outside. It may still have been too cold for morning walks, but Maggie was tired of being indoors and the spring had been miserable for too long.

She was at the door when she stopped at the thought of leaving something behind. She hurried upstairs to the master bedroom and went to her dresser. The top was bare. For a moment she was confused, and then she realized she was looking for a detective's shield and identification that weren't there anymore. After almost two years she forgot, and now she stood in the bedroom laughing at herself for thinking it was time to get back on the job.

The girls waited patiently for her when she returned. "I almost took you two to work," Maggie told them. "You want to do paperwork all day? No? Okay, then, let's walk."

It was after ten in the morning, and the bedroom community of the Parish at Beverly Point had gone mostly quiet. The hustle came at the beginning and end of the day, when SUVs and expensive sedans plied the clean and orderly streets to and from work in nearby Castletown. For the housewives like Maggie who stayed behind, the neighborhood grew too still and on a chilly morning like this one the fieldstone faces of the sprawling, four-thousand-square-foot houses on her street seemed as gray as tombs. A security company sent a car to lazily patrol, but it was for appearances only. Maggie rarely saw it.

Maggie didn't listen to music while she walked, preferring the quiet chirping of her daughters as Lana and Becky babbled to each other in twin-talk. A few birds flickered through the leaves of trees struggling into life against the weather. The drone of the stroller's rubber wheels was unchanging.

She reached the end of her street and chose another at random. Her walks could take an hour or more, and range all over the development. The Parish covered a lot of ground, and even after having lived there eighteen months Maggie was not familiar with every house or every family. Something about that itched at the back of her brain, as though she *should* know and it was unacceptable not to.

Somewhere a dog barked. The clouds lay heavy in

the sky, threatening rain. The pavement was already dark from an overnight drizzle. Maggie's attention wandered, and she barely heard the engine creeping up on her from behind until the car was right beside her.

The Mercedes limousine was glossy, as if a fingerprint had never been left on it. The windows were impenetrably black. Maggie started when she saw it in the corner of her eye and she stopped as it cruised past, not speeding up nor slowing down. Its taillights were brilliant, and they flared as it reached the far corner of the block and turned, coming to a stop along the curb in front of a redbrick house with its porch light still burning.

Maggie was within a few yards of the limo when the driver got out. He was clad in a gray uniform with a cap, and his face was set in stone. He barely glanced at Maggie when he rounded the limo's tail to reach the curb. He opened the rear door and said nothing, staring straight ahead.

The woman emerged. Maggie saw her hair first, striking and red, then the sooty black of her expensive dress. The woman stepped up on the curb and Maggie saw only the back of her head as she told the driver good-bye. The door was closed. The driver got back behind the wheel. The limousine pulled away. It was an efficient transaction, and now Maggie was alone with the woman and the girls and the quiet neighborhood.

Bare arms and heels, a high skirt with a girlish flounce. A dress suitable for a party, but not for the chilly morning. The woman looked left and right, and only then noticed Maggie there. She jumped and put her hand to her chest. Maggie saw the woman had a red mark around her wrist. A binding mark. "Oh, my God, I didn't even see you there," the woman said. Her voice was slurry from drink and tiredness. She had the air of someone who'd been up all night. Her makeup was mussed. Maggie's eyes flicked to the woman's other wrist. It was marked, too.

"We didn't mean to startle you," Maggie said. "We're only passing through."

The woman was in her mid-forties, maybe four or five years younger than Maggie, who was nearly fifty. Her lipstick was smeared. She smiled broadly. "Babies! Oh, what cute ones! How old?"

"Thirteen months and three weeks," Maggie replied. She looked at the woman's neck now. More red marks around her throat, subtler, but still visible. Maggie made out what might be the pattern of fingers. All these marks would inevitably bruise.

"So cute," the woman said again, and then she wobbled.

Maggie rushed forward and caught the woman before she stumbled off the curb. Up close she smelled alcohol and perfume in equal measure. "Busy night?" Maggie asked her.

"I can't keep up like I used to," the woman said. She dropped her clutch purse.

Maggie picked it up. "Maggie Denning," she said. "My husband and I are kind of new. I've never even been down this street before."

"Denning? Oh. Oh, I'm Holly," the woman said. Maggie noted a slight puffiness around the woman's eyes and in her cheeks. It went with the territory when blood flow was interrupted.

They shook hands. Holly had hardly any grip. "You should probably get some rest," Maggie suggested.

Holly laughed brightly and a little too loud. "I think that's a *great* idea. Nice to meet you, Maggie. Bye, little ones!"

The twins gabbled back. Holly walked away, unsteady on her heels. At the front door of her house, she struggled with her keys, but she managed to get in anyway. Maggie watched her go, and wondered if Holly was pay to play or strictly recreational.

Either way, it was none of her business.

CHAPTER 2

SHE'D PUT HOLLY OUT of her mind by breakfast the next morning. She got up early while her husband, Karl, was still asleep, juiced a half-dozen oranges and made omelets with cheddar and ham. She slid the food onto plates at the moment Karl entered the room, still putting on his tie. He hadn't donned his jacket yet, and his badge and weapon were visible at his waist. Maggie tried to shake the wistful feeling she got when she saw them. It never went away. "Morning," he said.

Maggie laid out the feast. She put a handful of plain Cheerios on each girl's tray to chase and eat. "Morning," she replied. She kissed Karl on the cheek. "I should say, 'Morning, stranger,' because I haven't seen you awake for two days. What kind of schedule does Collins have you working?"

"The busy kind. He's not a nice boss like you were."

"Maybe I should come down there and tell them I'd like to see my husband once in a while. I saw you more when we were on the job."

"Yeah, I know. It was a late one last night and we have briefings this morning I can't skip, otherwise I'd stick around and help you with the laundry. That pile is as big as I am."

"I'm working on it."

They sat and ate. Karl looked at his plate while he chewed, and he slurped the juice. "Coffee?" Maggie asked him.

"My blood is half caffeine at this point, but I probably should. I don't know how long this day is going to last. If I miss dinner again tonight, I apologize in advance."

Maggie poured the coffee. Her husband slurped that, too. He was a noisy eater, and he snored, too. They'd been married four years. "Gardening club tomorrow," she said by way of conversation.

"Isn't everything frozen?"

"If we don't start the community garden now, it'll be too late. We have ten volunteers this year."

"That's my wife, from chief of detectives to Mother Nature's assistant." Immediately his expression changed. He had brown eyes she found soulful, and an earnest face. He reached across the table to put his hand on hers. "I'm sorry. That was a dumb crack. Put me on the shittiest case you can find."

Maggie nodded to shake the sting. "It's a black mark in your file, Detective. It's not going to look good when it's time for your review."

"Is there anything I can do about it, boss?"

"Tell Collins to lighten up. When he took my job, I didn't think he'd take you, too."

Karl squeezed her hand and tried a smile. "I'll tell him the woman who gave him his detective's shield said so."

"That'll get him where it hurts." She smiled back, though she didn't feel it.

"In the meantime, can you keep from going crazy at gardening club?"

"Sure. It's something to do, right?"

He looked at her then. "I know it wasn't your idea to be a stay-at-home mom, but it's for the best. You put in your twenty and you don't have to go back to that. Besides, if you were on the job, you'd never see Lana and Becky and before you know it they'd be eighteen and out the door. Right?"

Maggie nodded slowly. "Right," she said without enthusiasm. "I just need to forget what it was like to accomplish anything."

Karl's smile faltered. "I know you think it should have been me who stepped back."

"No. You have room to grow. Collins's job will be yours. You want to be C of Ds? You have to stay."

"Are we going to be okay?"

"Sure."

Karl squeezed her hand again. "*Really* okay?"

"Really okay. Now finish up and go to work. You have bad guys to catch."

Her husband drained the last of the coffee. He snagged his jacket off the back of an empty chair. "I promise if I can get home early, I will. I'll even pick up from that Italian place and we can eat in front of the fire. It's still cold enough for a fire."

Maggie didn't smile. "Be careful out there."

"Always." He bent over the girls to kiss their heads. Lana giggled and Becky spit out a slimy Cheerio.

CHAPTER 3

SHE WAITED UNTIL SHE heard his car start in the driveway before she got up to clear the table. She washed the plates and the pan by hand and wiped them down before putting them on a rack to dry. Everything in the kitchen was in its perfect place. It had been her mother's doing, from the furniture to the towels. It looked like a model home and sometimes it felt that way, too.

When the girls were done playing with their food, Maggie took them to the front room, where they could frolic on the floor with their toys. Sometimes when they played Maggie tried to read a book, but she'd only ever gotten about two-thirds of the way through a page before some diaper or crying or toy emergency put an end to her reading time. She'd had more free time to read books as chief of detectives than she has as a mother. The book she'd been trying to read, two-thirds of a page at a time, was called *IQ,* a Sherlock Holmes–inspired comedy about a brilliant man in Los

Angeles who took on the cases the LAPD couldn't, or wouldn't. Maggie appreciated it as fiction, but she knew that if she had found a civilian poking around in police business under her command, she would have brought the hammer down so quickly the vigilante detective wouldn't know what happened.

The curtains were pulled back from the bay window at the front of the house, and the street was visible through it. The first police car passed almost before Maggie had a chance to catch the flicker of its lights. She looked up and a second followed closely behind. She heard no sirens, but the lights were unmistakable.

Her heartbeat picked up. She put down the book and walked to the window. She stepped on a Duplo block and cursed out loud before putting her hand over her mouth. The girls didn't seem to have heard. Maggie looked up and down the street. A third police cruiser came along, red and blue lights also flashing, and passed as silently as the others.

A few minutes passed without another car appearing. Maggie didn't leave the window, staring the way they'd come as if to will something new into happening. It didn't. Maggie caught herself chewing her lip. She stopped.

The phone rang in the other room. Maggie glanced down instinctively, but the girls weren't bothered. Maggie hurried into the hall and deeper into the house to find the phone. She answered.

"Maggie?" asked a woman on the other end.

"Yes. Who is this?"

"It's Helen. Helen Spirra. From the gardening club?"

Maggie saw Helen in her mind. Younger, dark-haired, and tan-skinned. She had a boy about the girls' age. "Oh, right. Is everything okay? I mean, is there a problem?"

"I'm calling because I got a call from Julie Rhodes. She's calling all the ladies in the phone tree to tell them the news."

"What news?" Maggie heard Lana laugh in the front room.

"It's right on Julie's street. There was a murder."

CHAPTER 4

WHENEVER THERE WAS A dead body, there was a crowd. It was as true in the Parish as it was in the city, and though there were only a dozen onlookers it was enough to require a couple of uniforms to hold them behind the line of yellow crime scene tape and maintain order.

Maggie brought the girls in their stroller, and felt slightly ridiculous rolling up behind the rubberneckers with twin children in tow. She'd taken directions from Helen on the phone, and when she turned onto Julie Rhodes's street, she realized she'd been there the morning before. This was the street where she met Holly, the partier. And when Maggie saw the house cordoned off by the uniforms, it was Holly's. Her breath quickened.

Most of the people watching the proceedings were women, and most of them were familiar to Maggie from the gardening club. They came from mid-thirties to mid-fifties, no one too young and no one too old.

Maggie tried to approach quietly, but Lana made a noise and one woman turned to look.

Carole Strickland was tall and blond and fortyish. She lived two blocks over from Maggie. She stepped away from the watchers and met Maggie halfway. "Isn't it crazy?" she said by way of a greeting.

"They said it was murder," Maggie replied.

Carole moved close to Maggie and kept her voice down. "They say the husband came home this morning from a business trip and found his wife dead. Murder for sure. You see? Oh, look, the crime scene people are here. It's just like TV."

Maggie kept her encounter with Holly to herself. She watched the crime scene investigators' van pull up to the yellow tape. Two men and a woman got out and gathered equipment from the back. They were quick and efficient. Maggie appreciated that.

"There's the husband," Carole said, and she pointed.

The man sat on the front steps of the house. He was in a suit, his jacket unbuttoned and his tie askew. His face was in his hands, and it was difficult to tell whether he was crying. Maggie thought not. His posture was right, but his shoulders didn't move. He seemed tired, but not distraught.

"And there's one of the detectives."

A black man stepped out of the open front door. He was tall and broad through the shoulders, and it was possible even from a distance to see how his hair was shot through with white. Maggie stiffened at the sight of him. "I need to get over there."

"I know, I want to see when they bring the body out, too."

They joined the crowd. Maggie watched the detective talk to the husband and make notes with a tiny pencil on a small pad. She couldn't hear what they were saying, but she was right about the husband: he had a resigned look, but lacked sorrow. A third of women were killed by an intimate partner.

The crowd was in a steady murmur, theories bouncing back and forth, and new flurries of noise whenever the crime scene investigators came out to gather some new piece of equipment from their van.

"Will you watch the girls?" Maggie asked Carole.

"What? Oh, sure. What's happening?"

"I'll be right back."

She pushed her way to the tape. A uniformed cop was only a few feet away. Maggie caught his eye and beckoned him closer. A frown creased his face. "May I help you, ma'am?" he asked in a distracted voice.

"May I speak to the detective?"

The cop glanced over his shoulder. The detective and the husband were still in conversation. "He's interviewing a witness."

"May I speak to him anyway?" Maggie asked, and her tone hardened.

The cop blinked, but didn't say no. "Do I know you?"

"Maybe. May I speak to the detective?"

"Hold on a minute," the cop said. He stepped away. He looked back once, his brows knit. He conferred with the detective. The detective looked up and Maggie saw his face change when he recognized her.

When the detective came for Maggie, a fresh stir passed through the rubberneckers. Maggie tried to ignore them. Once she and the detective were face-to-face, Maggie tried a smile. "Hi, Mike," she said.

"Chief, what are you doing here?"

Another murmur around her. The word rippled out from Maggie and the detective. *Chief*.

"It's my neighborhood," Maggie said. "Kind of hard not to hear."

"Does Karl know you're out here?"

"No. Does he have to find out?"

The detective cast a look toward the house. His name was Mike Cooper, and they'd known each other fifteen years. "He won't hear it from me, but you need to make yourself scarce. Where are the girls?"

"Over there. It's okay, someone's watching them. Tell me what's happening."

Mike frowned at the people around Maggie. "Let's talk somewhere else."

They walked down the line of tape until they were alone. Maggie looked toward the house. The husband watched them. His face was drawn, but that was all. Maggie got the impression he was examining her, though for what reason it was impossible to know.

"You know these people?" Mike asked.

"No, but I'm pretty sure I met the victim. Holly?"

"That's right. Holly Gibbs. That's her husband,

Bryant Gibbs. Husband does a lot of work out of town, owns his own business. Wife's a stay-at-home. You say you saw her yesterday?"

"In the morning, about ten. She came in a limousine, all dressed up for a party. I got the feeling…"

"What?"

"The husband was away?"

"He was. Got back this morning. Why?"

"She had party all over her. Smelled of liquor, marks on her wrists and neck."

Mike made a note. "Into the rough stuff?"

"Husband seem like the type?"

"I don't know. Maybe. Hard to tell. You see the driver?"

"Yeah. Mid-thirties, about five ten, white, clean-shaven. Dark hair, but I couldn't tell you if it was black or brown."

"Think you could recognize him if you saw him again?"

"I do."

"Okay, listen, I'm gonna—"

Maggie interrupted him. "Oh, shit."

They looked together. Karl was on the steps with Bryant Gibbs. He saw them when they saw him, and his expression turned dark. "You better go," Mike said. "I'll hold him off."

"No, let him talk."

When Karl was within earshot, he said, "Hey, Mike, can I talk to my wife for a second?"

The tone was cheerful, but the darkness remained.

Mike cast a warning look toward Maggie. She waved him off.

"Why are you here?" Karl asked her once Mike was gone.

"News travels fast."

"No, I mean, *why are you here?* You're not a murder junkie. The rest of the people, I can understand, but not you."

"I wanted to see what was going on. I didn't even know you'd be here."

Karl's jaw set. "Well, I am here. And Mike's here. And so are a lot of other people, and one of them might say you were poking around, which means I get my ass chewed out."

"I'm not poking around. Everyone else is here, and it would be strange if I didn't show."

"Do you even have the girls with you?"

"What kind of question is that?" Maggie returned. "Of course I do."

"Look, you have to go. Take the girls and go home. Don't talk to anyone about this. As far as I'm concerned, you were never here."

Maggie felt a stab of anger. "You don't get to tell me what to do, *Detective*."

"Yes. Detective," Karl said, and he tapped the badge on his belt. "Detective. As in official business. You're not the assigned investigator. You're not the supervising detective. And you're *not* the chief of detectives. You do not belong here, and if you want to fight about it, we can fight at home, but it's not happening right now."

"My neighborhood," Maggie said.

"But not your problem," Karl replied. His tone softened. "Just go. Go home."

"Tell me this: do I have to be worried?"

Karl didn't hesitate. "No."

He walked away without a good-bye. Maggie watched him go. Hot feelings stirred around inside her. She saw him stop to talk to Mike and the husband on the steps, and then all three went inside. She was aware of people in the crowd watching her. Her hands were in fists at her sides.

She made herself go.

CHAPTER 5

KARL DIDN'T COME HOME that night. He called, but Maggie ignored it. He left a voicemail and two texts. She didn't respond to either of them. She put the girls to bed, made herself dinner, and then slept restlessly all night. In the morning she did the rote tasks she'd come to hate: laundry in the washer and beds made and sinks scrubbed. Karl offered her a maid once. She'd turned it down.

Lunchtime and there were no calls, no texts. Maggie had another meal with the girls, and played with them in the front room while they played and she thought about her book. When the clock ticked over to one, she gathered Lana and Becky, dressed them for playtime outside, and made the four-block walk to the community garden.

The garden was meant to be mostly flowers, taking up the space of one of the Parish's huge houses. There would be a few vegetables to liven things up, all chosen for their color and not their popularity. It was maintained by the club with money from the homeowners' association, which claimed three hundred dollars every month. A half-dozen women were already there, including Julie, who lived on Holly Gibbs's street, and Helen, who'd told Maggie about the killing. Maggie had her jeans on and the weather was crisp, but not cold. The sun dazzled from a perfectly blue sky without a cloud.

Lana and Becky were not the only little ones. Three other children, none older than four, crawled or scampered on the green grass while one of the ladies from the club supervised. The women took turns at this duty. Last week it had been Maggie who sat and minded while the others toiled.

Maggie never knew so many weeds could sprout in seven days. The grass was hardly growing yet, but the weeds were everywhere. She worked with gardening gloves alongside Helen. Conversation passed over the rows, ranging from childcare to the weather to television shows. Maggie realized after thirty minutes that no one had said a word about the murder.

She broke the seal and spoke to Helen. "Did anyone hear about what happened yesterday? To Holly Gibbs?"

Helen didn't look up. She raked at the black soil with a cultivator. "Did you know her?"

"No, but I saw her once."

"Not many people knew her. She and her husband went to all the dinner parties and barbecues when they first moved into the Parish, but they didn't keep it up.

I can't believe something like this would happen to either of them. But I guess I shouldn't be surprised."

"What do you mean?"

Now Helen stopped. She looked left and right before leaning closer. "Apparently they had an open marriage. And you know how people like that are: they get into trouble with strangers they meet online. That sort of thing."

Maggie didn't go back to her weeding. "How do you know about this?"

Helen gestured vaguely with the cultivator. "Oh, you know, it's the kind of thing that gets around. Julie knows about it. And Robin. Have you met Robin yet? She has a little party animal in her, too. And you *know* the husbands know about it. They have a nose for this stuff. I'm pretty sure Holly got around to a couple of them. Always flirting it up at the barbecues. I think that's why they stopped coming. You can't make the wives jealous."

"What else do you know about them? I mean, the development isn't *that* big. You know about that, so you have to know more."

Helen went back to digging. "It's none of my business. I stick with the gardening and the ladies' golfing club and try not to worry about what other people are doing. It's better that way. All I know is that if I ever caught Devin looking Holly Gibbs's way, he'd have an appointment with a sharp knife when he was sleeping."

They both laughed. Maggie thought a bit, absently

gathering weeds into a small pile. "Is there anybody here who might know more?"

"Here? No, but you're friends with Carole Strickland, right? Apparently she and Holly had…similar interests."

"You mean…?"

Helen shrugged with exaggerated casualness. Her tone was coy. "Like I said, it's none of my business, but you hear things. And maybe I heard something about Carole. I'm just saying."

Maggie didn't reply. She looked out over the garden, at the bent backs of the neighborhood ladies working diligently in the soil. She thought of Carole and she thought of the limousine and Holly Gibbs, the woman with the lavish red hair. And then she thought about Karl, and the idea turned in her mind.

CHAPTER 6

KARL CALLED AHEAD. "I'M coming home late," he said.

"I'll be waiting."

Maggie bathed the girls and put them to bed. She let a casserole warm in the oven while she had a glass of wine in the darkened front room. The streetlights glowed. She waited until the flash of headlights let her know Karl was nearly there, and then she went outside to meet him.

He wore exhaustion heavily around his shoulders, and his clothes were rumpled from two days of solid work. Maggie said nothing when she came to him and put her arms around his waist. He encompassed her body in his embrace and they stood that way for a long while in silence.

Finally, Karl kissed her and said, "It's good to be home."

"Let's eat."

"No, I have a better idea."

Karl bent his legs and scooped Maggie up with an

arm behind her knees, another at her back. She laughed at the extravagant silliness of the gesture, and they only made it a few steps before he had to set her down again. Maggie took his hand and led him in. They locked the front door and proceeded up the stairs to the second floor without turning on any lights. In the bedroom he shrugged off his jacket and there were more kisses and the hush of his breath in her ear as he lowered his lips to her neck.

On the bed they undressed each other. He touched her and kissed her, and she responded in the way she always did. He had the thing that worked for her. It had been this way from the start. When he pressed her back on the mattress and slipped between her parted knees, they made as little sound as they could. The rhythm began slowly, not urgent. Karl was good about taking his time. She put her hands on his arms on either side of her, looked up into his face as the tempo notched up bit by bit until there was the sound of skin striking skin and the give of the bed.

His breathing roughened, and his forehead began to shine with perspiration. There was heat and wet and body against body. Maggie gasped, the air driven from her, and then she felt his hand close around her throat.

Karl didn't squeeze hard at first. His fingers rested against the thudding pulse in her neck, his thumb on the other side. Maggie saw a certain darkness fall across his eyes and then he closed his grip. Her windpipe constricted and she felt the blood rushing in her head. She grabbed at his wrist, but he didn't let go. "Karl…" she tried, but her voice was weak. Karl's face was a twisted mask of exertion and then his breath exploded in her face and the moment passed. He let go. The motion of his hips slowed and stopped. They lay together still joined. Karl rested his forehead in the crook of her shoulder. Maggie put her hands on his back, feeling the sweat there. Her neck throbbed.

After a while, she asked, "What was that?"

"I'm sorry," he whispered in her ear.

"That was…new."

"I wasn't thinking about it. Or maybe…I don't know. Did I hurt you?"

"No, but don't do it again. That's not me."

"Okay."

They stayed together, unmoving.

"Are you going to fall asleep there?"

"Can I?"

"If you want, but dinner is going to dry out."

Karl rolled away from her. They lay side by side on the bed, looking up at a still ceiling fan in the shadows. They held hands. "I couldn't eat right now anyway."

"It wasn't that bad."

"No, I'm sorry. I let it get away from me. I'm in my head too much."

"Is it getting to you?"

"I only wonder how we kept it up all this time. The hours and the reports and the BS. I don't know."

"You can talk about it if you want."

Out of the corner of her eye, she saw him glance at her. His hand twitched slightly in her grasp. "Yesterday…I know you were just trying to help, as a witness, but it was awkward to have you asking Mike questions, acting like you're still on the job. You know how it works, Maggie."

She didn't look at him. "Someone dies in our neighborhood, it's hard to look the other way. You wouldn't."

"I'd remember where the line is. There are cops and there's everybody else. You're a special case, but you're not on the inside. You knew it was going to be like this. We talked about it."

"I didn't need you throwing it in my face like you did," Maggie replied. "I used to be your boss. I used to be Mike's boss. I was *everybody's* boss. That's not something you can turn off like that. Two years away isn't that long."

Karl turned on his side to face her. He put one leg over hers and a hand rested on her belly. She'd worked hard to make it flat again, but she wasn't so young anymore and it wasn't that easy. Karl kissed her shoulder. "What do you want to know?"

Maggie paused. Questions surged up, and she held them back. "I can't. You're right, I can't. You'll catch so much hell if you start talking about the case. I would have pulled your guts out if I were still in charge."

"You can talk to me," Karl said. "And I know you asked around. I *know*. Because you can't help yourself. That thing last year with the kid and the glass cutter? I didn't forget about that. You were all over it."

"A teenager cutting his way into houses to steal a few things isn't the same as murder, and you know it."

"But you still asked."

"Okay, I asked!" Maggie admitted. "I dropped a couple of questions at the gardening club. I wanted to see if anyone knew something."

Karl breathed quietly, and she felt him thinking. Then he said, "What did they say?"

"They said Holly Gibbs slept around. And maybe her husband was okay with that."

"Mike said you spotted some marks on her."

Maggie nodded. "She was tied up at some point. And she had...other marks."

"She's not the only one to be into that."

Maggie touched her throat. "No, but one day she's coming home from an all-night party, the next she's dead. And if she was taking scalps in the neighborhood, maybe her husband wasn't as cool about it as people think he was."

Karl chuckled. "'Taking scalps'? That's one way to put it."

"You know what I mean."

He got up. Maggie stayed where she was.

"Unfortunately I can't arrest a guy on suspicion of being kinky."

"It's an angle you can work, Karl. Sweat the husband. Nine times out of ten, the husband knows more than he's saying."

"Yes, boss. But you remember I've been doing this awhile, right? So relax. I had Mike stick his nose into the guy's business right away. You know how Mike has a soft touch. Gibbs probably didn't even realize we were checking him out."

"And?"

Karl got a robe from the closet. "Didn't you just say you'd string me up if I talked about a case with my wife?"

Maggie hit the bed with her palm. "All right, fine. Let's talk about something else."

"I want to talk about a shower and maybe somebody in the shower with me," Karl said. He came to the bed and bent to kiss her softly. "And then we can talk about how dry dinner got while it was waiting. Deal?"

She sighed quietly. "Deal."

"Great. I'll run the water."

He went into the bathroom and pushed the door closed. The lights switched on, and a rectangle of pure gold lit up around the edges of the door. A few seconds later, Maggie heard the shower's spray.

"Nice and warm," Karl called from the bathroom. Maggie went to join him.

CHAPTER 7

ON MONDAY, SHE WAITED until Karl was gone for the day, and then she went to work.

Maggie googled Bryant Gibbs, discovered he was forty. She looked for more information about him. She found a few pictures of him with different men, always in suits and always in settings of dark wood or brilliant glass. He was featured on the website of a business called Kirby Development Leasing. Gibbs was friends with bankers and politicians, or so the pictures told the story. His wife never appeared in any photo, no matter how deeply into the search results Maggie went.

She dressed to go out, got the girls ready, and packed them away in her small SUV with snacks for the ride. On her phone she had directions to the offices of Kirby Development Leasing. The drive was only thirty minutes in midday traffic. She kept to the right lane and drove the speed limit, both hands on the wheel as the miles ticked off on the phone's GPS.

She found the offices in an unremarkable business

park not far from the highway. The buildings were single-story, made of brown brick, and had muddy, tinted windows. Perhaps half the units she saw were empty, but others had simple signs designating what went on within. Nothing flashy, or anything that might call attention to one business over another.

Kirby Development Leasing's sign had the letters KDL at the top, with the full name in smaller letters. There were no cars parked in the spaces out front, and only a scattered few others were there. Maggie went by slowly, then cruised back again. She thought the lights might be on inside. She slipped into a space in front of another, unoccupied unit and left the engine running. She looked to the girls in the backseat. *You cannot leave your kids in the car,* she thought. *People go to jail for that.*

But Becky was asleep. Lana stared idly out the window, her eyelids promising a nap, as well. *One minute. Sixty seconds to look around. That's reasonable, right?* "I'll be right back," Maggie said to Lana. "Behave."

She got out and looked around. Nothing moved. No one was outside. The SUV idled, the compressor switching on and off as the air conditioning cycled. She felt a nervous sweat under her clothes. It was an old sensation, one she'd almost forgotten after being on the job more than twenty years. It was back again, as if she were starting all over.

The decision was made. She walked deliberately, controlling her speed and counting down the seconds. When she reached the door of KDL, she gripped the handle and immediately froze. A thought knifed through her mind: she'd seen Bryant Gibbs at the crime scene, and they were barely fifty feet apart. He'd looked right at her. Maybe he wouldn't remember the details of her face. Or maybe he would know her instantly.

A second ticked past, and another and another. She didn't move. A droplet of perspiration ran down her side beneath her clothes. She screamed at herself to move, to simply move. She willed her shoulder to flex, and then her bicep, and then her forearm, all the way down to her hand. She pulled the door open, and a vaguely antiseptic smell rushed out to greet her.

Inside she found herself in a small waiting area with a couple of chairs, a table stacked with magazines, and a potted plant that might have been artificial. A receptionist's station faced the door, but it was empty. Maggie stepped in farther, until she put her hands palms-down on the cool counter. She made herself breathe.

"Is someone out there?"

A young woman's voice carried from a side hallway, and Maggie heard the thump of footsteps on carpet. Moments later a slim, dark girl no older than twenty-five appeared. She had her hair pulled back conservatively, but her makeup was a perfect mask of delicate beauty. Her lips glistened when she smiled, and her teeth were flawless and white.

"Hello," Maggie said.

"Hello! I'm sorry I wasn't here. The office is closed for lunch and I'm…you know."

Maggie recalled the details on the website. "This is a commercial leasing office, right?"

"That's right."

"You said the office is closed for lunch, but is Mr. Kirby in?"

The woman blinked, her smile faltering before it came back stronger than before. "Oh, there's no Mr. Kirby anymore. He retired. Mr. Gibbs runs the business. I'm Rachel, by the way. I didn't get your name."

"Alyssa," Maggie said. "Mr. Gibbs is out, too?"

"I'm afraid so. If you'd like me to leave a message for him, he'll be back in thirty minutes or so."

"No, that's all right." Maggie's voice strengthened into the cover story she'd concocted on the drive. "I'm just stopping by to check it out. I saw on the website...well, I'm just interested in finding a space for my real estate business. I'm opening my own office."

"That's wonderful! I have a folder with a number of properties you can look through, and then you can call back and make an appointment to see Mr. Gibbs."

Rachel stood behind the counter and gathered papers. Maggie leaned forward to see if she could peer down the hallway. It seemed dark there, with offices behind glass, but none of them lit. "Are there other associates?" Maggie asked.

"No, it's only Mr. Gibbs and me. Here you go."

Maggie accepted the folder without glancing at it. She smiled as easily as she could muster. "Thanks so much. I have to get going now, my kids are waiting. You've been a big help."

She headed for the door. Rachel called after her. "Are you sure you don't want to leave a message?"

"No, thank you. I'm sure I'll see him very soon."

Outside she walked away quickly, almost jogging back to the SUV, where the girls hadn't moved. She climbed in, took deep breaths and tossed the folder on the passenger seat. Both Lana and Becky were asleep now. Maggie buckled herself in and backed out of the spot. She made sure to drive past the window of the office for the benefit of Rachel inside. She went around the corner and swung toward home. The girls would be getting hungry and tired, and she knew her mother, who'd just returned to town, would be happy to take them for a few hours.

But she hadn't lied: she would see Bryant Gibbs soon. And then she would be his second shadow.

CHAPTER 8

WHEN MAGGIE RETURNED EXACTLY thirty minutes later, she didn't have to wait long for Bryant Gibbs to show. True to the receptionist's word, he was back within the hour, driving a dark Lexus whose license plate number Maggie took down. He went inside, and then the monotony set in.

Maggie hadn't run a stakeout in years. Before she sat behind the desk of the chief of detectives, she'd spent ten years working cases, and sometimes that meant long hours in one place, waiting for the one moment on which everything would hinge.

It was late in the afternoon before she saw more action. No one had gone in or out for hours. Karl called twice, but Maggie sent him to voice mail with a text message assuring him she'd call back.

The receptionist's ride came first: a blue Hyundai sedan with another young woman behind the wheel. Rachel got into the Hyundai without a second look back toward the offices of KDL, and then the car drove away. Gibbs still didn't emerge.

Maggie exhaled in disappointment and put the SUV into Drive. Her foot lifted off the brake pedal and then she stomped down on it again.

When she saw the limousine, she gasped out loud. Adrenaline made her flesh tingle. Maggie grabbed the wheel in both hands and held on tightly as the limousine slowed in front of KDL. She tried not to hold her breath, but Gibbs emerged and she realized she was doing it anyway. Everything in her lungs came out at once when the limo driver stepped out from behind the wheel and opened the rear door for Gibbs.

Maggie quashed an internal reprimand. She already felt guilty for disposing of the twins for this fool's errand. It would all be better after this, she promised them silently.

The limousine eased into motion. It made a looping turn in the lot outside the offices and headed away in the failing daylight, taillights flashing. Maggie let the SUV roll out, keeping a good distance and leaving her headlights off.

She followed them all the way to the highway, and then onto the busy lanes. Once she was submerged in traffic, she turned her lights on. They moved faster.

It was full night by the time they reached the city. Karl called again. A text came and then another. *Where are you?* Maggie didn't have time to respond.

Into the warren of tightly packed blocks and painful congestion. The limo was four car lengths ahead, farther than she would have liked. When she had a chance, she barged between a taxi and a bus, changed lanes sharply in a swirl of horns, and then rushed up to within two car lengths. She couldn't see inside the limo, but Gibbs hadn't gotten out.

Maggie recognized the Ambassador from a block away. She was almost on top of Gibbs's ride now, so close she thought he might recognize her if he happened to glance back. Her heart tripped as they made the last intersection a hair before the light turned red. They came closer. The limo slowed. A gap cleared between Maggie and the limousine and then she was on the rear bumper.

The limousine stopped in front of the Ambassador, where lights dazzled off brass and the bright colors of the doorman's uniform stood out starkly against blacks and grays. The driver got out and opened the door. Maggie was trapped behind the limo. She put on her signal and tried to merge into the next lane. She couldn't stay here. Cars started flashing their highs at her, and there were new horns.

Gibbs didn't get out. Instead, a woman emerged from the hotel lobby. The woman was tall and athletic, with hair the color of pale straw. Maggie almost didn't realize who she was looking at. In a red dress, makeup perfect and hair sculpted to fall to her shoulders, Carole Strickland looked like a different person altogether.

Carole got in the limo. An opening in traffic appeared in the adjoining lane. Maggie swerved into it, pulling past the limousine and letting the flow of cars sweep her away. When she looked into the mirror, the limo was lost in a constellation of headlights.

Her phone rang. Maggie glanced down and saw Karl's face on the screen. She touched to answer.

"Where *are* you?" he asked.

"I'm running some errands."

"I've been trying to get ahold of you for hours. How many errands do you have?"

"Only a few more. Why don't I call you after I pick up some dinner?"

"What is going on?" Karl asked.

"It's nothing."

"Are the girls okay?"

"They're fine, they're with my mom. Look, I'll be home soon. Chicken okay?"

"Fine, but it's getting late."

Maggie saw a sign pointing the way out of downtown. If she doubled back she could get on the highway well before the limo. She calculated the time she'd have to get where she needed to be, and what she would do when she got there. The decision was made.

"Maggie? Hello?"

When Maggie answered, she heard something in her own voice, and she realized it had been absent for a long time: the sound of steel. "I'll be home soon. Take off your shoes and relax. I've got this."

She ended the call before he could say anything else.

CHAPTER 9

ONCE SHE REACHED CAROLE'S street and set up three houses down it took longer than she anticipated for the limo to arrive. Before it appeared, her confidence began to falter, but when she saw it, a new surge passed through her.

The limo stopped on the curb. Gibbs got out. He offered a hand to help Carole onto the sidewalk. They walked to the house together. The lights were on in every window, and cast warm yellow light on the perfect lawn. The front door opened before they got there. Maggie saw Philip, Carole's husband. He kissed Carole on the doorstep, and then they all went inside.

Maggie started the SUV's engine and crept up on the house. It had a picture window in front, framed by curtains on either side. When drawn it was impossible to see inside, but when they were open by night the living room was clearly visible.

Three figures moved in the frame of the window. Maggie eased her vehicle to a stop directly opposite the house and hunkered down in her seat. She watched Philip laugh and put his hand on the small of Carole's back. She saw Carole open the small purse she carried. An envelope came out. Carole handed it to Gibbs, who peeled it open. Maggie saw the cash come out. Gibbs counted it. Eight bills. He gave four to Carole's husband, and put the rest inside his jacket.

They were close together now. Maggie saw Philip move behind Carole and kiss her neck. He smiled while Gibbs talked, and Carole laughed silently, every sound absorbed by the glass. Gibbs moved toward her. Maggie realized Philip was unzipping Carole's dress.

None of them seemed to notice or care that they were showcased in the golden illumination of the living room. Maggie watched the first part of the spectacle unfold, and by the time they moved out of sight, likely to a bedroom on the second floor, she realized the view was simply part of the thrill.

CHAPTER 10

SHE FELT FOR CERTAIN Karl would be full of angry questions when she returned home after meeting her mom to pick up the girls, but he was strangely subdued. He took the girls in to change them for sleep while she defrosted the chicken. Maggie hoped for something to break the stalemate, but she knew when he wasn't ready to talk and she didn't know what she'd tell him, anyway. It was very quiet as they sat opposite each other in the girls' bedroom in twin rocking chairs with the lights turned off, and only the night-light glowing like soft star-shine. Karl murmured to Becky and Maggie cuddled Lana against her shoulder until both children were asleep. Maggie switched on the baby monitor and they moved to the table to eat, the bare minimum of small talk between them.

An hour later, Maggie lay on her back looking at the ceiling, and she knew without looking Karl was doing the same. Neither one of them would sleep until the words were said.

"I'm sorry," Maggie told him.

Karl was slow to respond. "I guess I don't understand."

"It wasn't a big deal. I was doing something for myself and I didn't think. Before I knew it, the sun was down and...you know."

"I guess we should talk about it," Karl said.

"There's nothing to talk about. I was running around too late. You're right, I should be thinking about what has to happen at home."

Her husband turned toward her on the bed, his head resting on his pillow. They didn't touch. "We went over it a thousand times, but sometimes I think we were wrong not to just hire a nanny. I know we didn't want that for our children, but you don't ask the chief of detectives to turn into a stay-at-home mom overnight while her husband stays on the job. It's like putting a wild animal in a cage. They might get used to it after a while, but they're always going to want to be out there. And I'm sorry about that. I really am."

He put his hand on her, resting his palm on her belly through the covers. After a while she put her hand on his. "I get a little crazy sometimes. It's true."

"You need to get out. I understand."

"It's not just that. I'm still thinking like a cop. I hear things and I see things and I can't stop wondering what's going on. It's like this whole situation with Holly Gibbs."

She felt Karl's hand twitch under hers, but when he

spoke his voice was careful. "I thought we were going to steer clear of that."

"We are. We are. It's just that the ladies around here all know one another and word gets around. When something like this happens, it's all anyone wants to talk about and it gets me going. I want to know more." She looked at him. "Do you understand I need to know more?"

"You know I can't talk about it. And Mike can't, either, so don't think about doing an end-run."

"Did you set him straight?"

"We talked. He agreed."

Maggie nodded slowly, then turned toward the ceiling again. "Holly Gibbs and her husband definitely had an open marriage. It's not just a rumor."

"Do I want to know how you know this?"

"The first things I heard could have been speculation, but I have corroboration now. I don't know how extensive it is, but he was just as much into it as she was."

"Who are you getting this from? Who *exactly*?"

"I'm not ready to talk about that yet."

"Protecting your informant?"

"Something like that. What did you get out of Gibbs about it?"

"It didn't come up during our interview, that's for sure."

"I guess it wouldn't. Because then he'd have to explain that she was out with other men and he was out with other women and then the pool of suspects gets bigger and more complicated. It's probably not what he wants. He seems to like his privacy."

"All the more reason to give it to him. The man just lost his wife. And like I told you before, I can't arrest the man on suspicion of being a sexual deviant. We don't exactly have laws against that anymore. As long as he and his wife were consenting adults involved with *other* consenting adults, there's nothing actionable."

"Let me ask you this, then: would you let me run around on you?"

"What kind of question is that?"

"I'm only wondering what husband lets his wife out to play like that. I mean, I can get it when one spouse cheats without the other one knowing, but they were totally up front about it. And they're not the only ones out there doing it. Maybe not even in the neighborhood. So when you put yourself out that far, with so many people who might get jealous or crazy...it's something worth looking into."

Karl slid his hand away. When he spoke again, Maggie heard a different note in his voice. "I don't think we should talk about this anymore."

"Why not?"

"Because you're doing exactly what we decided you shouldn't do, which is investigating this on your own. It's one thing if you want to pass along little bits of gossip that I can use, but it's something else if you're out there looking for suspects and building cases. I shouldn't have to explain this. You should know even better than I do that sort of thing causes headaches for everybody. Amateur detectives."

Now Maggie stiffened. "'Amateur detectives'? I had my gold shield before *you* did. Mike, too. I busted my tail to make chief of detectives when I did. And I was—"

"The youngest chief of detectives in the history of the department," Karl cut in.

"I was, Karl. I'm a professional, not an amateur."

"I'm not saying you don't know the procedure. You know what I mean. I'm talking about people on the outside who want to get a piece of the investigation. They could contaminate evidence, or interfere with witnesses and make the whole case fall apart."

"You think I'd let that happen? You think I'd kill your case?"

Karl rolled on his back. "I can't believe we're even having this discussion. You need to stay out of it, and I don't care what you heard about Holly Gibbs or what you think of her husband. And whatever freaky sex stuff they were into might make for juicy chitchat at the gardening club, but it's only relevant if I can make a better case out of it."

Maggie was quiet awhile. Karl said nothing. Finally she said, "But you're going to look into it?"

Karl sighed. "I have to now, don't I? It's information provided from the community. Yes, I'll ask him about it. And if it's relevant, we'll open a line of inquiry and see who she was with and whether any of them had anything to do with her murder. I *swear* I'll look into it."

"Okay."

"Okay."

"But you didn't answer my question," Maggie said.

"What question?"

"Would you let me run around on you? Is that the sort of thing that'd be okay with you?"

Karl fell silent again, and this time Maggie thought he would avoid the question altogether. He turned so his back was to her. She listened for the soft sound of his sleeping breath, but he was still awake. "No," he said. "That's not something I would do. And I don't think it's something *you* would do."

"I wouldn't," Maggie said. "I love you."

"I love you, too. Go to sleep now. We'll pretend like today never happened. Good night."

"Good night," Maggie said. She said nothing else, and eventually Karl did sleep, but she was still awake, the ceiling hovering above her, and the image through the picture window of Carole's house.

CHAPTER 11

MAGGIE'S MOTHER CAME THE next day. She set up in the guest bedroom, and buzzed around the house tidying up and making meals and fussing over the twins for three days. Karl came and went, but Maggie stayed home. They didn't talk about Holly Gibbs again. She thought several times about revealing what she'd seen at Carole's house, but she didn't want a repeat of the night she'd seen it all, so she kept it to herself. He said nothing to her about what he might have learned from Bryant Gibbs. Maybe he hadn't asked the question at all.

On the fourth day Maggie called Carole and caught her at home. "I was thinking about lunch at DiMaggio's," Maggie said. "Are you busy?"

"Of course not! Are you kidding? I'll be watching reruns of *Dr. Oz* all day if I don't get out of the house. Meet you there around one?"

"Sounds great," Maggie said brightly.

She found the twins and their grandmother in the

backyard, crawling on the grass. Already they had grass stains on their outfits, but they didn't care. Maggie's mother looked up. "What's wrong? Did you get some bad news?"

Maggie pretended a smile and injected cheeriness into her voice. "Oh, no, it's great. You know I love having you here. It makes things a lot easier."

"Happy to help. And look at these two! They're natural explorers!"

"Hey, listen," Maggie said casually. "I was thinking about having lunch with a friend. Do you mind if I'm gone for a couple of hours?"

"Not at all. We'll eat our own lunch and have naptime and then we'll play the afternoon away. Take all the time you want."

"Thanks, Mom."

"Don't worry about a thing. Have some fun."

When noon arrived, Maggie's mother was in the kitchen feeding the twins. Maggie dressed for the weather and the restaurant, kissed the girls on the head, and told her mother not to worry. She was on the road soon after, the radio playing light pop and everything seemed as normal as any other day. It might even have been boring, but she hadn't reached that point yet.

It was warm enough in the afternoon, and the sun bright enough, that the patio at the restaurant was open. Maggie saw Carole as she walked in from the parking lot, waving from a table beneath a gaily spreading yellow umbrella with a green stem like some giant, exotic flower. Maggie went straight to her. Carole hugged her loosely and they sat down to-gether.

"I ordered something already," Carole said. "A Long Island iced tea. You want something? Not too much, I know, but it's nice out."

The server came, a young woman with a ponytail and a crisp uniform. The restaurant wasn't fancy, but threaded the line between upscale and casual well enough to attract the suburbanite crowd. People with money, but not true wealth. That described the Parish very well. Maggie ordered a lemonade and a bottle of sparkling water. "I want to look at the menu for a little bit," she added.

When they were alone, Carole sat picking idly at the edge of her menu. She looked strikingly normal in a pink golf shirt and white slacks. She had a yellow neck-erchief tied around her throat, and its tail flicked in the light breeze. Her hair was up and her makeup conser-vative. When Maggie looked at her, she could hardly square the image of this woman and the woman in the limo. The woman who'd take two men to bed, one who wasn't her husband, and maybe more Maggie didn't know about, all on the same night. And the neckerchief made her think. "You're looking at me like I have two heads," Carole remarked.

Maggie flushed. "I'm sorry. I was spacing. So busy with the girls, and now my mother's staying with us for a little while. It's crazy."

"You have to get out sometimes," Carole agreed. "Take some time for you. I know that's how I am.

Philip's at work half the time, so you'd think I'd have all these opportunities to go crazy, but I stay cooped up in the house until I just *have* to go out, you know?"

Maggie saw Carole kissing Bryant Gibbs. "I understand completely," Maggie said. "It's like prison sometimes."

"Exactly. What are you going to have? I'm going to have the lunch omelet. I should watch the calories, but you have to live a little."

When the server returned, they ordered, and then they were left alone again. Maggie stirred her lemonade with a straw, paying closer attention to the swirling ice than she might otherwise. She didn't want to look directly at Carole, because she didn't want anything to show. The need to know was stronger every minute they sat together, but it wouldn't do to crash directly into it.

"So…how is Karl?" Carole asked.

"He's good."

"*Good* good, or not-so-good good?"

Maggie still averted her eyes, but she hoped Carole would misread it. "We have our ups and downs. He's like Philip: always working. I used to be that way, too. When I was in my last job. When we saw each other outside work, it was kind of like a surprise."

"Surprise is good. Keeps things lively."

Something clicked for Maggie. She looked at Carole directly. "I think that's the whole thing, you know? Keeping it lively. I mean, Karl and I have been married for four years, and we were together five years before that, and now we have the girls and it can be hard to hold on to the spontaneity."

"I know exactly what you mean."

"Do you?" Maggie asked. She let nothing of the truth bleed into her voice.

"Oh, sure. You do this and that."

"In bed," Maggie said.

"Where else?"

"So what do you do?"

Carole shrugged. "What you'd expect, probably. Playacting. Costumes. I don't want to be crude but, you know, sometimes he ties you up, sometimes you tie him up. Stuff like that. I mean...that *is* what you're talking about, right? Oh, God, I'm running at the mouth."

"No, no," Maggie said quickly. She put out a hand and touched Carole's across the table. "That's it. You want to keep it fresh, and it's hard to do that when you're washing baby clothes all day and scrubbing mashed peas off the counter. Karl comes home, we talk a little, we're both too tired to do anything, and then we fall asleep. Same thing every day. And after a while you don't even want to look at each other anymore because we're so familiar."

Carole looked at Maggie with a careful expression. Maggie thought she saw something glimmer in the other woman's eye. "You aren't thinking about having an affair, are you?"

"What? No! I mean, who with? I don't see any eligible men around."

Carole shrugged and drank the last of her drink.

"Depends on what you mean by 'eligible.' Does that mean single? Because that's usually not a problem. Single or not, if you put the signals out, they respond."

Maggie leaned in more closely. "You sound like you're speaking from experience."

"Maybe I am," Carole said, and the corner of her mouth curled up only a bit. "But my life is a lot more boring than yours. I don't even have kids to keep me distracted. I mean, thank God for that, because I'd be a terrible mother, but at least I'd have something to do."

"I heard some things about Holly Gibbs from the ladies at the gardening club," Maggie said conspiratorially. "She wasn't only thinking about it. She was *doing* it."

Carole flagged the server down and ordered another Long Island iced tea. Once the girl left, Carole said, "I heard the same thing. But, you know, people talk. Especially housewives with nothing else to do."

"They say her husband knew."

Now Maggie saw something else behind Carole's expression, and when Carole spoke again, her tone was measured. "Who told you that?"

"Somebody. I guess it wasn't a big secret. I just don't know how he could let her do it. If he did, anyway."

"Husbands do a lot of different things," Carole said. "They like to play around, but they usually keep it a secret, you know? And when wives play around, they keep it a secret, too. But sometimes it's better to know. Sometimes knowing about it is more exciting than anything else."

"Do you—?" Maggie started, but she was interrupted by the arrival of their entrees. By the time they were alone at the table again, Maggie sensed the moment had passed. But Carole looked at her differently now, more carefully, and Maggie knew something had come close to the mark.

CHAPTER 12

SHE LEFT CAROLE WITH more questions than answers,
but the answers she didn't get were bracketed by the
things Carole let slip and gave room for examina-
tion. Maggie had been a cop for twenty-four years,
and a detective for half that time. More often than
not, the first things out of a subject's mouth were
lies, and the second things, too. By the third repeti-
tion, it was the gaps in the misdirection that told the
rest of the story. A good investigator could wedge
into those gaps, prize them apart, and finally get at
the truth.

Carole didn't have to tell her what went on with her
husband and Bryant Gibbs. She didn't even have to say
it had happened more than once. The hints had been
enough. Maggie didn't understand the desire this ful-
filled, but understanding that was not the issue. If two
adults, or three adults, wanted to do something in private that was their concern. But when one turned from
the arrangement…that was when things turned out in

a bad way. It had happened time and again, going all the way back to the Bible.

It was time to get back to her mother and the girls, but Maggie drove aimlessly instead, turning over facts and assumptions in her mind. She had to set aside any judgment. All that mattered was the meaning, and from that meaning a resolution. After an hour and a half, something concrete had begun to form. She pulled over into the parking lot of a Speedway, brought out her notes from her time outside Gibbs's office, and dialed a number she shouldn't.

Mike Cooper answered her call. When he heard her voice his tone shifted from business to personal, then immediately dropped into neutral. "I can't say anything," he said, unprompted.

"Have you been talking to Karl?"

"Of course. He's my partner."

"Did he tell you about Holly Gibbs and her husband?"

"Ye-ess," Mike said carefully. "And we're looking into it. Something like that, you don't want to drive in too quickly. We don't want to spook him."

Maggie nodded, though she was invisible to Mike. "So you're watching him."

"We have a cruiser go by a couple of times a night. Karl checks in with Mr. Gibbs every day. He makes like it's a condolence call, but you know."

"Sure. He wants Gibbs to know he's paying attention. Listen, Mike, I wanted to get some background on Gibbs."

"Maggie, I *just* told you—"

"Hear me out," Maggie interrupted. "Gibbs runs a business called Kirby Development Leasing. It's some kind of commercial real estate venture. But here's the thing: no one works there. His main office is empty. There's him and there's his secretary, and nobody else. Don't you think that's odd?"

Mike didn't answer for a beat. "Do I even want to know?"

"I did some digging."

"Why? Why would you do that?"

"Mike, I don't need a lecture. I have Karl for that. What I need from you is the Mike Cooper magic, okay? I know you can get anything from anybody, and all I want right now is a look at Gibbs's financial records. I want to know who he's doing business with and what kind of money he's making. Where are his properties? What are they going for? How much is he pulling in?"

She heard him sigh. "That'll take time."

"I'm a housewife in the suburbs, Mike. Once the girls are asleep, I have nothing *but* time."

"Okay, I'll do it, but keeping Karl out of the loop is gonna be tough."

"You never kept a secret from Karl before?" Maggie teased.

Mike didn't answer the question. "I'll call you back."

Maggie put her phone away and left the Speedway. She drove all the way home with her mind ticking over the facts she had thus far. The fact that Bryant and

Holly Gibbs were unfaithful to each other wasn't a secret to anyone, even in a place like the Parish, but three days after his wife has murdered? Twice Maggie had seen a limousine ferrying women involved with Bryant Gibbs, and on one occasion money had changed hands. Gibbs's offices were empty, but his mortgage was still being paid, while he owned a nice car and wore nice clothes. That raised questions, but if you looked at the obvious, the man wasn't mourning his wife at all. To Maggie this amounted to more than simple adultery, more than sex games, and became something else. It became a crime.

CHAPTER 13

SHE PLAYED WITH THE girls in the backyard, then put them down for a nap. When they were asleep, she joined her mother in the kitchen to make dinner. Maggie saw her mother out of the corner of her eye, casting glances, until finally Maggie stopped in the middle of deboning a chicken thigh to ask, "What is it?"

"You didn't go out to lunch," her mother said.

"Of course I did. I had lunch with Carole Strickland at DiMaggio's."

Her mother's face tightened with scrutiny. "No, there's something else. I can read it all over you."

Maggie turned back to the chicken. "It's just your imagination," she said breezily. "It was lunch with a friend and that was it. Girl talk."

"Oh, please, you never did girl talk even when you *were* a girl. No, this reminds me of when you first started poking your nose into things back in third grade. Somebody stole somebody's favorite action figure. Somebody was getting into the lunches in the cubbies. When you went to the academy it was only a formality. You were a cop long before that."

"Well, I'm something else now."

"My foot."

Maggie put down her knife and washed her hands without looking at her mother. "Would you excuse me for a minute? I need to check up on Karl and make sure he's still on time."

"I'm sure that's it, sweetie," her mother said with false cheer.

She turned away so her mother wouldn't see her scowl, and she fled into the other room. Standing in the rubble of the twins' Duplo battlefield, she dialed Mike's mobile number. Outside on the street it was gathering dark and all the streetlights were on. One by one, the houses' windows began to glow. Once more, unbidden, the image of Carole with her husband and Bryant Gibbs.

The phone rang for so long, Maggie expected voice mail, but Mike answered. "I was going to call you," he said.

"I'm calling you. You have something?"

"I do. Do you want me to tell you, or do you want me to e-mail it?"

"Both. Give me the highlights now."

Mike spoke quietly on his end. Maggie couldn't be sure where he was. She thought she heard voices, but it could have been the bull pen or it could have been somewhere else. "Bryant Gibbs hasn't made a nickel from commercial leases in four years. Not since he moved into the area."

"Is that when he bought Kirby Development Leasing from the guy who started it?"

"What guy? Gibbs filed the incorporation paperwork himself."

Maggie sat down on the edge of a chair. "Wait a minute, that business is all his? There's no Kirby?"

"No."

She thought. Why the subterfuge? Why create a man who didn't exist, and why keep this information from the one woman who seemed to work in the office? The envelope of cash Carole gave him was part of the answer. "Tax returns," she said. "Did you get tax returns?"

"Those are harder to get hold of."

"Listen, Mike: this guy is making money, but it's all off the books. From everything I can tell, he is running women, and one of them was his wife. You hear what I'm saying? He's a pimp."

"His wife was a part of his stable?"

"It has to be," Maggie said. "I knew something wasn't right when his office was empty. He rents this place and he has a website and he puts in appearances at Rotary Club get-togethers or whatever, but he's pulling in his income from another source. They say he was out of town a lot. Doing what? Maybe this is something he does in multiple cities. You need to coordinate that. And there's more."

Maggie told Mike the rest of it. What she'd seen of Carole, what she'd gleaned from their lunchtime conversation, and the inevitable conclusion she reached.

Mike grunted on the other end. "Suburban pimp," he said.

"But now we know. And that opens the whole thing up. If it was just a husband and wife situation, I would suspect him for the doer no matter what he said, but this changes everything. Pimps have competition. They get money from bad dudes. Sometimes that blows back on them. People get killed."

"You know I'm going to have to tell Karl this."

"I know. He *should* know. It's the next step. You have to bring Gibbs in. You have to sweat him. You have to—"

Mike cut in. "Hey, Chief, hold up for a minute. You don't need me telling you this, but Karl's the lead. I have to make like I uncovered this on my own, and then I have to make sure he doesn't put two and two together. We'll get Gibbs in and we'll question him, but we got to work through the steps first. You know how these things go."

"Goddamnit, Mike," Maggie said. Her voice was rising, but she knew already he was right and she was wrong. She forced herself not to say more.

Mike's tone was soothing. "This stuff is great. You've still got it, Chief. Now let us handle the rest of it."

"I can get more," Maggie said before she could stop herself.

"Hey, I know you can. The question is how deep you can get before you don't have any cover. I can play this so your name doesn't come up, but if you keep pushing, Karl *will* find out, and I know he's already a little hot about how strong you're coming on."

Maggie stopped. "He told you?"

"He tells me everything. We're partners."

She didn't know whether to be angry or relieved. She opted for neither, and pushed neutrality into her voice. "Mike, this is happening in *my neighborhood*. Do you think for a second Karl would let this slide without doing something, even if he wasn't on the case? Or you? And I can't sit on my hands. You can't ask me to do that, Mike."

"Chief," Mike said, "I have to tell you no. And if you were still my boss, you'd *want* me to tell you no. There's no room in this kind of thing for people putting their noses in. Not even you."

"Mike—" Maggie started.

"I gotta go. I'm sorry, Chief. I'm real sorry."

CHAPTER 14

MAGGIE AND HER MOTHER took turns reading silly stories to the girls. Neither Lana nor Becky understood a word of it, but they understood the whimsical tone, and that was enough to make them laugh. Eventually it was bedtime. Maggie bathed the girls herself, dressed them for sleep, and turned out the light.

Karl didn't come home for dinner. Maggie ate with her mother and checked on the girls, sleeping soundly. She found her mother in the kitchen with an open bottle of wine on the center island and two glasses. Only the light over the sink was on. "You looked like you could use a little nip," her mother said.

Susan Gilcoe was only eighteen years older than Maggie. Unlike her daughter, Susan had children early. Maggie thought of that often as the years went by and there was still no child in her life. And even when Karl entered it seemed like a remote possibility that eventually crumbled into nothing.

They drank together in the shadows. "I'm glad you waited to have kids," Susan said.

"Are you reading my mind?" Maggie asked. "I was just thinking about how I thought they'd never come."

"Modern science can do wonderful things," her mother replied. "And you weren't quite ready yet, I don't think. Not until you were able to let go of that job."

Maggie finished her glass and had another. Her mother watched her carefully. "Sure," Maggie said, and she smiled. "I'm a happy homemaker now."

"Hm. Now I'm going to go to bed because a glass and a half does it for me these days. You should get some rest, too. You look harried. Relax and enjoy life a little. I won't be around to help forever."

"Thanks, Mom," Maggie said. "Good night."

They parted. Maggie lingered in the kitchen alone. Finally she sat down at the table in the breakfast nook and finished off the bottle of wine on her own. She rinsed the glasses, put the bottle in recycling with a reminder to herself to put it on the curb in the morning, then went to bed.

She woke to the sound of Karl's car in the driveway. A few moments later she heard the garage door open and then close. Karl's key was in the kitchen door. Maggie sat up in bed. Karl never parked in the garage.

He came up the stairs and Maggie realized he was trying not to be heard. He eased their door open. Maggie saw him as a shadow on shadows.

"I'm awake," Maggie said.

Karl jumped. "Goddamnit."

Maggie reached for the bedside lamp and turned it on. "What's—what the *hell*?"

He had his jacket off, but the cuff of his right sleeve was deep red with blood. He had blood on his knees and on his hands, though it looked as though he'd tried to wash them clean. He recoiled from the light, clutching at his jacket; she saw it was bloody, too. "Turn the light off," he said. "Turn the light off!"

Maggie didn't obey. "What is going on?"

"Get me a plastic bag, will you?" he asked, and then he retreated into the bathroom. Maggie heard the lock click. Seconds later the shower ran.

She realized she was calm. Her hands didn't shake. She was alert and awake, but there was no panic. It was the instinct that carried her in her years behind the badge, but at the same time it was the thing already scrabbling at the back of her mind about what she'd seen and what it meant to have seen it.

While Karl showered, she went downstairs and fetched a plastic garbage bag. She sat on the edge of the bed until he emerged, still steaming and wet, with a towel around his waist and his clothes in a ball. The blood was gone from his hands. He stuffed his outfit into the bag when she gave it to him, then cast the bag in a corner. He sat down heavily beside Maggie and stared at the shapeless black plastic.

"What is going on?" Maggie asked, and the calm in her voice surprised even her.

"It's not what it looks like."

"It looks like you're eliminating evidence. I'm calling Mike."

"Mike already knows."

"Whose blood is that?"

"Carole Strickland's."

Maggie started, and her heart clutched in her chest. She felt electrocuted, breathless, and for a moment she thought she couldn't see. The moment passed quickly. "How did you get Carole's blood on you?"

"A call came in," Karl said steadily, without looking at her. "An anonymous tip about Carole being in danger. I went to her house. I found her husband in the living room, dead. I found her in the master bathroom. You could hardly recognize... And I..."

He covered his face with his hand. Maggie wanted to touch him, but she couldn't do it until she heard the rest. "What did you do, Karl?"

"I slipped. I came into the bathroom to investigate, and I took one step too many and I slipped. I fell right into it. I contaminated the crime scene. Fibers from my jacket are going to be all over the place. Hairs and maybe skin. By the time backup came, it was too late. They found me like that, with blood all over me. And then Mike came. It was a mistake. It was a *rookie* mistake. No, it's worse than that, it was stupid. Stupid and careless."

Maggie finally put her hand on his bare shoulder, gently and then with more pressure. "Is that what happened?"

He looked up sharply. "What are you saying?"

"You don't make mistakes like that."

"No, I don't. But it *was* a mistake. A huge mistake. Do you have any idea how humiliated I am?"

"Did you explain what happened?"

"Of course. But you should have seen their faces. This is going to come back at me hard. You can forget a gold shield. That's gone."

She felt him slipping on the edge of something, an out-of-control tailspin that would make it impossible to learn more. She'd seen it in the interrogation room, read it in transcripts, heard it in recordings. She kept her hand on his shoulder, but they were far apart.

"You need to tell me the whole thing," Maggie said. "All of it."

CHAPTER 15

"WE'VE BEEN LOOKING FOR Gibbs," Karl said after a long pause. "Everything you said about his open marriage made sense, and I had Mike start digging into the Gibbs's associates. There didn't seem to be a lot of people they knew closely, but they had enough friends to make it worthwhile. Any one of them might have been the jealous type. You know how it is: all it takes is one person who wants more than they're getting and it all goes sour."

"If Mike was doing that, what were you doing?" Maggie asked.

"He worked that angle, while I tried to pry something loose on my own. I looked into Gibbs's business record. Did you know he owns a commercial real estate business that doesn't have any clients? That's *never* had any clients?"

"No," Maggie said, and gave nothing away.

"Yeah, so that got me thinking how he makes his money. He couldn't afford a house in the Parish if he doesn't have an income, and as far as I can tell he's not living off a trust fund. So the cash was coming in. So what if the whole thing wasn't just an open marriage? What if he was renting his wife out? She wasn't young anymore, but she was good looking and they were the type. She goes out, makes the money, and he cashes in."

Maggie got up from the bed and found pajamas for Karl. She lay them down beside him. "Did you talk this over with Mike?"

"I did. He said it was a good angle. It's like you said before, it's a big game to them. Where have you been? What did you do? Who'd you do it with? And if you can make a living at it, so much the better."

She watched him get into the pajamas. Everything about him denoted shock. A homicide detective didn't display such reactions. She thought of the blood on his clothes. No one had seen him go in. He'd been totally alone with the victims, and by his own admission traces of him were all over the scene. "Was there anyone who saw you with Carole or Philip?" she asked.

"No. They were already dead when I got there. I was first through the door."

"How did you get in?"

"The front door was open." Karl's eyes narrowed. "Why would you ask me that?"

She skipped over his question. "You said it was an anonymous tip."

"That's right."

"Left for anyone?"

"No, they said to give it to me."

"Who was the caller? A man? A woman?"

"A man. He used a prepaid cell phone. No way to follow the chain back from there. Listen, I don't like the way you're looking at me. I'll admit it: I screwed up tonight. I should have waited for the uniforms to arrive. I shouldn't have gone into that bathroom until I had someone watching my back. So if you want to come down on me for that, you can, but I'm already angry with myself. I am screwed."

"This isn't all about you, Karl."

"What's *that* supposed to mean?"

Maggie moved past it. Her mind kept working. "You think the man who called it in was the doer?"

Karl's face was twisted, but he answered straight. "Could have been. Or someone else."

"When will you get prints back?"

"In the morning, probably. You know how it goes. Why?"

Maggie was slow to speak. Karl's attention was on her, probing her the way she had done to him. It could not all be hidden, but some part of the truth could be kept secret. "I saw Bryant Gibbs in Carole's house. With her husband. Five nights ago."

"How did you see this?" Karl asked.

"The night I was out late with the girls. I drove by Carole's house and they were in the front room, and they didn't care who was watching."

"They were…close?" Karl ventured.

"Yeah, you could say that. And while I was watching, Carole made a cash payment to Gibbs, and I don't think it was HOA dues. If you were looking for evidence of prostitution going on, it wasn't restricted to Holly Gibbs. Carole was a part of it, too, and her husband knew. Whether he was in it because that's how he got his jollies, or because he liked the cash, I don't know, but that's three bodies on Bryant Gibbs and all of them connected to one thing."

Karl sat back on the bed. His mind was working, every thought written on his face. Maggie glanced at the bag in the corner, then back toward him. No one saw him go into Carole's house. No one. She chastised herself for even daring to think of the possibilities stemming from that.

"How many wives do you think are in on this?" Karl asked finally.

"I don't know, but someone told me not to get involved, so I'm taking a step back."

"But you uncovered this! Mike and I had suspicions, but you provided the corroborating evidence. You need to make a statement and we need to come down on Gibbs hard. He's the key."

"If I make a statement, then I have to admit I was colluding with the lead detective," Maggie said. "I can't do that. You think tonight's mistake made you look bad? People will forget it someday. But letting your wife run part of the investigation on her own? That's not going to fly, and I don't care how you gussy it up. No, you have to keep my name out of it."

Karl nodded. "Okay. We'll make our case some other way. But that means you have to step back. You got us part of the way, but we can handle the rest. There's no need for you to stick your neck out. We have three victims, and if things go any further…I don't want to think about what could happen. The girls. You. It's not worth it."

"No, Karl, that's exactly why it's worth it. Because it could have been any of us."

CHAPTER 16

THEY SPENT A RESTLESS night together. Maggie didn't sleep, and she suspected Karl didn't, either. She knew he was thinking about what came next. A mistake like the one he made wouldn't cost him his badge, but it would be bad. How bad depended on how the new chief of detectives felt about making examples. Collins liked making examples.

In the morning she made wordless breakfast for the family. Her mother puttered around the kitchen making small talk. Karl tried to play with the girls. From the outside they were okay. On the inside it was different. When Karl's phone rang, a veil of darkness passed over his features. "It's the chief," he said dully.

"Take it in the other room," Maggie told him. It was not a suggestion.

She cleaned up the table, her mother beside her. Still Susan appeared to know nothing, or if she did it was so well-hidden even Maggie couldn't pull it to the surface. "What are your plans today?" her mother asked airily.

"I hadn't thought about it."

"I was thinking I'd take the girls to one of those activities classes they have. Gymboree. They can play with the other babies. You can have some alone time."

Maggie looked at Susan out of the corner of her eye. Again there was nothing, but she had to have known. She realized her mother would have made the perfect interrogator: everything was concealed, and her mother gave nothing away. "That would be nice," Maggie replied. "But don't put yourself out."

"Nonsense. It's what grandmas live for."

With that, Susan swept the girls out of the kitchen like a gentle whirlwind, leaving Maggie alone. She was conscious of Karl speaking quietly in the other room, and then the fun-filled tone of her mother talking to the girls, one tucked into the crook of each arm. Maggie didn't think she'd have that much left in her when she was Susan's age.

She poured herself a cup of coffee and waited at the table for what came next. Finally Karl returned. "Okay," he said.

"What will he do?"

"First he wants a statement on the record. Then we'll see about an official hearing."

"Do what they tell you to do. Say what you said to me."

Karl nodded. He was not like Susan. He wore guilt and darkness around him like a shroud. "I have to go," he told her.

She let him kiss her on the cheek. She stayed at the

table until he was gone, then rinsed the coffee cup in the sink and went upstairs. The plastic garbage bag was still in the corner. She carried it into the bathroom.

Laying the clothes out on the bright white tile made them seem gorier than they were. It seemed as though Karl had bathed in Carole Strickland's blood. It was spattered and smeared on his clothing. She pictured how each mark came to be. A knee down on the floor. A hand slipped in the puddle of blood. The cuff soaked, the sleeve tagged. He'd wiped a hand on his stomach unconsciously. The department would want all of this, and they would want to know what Maggie had seen.

When she was done, she put it all away. She dressed mechanically, because her mind was somewhere else. She wanted to be where Karl had been, seeing everything exactly as he'd seen it on the night in question. Failing that, she wanted the pictures. Large glossy photographs in living color. Every droplet of blood. Every inch of pale, drained flesh.

"We're going!" her mother called to her.

Maggie started. She looked at the clock and realized she'd been standing at the open closet door, staring at herself in the body-length mirror, for most of an hour. "Okay," she called back. "Drive safely!"

A thump of the front door closing. The sound of the girls babbling while Susan got them in their car seats in the rental car outside. Then fading engine noise as they drove off.

Maggie went to the ground floor. She stood in the

middle of her foyer with indecision stretching away from her on every side. The options were many, but the realistic ones few. Suddenly she heard another thump downstairs. A door closed firmly. She went to the front window, but Karl's car wasn't in the driveway. Her mother hadn't returned.

She dropped a hand to her hip, but there was no weapon. The only pistol was locked in a box upstairs in the closet. A Colt Detective Special she'd gotten from her father on her eighteenth birthday. A traditional gun. A cop's gun. A gun she did not have.

The sound was quiet, but instantly identifiable: a heel falling on concrete in the garage. Then silence. Maggie swallowed and felt her dry mouth and the sound of the swallow in her ears. Her heart didn't race. She was closed and calm and unshaken.

She went into the formal living room, silent on the carpet. The fireplace waited, clean and empty. She took a brass-handled poker from its rack. It was not a perfect weapon, but it was enough.

Not a single new sound came from the garage. Maggie thought about calling 911. Her phone was in her pocket. Dialing it would be simplicity, but she didn't. A faint hum had begun in the back of her head. She breathed in through the nose and out through her arid mouth. She didn't want anyone's help.

She made no sound on the walk to the kitchen. At the edge of the tile she used her toes to slip out of her shoes, so she wore only socks when she stepped out like a whisper. The door to the garage had a dead bolt, but she saw from the position of the knob that it was open. Karl had forgotten to secure it when he left the house.

Maggie approached the door. She put out her free hand and raised the poker with the other. She clasped the doorknob and turned. It made the sound of a gunshot, deafeningly loud. She pulled the door. It swung inward.

Bryant Gibbs stood on the other side with a gun in his hand. He was slick with sweat.

Maggie hit him with the poker.

CHAPTER 17

SHE WANTED TO KNOCK the gun from his hand, a compact Glock the color of coal. He cried out when the iron poker crossed his forearm, but he didn't let go of his weapon even as he reeled away. Maggie came after him into the darkened garage, the only light coming from the high windows on the door. She struck again and again, catching him across the shoulders, landing a glancing blow on the side of his head, which drew blood. She went for his knees and he went down.

"Goddamnit!" he shouted. "Goddamnit, *stop!*"

He brandished the Glock and Maggie saw his finger on the trigger and his knuckle whiten. She raised the poker once again, but didn't strike. "You know how to use that thing?" she asked him.

"You want to find out? Try to hit me one more time. Try it."

Maggie lowered the poker.

"On the ground."

It clanged when it hit the concrete floor, and echoed in the open space of the garage. Gibbs nodded. He touched his bloody temple. "Damnit," he said.

"Put the gun away," Maggie told him. "I'm unarmed. You don't need to have the gun out."

"I think I do." Still, Gibbs turned the muzzle away from her. He was on one knee, and if she moved fast enough, she might have been able to get hold of him and even disarm him, but she wasn't as young or as fast as she used to be, and she wouldn't die here in her own home where her mother would find her dead, where her children might see.

"People are looking for you," Maggie said.

"I know. That's why I came here. You used to be a cop, right? You are one big, happy cop family. That's right, isn't it?"

"Yes."

"You knew Carole and Philip."

"I did."

"I didn't kill them," Gibbs said.

Maggie didn't look away from him. Her voice betrayed nothing. "I believe you."

Gibbs laughed at that. "No, I don't think that's true. But I don't care. I care about people knowing the *truth*. And you're going to help me do that. You're going to help me uncover the whole thing. So we're gonna walk in and sit down and I'm gonna tell you what happens next."

"You're the boss," Maggie said.

"I *am* the boss. Walk in front of me."

They went inside and he directed her to sit in a kitchen chair. He was careful to sit on the far side with the gun resting on the table, but not out of his reach. The wound in his head was bleeding more. Red had run down the side of his face and neck, and stained his collar. It made Maggie think of Karl's suit. Gibbs's clothes were rumpled, as if he'd slept in them. His face was shadowed with stubble.

"I know you said you believe, but I know what you're really thinking," Gibbs said after they looked at each other for a while.

Maggie didn't reply. She had both hands on the table, both feet firmly on the floor. She calculated the weight of the table. How easily could it flip? How badly would Gibbs be startled? She did nothing.

"You're thinking I killed my wife, and then I killed Carole and Philip to cover it up."

"Did you?" Maggie asked.

"No. I'm not a killer. That's not my thing."

"What is your thing?"

"Money. Sex. A little blow if I'm feeling like a party. I'm a simple guy. You understand, right?"

"Sure," Maggie said. "I saw you partying with Carole and Philip a few days before they died."

A smile almost lifted Gibbs's face. "Phil liked to watch her with me."

"And now he's dead," Maggie replied.

Gibbs scowled. "Not because of me!"

Maggie soothed him with her tone. "If everyone was a consenting adult, there's no crime. The police might even overlook the money if that was just part of the thrill. You need to do yourself a favor: put down the gun, let me call 911, and then you can tell your whole story."

The man shook his head emphatically. "No. *No*. You don't get it. I can't talk without any proof, and even then they're gonna call me a pervert and a liar. People will listen to you. I'll show you everything, and then when *you* take it to the cops, you won't get pawned off on some pencil-pusher who thinks it's all a bunch of bullshit. Carole said you were asking around. She knew you were interested in playing. She had you all figured out. I would have come to see you sooner or later. Then you'd know."

"What is there to know?" Maggie asked. "Who killed them? Who killed your wife? I can't help you if I don't know."

"Right," Gibbs said, and his chin bobbed up and down. "You need to know everything. And I'll tell you, but first we have to get everything together. So you come with me and we'll get it. I have something I need to check, and then I'll know for sure. Let's go."

"I'm not going with you anywhere," Maggie said firmly.

"No, you *are*. You're going to come with me, or I'm gonna…I'm gonna…"

He faltered. Maggie leaned forward in her seat. "What are you going to do, Bryant? You said yourself you're not a killer. You're a suburban pimp. Are you going to kill a cop's wife? Is that how you're gonna play it? Because they'll give you the needle, Bryant. They'll put it all on you, and then you'll die."

She saw his lips tremble, and then his mouth hardened. He lifted the gun from the table. "No. You are coming and I will kill you if you don't. Because I don't have anything to lose, baby. So get your shoes and grab your keys. We're leaving now."

CHAPTER 18

HE WAS SMOOTHER GETTING it done than Maggie expected. Maybe he'd seen the technique on TV, or maybe he was a natural. Whatever the case, they got into the SUV without him ever taking the gun off her. She couldn't have run if she wanted to, and right now she wasn't sure she wanted to. Bryant Gibbs was leading her to something, and the magnetic pull of knowing, of finding the solution, was like welcoming an old friend.

Gibbs directed her through the streets. At one point they passed the community garden and Maggie saw the housewife volunteers working. No one spotted her. She could have driven up on the curb and alerted all of them, but she opted not to. With every turn they made, the attraction to the truth grew more irresistible. She knew exactly where they were going.

"Stop here," Gibbs said.

Maggie obeyed. She left the engine running. "Why are we at Carole's house, Bryant?" She had to keep using his name. If she used his name it would subtly reinforce the notion that they had a relationship, that they were working together toward a common goal. He would be less likely to use the gun, at least until the moment arrived when she could take it from him.

Gibbs looked at the house. It was quiet from the outside, as if nothing untoward had ever happened there. Where were the police? Bryant must have waited until the crime scene was cleared, but she couldn't believe they had vacated the premises. How had they kept this story from the press? Even the yellow tape on the front door was barely noticeable, placed discreetly like so much else in the Parish.

"Bryant? I asked you why we're here."

"Carole was one of my top earners. She was like Holly: doing the weird stuff, the harder stuff. And Carole's husband, Philip? He got more out of it than anyone. But he was nosy, and looked into matters that weren't his concern. Carole let it slip the last time I was with her."

Maggie checked the rearview mirror. The street was clear. She hadn't seen the security patrol on their ride, and it was nowhere now. It wasn't around when Holly Gibbs was killed, and it hadn't stopped Carole and Philip Strickland from dying. Now Maggie wanted it to stay away because this was handled. She could handle it. She breathed steadily and her heart beat in a regular rhythm.

"We're gonna get out now," Bryant said. "Then we're going to go inside and get some things. I have a pretty good idea where he's keeping them."

"Whatever you want to do, Bryant," Maggie said.

"Goddamnit, stop calling me by my name."

"I'm sorry. I won't do it again."

They got out as smoothly as they got in. Bryant was careful, and steadier than she would have expected. He waited until she came around the nose of the SUV, then gestured at her with the gun held close to his body. The blood on his face was dry. "You stay ahead of me," he said. "And when we get to the door, you turn your face to the wall while I get it open."

She obeyed. They crossed the broad lawn, passed the little sign with the security company's name on it, stepped under the cover of the eaves in front of the large front door. It had glass on both sides, and when Maggie moved to comply with Bryant's directions, she was able to see inside to the foyer, which was clean and perfect and gave nothing away. This house didn't look like a double murder had been committed here.

Bryant cut the tape with something sharp. She heard the edge slice through the adhesive plastic. Afterward he worked the lock. Maggie couldn't see what he was doing. "How did you get inside my house?" she asked.

"The same way I'm getting into this one. With a key."

"Where did you get a key to my house?"

"Enough questions. I'm opening the door. You go in first. There's a table by the stairs. Put your hands on it."

The door opened. Immediately a regular beeping sounded from just inside. Maggie went inside and her nose was filled with the scent of potpourri. She saw the small table cradled in the arm of a curving staircase climbing upward. On her left was the alarm system panel. The distance to the table was six feet. She was too far from him.

Bryant entered the code. The alarm went silent. He closed the door.

"You know how to do this pretty well," Maggie said calmly. "You handle a gun like a pro. You know how to keep someone under control. Where'd you learn all that?"

"From *cops,*" Bryant said, and she heard the sharp tone in his voice. "They're always talking, always wanting to show you this or that. The only thing they like more is taking my money. We're going up the stairs now. Turn to the left, walk all the way to the master suite. Stop by the bed."

"If you try to do something to me there, Bryant, I can't let you," Maggie told him.

"What? Please. I get it whenever I want it, however I want it. I'm the king, lady. Up the stairs. And what did I say about my name?"

She took the steps with him behind her. She kept her hands where he could see them. "I thought kings didn't like to share," she said. "Holly was out there working for you. It must have been hard, knowing what she was doing. Makes you wonder if she really liked it when you were together."

"You don't know what you're talking about. What we did made it *better.* Don't you get it? It's all about making life better. Hotter. Everything you think you know about all of this? It's bullshit. You're as much in the dark as everyone else. But it doesn't matter. You're my shield, because no cop is going to do anything with a cop's wife on the line."

They went to the master suite. Maggie walked forward until her knees touched the bed. "You don't know my husband."

"You think so?" Gibbs asked.

She heard him step close to her in the moment before he struck. The hard frame of the pistol clipped the side of her head and she saw explosions of white in her vision. Balance fled. Blood rushed in her ears. She reached for her temple, but before she touched it, she was gone.

CHAPTER 19

SHE WOKE UP SLOWLY. The floor tilted underneath her, swaying this way and that, an unsteady platform she had to cling to or be thrown from. She felt the carpet fibers clutched in her fingers. Her ears still rushed. She opened her eyes and tried to find focus.

Gibbs wasn't in sight. Maggie rolled onto her back and tried to sit up, but the movement made her feel violently ill. She tried a different tack, grasping the edge of the bedspread and levering herself up on one knee until she could use the bed to support her as balance returned. Her skull throbbed.

The room had been tossed. The job was thorough, but amateur. A cop could take a room apart completely without destroying much of anything. Gibbs had torn everything to shreds. Pictures were off the walls. The bed was partly denuded, the mattress not on straight. He'd turned over the chairs and emptied every drawer. And now he came in the room and sat across the room from her with a ledger across his knees and the gun

atop the leather cover. The door to the master bathroom was closed, but there was a bloody handprint
two-thirds of the way down. Immediately Maggie
knew it was Karl's.

Maggie looked back to Gibbs, and he looked back
at her with an intensity she hadn't seen before. His
hand rested lightly against the pistol, but wasn't closed
around the grip. Even so, he was too far to reach, and
she was too unsteady to risk it. She sat on the bed
instead, and from the corner of her eye gauged the distance to the bedroom door.

"Why was Karl here?" she asked.

"Good question. Why are any cops involved in my
business at all? Until recently, everything was running
smoothly. Sure, the kink is there, and that's gonna
bring out some of the freaks, but this wasn't like that.
This was about money, and money beats sex every
time.

"Holly wasn't the first casualty," Gibbs said. "But
nobody knew that. The first casualty from the women
who worked for me was Melissa Mason. Her husband
told everybody she left him. He got pictures of her
body in the mail."

"Why would someone kill her?" Maggie asked.

"I didn't know. I thought it was a job gone wrong.
I was freaked out, but tried to be even more discreet. I
didn't know who I was reporting to. It was just business, and eventually I expanded my business. And
maybe I didn't report all of my profits."

He still hadn't touched the gun. Maggie didn't look

directly at it. Her vision was clearing, and her head no longer swam. The pain was still there, but that could be beaten.

"Then they came for Holly, and that's when I knew this was about me."

"The police wanted in on your business," Maggie said. "Payment to look the other way."

"Yeah. I don't know exactly who, because I paid the way they asked: anonymous cash at a drop in a park in Castletown. Everything was fine. Then I get a call saying the price is higher now."

"You didn't pay."

"No, I paid, but I guess I didn't pay fast enough. That's when they hit Holly."

"And Carole? Her husband?"

Gibbs shook his head. "It's not about payoffs anymore. It's about taking over. That's how I know it's cops: They know my business, they know my women. They're on the inside. They're customers. They've destroyed my business, and they've murdered my wife. And if I'm going down, so are they."

Maggie noticed his pupils were enlarged. He was on edge.

"The question was whether I could prove it without a doubt. Audio is good. Video is better. But you know what really gets people like you off? *Corroborating evidence*. Two people who tell the same story. Problem is, Philip's not alive to tell his side of it. But I have this."

He tapped the ledger again. Maggie risked a more direct glance toward the door. She could make it. She nodded to the ledger. "You have what you need in there?"

"I do. Put what I have together with what he had and you have a case. Police corruption. Murder. You and me, we're going to go get the rest of the evidence. You're more important than ever now."

"How can you be sure you're right?" Maggie asked.

He'd taken something while she was out. It could have been anything, from street drugs to something gotten with a prescription. Sometimes they were almost the same thing. He said he liked cocaine. "When Philip got involved, he started talking to all my ladies. It started with Carole, but he branched out. He wanted it all: where, when, who, what. He said he had it written down and all recorded. Exactly what I didn't want, but I let him do it when he promised to keep it hidden and on paper. And now I'm glad he did, because it's my proof, don't you get it? It backs up everything I figured."

"You have blackmail material?"

Gibbs made a face. "I'm not a blackmailer. Blackmailers are scumbags. I'm not a scumbag."

"I didn't say you were. So what are you going to do, Bryant?"

"We're going to get the rest, and then I'm going to use you to get the story out."

"What—?" Maggie started.

Something banged downstairs. A foot struck against wood, and then again. The distinct sound of a doorframe shearing followed, and then a bellowing voice.

"Police! Get down on the floor and put your hands on your head!"

Maggie moved. She surged toward the door, aware of Gibbs springing out of his seat with the gun, the ledger falling to the floor. He shouted, but she ignored him. "Second floor, second floor!" she yelled. "White male armed with a handgun!"

She saw a uniformed cop in the foyer. Two more men bulled in behind him, black and white. They looked up and Maggie saw Karl and Mike. Karl called her name.

Gibbs caught up to her when she was two steps from the top of the stairs. He grabbed her by the hair and pulled sharply. Her scalp shrieked with pain and she felt some hair come loose. She crashed back against him. He put the gun in her ear and whispered, "Told you they were watching me." Then he raised his voice. "Cops! Back off or she dies! I'll kill her!"

"Stay back," Karl commanded the uniformed officer. He had his weapon out. Mike held his low to his side. When Karl addressed Gibbs, he did so in a smooth tone. "Nobody needs to get hurt. Maggie, are you hurt?"

"I'm fine. Relax."

"I will kill this bitch. And you'll deserve it!"

Karl put his foot on the bottom step. "I don't know what you're talking about, but take it easy, okay? Nobody's going to kill anybody."

Maggie felt Gibbs's body against hers, muscles electric with tension. His breath came sharply in her ear, just above the muzzle of his Glock. She saw Karl rise one more step. She set her feet apart slowly. Gibbs noticed nothing.

He whispered into her ear, his voice barely audible: *"There he is."*

Maggie started to move, but stopped when she saw Karl come up another step. She felt Gibbs touch her hip.

"Everything's cool," Karl said.

"Back off and do what he says," Maggie told Karl.

Gibbs spoke up, louder than before. "Yeah, do what I—"

Gibbs didn't finish. Maggie drove her heel down on Gibbs's instep, and pivoted in the next moment, driving the gun up and away from her head. It discharged into the ceiling as Gibbs stumbled, his foot broken. He reeled, but his scream was cut off by the thunder of Karl's service weapon. Gibbs toppled over with a hole punched in his skull.

CHAPTER 20

MAGGIE SAT IN THE back of an ambulance with a thermal blanket wrapped around her. An EMT had made a dressing for the injury to her temple. She still had a terrible headache, and they told her she would need to go to the hospital for X-rays and tests. That was fine for now.

The house swarmed with people. She saw Mike Cooper on the lawn.

She blinked and Karl was there. "What are you doing here? Aren't you on desk duty, pending investigation of your accident at the crime scene?"

He shooed the EMT away and hugged her. "I could never sit at a desk knowing you were in danger," he said. "I don't care what the repercussions are for me. I was so scared and I am so glad you're safe."

"I'll always be fine," Maggie said. "I'm the chief." She smiled faintly, but doing it made her hurt. She wanted sleep, but first they had to find out if she had a concussion. Sleep with a concussion might never end. "Got to watch my people work."

"You know, I'm not even going to argue," Karl replied. "As long as you're okay."

Maggie looked at him. She searched his face seeking something she wasn't sure about herself. She wanted to ask him questions, and she wanted to see his reactions. Guiltily she realized she wanted to see him on the other side of an interrogation table, and herself opposite him. What did he know? When did he know it? What was Bryant Gibbs trying to tell her?

Instead, she said, "You're still a good shot."

"Tops in the unit."

"Don't brag."

Karl's expression turned serious again. "You talk to your mother?"

"Yeah, they loaned me a phone. The girls are fine. She's fine. I told her to have someone come by today and change the locks. Gibbs isn't coming back, but that doesn't mean no one else will."

He glanced away. She thought she saw something then, but it was hidden when he turned back to her. "No one's coming, because Gibbs is the one. I don't know what he wanted with you, but it's pretty clear he did his wife, then Carole and Philip."

"She was definitely working for him. One of his better earners, he said."

"I don't doubt it. He had a key to their house and he knew the alarm code. He'd been in there plenty of times before. If he got around the way you said he did, it's likely he was in the sack with Carole on a regular basis."

"He had a key to our house, too," Maggie said. "Was I sleeping with him?"

The question was delivered with no emotion, no accusation. Maggie put it to him directly, the way she would with a suspect in interrogation. In such a situation, empathy was essential. If the subject thought they were being grilled by someone already convinced of their guilt, they'd shut down. The accusations came later, when trust was built.

She watched him closely without appearing to do so. The narrowing of his eyes, and the way his lips pressed together. He shifted on his feet. Only a little, but she noticed. She could tell he wanted to look away again, buy a second or two to formulate an answer, but she also saw he knew what she was thinking, and he couldn't do it without being caught. "I don't know how he got our key," he said.

"You knew him before all this started?"

"No, I didn't know him."

"His wife?"

"What is this? Am I the suspect here? I didn't know either of them before the day Holly Gibbs was killed. I didn't hear any of the gossip about them, I never even spoke to the man at a party. He was a total stranger to me. And he was to you, too, right?"

Maggie didn't fire back right away. When she spoke again, it was the same as before: no investment, no passion. Anything she felt she kept inside. He'd know she was doing it. Maybe it would make him angrier. Maybe it would do something else. She said, "So we don't know where he got the key, but he had it. And he came looking for me. He came for me specifically. I don't know why that is. Why would he do that, Karl?"

She saw him stamping out an internal fire. He assembled a calm face, but he had never been as good at it as she was. "He knew you were a cop's wife. He knew you were *my* wife. He thought he could use that if he had to. But he was wrong. He messed with the wrong lady. And the wrong man."

"I'm going to want to talk about this some more when we're home again," Maggie said. "I don't want there to be any secrets here. We'll talk and we'll put it all on the table. I don't care what it is."

Karl breathed sharply through his nose. "I'm telling you there's nothing to hide. It's because he was the doer and I was the investigating detective. If Mike were still married and living in the Parish, Gibbs probably would have gone after Kelly. It's bad luck, that's all."

"Okay," Maggie said.

"Okay?"

"Okay. Tell them I'm ready to go."

He kissed her on the forehead, gently. "Don't die on me, all right?"

"Go do your job, Detective."

She held a breath that she did not exhale until he left. Her lungs shuddered with released tension. The EMT and her partner came to secure her in the back of the ambulance. Soon they were under way. Maggie listened to the mumble of the radio, rested her aching head on the pillow, and thought.

Neither of the EMTs had anything to say. Maggie was glad they weren't sitting with her. She put her hand in her hip pocket and there was something there that hadn't been before, that must have been put there when Gibbs touched her hip at the top of the stairs: a steel key with a barrel shaft and a red bow marked with a simple number. Maggie gripped it tightly as the ambulance drove on.

CHAPTER 21

IT WAS THE NEXT day before Karl was allowed to bring her home. The hospital found she had a mild concussion, and monitored her all night, but nothing came of it. They stopped at the pharmacy for a bottle of pain pills, which she didn't plan to take. Drowsiness was the first and most significant side effect. She wanted to be awake.

Karl wanted to support her as they walked from the car to the front door, but she shook him off. She went into the house under her own power. Her mother waited just inside with a girl tucked under each arm. When she saw them, Maggie felt a surge of emotion that had been missing before. She felt herself tearing up, and she put her arms around all three of them.

"It's over now," Susan said into her ear. "All over."

The girls made happy sounds. It almost made her knees buckle, she was so glad to see them. Maggie kissed them both, then bussed her mother on the cheek. She stepped back and saw Karl watching. His face was soft, his eyes taking in the scene with warmth. This man she knew well. This man she loved. Despite herself, she hugged and kissed him, too, as if they had been apart until now.

"Home again," Karl said.

"Right."

They gathered around the kitchen table. Her mother made a breakfast feast with enough food for six people.

For an hour it was enough to sit and talk as though nothing had transpired to disturb this home. Susan wouldn't allow Maggie to help clean up. Karl insisted Maggie go upstairs to lie down. "I'll make sure the girls are okay. When your mother's done I have to go back to work, though."

"Of course," Maggie said. She kissed him.

She undressed with some help and Karl assisted getting some flannel pajamas on her. They were too heavy for the season, but they felt soft and comfortable and that worked for her. Maggie's arms and legs had begun to feel leaden, and she sat dizzily on the edge of the bed while Karl filled a glass of water for the side table. "You all right?" he asked when he came back.

"I'm feeling out of it all of a sudden."

"You want me to stay?"

"No, you go."

Karl took the bottle of pain pills out of his pocket and set them by the bed with the water. "Take those if it turns out you need them. Gibbs popped you pretty good, so don't try to be a tough guy."

Maggie nodded. She pulled back the sheets. Karl tucked her in. "Be safe," Maggie said, and she touched his face.

He clasped her hand. "Always. Sleep now."

She closed her eyes without even realizing it was happening. She heard him walking away. Sleep pressed down on her firmly, forcing her into the mattress. Maggie edged toward surrender until a sudden spark of awareness flashed in her mind. Her eyes snapped open.

The bottle still stood by the bed. She looked at the label for the first time. The prescription called for medication twice a day for a week. Fourteen pills. Maggie twisted off the cap and poured the pills onto the side table. It was hard to focus, but she counted an odd number: thirteen.

She read the label again. DO NOT CRUSH.

Her mother served orange juice with breakfast. It tasted fine, but a little chalky. She picked up one of the pills and touched it to her tongue. The bitterness would have been hidden, but that chalky flavor was distinct.

Karl's engine hadn't started outside. He was somewhere in the house, and for some reason it didn't feel right that he was there. Maggie fell back onto the mattress. She was fading despite herself. She turned on the bed and saw the landline phone on the other side table. She made her way to it like a swimmer crossing difficult water. Her hand fell on the cool receiver. She dragged the whole phone to her and dialed from memory.

"Cooper," said the man on the other end.

"Mike," Maggie said. Her voice sounded like a breath.

"Chief? Hey, Chief, are you okay? Where are you?"

"I'm at home. Listen, Mike: what happened to that ledger Gibbs took from the Stricklands' house?"

"Chief, I don't think you should be worried about that kind of thing. Are you calling from home? Where's Karl? Do I need to call Karl?"

"No!" Maggie said too sharply. "I don't need Karl. I need you, Mike. The ledger. Is it in evidence?"

Mike paused. Maggie faded further. She thought she would fall asleep with the phone against her ear. "I'm not really sure what ledger you're talking about," he said at last.

"In the bedroom with Gibbs. He had it. He found it somewhere in the house."

"Chief, I'm going to call Karl. Something's wrong here."

"Goddamnit, don't call him! Who had access to the room? Who was the first one through the door?"

"It was Karl."

Maggie pressed her forehead against the sheets. She was almost gone. "You have to find that ledger. You have to…"

She didn't finish. She was gone.

CHAPTER 22

MAGGIE AWOKE IN FULL darkness. She didn't have the phone in her hand, but she heard the steady alarum of the off-hook tone throbbing from the abandoned receiver. Her mouth tasted like a desert, but her head didn't hurt at all. The room was unusually cold, and she knew it was because her mother had turned down the thermostat, knowing Maggie slept better in cold surroundings.

First, she hung up the phone. Second, she got out of bed. Somewhere downstairs, Susan was talking brightly to her grandchildren. Maggie moved quietly, so they wouldn't know she was awake.

Her clothes from the day before were in the hamper. Maggie dug through them, aware of the little desperate sounds she made as she clawed through the laundry. She found her pants and plunged a hand into both pockets but found nothing. She stifled a cry, then overturned the hamper completely.

Once she had everything spread out, she found the

key. It had fallen clear of her pants, but still inside the hamper. In the dryer it would have made a distinctive rattle and couldn't be hidden. In the hamper it was a secret.

"Maggie, are you awake?"

Her mother's voice carried from the stairs down the hall. Maggie froze, then cleared her throat. "I'm up," she said.

"Someone's here to see you. Are you decent?"

"Who is it?"

"It's Mike, honey."

"Tell him I'll be right there."

Maggie looked around herself. She went to her dresser and opened the top drawer. She rummaged around inside until she found a small, flat case. Inside was a velvet bed supporting two teardrop pearl earrings. Maggie lifted the bed, put the key Gibbs gave her underneath and then put it all back as it was. Only then did she shut the drawer, grab a robe off the bathroom door, and leave the room.

She found Mike sitting on the floor in the front room with the girls. Lana had the side of a large plastic block jammed against her mouth, but had no way to understand that her jaw would never stretch wide enough to engulf the whole thing. It glistened with drool. Becky giggled as Mike played with a hand puppet of a fluffy lamb, talking in a high-pitched voice and making silly sounds that turned giggles into peals of laughter. Susan watched it all with delighted eyes.

Mike laughed, too, but when he saw Maggie, his face turned serious. "How you doing?" he asked.

"As well as I can be."

"Mrs. Gilcoe," Mike said to Maggie's mother, "do you mind if the chief and I talk in another room?"

"No, of course not. But don't get her into any trouble."

"No trouble, ma'am."

Maggie beckoned Mike out into the hall. They walked to the formal dining room. It had double doors that could be pulled together. Maggie did that now. "Mike…" she said.

"I got that call, and I didn't know what to think. You panicked me, Chief."

"It's Karl," Maggie said. "He…I don't know. I'll figure it out on my own. But I have to find out about that ledger."

Mike's face was engulfed in shadows. She could see the concern in his eyes, the edge of his face limned by the streetlight. "What's the story with this ledger? You call me up, you sound like you're in a panic about it. What is it? Where is it?"

"I thought you'd be able to tell me," Maggie said ruefully. "It's part of what Gibbs wanted out of Carole Strickland's house. And I'm pretty sure it's some of what the killer wanted, too. A record of Gibbs's business. Who was in his stable. Who their clients were and what they wanted. It's the kind of thing we need to start pulling this together."

"Hold on a second, Chief," Mike said, and he raised

his hands. "*We* don't need anything. Everything that goes on here is strictly off the books. Karl and I are still the detectives on this case."

Maggie swallowed. She didn't want to say the next thing. "Mike, why didn't Karl wait for backup before he went into Carole's house on the night of the murders? When you found me there, you had backup. He didn't go in for *me* without backup, but he went into Carole's house with no one else behind him. And he got Carole's blood all over him without anyone seeing what happened."

"I don't know if I like where this is headed," Mike said. His voice was careful.

"I'm not accusing him of anything. All I want is to put the pieces together. Karl's a good cop, you and I both know that, so it's sloppy work at best. And you don't have the ledger? It's not anywhere? No one said anything about it?"

Mike shook his head. "No. Chief, what you're saying—"

"He's not a killer," Maggie said quickly. "He might take someone down in the line of duty. Like Gibbs. It was a righteous shooting. No one's going to fault him for that. Whatever else he might be, and I'm saying this because he's my husband and you'd expect me to, he's not a killer. That's not in him."

"Chief, you've been on the job long enough to know that you can't always figure who's a killer and who's not. I've seen it, and I know you've seen it. I don't want to believe Karl's anything but a straight-ahead cop, but you're making me ask questions. Maybe he's not taking anyone out, but…"

"He's hiding something," Maggie said.

"Any guesses as to what?"

"I'm not sure yet, but we have to find out. He put something in my drink, Mike. He made sure I was asleep for whatever he had to do next. And if he wasn't bringing the ledger in to you, that means he took it somewhere else. It might even be in the house."

"You'll look for it?"

"When I can. My mother's here, and as long as you warn me when Karl's headed my way…"

"So I'm your lookout," Mike said.

"You have to watch him. You can see him when I don't."

"This isn't right, Chief."

"You can't clear a suspect without looking into him first. That's the rule."

A sudden glare of yellow light exploded between them as the double doors were slid open from the other side. Karl stood there. His face was grave. "Honey. Mike. Am I missing a meeting?"

CHAPTER 23

MAGGIE SWALLOWED EVERYTHING AND put on the face she knew Karl expected: surprised and pleased, but also tired and in pain. Karl's expression was something else entirely: a thicket of emotions from annoyance to anxiety. "Karl," Maggie said, "Mike came by to see how I'm doing."

Karl looked at her, and then at Mike. Maggie saw Mike had turned studiously neutral. He turned it on in a second, and Maggie would never have known the difference if she hadn't seen it happen in the moment. "How is she doing, Mike?" Karl asked.

"Good, man. Good."

"I think Mom's got some dinner for us," Maggie said, and she kissed Karl on the cheek. His skin was almost imperceptibly moist. When Maggie touched her lips with her tongue, she tasted salt. Karl was holding on to something, too, but he wasn't so skilled at it. Maggie showed him nothing with her eyes or her voice. "Do you want Mike to sit down with us?"

"Sure," Karl said. "Come on and have some dinner, Mike."

They sat around the table with Susan and the girls. Dinner was a hearty soup with chunky, hand-chopped vegetables and a homemade stock. Maggie sat opposite Karl with Mike at the end of the table. Maggie's mother sat beside Karl and the twins had their own dedicated space. Very little was said. There was the clink of spoons and the sounds of Lana and Becky babbling to each other and to the grown-ups at the table, but not much else.

"Does anyone know any good jokes?" Susan asked brightly, but dead looks silenced her.

Mike pushed his empty bowl away. "I should get going. I have some things to check in on, and then I got to catch some shut-eye. I've been burning the candle at both ends."

"I'll walk you to the door," Maggie said.

Karl stood up sharply and jostled the table. The girls stopped what they were doing and gaped. "No, I'll do it," he said. "Mike, come on. I've got to talk to you about something anyway."

Mike glanced toward Maggie. Maggie saw her mother watching. "Feel better, Chief," Mike said, and then left.

When they were both gone, Susan turned to Maggie. "Is there something happening here I ought to know about?"

"It's better if you take care of the girls and let me handle it."

"Is this personal or professional?"

"I'm not a cop anymore. It's all personal."

Susan reached across the table and put her hand on Maggie's. "Whatever you think is going on, don't let it ruin what you have here."

Maggie slipped her hand free. "That's not up to me."

She left the table without offering to help clean up, stopping to kiss each of the girls on their heads. Karl hadn't returned. She went up to their bedroom and sat, thinking, her mind exploring the house through memory. All the hidden places, all the little-used corners. Each one would have to be checked.

Karl's footfalls sounded in the hallway outside the room. He appeared. "I have to go back in."

"You just got here."

"I know, but I have to go back in. I'm sorry."

Maggie only nodded. She said nothing.

"I'm not sure what's going on here," Karl said quietly. "I know somewhere along the line I started to lose your trust. If you'll give me a chance, I'll earn it back. Whatever you think I'm doing, or you think I've done, you're wrong. I'm still the same man I've been all along."

Now Maggie looked at him. He stood in the doorway hesitantly, as if afraid to set foot inside the room. "I want to know one thing," she said.

"Okay."

"If I look, if I ask, will I find out you were sleeping with someone else?"

"Who else would I sleep with?"

"Carole. Maybe Holly Gibbs. Have you ever heard of Melissa Mason?"

Karl shook his head slowly. If before he had been easily read, now he was perfectly in control. Maggie couldn't decide if she believed the mask he wore now. She couldn't even be certain it was a mask at all, but she wore one with him, and it made sense he would wear one for her. Especially now.

"Go do what you have to do," Maggie said when the silence went on for too long.

"I do love you," Karl said.

"I know, Karl. But you should probably go."

He did go, and she was alone. This time she waited until she heard him drive away. Her mother's sing-song talk as she put the girls to bed floated up to her, reminding her the house was alive even if Maggie herself had begun to feel differently. It had come on abruptly in the death of Holly Gibbs, and now it threatened the bubble of peace that surrounded her family.

She waited a full ten minutes to be certain he wasn't going to come back, and then she went to work.

CHAPTER 24

SHE STARTED ON THE second floor so as not to disturb her mother. The bedroom was her first target, though she was reasonably certain nothing was hidden there. She would have seen Karl do it, or she would have heard him, and even being doped up on the pain pills would not be enough to dull her senses that much. Or at least she hoped so.

The closets and drawers were clear, the space under the bed unoccupied by anything except dust bunnies. She halfheartedly searched the master bathroom, but again she found nothing. Then it was on to the hall, the closets, checking between linens and inside boxes of Christmas decorations and wrapping paper.

In the guest bedroom where her mother slept, Maggie was careful not to disturb anything that might give the search away. When she got downstairs, she'd have to figure out a way to distract Susan until she could clear the first floor. Maggie's mother had an eye for anything out of the ordinary. She knew already there was more happening than she was being told, and maybe she knew far more than she let on.

The guest bedroom was clear. The second bathroom was clear. Maggie stood in the hallway, thinking. She looked at the door to the girls' room, and a curtain of darkness draped over her. "No," she said to herself. "No way."

Maggie reluctantly stepped up to the door, step by slow step. The door itself was half-closed, the lights switched off. She saw light from the window, but there was deep shadow. She put her hand on the panel and pressed lightly. The door came open. She saw the matching cribs with sleeping forms, the dressers, the changing table, the toy box.

"Goddamnit, Karl," Maggie said without anyone to hear. "Please don't…"

She didn't finish the thought. She turned on the night-light and went inside, closing the door behind herself, because this felt wrong. She scanned the room slowly once more, and then she made herself move.

Under chair cushions and inside the toy box and dresser drawers, but nothing—perhaps she'd been wrong after all. She opened the closet to find the neat racks from IKEA, which organized the interior. Maggie looked behind and beneath, but there was nothing. She looked up to the shelf running above the closet, straining to see in the dim light. Blankets were stacked there, and additional sheets and supplies. She put her hands between the folds of a soft white blanket they'd gotten from Karl's aunt, and then she felt it.

Maggie made a sound like crying, then remembered to be quiet. She pulled back and held her hand as if she'd been cut. Something blurred her vision, and when she wiped her eyes her fingers came away wet. She made herself reach up again and pull the ledger out into plain view. She brought it down and gripped it tightly in both hands. Even in the dark, she knew her knuckles were white. She shook, though whether it was from anger or sadness she didn't know.

She wouldn't look at it here. She walked out, closed the door, and took it into the master bedroom instead. There she sat on the end of their bed and opened it. She saw handwritten notes, dense letters not entirely even, the lines meandering up and down on the unlined pages.

If she'd hoped for names and pictures, she was disappointed. Philip Strickland was thorough, but he seemed to have some strange hesitation about the last veil of privacy. The women were marked with the symbol for female and referred to by initials. The men had their mark and initials. The rest of each entry was a detailed account of what acts had been performed, what money had changed hands.

Maggie found Carole's entries easily, because instead of the mark for a woman, Philip had placed a heart. The things he wrote about her made Maggie draw a sharp breath. Everything she had done or had done to her. Every moment, it seemed, catalogued in a hand that became more fevered as the specificity increased.

She must have told him everything, and he wrote it all down to pore over again and again.

Some entries had notations, either *A* or *V* or both together. It didn't take much imagination to understand what these meant. Maggie brought out the key. She remembered what Gibbs had said. Carole was the most-recorded of all of them, which made sense in its own way. *CS* met with *KD* many times, and each visit was recorded. *KD at CS home,* said a dozen entries.

Gibbs had a key to Carole's house. He had a key to Maggie's house.

Karl Denning.

Maggie put her face in her hands and cried, but cried quietly. Even now she didn't want her mother to hear, because then she would have to say it all out loud and it would become real.

CHAPTER 25

"MAY I SPEAK TO Amanda?" Maggie said to the officer on the other end of the line. The steadiness of her voice was surprising even to herself. She waited until she hadn't cried for an hour before making the call. Whenever her mother came up to check on her, she made certain she was in bed with the covers pulled up and the ledger hidden under her pillow. Once she feigned sleep.

The line clicked. A woman answered. "Sergeant Knight," she said. "May I ask who's calling?"

"Amanda, it's me. The chief."

Before, Amanda sounded bored. Now her tone brightened. "Chief! Hey, Chief, I heard what happened, but you're okay. Everybody's talking about it. I mean, you *are* okay, right?"

Maggie imagined Amanda: thirty years old, going thick despite her relative youth, betrayed by hours upon hours of desk work. Amanda was always on a diet, always trying to exercise. One month it was power walking. Another month it was yoga. Nothing ever seemed to help. "I'm okay," Maggie lied. "Everything's okay. But I wanted to know if you could help me. I can be down there in an hour or so."

"You need to come in?"

"I'll explain when I get there. But keep it to yourself, okay? Not a word to Karl."

"Lips locked and the key is gone."

"I'll see you soon," Maggie said.

She ended the call and got dressed. She tucked the ledger under her arm. Downstairs her mother was folding baby clothes. When she saw Maggie, her eyes narrowed. "What are you doing out of bed?"

"I have to go out."

"No, you have to rest."

"I have to go out."

Her tone was flat. Her mother looked at her, seemed to think, and then nodded. "Don't stay out too long."

"If Karl calls, I'm sleeping."

Maggie drove with the ledger on the seat beside her. She thought she could still smell Gibbs, but she knew it was her imagination. It was almost ninety minutes to the second since she talked to Amanda when she pulled into the lot outside the station. She almost parked in a space allotted for department vehicles before she checked herself and moved on to the civilian area. It had been six months since she'd been here.

The building was sandy, with windows tinted dark brown, giving everything a sort of dull appearance, even on a sunny day like this one. Cruisers were in and out, and though Maggie looked, she didn't see a single familiar officer behind the wheel of any of them.

She went inside and was allowed through the metal detector by more officers she didn't know. She felt like she was on some alien planet. In two years everything had changed except for the sounds and scent of the building. These were not her imagination, and were as familiar to her as the beating of her heart. She went to the elevator and pressed Down.

On the sub-level she found Amanda's lab at the end of a long corridor. It had the look and feel of a campus research facility, markedly different from everywhere else in the station. Here no one wore uniforms, but white coats instead. They had a tank for discharging weapons, they had more computers than there were people, and a self-contained lab for chemical analysis. Anything they couldn't handle, they would send out, but Amanda prided herself in keeping most forensics work in-house.

Maggie found her at a workstation filing a report. She stood at the desk for a minute, waiting, until finally she cleared her throat. Amanda jumped, then smiled. She got up to give Maggie a hug. She was much shorter than Maggie. "Chief," she said, "you look great. I mean, really great. Nothing sticks to you."

"You look good, too," Maggie replied. "You lost weight."

Amanda patted her hips. "Zumba classes."

"They work."

Amanda looked at the ledger. "Is that for me? Is

this for a case? Oh, are you doing private investigations now?"

"Nothing like that. It's actually this I need help with."

Maggie brought the key out of her pocket. She gave it to Amanda, who held it up to the light. "Safe deposit box key," Amanda said immediately.

"That's what I thought. It has a serial number. You can use that to narrow down the facility, right?"

"Oh, sure. And the key's pretty new, so that means the boxes were installed within the last couple of years probably. That'll help a lot. Let's check it out."

Amanda went to another workstation. Maggie watched her navigate screen after screen full of things she didn't know or understand. Many times investigations could not proceed without forensics, and the reverse, but they remained separate disciplines. Finally, Amanda settled on a database where the key's serial number could be entered.

The result took half a second. "We have three banks in the tri-county area with safe deposit box installations to go with the key," Amanda said. "It's impossible to know which one until you check them out, but you could probably hit them all in one day if you hustle."

Maggie took the key back. She put it in her pocket. "Great—would you give me the addresses?"

CHAPTER 26

AFTER A RESTLESS NIGHT of feigning sleep to avoid Karl, Maggie started on the list the following morning. She found the vault under Karl's name in the second bank. Maggie played dumb, said she found her husband hiding something, and she wanted to know what it could be. To do this required a warrant, she was informed, and there was no way around it, husband or not. Maggie called Mike.

The process took a long two hours, but Mike got the ADA to find a judge willing to issue a warrant for the contents of whatever box the key opened. Maggie waited in a chair by the windows with the ledger on her lap. Occasionally she looked at the litany of initials: *MM, JE, RL, MC,* and *KD*. Always *KD*. *MC* was the only set of initials that appeared as often. Clearly *KD* liked Carole, or Carole liked *KD*. It didn't matter. Only *KD* mattered.

She saw Mike when he parked in the lot. He came in through the doors and spotted her. She met him halfway. "Do you have it?" she asked.

"I have it. But Karl's gonna find out as soon as he

comes back from his meeting with Collins. I can't keep a lid on that. And he's gonna be pissed, Chief. There's no two ways about it."

"I don't think it's going to matter," Maggie said, and her vision clouded again. She turned her head. She didn't want to cry in front of Mike. She was still the Chief to him, and the Chief never cried.

Mike waited until she could look him in the eye again. "That's the book?"

"Yeah."

"Mind if I look at it?"

"Be my guest. I'll deal with the manager."

She left Mike and made the arrangements. When she came back, Mike's expression was grim. "He's the one," he said. "He's got to be the one. And you think this safe deposit box has the audio and video to prove it?"

"I do."

"Then let's look."

The manager bent to the warrant and let them into the vault. The box was located, and it was much smaller than Maggie expected. Maggie opened it. Inside was a single thumb drive and nothing else. "You got something that can read that?" Maggie asked.

"My laptop's in the trunk."

"You're taking it?" the manager asked.

"That's what the warrant's for," Maggie returned. Mike took the thumb drive and nodded to her. They left together.

They sat side by side in the car when Mike accessed the drive. The file revealed a screen full of folders marked by dates. "Give me one of the dates where KD was with Carole Strickland," Mike said.

Maggie did. They saw MP3 and MP4 files available. Maggie felt her stomach turn. "I don't think I can watch a video," she said.

"I understand," Mike said, and he patted her on the arm in a familiar way he had never done before. "But if KD is Karl, then we're going to have to look at everything, Chief. You know that."

"I know. Put it on."

He clicked the icon, and the audio began. Maggie heard a man say, *"Is it on?"*

"That's Philip Strickland," Maggie told Mike.

"Yes, it's on."

"Carole," Maggie said.

"Okay. Press the button on the camera when you put your purse down."

"I know how to do it, Philip."

Kissing. A moan. Philip chuckled. *"Yeah, you know how to do it. You ready for it?"*

"You know I am."

"I want to see and hear it all."

"Is that all you want?"

"No, but I can wait."

The audio rustled, and Maggie surmised the microphone had gone inside Carole's purse with whatever small camera they were using. Video quality would be terrible, and the audio wouldn't be much better, but they used such things in the department all the time. So long as the basics were distinguishable, it could be used in court.

She heard the murmur of voices and the sharp click of heels on marble. Maggie imagined Carole inside the Ambassador, moving through the lobby. The ping of an elevator. Light music, muffled by the purse.

Maggie realized she was holding her breath. She let it out. Mike was watching her. "You know, you don't have to listen to this, either. I can do it all on my own."

"Keep going," Maggie said. She had to make herself inhale and exhale. Her heart beat too quickly.

No footsteps anymore. Carole would be on carpet. A rapping on wood. A man's voice. Karl's voice. Maggie felt her insides fall through the floor of the car. She gripped the armrest as Karl spoke to Carole in familiar terms, then in rawer language. The volume rose and fell as they moved around the room relative to the purse-bound microphone.

Maggie listened to them together, and then Carole said, *"Is that all you want?"*

"No," Karl said.

Carole laughed the kind of laugh Maggie had never heard from her. The private laugh of people who knew each other intimately. Maggie remembered laughing like that once a long time ago, when she and Karl saw each other in secret, boss and subordinate, in motels and hotels and in apartments where they didn't dare turn on the lights.

They began again. Maggie grabbed for the door handle with her eyes burning and fled the car with Mike calling after her.

CHAPTER 27

THE DAYS OF STICKING a wire to an informant with tape were long gone. A few hours after she and Mike had listened to the recording, Maggie was donning a slightly padded bra with pockets specifically to hold the recording device and microphone in place. With a loose-fitting blouse on, the difference wouldn't be noticeable. She put the bra on in the bathroom then went out to Mike in the bedroom to place the device.

"You sure you don't want backup for this?" Mike asked her.

"I'm sure. If he's the one, then we have to be the people who bring him in. This is family."

Mike closed a Velcro flap. "Except I'm not family."

Maggie squeezed Mike's arm. "You're the only one we can trust," she said.

They looked at each other for a beat. Mike's eyes were dark. A flicker of emotion showed there, but he kept it down deep where it could barely be seen. Maggie hoped she looked the same, but she knew her face was a mass of tics and feelings. When Karl came, she would have to pull it together.

"Done."

Maggie buttoned up her blouse. The recording device felt like a brick pressed against her ribs under her breasts. The microphone was imperceptible. "Okay," she said. "Let's test it out."

Mike put an earpiece in. The wire trailed to a digital receiver and recorder only a little larger than a pack of cards. When Maggie started on the force, such a thing would have been ten times as large, or maybe more, and would use cassette tape. Soon perhaps there'd be no need for a device at all, with words plucked from the air and whisked off to a secure server somewhere on the internet.

"Test, test," Maggie said. "Test."

"It's good. I'm gonna set up two houses down. The one that's for sale? Nobody in there, nobody to notice me in the driveway. When you say, 'I think I need a drink,' I'll come running. I have the key in my pocket. Okay?"

Maggie nodded. "Okay."

"You can do this, Chief."

Her face felt hot. She touched her forehead. She was perspiring, but only a little. "I know I can."

"It's almost time. I'm gonna move."

She waited until Mike left and then she sat on the end of the bed. She hugged herself to stop the trembling she felt in her limbs. It took some time, but bit by bit she stilled and the anxiety shrank. She kept it wrapped up inside her core, crushed tightly, and then tighter still. The sweat dried on her skin. Her mouth still felt papery, but that was all.

When she was ready, she went to the closet. She found the lockbox and opened it with a small key. The Detective Special her father gave her was inside, the trigger locked for double safety. Maggie took the gun and returned the box to the top shelf. At the bedside table she unfastened the trigger lock, put it away, and retrieved a speed-loader from her pocket. Six .38 caliber rounds, their casings a brilliant, untouched gold shade. Unsullied brass.

She snapped the cylinder back into place. With the tail of her blouse untucked as it was, she was able to pin the gun against her flesh at the back of her pants. It felt startlingly cold. Her spine crawled, and then the sensation faded.

Finally, there was the sound of Karl's engine. Maggie tensed at once. Conscious will forced looseness back into her arms and legs. She rolled her head and shrugged off the tightness in her shoulders. "It's on," she said to the empty room. Mike couldn't reply, but she knew he heard her.

Karl's key in the door, and then his voice. "Maggie?"

Maggie stepped into place at the foot of the bed. "Up here," she called back.

Footfalls on the stairs. Karl appeared in the hallway. He looked toward the twins' room, where the lights were out. "You said there was something wrong. Where are the girls?"

"My mother took them out," Maggie said, and then she cleared her throat. "They'll come back when I call them."

Confusion crossed his face. He approached her slowly. "Why would you send them out? What's going on here?"

Maggie kept her arms loose at her sides. The gun at her back was a solid reminder. "We have something to talk about. It's important."

He stood at the bedroom door. "What do you want to talk about? What the hell is happening?"

"Carole," Maggie said with too much force. "It's Carole."

Karl blinked at her. His expression didn't change, but now Maggie knew it was because he had closed himself up the same way she had. It wasn't real calm, but outward calm. When he spoke again, it was in a softer tone. "I'm not sure what you mean. What about Carole?"

"Were you seeing her?"

She caught the faintest register of something like surprise, but it was gone before it had a chance to take shape. "Who have you been talking to?"

"Carole's husband, Philip, kept a ledger with the names of the people she slept with. He wrote down everything they did. He got video and audio, too. He was watching all the time. He knew about you, Karl. He knew it all."

Karl straightened up, but didn't come closer. "Where is it? All this proof."

"I found where you hid it, Karl. I've seen and I've heard it."

He turned on his heel and dashed toward the girls' room. Maggie went after him as he disappeared through their door. She heard the closet flung open and the soft avalanche of blankets and linen falling to the floor. He reappeared, and the artificial calm in his face was utterly gone. He stepped toward her, and reflexively Maggie stepped back to keep distance between them. "What did you do with it, Maggie?"

"It's safe."

"Safe? Who has it? Where's the video? Where's the *evidence*?"

She heard something else in his voice now, something she didn't hear in the tone of a guilty man. Her response was slow. "I've been talking to Mike," she replied.

"Mike? Mike!? I knew it. Oh, my God, Maggie, what did you do? Why didn't you come to me? Why couldn't you *tell* me?"

He came at her. She backed off fast.

"I need a drink!" Maggie shouted. "I need a drink!"

CHAPTER 28

KARL BACKED HER INTO the bedroom. "You're wearing a wire," he said. "Jesus Christ, Maggie, don't you understand what's happening?"

She put the corner of the bed between them. She didn't reach for the Detective Special yet. "You were having an affair with her. You were *paying* her, Karl, and you were taking money from Bryant Gibbs."

"No! I mean, yes, I was seeing her. I needed an outlet, something that was just sex. It wasn't complicated. But I never took money. Not once. But I knew someone was. Gibbs talked to his wife. His wife talked to Carole. They had their ideas and I looked into it. I need to know, Maggie: did you give it all to Mike?"

"He's the only one I could trust to keep it quiet."

"That's because *he's the one!*"

Maggie froze. She remembered Gibbs whispering in her ear. At that moment it had been Karl in front, but he wasn't alone. There was a uniformed cop with him. And Mike. *He's the one*.

271

Karl moved closer. Maggie kept a gap between them, but she was running out of bedroom. "If you looked in the ledger, then you know Carole had a regular. The initials *MC*. I know you saw it. *MC*. Do you remember?"

"I remember."

She didn't know where Mike was. This was taking too long.

"I'm *KD*. You know that. I'm not denying it. But *MC?* Mike Cooper. Mike Cooper! They thought it was a cop putting pressure on them. They'd seen it before, but they didn't know who. First they thought it was me, but I told them I'd help if they kept things quiet for me. Mike was a regular, Maggie. He was with Carole before I ever was. Philip was right in the room with them! They would have known his face. They'd let him into their house if he called for a date. That's how he got in and out without a problem."

Maggie faltered. Karl's closed face had fallen apart. She saw all of him now. "How did you get her blood on you?"

"I slipped. I told you I slipped."

"But it's bullshit, Karl!" Maggie exclaimed. "No more bullshit!"

"She was still alive when I got there! I went into the bathroom and I *slipped*. I got my hands dirty trying to stop the bleeding, and when she died I put her back the way I found her. It was too late to get the blood off me."

"You are lying," Maggie said. Her voice shook, and she couldn't stop it. "You're a liar, Karl!"

"I'm telling you the truth! I knew there were recordings. I needed to get them before they disappeared. But you gave them to Mike, Maggie. He's probably destroyed everything with him on it already. We have no way to show he's connected to them. All the witnesses are dead. He's gonna get away with it. Don't you see? He's gonna put it on me. He's *already* put it on me. You helped him."

"She's the chief. She knows how to put a case together."

Mike was at the door of the bedroom. His weapon was out, ugly and black in his hand. Karl turned, reaching for his gun at the same time. Mike shot him once and Karl fell. His Glock tumbled away.

Maggie rushed forward, but Mike turned his weapon on her. "Stay right where you are, Chief. Don't make this difficult."

Karl made a sound. He breathed, but roughly. Maggie felt her heart clenching in her chest. "Mike, he's down. It's over. All I want to do is make sure he doesn't die."

"Then we have a problem, because I kind of need him to die to close all this out."

He said it flatly, and in that moment Maggie understood it all. "You are the one," she said.

Mike shrugged. "I guess it doesn't matter now."

He walked over to retrieve Karl's Glock, and when Maggie moved toward the door, he regripped the gun he was aiming at her, as if to say, "Don't try it." But now he had his back to Karl.

Karl was still moving. He was reaching toward his toes, and it broke Maggie's heart to see him moving with such slowness, in such agony. Maggie couldn't breathe, watching him. Mike didn't turn around. "Whatever you're thinking, it's not going to work," Maggie told Mike. "How are you going to explain it?"

He didn't take his weapon off her. "It won't be hard. I've got the book, I've got the recordings. You confronted him. He shot you. I shot him. It all goes in the report, and I walk away."

The carpeting beneath Karl was soaked with crimson. Maggie tried not to look at him. She wanted Mike's eyes on her. "Don't do it, Mike. I'll back you."

"Why would you do that, Chief?"

"I have kids. I have the girls. I don't want them to go without a mother or a father. They won't even remember Karl. He's gone all the time. But they need me, Mike. They need their mother. Don't make them grow up without me."

Karl finally managed to reach his ankle. Maggie braced herself. She raised one hand high, and the other only halfway.

"Let me raise my girls," Maggie said.

She saw hesitation in Mike's face for the first time. The muzzle of his weapon dropped two inches. "Chief—" he started.

Karl shot him in the back with the .32 automatic he kept in his ankle holster. Mike cried out, reeling.

Maggie drew in the same moment. The Detective Special came up smoothly. She closed one hand over the other. She sighted without conscious thought and unloaded the weapon into Mike's chest at a distance of six feet.

CHAPTER 29

MAGGIE STOOD LOOKING OUT the window of the front room at the white truck parked on the curb. It was heavily laden with wooden L-frames, and as she watched, the driver finished using a post-hole digger to make a place for the one he'd put in front of her house. The whole process was quicker than she expected, only ten minutes from start to finish, and at the end he hung a metal sign from the frame showing the name and face and number of a Realtor. He wiped his dirty hands on his jeans, got into his truck, and left.

"Is it done?"

She turned away from the window. Karl sat on the floor with Becky balanced on one leg while Lana chased a ball around the carpeting near at hand. He had a cane to help him walk, and she still had to assist him when he got up or sat down, but the doctor said it wouldn't be long before he would be able to do everything himself. He peered up at her now with the sun casting down from the window onto his face, and the room looked warm and golden and perfect. It was moments like this one that brought them to the Parish in the first place, but they had no real hold anymore.

"Hello? Earth to Maggie."

"Yes, it's done."

"Good. They say we're asking a good price and it'll move quickly. We won't be here much longer."

Maggie nodded absently before sitting down on the carpet opposite him. "Are you going to like the west coast?" she asked.

"I guess I'll find out. That's not really what's important anymore."

She didn't disagree. She looked at him and he at her, and after a moment Karl put out his hand for Maggie to take. They held on tightly for a long time, saying nothing, until Becky squalled, demanding to be allowed down. Karl laughed softly and did what she wanted.

Maggie's mother appeared in the doorway to the hall. She had on an apron and looked so much like a housekeeper Maggie felt suddenly guilty about what she demanded of her. "Lunch is almost ready," Susan said. "I hope you two are hungry, because the recipe's supposed to serve six."

"I could eat," Karl said.

Susan regarded them without saying anything. She looked about to speak, but she didn't, turning away and disappearing again.

"She wants to follow us out there," Maggie said.

"Is that what you want?"

"I don't know. Maybe. It'll be good to have someone to be close to."

She saw the hurt in his face, but he didn't put it into words. Their counselor said everything would take time, maybe more time than either of them expected or realized. If they were willing to put in the work. Karl said he was. Maggie agreed. The end seemed like a long way away.

Karl changed the subject. "I heard from Chief Collins today."

"I thought he wasn't speaking to you anymore."

"Me, neither, but I guess he wanted me to hear it direct from him. The DA's officially closed the case. They found no wrongdoing on your part, like I told you. I'm the one they hung out to dry. I was hoping he was going to tell me I could still get my pension, but that's not gonna happen. But there's plenty for ex-cops to do out west. I could be a security guard at the mall."

He smiled as if it didn't bother him, but Maggie knew it did. She couldn't smile back, even though she knew it would make him feel better. Everything in time. Everything in time.

"I'm going to see if Mom needs any help," Maggie said.

"Okay. We'll be here."

She left him in the front room and went to where her mother was washing out the kitchen sink, her hands clad in rubber gloves. Susan turned to her when Maggie stood beside her. Her mother didn't smile, either, and Maggie was glad of that. "You know it'll get better," Susan said. She took off a glove and squeezed Maggie's arm. "It always gets better."

"I can't forget what he did," Maggie said without looking at her mother. "I know I'm supposed to keep trying, but I can't forget."

"No one says you have to. The important thing to remember is in the end he loves you. He loves those girls. And he may have tried to save his own skin, but he also wanted to protect you."

Maggie looked her mother in the eyes for the first time. "I don't need to be protected. I want to be trusted."

Her mother made an expression that might have seemed like a smile but didn't quite get there. "He knows that now. And the fact that he's still here and you're willing to have him...that's going to make all the difference."

"So where do we go from here?" Maggie asked.

"Wherever feels right. But you're making a good decision to leave this place. It's no good for you. It never was. You're not a homebody. It's not the kind of thing that fits you."

"What does?"

"Being a cop."

Maggie let her gaze slide toward the window over the sink. "So that's all I was ever good at?"

"Of course not. You're a mother, too. And a troubled man's wife. You're going to see him through. It's only that people don't see that the way they see a uniform. The decorations you get, you don't wear for everyone to see."

Maggie had no reply for that. She continued to look out the window at the serene and sun-splashed neighborhood. It had all seemed so ideal once, but now she saw the falsity of it, from the brick façades to the people who called it home. No one was quite right. No one was wholly honest. In the end it was like everywhere else, every dark place she'd ever gone, but the darkness had never gotten inside before. Not into her own home. And she wasn't going to let it happen again.

"Are you going to be okay?" her mother asked.

"I think so," Maggie said.

"Try again. Be a mother. Be a wife. But don't forget who you are when somebody steps out of line."

"I could get into trouble again."

"Then get into trouble. And if they say you can only be a housewife, you tell them—"

"I was a cop first," Maggie cut in.

"You were, and nothing's ever going to change."

They hugged. Maggie felt a wet glove on her shoulder. "I *am* a cop," Maggie agreed.

And that was all right.

ABSOLUTE ZERO

JAMES PATTERSON
WITH ED CHATTERTON

CHAPTER 1

THURSTON'S BEEN DOWN TOO long. Thanks to the hypersensitive security sonar in place, the use of standard-issue dive gear has been ruled out for this mission. Thurston's operating on lung power alone.

Lieutenant Hardacre, the whites of his eyes flashing against the night camo makeup, glances at Green at the tiller of the rigid-hulled inflatable boat. Green shakes his head and checks his watch.

"Seven minutes twenty. Not looking good, sir."

Hardacre glances across the water at the black mass of the target vessel. They're less than forty meters from the Karachi Naval Yard perimeter. Their target—Thurston's target—is the *Khan,* a Pakistan Navy Tariq-class frigate whose captain has distinct al-Qaeda leanings. US Intelligence suggests in no uncertain terms the rogue officer is contemplating a major attack on US assets in the Gulf. Exactly what those assets might be, nobody is too sure. But with the frigate packing as much firepower as it does, no one back at Command is taking any chances. In normal circumstances, a black ops team might make the captain disappear, or a drone could disable his ship from the comfort of a bunker in Washington.

But these are not normal circumstances.

Because the captain of the *Khan* is the nephew of an extremely high-ranking and well-connected family. For reasons far too complicated for all but the mandarins at Langley to comprehend, this must look like an internal attack: there can be no traceable links back to the US. Hence the use of an Australian team as the pointy end of a dirty spear. None of Hardacre's team are wearing uniforms. This mission is as off the books as it is possible to be. Get caught here and there'll be no trial, no covert handover at a checkpoint in the Sinai. It'll be a long dusty trip to some Pakistan Intelligence torture camp and the distinct possibility of starting World War III. All three men wear cyanide capsules on a chain around their necks and none would hesitate to use them. They've seen the results of concerted torture before.

"Jesus Christ, Thurston," mutters Hardacre.

Green looks up at his boss. "Eight minutes ten."

"He's dead. We've got to cut and r—"

"There!" Green points at a spot of black water some twenty meters away. Hardacre can't see a thing but Green is part owl when it comes to night vision.

They paddle the RHIB toward a flurry of rising silver bubbles and arrive as Thurston's head breaks the surface. He throws open his mouth and sucks down a lungful of air. Hardacre leans over and pulls Thurston aboard.

"All good?" says Hardacre.

Thurston, unable to speak, raises a thumb.

"Go," says Hardacre.

Silently, Green paddles the RHIB out of the dock, past the Pakistan Naval Academy and out into the main channel. Only when the boat is out of earshot does Green start the muffled engine and head slowly and quietly down toward the Marho Kotri Wildlife Sanctuary where they have established a camp. After a switch into civilian clothes they'll sink the RHIB in the mangroves and slip into Karachi in a day or two to resume their cover work as liaison officers at the Australian embassy.

They've just turned the first corner when the blast comes.

"Nice work, Thurston," says Lieutenant Hardacre.

Thurston nods. "Thanks, sir."

"Nine minutes," says Green. "You were down nine fucking minutes, mate!"

"Seemed longer," says Thurston, as the sky erupts behind them.

CHAPTER 2

THEORETICALLY, A TEMPERATURE OF absolute zero is a physical impossibility. But rounding the corner of Hackney Road and copping the whip of the sleet-streaked wind directly into his face, Cody Thurston is pretty sure he's found it.

Jesus, London in January. It never gets any easier.

Not for a boy brought up in Byron Bay anyway.

Thurston tucks his chin deeper into the cowl of his North Face and conjures up memories of a seemingly endless parade of sun-kissed January days on the far north coast of New South Wales.

He checks his watch. Eight o'clock on a dog of a night in Hackney, five in the morning Down Under. The first surfers will already be in the water at the Pass or down at Tallows. Thurston allows himself a brief moment of wishful thinking before shouldering his gym bag and picking up the pace.

Screw that nostalgia shit. The teenage Cody Thurston who surfed like there was nothing else worth living for is long gone. *This* Cody Thurston is right here, right now. And all he's got to look forward to is another shift at The V and the usual sh—

"Mother*fucker!*"

Thurston feels a sharp pain in the back of his kidneys and looks down to see a young guy in a wheelchair cocking his fist for another punch. Thurston swivels out of the way and gives the guy a slap across the back of the head. Not too hard, but enough to let him know Thurston's there.

"Hittin' a cripple, hey? Nice fuckin' work, man! You smack every disabled person you see?"

Thurston shakes his head. "Only you, Lenin. Only you."

Lenin smiles, brushes some sleet off his dreads, and swings his chair next to Thurston. "You goin' to The V?"

"Same as every night. How about you?"

"Same as every night, man."

Lenin puts on a spurt. "Race you!"

Thurston watches him go. "Fuck you. You *hurt* me."

"Loser!" shouts Lenin, as he turns into the warm yellow light spilling out of the door to The V. The crumbling Victorian bar halfway down Hackney Road has been Thurston's workplace for almost two years. He lives in a cramped two-room attic shoved up under the leaky roof.

It's home.

CHAPTER 3

"YOU'RE LATE, DICKHEAD. THINK I'm made of fuckin' money, Buster?"

Barb cackles, making a sound like a parrot gargling nails.

The owner of The V is in her regular spot, perched precariously on a stool in the corner of the bar on the customer side. Barb Connors must be eighty-five if she's a day but there's still something of the King's Cross hooker about her, and it's not just her filthy mouth. She wears a yellow wig that looks like it would survive a nuclear attack and makeup half an inch thick. Her choice of lipstick, as always, is crimson.

Thurston acknowledges his boss but doesn't say anything. As long as she keeps calling him "Buster" he's going to keep right on saying zip. Barb had watched a documentary about silent movies last year and has been trying to make the Buster Keaton thing stick with Thurston ever since. He's having none of it—as much to annoy Barb as to any objection he has to being called Buster. Ignoring the military-grade laser death stare coming at him from Barb's direction, Thurston flips up the bar lid and hangs his sopping jacket behind the door to the cellar.

"Hey, Janie," says Thurston to a thin blond punkette with tattooed cleavage who is placing fresh bottles in a cooler cabinet. Thurston makes a point of staring directly at Janie's chest.

"Evening, girls," he says and waggles his fingers.

Janie Jones reaches down and casually grabs Thurston's nuts.

"Evening, boys," she replies and squeezes. Hard.

"Jesus!" gasps Thurston.

Janie releases her grip with a sweet smile, flips Thurston the middle finger, and continues her task. On the other side of the bar, Lenin laughs and bumps fists with Janie.

"Man's a Neanderthal, Janie."

Janie doesn't look up. "He's Australian. What do you expect?"

"I was being ironic," says Thurston.

"Well consider that nut squeeze my ironic reply, okay?" says Janie.

"Fair enough," says Thurston. "How's it been tonight?"

Janie stands and looks at Lenin, not quite ready to restore peace with Thurston. "Usual?"

Lenin is staring at Janie's chest so she snaps her fingers in front of his face twice. "Hey. Hey. Up here. There's nothing ironic about you, Lenin. Usual?"

"Uh-huh," says Lenin, his eyes remaining glued to Janie's breasts. While she pours, Janie turns to answer Thurston's question.

"It's been quiet," she says, shooting a glance at Barb. "Kind of." Barb looks at Janie and then back at Thurston. Something's up.

Thurston slides his plastic cash register ID into place and punches in the code. While Janie pours Lenin's drink she taps Thurston with an elbow and flicks her eyes toward a knot of men near the pool table.

There are four of them, all in suits, all in their thirties; beered-up, red-faced, peaking early. Thurston's seen the sort down here plenty of times before; businessmen coming to The V for a bit of authentic old London boozer flavor. Slumming it before the inevitable gentrification takes place. They're loud and look like they could easily be a bunch of dicks but Thurston can't see what the problem might be. Two local girls are with the group but they look happy enough to be there, if a little bored.

They also look about fourteen years old, but Barb has a liberal approach to the drinking age laws.

Thurston raises his eyebrows in a question to Janie. "Problem?"

Janie shrugs. "They haven't been here long. Couple of beers, nothing much. Out-of-towners. Tourists. Probably nothin'."

"They don't look like fuckin' tourists," says Lenin. "I don't like 'em."

Thurston agrees. Now he's had a chance to study them a little longer the group don't look like tourists.

They look like trouble.

One of them, a guy with cropped hair and a thick black goatee, sees Thurston looking their way. Black Goatee holds Thurston's gaze for a few seconds, smiling without warmth. Thurston looks away. There's never any point getting into a pissing contest with a drunk.

"There's another one," says Janie. "You'll see. He's in the bog."

Two more customers come to the bar and Thurston serves them. Sofi Girsdóttir, The V's chef for tonight's shift, comes up shivering from the cellar carrying a can of cooking oil. She mutters something sweary in Icelandic and pats Thurston on the shoulder before heading back into the kitchen.

Which is when Thurston sees the monster.

CHAPTER 4

THE GUY WHO COMES out of the bathroom, dipping his head under the door frame, is huge.

A giant.

Thurston hesitates for a fraction of a second and then resumes pouring drinks.

"Unbelievable, hey?" says Lenin. "Incredible 'ulk, innit?"

Thurston shakes his head a fraction and glances again at the big man as he joins the rest of the crew at the pool table. Thurston sees Black Goatee point to the giant's upper lip. The guy wipes something off with a hand the size of Nova Scotia. Black Goatee laughs and says something to another guy in the group.

Janie's right; these fuckers are trouble.

As another evening wears on, The V fills, the noise level rising steadily as the alcohol takes hold. Thurston likes it fine that way. The more noise the better, the busier the better.

Less time to think.

An hour in, Black Goatee rocks up to the bar with another guy. The group has been ordering drinks from Janie so far, so it's the first time Thurston's had any reason to hear them speak.

"Five beers, three double Jack and Cokes, *mate*." Black Goatee speaks in an American accent and says the word "mate" in what he imagines is a London accent. He stares at Lenin coldly.

The American voice surprises Thurston.

Black Goatee's skinhead sidekick mutters something under his breath. Thurston can't make it out but hears a Russian accent. They are talking about him— that's clear—but Thurston lets it go. It happens every night.

Thurston completes the order in full Buster Keaton mode. When he asks for the money Black Goatee looks up.

"What's your accent, champ? Scottish?" He hands over a fifty.

Thurston notices a faded tattoo creeping out of the end of his sleeve: an eagle of some kind with German-looking text underneath.

"Aye," says Thurston, handing over the change but saying nothing else. Black Goatee frowns, aware he's being punked but unsure exactly how.

"Yeah? Don't sound real Scottish now I hear it again."

Thurston shrugs. "Born and bred." He turns to another customer. In his peripheral vision he sees Black Goatee getting wound up.

Before anything else happens, Sofi pushes open the door to the kitchen.

"Cody," she says, "have you—"

As she sees the American on the other side of the bar, Sofi stops dead, the color draining from her face.

"Hey, lollipop," says the American. He's smiling.

Sofi Girsdóttir turns without speaking and stumbles her way back into the kitchen.

"Sofi?" says Thurston.

"We got to catch up soon, honeybun," says Black Goatee to the closed kitchen door. He mimes putting a phone to his ear. "Call me, y'hear?" He and the Russian crack up.

"Do we have a problem here?" says Thurston. There's an edge to his voice that wasn't there before. The exchange worries him. Thurston knows Sofi well enough: she's feisty, independent, and not the sort to scare easy.

"No," says Black Goatee. "No problem, chief. Just one old friend catching up with another in jolly old England." The guy stares at Thurston for a few seconds before letting the Russian drag him back toward the pool table. Thurston has to fight the urge to leap across the bar and wipe the smug smile from Black Goatee's face.

"Forget it," says Janie quietly, appearing at Thurston's shoulder. "But keep an eye on them. They give me the creeps. I'll go and check on Sofi."

Thurston walks down the bar and takes an order from another customer.

Tonight's going to be a long one.

CHAPTER 5

JANIE HAD BEEN RIGHT predicting trouble, but when it comes, it isn't from the direction Thurston had been expecting.

Three guys in rugby shirts, who'd been drinking heavily all night, get into a political debate with, of all people, Lenin. Things escalate when an enraged Lenin punches one of them in the nuts. The men laugh, but the guy who was hit tips Lenin out of his chair.

Thurston is around the bar before Barb gives him the nod.

"Out," he says, his voice flat. It's a statement, not a question.

"Fuck off, Crocodile Dundee," says the guy who Lenin hit. His voice has the plummy English accent Thurston hates.

"Out now," he says.

"Or what?" says one of the others. "What, precisely, will you do, *cobber*? Throw another shrimp on the barbie?"

Thurston doesn't reply. Instead he steps forward, pulls a pen from his pocket, and jams it tight against the throat of the guy who'd tipped Lenin from his chair. With his mouth close to the guy's ear, Thurston whispers:

"Apologize. Or you get a second hole in your windpipe."

The plummy-voiced loudmouth is about to react when he looks at Thurston and sees something in the Australian that keeps him still.

"Get your hands off him, you fucking oik!" One of the others takes a step forward. Thurston stops him with a quick shake of the head.

"The night's over, gents," says Thurston. He drops his hand to his side but knows he'll have no more trouble. "Go on, out you go. Nice and quiet."

"Yeah, fuck off," hisses Lenin, back in his chair. He singles one out of the group and points a finger. "Come the Revolution, bro, you're going down. Believe it."

Thurston closes the door of The V behind the troublemakers and returns to the bar.

"A pen?" says Barb, one thickly-drawn eyebrow raised to within an inch of her dyed hairline.

"Worked, didn't it?"

Thurston looks toward the pool table and, as he knew he would be, Black Goatee is looking in his direction.

CHAPTER 6

THE ALREADY FERAL ATMOSPHERE in The V curdles further as the night wears on. From what Thurston can see, a blizzard of coke is being snorted in the toilets. One sneeze and there'd be a whiteout.

"You want me to do something about this?"

Like everyone at The V, Thurston knows coke is a fact of London life. Mostly, so long as there's no obvious dealing taking place, the cops turn a blind eye to the occasional recreational toot. Tonight though, the group at the pool table are flat out taking liberties and Barb could find herself shut down so fast it would make her nose bleed. Which, from the look of some of the customers, is also a fate they'll be experiencing soon.

"You better tell them to go." Barb looks at Thurston. "You sure about this one, Buster? These guys don't look like they'll take a hint."

"I don't plan to be subtle," says Thurston. "There won't be any hinting."

Thurston wipes his hands on a cloth and moves toward the bar flap. He's about to go through when he stops, hearing a muffled noise in all the cacophony that, without knowing exactly why, sounds out of place. *Wrong.*

"What is it?" asks Barb.

"Where's Janie?" says Thurston, but doesn't wait for an answer.

Following some base-level instinct, connecting the dots as he runs—Janie taking a cigarette break, the giant glancing her way as she heads to the back of the pub, a couple of knowing looks between Black Goatee and the Russian—Thurston ducks past the toilets and pushes open a fire door to the alley.

Next to the Dumpster, Janie Jones is on her knees. The giant from the troublemakers inside is holding her hair bunched in his massive fist. His other hand is unzipping his fly.

"Private party," rumbles the giant. "Fuck off."

Janie, tears running down her face, moans. She moves her mouth but no words come.

"Shut up, bitch!" growls the giant.

Thurston retreats. "This isn't my scene, man," he says, holding up his hands. He turns to go. "Sorry, Janie."

"That's right, little man, run along and let the grown-ups play."

Thurston moves away and then, as the giant turns his attention back to Janie, picks up a length of wood leaning against the Dumpster, whirls around, and cracks it across the man's windpipe.

If a normal human had received the blow, it would have killed them. Instead, the giant buckles at the knees, his hands clutching his throat. Thurston takes two steps forward and, two-handed, cracks the wood over the man's skull. He falls to the floor, motionless.

Janie Jones gets to her feet and kicks the guy full in the face. His nose explodes. She leans over him and spits at him. "Mother*fucker!*" she howls and kicks him again.

"C'mon, Janie," says Thurston softly. "Let's call the police."

"No!" Janie jabs a finger in Thurston's chest. "No fucking police! Have you got that, Cody? No police!"

"Okay, Janie," says Thurston. "Whatever you want. No problem."

He guides Janie back to the door of The V. Sofi and Barb appear in the doorway, their shadows dancing across the body of the fallen giant.

"Jesus," says Barb. "Is he dead?"

"I fucking hope so," says Janie and pushes through into the bar.

"This is bad," says Sofi. She puts a hand on Thurston's arm. "What does Barb want you to do?"

"I'm getting those lowlifes out." Thurston looks at Sofi and raises his eyebrows in a question.

"What?" says Sofi.

"Are you going to tell me?"

"Tell you what?"

"What all that stuff was back inside with your beardy friend?"

Sofi's eyes flash. "He's no friend, Thurston." She turns back and starts walking toward the kitchen.

"So that's it?" says Thurston.

Sofi stops.

"Be careful," she says.

CHAPTER 7

THURSTON WALKS DIRECTLY ACROSS to the group of Americans and Russians, takes the drink out of the hand of Black Goatee, and jerks a thumb at the door.

"Get the fuck out. Right now. All of you."

The American starts to speak but Thurston talks across him.

"No. Nothing to say. Get out before I hurt you. If that overgrown bear you've been hanging around with is still alive, take him with you. He's in the alley considering his life choices."

Black Goatee looks steadily at Thurston. Behind him, the Russian is thoughtful.

"Come on, Nate," says the Russian. "We don't need this, right?"

Black Goatee waits a couple of beats. "Okay, *cobber,*" he says, smiling. "We'll go."

He waves a couple of his boys toward the alley. "Go get Axel." He turns back to Thurston.

"Listen, man. No hard feelings, okay? We're all

grown-ups here, right? You ever need a job, call me. Always on the lookout for someone who can add experience to the company." He holds out a hand. "Nate Miller."

Thurston looks at Miller's hand like it's been dipped in manure.

"I wouldn't touch your hand if you were pulling me out of the wreckage of a burning plane. Get the fuck out of here before I lose my temper properly and embarrass you in front of your dickwad buddies, *Nate*."

"Okay, chief," says Miller. "All I'm gonna say is you might have call to regret that decision someday." He pulls back his jacket to show the handle of an automatic tucked into his waistband.

"Good for you. SIG Sauer SPC 2022, nine nineteen," says Thurston. "I wondered what model it was. Must be kind of awkward walking around with one of those stuffed in your panties? Although I guess there's plenty of room down there. You ever use that thing or is it for decoration only?"

Miller nods like Thurston has confirmed something.

"Not bad," he says. "Not bad at all." He holds Thurston's gaze for a few seconds before brushing past followed by the rest of his crew. He is almost to the door when he spots Sofi huddled with Janie and Barb behind the bar.

"You and me got some unfinished business, Ice Queen. You dig?" Miller smiles and cocks his fingers into a gun. "Bang, bang."

CHAPTER 8

"YOU GONNA TELL ME NOW?"

Thurston and Sofi are the only ones left at The V. Barb's gone to bed and Janie's been put in a taxi back home. She'd continued to refuse any contact with the police. Thurston's locked up the darkened bar and is leaning against a steel table watching Sofi make her final cleanup in the kitchen.

"Tell you what?" Sofi doesn't look up from her task. Her arm sweeps back and forth furiously. Thurston waits patiently for her to slow down.

"C'mon, Sofi," says Thurston. "You know exactly what I mean. You've got history with the guy with the beard. Miller."

Sofi stands upright and breathes deeply. Her dark eyes glitter. She's been crying.

"Okay," she says. She puts down the cloth and runs the back of a hand across her brow. "I know him, yes. From Reykjavik. A long time ago."

Sofi takes off her chef's jacket and hangs it on a peg.

"And?" says Thurston.

"And what?" Sofi pulls up a stool at the table and opens her ledger. "It is late, Thurston, and I still have to do tomorrow's orders for Barb."

"I'll quit bugging you if you give me some more information."

"This isn't a movie, Thurston. Miller is bad news. Okay? This I can tell you. Very bad news. And you being a big hero man didn't help anything, you know? Not a thing. In fact, if I'm honest, it makes things worse. We done? I can finish my work now?"

Thurston pushes himself upright from the table. "Okay, Sofi. I'm done. I don't know why I'm asking. We won't see Miller again."

Sofi shrugs. "Maybe."

Thurston stops in the doorway. "You good to lock up on your way out? How're you getting home?"

"I have my motorbike."

"Okay. Good night, Sofi. And, so you know, I wasn't being any kind of hero out there. I did what I had to, nothing else."

Thurston opens the kitchen door.

"Thurston?" says Sofi. He turns back and sees tears welling in the corners of her eyes.

"Yes?"

"Miller…"

"Miller what?"

Sofi Girsdóttir shakes her head. "Nothing. Forget it."

CHAPTER 9

THURSTON IS WOKEN BY a monster prowling outside his room.

He hears someone screaming and opens his eyes to see fingers of flame creeping around the edges of his door. Below, a malevolent red line throbs. His room is full of smoke from the ceiling down to about two feet from the floor. An ominous, restless roaring comes from the landing. The fire sucks up every available scrap of oxygen, gathering its strength for an all-out assault on his room at the apex of the house—the worst place possible in this situation.

Coughing out smoke, Thurston rolls out of bed, dropping to his elbows. The floor is hot to the touch.

A woman screams and Thurston hears the door to his room start to buckle. He has seconds, no more.

Another scream. A sound from Hell.

"Barb!" shouts Thurston and chokes on a lungful of smoke. Coughing, his eyes tearing up, he crawls to the bathroom and finds the bath taps. Thurston drags the

305

towels under the water and soaks them. He wraps one around his head and another around his upper body. When he turns back to his bedroom, flames are licking hungrily under the bottom of the door. The pressure from the inferno on the landing bends the flimsy wood. If he opens the door to get down to Barb, the backdraft will blow him straight through the opposite wall. And keeping the door closed won't be an option much longer.

Thurston can't hear any more screams from Barb but knows he has to try something. He makes his way to the window and punches out the glass, his hand wrapped in a T-shirt. Smoke is sucked upward, giving him momentary relief, but the ventilation creates a sudden rise in oxygen. The fire on the landing howls in fury and renews its assault on the door.

Thurston steps out onto his tiny balcony and looks down. Barb's room, one floor below, has an identical balcony some two yards to Thurston's left. Flames are already rolling upward and over Barb's window.

Thurston doesn't hesitate.

He makes the calculation and leaps down, landing square on Barb's balcony. The old concrete threatens to pull away from the brick wall but it holds. Just. The heat here is intense. Thurston puts his back to the wall, the bricks hot against his skin.

"Barb!" he shouts. *"Barb!"*

Nothing.

Thurston braces himself. He ducks as low as he can and tries to look inside.

It's like looking into a blast furnace.

Even with the wet towel wrapped around his face, Thurston's hair soon starts to smolder.

"Barb!" screams Thurston, but gets nothing back. He knows Barb Connors is dead already and that he won't be far behind if he doesn't get off this balcony. The concrete shifts below his feet and Thurston feels the whole structure start to give. The V is disintegrating around him.

Above him, the fire outside his bedroom finally breaks down the door, and a massive backdraft blows a spume of glass and wood and flame into the cold night air. The blast knocks Thurston off balance. He stumbles dangerously, inches from tumbling over the edge of the balcony.

Sixty feet below is nothing but hard pavement.

Thurston registers people running across the street. Someone screams and Thurston feels the skin on his fingers start to burn. In a second or two he won't be able to hold his grip. Things become simplified at these moments: do something right *now,* or die.

Adrenaline works differently in different people.

Cody Thurston has always found when his adrenaline spikes, events around him slow to a crawl. So long as that slowness is not accompanied by paralysis, it can be a useful trait. In the sliced seconds of time he has left on the balcony, Thurston scans his surroundings for an out.

There'll be something. There has to be.

And then he sees it. Not much but it's all he's got: a phone line bolted into the crumbling brickwork a yard or so down to his left. It's too far to reach with his free arm, but, by swinging across and down, using his own body weight as a pendulum, Thurston manages to hook his feet around the wire. He locks his ankles together, takes a deep breath, and lets go of the railing.

For a dizzying second he drops before the wire cuts into his ankles but he holds on. Now he's hanging upside down from the burning building. He swings upward and manages to grab onto the wire. He clings to it like a monkey on a vine.

A slab of masonry topples from above and almost swipes him out of the sky.

"Move!" shouts a voice from the street and Thurston hauls himself hand over hand toward the steel telephone pole across the street. He's about twenty feet from The V when he's almost jolted off as a second piece of debris falls from the roof and bounces onto the wire. Thurston redoubles his efforts and, with each passing second, gets closer to safety.

Less than ten feet from the telephone pole, the wire finally pulls free from the crumbling brick and Thurston is free falling. He smashes backward into the steel pole and the wire almost jerks loose from his hand. He falls another ten feet before he's pulled up with a violent jerk as the wire finds its length.

The wire snaps and now Thurston is falling. He twists in midair and lands heavily on the roof of a car parked below. The sheet metal crumples and every last ounce of Thurston's breath is knocked from his lungs.

But he's alive.

As the buzz of unconsciousness closes in, he hears a rumble. He looks across at The V in time to see the roof collapse in an explosion of dancing orange sparks and blackened timber.

And then there is darkness.

CHAPTER 10

LIGHTS. VOICES. THE CLANG of metal equipment and that unmistakable antiseptic tang in the air. A gurney rumbles down a corridor, wheels squeaking on the rubberized flooring.

Hospital.

Thurston opens his eyes to see a young cop sitting next to the bed, his head bent over a phone, mouth slightly open.

"Is she okay?" says Thurston. "Barb?"

The cop looks up, startled. "What?"

"Barb Connors. She was in the pub. Did she get out?"

The cop doesn't answer.

"She didn't, did she?" Thurston lets his head sink back and closes his eyes. An image of Barb trapped inside her room comes into his mind. She's screaming, her clothes on fire. Thurston opens his eyes again and now there's a doctor leaning over him with a syringe.

"Wait," says Thurston, but the needle is already in his arm.

"How long will he be out for?" says the cop.

The doctor shrugs. "Six, seven hours maybe," he says.

"Tell m—" says Thurston but can't complete the sentence. He feels like he's underwater with some great beast dragging him down into the depths. He fights to keep his eyes open but it's no use. Blackness creeps in at the edges of his vision and his last coherent thought as he sinks back into unconsciousness is to wonder why there's a cop in his room.

CHAPTER 11

THURSTON'S IN THE HOSPITAL for three days. He'd banged himself up pretty bad getting out of The V but it mostly looks worse than it is. He's got nine stitches in a head wound and five more in his right hand. There's been some low-level skin damage on one side of his face. No broken bones. He'll live. The concussion had been what concerned the doctors most. Despite the fall being broken by the car roof, Thurston had hit hard. Internal bleeding had been a distinct possibility but that had not shown up.

As soon as he's given the all-clear he dresses in the jeans, T-shirt, and sneakers given to him by the cops, and two of them sign him out and take him in handcuffs to a patrol car. No one has answered any of his questions about Barb Connors and he'd been allowed no visitors. The patrol car takes him directly to Paddington Green police station less than a mile from the hospital.

Inside the station, Thurston is shown into an interview room and left to wait. He takes a seat on one side of a plain wooden table. Now he's away from the hospital, anger about his treatment is growing. They can't think he had anything to do with the fire, so why all this heavy-handed stuff? Thurston wonders if it could be related to something in his military past—the fire at The V bringing him to the attention of some shadowy black ops outfit. Almost as soon as he's thought of it he dismisses that as fanciful. Thurston knows too that these kinds of mind games are part of any interrogation process. Whatever's happening, his conscience is clear.

Eventually the door opens and two plainclothes cops come in. One of them, a beefy-looking guy with thin, reddish hair, and what Thurston guesses will be a permanently flushed face, sits down and places a file on the table in front of him.

"I'm Detective Sergeant Hall," he says. "This is DS Morrison. We'll be conducting this interview."

Morrison is a tall, bland-looking man in his early thirties. He says nothing and takes a seat next to Hall.

"You ready to tell me what all this is about?" says Thurston. "I need to know if Barb Connors survived." He keeps his voice level, respectful. No sense in pissing these guys off if all they're doing is their job. Still, Thurston has to repress the urge to shout.

"Interview commences 12:00, Monday, eleventh of January," says Hall. He shows no sign of having heard Thurston speak. "DS Hall and DS Morrison present. Subject, Cody Michael Thurston, formerly of 21 Hackney Road, London."

Thurston looks at Morrison but, seeing nothing there, keeps his mouth shut. There's a play going on here and Thurston can wait.

"Why did you do it, Thurston?" says Hall. "She knock you back? You try and screw her and she wasn't having any of it?"

"Excuse me? What are we talking about? *Barb Connors?* She's eighty years old."

"He's not talking about Barbara Connors," says Morrison. "At least, not yet." He looks down at the file. "We want to know why you raped and killed Sofi Girsdóttir."

"What?" Thurston sits up straight.

Hall makes a show of sighing. He exchanges a weary look with Morrison.

"Is this how you're playing it, Thurston?"

"Playing what?"

Hall leans forward and props his elbows on the desk. "Sofi Girsdóttir, your co-worker and ex-girl-friend—"

"My what? Sofi's not my ex."

"We understand you had a prior sexual relationship with her that ended recently."

"We went out once or twice. It didn't work so we stopped. She's not what I'd call an ex."

Hall leans farther forward. "Was the fire an afterthought? Something to cover your tracks after you'd raped and killed Sofi?"

"Let me get this straight," says Thurston. "Sofi's dead?"

Without warning, Hall slaps Thurston across the cheek. Thurston bites back the instinct to ram Hall's face into the table. Thurston sees Morrison tense and thinks: *he's not entirely on board here.* It's useful information.

"Okay," says Thurston. "You can have that one, Hall." He wipes blood from his cheek. His head wound has reopened. "Let's do things your way."

"While you've been in hospital pretending to be hurt," says Hall, "we've been busy out here building a nice, shiny, completely airtight case against you. Want to hear how it goes? After the pub shut down for the evening, you tried it on with Sofi Girsdóttir. Maybe you weren't happy about her breaking up with you. Maybe you are the kind of man who can't control himself around women. Who the fuck knows? But you tried and when you were rejected you raped and strangled her. Later, to cover your tracks, you set the pub on fire and staged your own escape. Barbara Connors, an elderly lady, your boss, was left to burn alive."

Hall pauses for emphasis and holds up a hand. He counts off on his fingers as he talks. "We have a petrol can with your prints on it. We have multiple witnesses who saw you arguing with her on the night of the attack. We have sexually threatening e-mails from you on Girsdóttir's computer. We have you alive and her dead. So, let's keep things nice and simple, shall we? Tell us why and how and it'll go easier on you, Thurston. Not much, but easier."

Thurston says nothing.

"No request for a lawyer?" says Morrison.

"He's upset, DS Morrison. I think he might cry."

Thurston stares at a spot on the wall somewhere past Hall's shoulder trying to put together something coherent from the information he's receiving. Barb's dead. Well, he knew that already. He'd heard the screams. Sofi being dead is a shock. And the crap about him raping her is doubly shocking. Thurston thinks about the evidence Hall had recounted. He thinks about that quite a bit.

It's the reason why he's not going to ask for a lawyer, because the torrent of shit coming out of Hall's mouth means one thing and one thing only: this is a grade-A stitch-up. There's no point in Thurston protesting his innocence, no percentage gained in whining. If someone's putting this much effort into framing him then he has to come up with something better than asking for a lawyer. No, Thurston keeps quiet because he isn't planning on sticking around.

Still, there could be advantages to talking.

Putting your opponent's mind somewhere else, for example. Thurston wants something from Hall but needs him off balance to get it.

"How much are you getting, Hall?" says Thurston. "Enough?"

Hall frowns. "Come again?"

"For the frame," says Thurston. He switches his gaze to Morrison. "You know about this, too? Wait, no, I'm guessing not." Thurston smiles bleakly and holds Morrison's gaze. "Your partner's for sale, Morrison. A cheap whore. There must be a part of you, deep down, that knows the little fucker's dirty, right?"

Morrison glances at Hall and Thurston sees the barb has hit home. Morrison isn't in on this—whatever "this" might be—but has enough suspicion about Hall already to figure he could be bent.

"Ah," says Thurston, "you do."

"Very funny, Thurston," says Hall. He leans forward close enough for Thurston to smell the cigarette smoke on his breath. "You're going down, dickhead," he whispers. "For a long time. And you know what they do with rapists inside."

Thurston lunges at Hall, grabbing him by his lapels and pulling him across the table. He moves so quickly, he and Hall are on the floor of the interview room before Morrison can react.

Thurston and Hall grapple for a few seconds before Morrison hauls Thurston off his partner. Hall staggers to his feet and punches Thurston hard in the stomach. Thurston drops.

"Steve!" spits Morrison. "Enough."

Hall, breathing heavily, controls himself with difficulty. He brushes his thinning hair back into place and adjusts his tie. Thurston is curled on the floor in a fetal position.

"Interview terminated," says Hall. He knocks on the door and two uniforms step in.

"Overnight," says Hall, bending over Thurston. "And we'll get you a lawyer, Thurston. You're not getting off on some technical bullshit."

Thurston says nothing. Instead, he concentrates on slipping the mobile phone he'd taken from Hall's pocket into his sock. He'll need it later when he gets out of here and comes after every last motherfucker responsible for the killings of Sofi Girsdóttir and Barb Connors.

CHAPTER 12

ONCE HE'S DOWN IN the cells, Thurston's chances of escape will reduce drastically. At the very least, Hall's phone will be discovered.

No, if he's going to get out of here, there's only going to be one opportunity: on the short journey between the interview room and the lower cells while the two cops taking him there assume the action is over. Thurston slumps between the two uniforms, waits until they pass the fire exit door. The cops aren't expecting any trouble from the hobbling Thurston so when it comes he meets little resistance. They haven't even cuffed him.

Big mistake.

Without warning, Thurston drives the point of his elbow full into the gut of the cop to his left and pops the knee of the other with a simultaneous downward heel kick. With both men disabled, Thurston smashes the fire alarm glass and pushes open the exit door. The bare concrete stairwell is empty but won't be for long. Thurston walks slowly down, pretending to look at

Hall's mobile. Cops begin to stream into the stairwell, barely giving Thurston a second glance—lesson one in the dark arts he's been trained in. If you look as though you belong somewhere, no one questions it, not even cops.

This strategy does have a fault: it is strictly a short-term solution. The fire alarm Thurston triggered to cause confusion works well. But by the time he gets to the fire exit door at the foot of the stairs he can detect a shift in the information spreading through the cops milling around outside. News of his escape is in the air. He hears voices raised, fingers pointed his way.

Time to go.

Thurston moves to the curb and waits a few seconds for what he wants on Harrow Road. Behind him he sees five or six cops moving toward him.

C'mon, c'mon.

A courier on a big motorbike weaves slowly beside a stationary BMW. Thurston steps out into the road and, in a swift movement, drags the courier backward off his bike.

"Stop!" yells a voice.

Thurston jumps onto the bike and guns it through the crowd of cops on the pavement. Without hesitation he roars straight down the steps of the Joe Strummer Subway, ducks under the Westway, and comes up the other side heading south on Edgware Road. By the time the first pursuit vehicle has been alerted, Thurston is at the northern edge of Hyde Park. He turns in through the gates and dumps the bike in a clump of trees. At a park café he swipes a blue zip-up wind-breaker and a baseball cap from the coatrack near the door.

Brim down, collar up, Thurston walks east toward the West End.

Six minutes after exiting Paddington Green, he's in the wind.

CHAPTER 13

OLD HABITS DIE HARD.

Thank Christ.

From Hyde Park, Thurston makes his way on foot to the rear of a gym at the side of St. Pancras station. He counts nine bricks up and nine along from the western corner, puts a finger in a crack in the mortar, and levers out a small plastic bag. Inside is the key to a locker stationed next to the Eurostar terminal.

Even though he's been out of the game for a decade, Thurston's kept a go-bag in the locker for the past two years. The bag contains a passport in the name of Michael Flanagan, a smartphone and charger, two thousand in cash, and a clean credit card, also under the name of Flanagan. The account the credit card charges back to has better than two hundred grand sitting there: the payoff for some security work Thurston did in Mozambique after leaving the forces. He hadn't done anything illegal but the payment and the client had left a bad taste in his mouth. He'd stowed the cash in the Flanagan account and told himself he'd only touch it on a rainy day.

Right now it's pouring down.

Thurston takes the bag from the locker and walks south from St. Pancras, stopping on Tottenham Court Road to buy a laptop and a holdall bag. He fills the holdall with clothes bought at the first department store he finds. He also buys a navy business suit, a pair of black brogues, and tops the purchases with a heavy overcoat and scarf, dumping the clothes he'd been wearing in the store dressing room. At a walk-in hair salon in Soho he gets his collar-length blond hair dyed black and cut short. The stubble he usually wears is shaved clean. At a large chain pharmacy he buys a pair of glasses with plain lenses. By four p.m., the Cody Thurston who escaped from Paddington Green earlier is almost unrecognizable.

Thurston takes a train to Heathrow and books into a chain hotel in sight of the runway. Airport hotels are the perfect place to hide. Too many people coming and going for anyone to get suspicious. In his room, Thurston charges his phone and laptop, orders some food from room service, and settles back on the bed to examine DS Hall's phone. One message in particular gets Thurston's attention, as does Hall's calendar. He opens his new laptop and spends three hours researching the information on Hall's phone. Around ten he turns off the lights and tries to sleep.

The next few days are going to be busy.

CHAPTER 14

FRIDAY MORNING. THE END of a nightmare week.

Four days after Thurston's escape and Steve Hall has got precisely nowhere in tracing the Australian. Hall's superior officer, Detective Chief Inspector Venn, flays him alive and tells him in no uncertain terms to get a result, or else get ready for a long stint down in Records.

"This is a departmental embarrassment, Hall. A man under your watch—a killer, no less—waltzes out of Paddington Green in broad daylight. Have you any idea of the mountain of shit I'm having to wade through because of this? Get him found and make it quick or I'll bury your pathetic fucking career so deep you'll need an archaeologist to find traces."

It's enough to drive a man to drink. Or, in the case of DS Steve Hall, to 22 Logandale Lane.

From the outside, 22 Logandale Lane looks like any other semi-detached in a quiet street off Fulham Road. To those in the know, the house is one of West

London's wildest knocking shops, with specialties in rent boys, pain, and coke, all of which tick Hall's recreational boxes. And, since Hall's patch covers the area, he can come and go as he pleases, his admission costs taken care of by ensuring what goes on inside number 22 doesn't come to the attention of the police.

By eleven fifteen, Hall, wearing only a blindfold, a gag in his mouth, is tied facedown on a bed. Work, DCI fucking Venn, and the entire debacle of Thurston's escape is forgotten. Hall's treated himself to Raul and Ricky, two of his favorites, and between the three of them they've made serious inroads into a baggie of top-class blow. Life, temporarily, is sweet.

Thurston comes into the room carrying a short-handled metal baseball bat. He puts a finger to his lips and indicates to the two naked rent boys that they should remain where they are. Thurston takes out Hall's mobile and shoots a short video, making sure he includes both boys and Hall. When he's finished he jerks a thumb at the door. Neither boy hesitates. They recognize real trouble when they see it. Gathering their clothes from an armchair, they slip noiselessly into the corridor.

Thurston clicks the lock shut behind them, although, after the forthright conversation he's had downstairs with Mrs. Murgatroyd, the owner of number 22, he doubts anyone will be riding in to rescue DS Hall anytime soon. Somehow, Mrs. Murgatroyd has been left with the distinct impression that Thurston works for the O'Learys—a legendary South London outfit, the mere mention of whom causes even hardened criminals to reassess their priorities.

Thurston pulls off Hall's blindfold and the cop twists his head to one side. His eyes widen as he sees Thurston.

"Hi," says Thurston. "Remember me?"

Thurston shoots some more footage of Hall's panicked face and pans across to the cocaine paraphernalia on the bedside table. Replacing the mobile in his pocket, Thurston picks up the baseball bat and, without preamble, cracks it down hard across Hall's shoulder, breaking his collarbone. Hall's anguished cries are mostly muffled by the gag in his mouth. Thurston waits patiently for the man to regain some composure.

"Just a taster, Hall," says Thurston. "To get you focused. I'm going to ask you some questions and you're going to answer them."

Hall responds angrily, spittle foaming around the sides of the gag.

Thurston hits him again on the same spot and Hall sobs.

"Wrong response. You need to concentrate. My offer isn't all warm and fuzzy. There are no gray areas. You tell me what I want to know and you live. You don't tell me and I'll kill you right here. You can tell I mean this, right?"

"Yeah," grunts Hall. "Jesus!"

"Mrs. Murgatroyd has been persuaded to give us some time," says Thurston. "So, when I take the gag out of your mouth, keep quiet."

Thurston removes the gag and Hall whimpers.

"How did you find me?" Hall croaks.

"Your phone. And some research. It wasn't difficult. Now, concentrate on the matter in hand. Think of your kids, Hall. Little Timmy and baby Natalie. And your wife, Sarah. You don't want news of this filth getting out there, do you?"

Hall shakes his head.

"Who framed me?" says Thurston.

"They'll kill me if I tell you," says Hall.

"I'll kill you if you don't. Your choice. Was it Miller?"

"Who?" says Hall.

"Don't," warns Thurston and shows Hall the end of the baseball bat.

"Yeah, okay," says Hall. "It was Miller."

"Tell me why."

"The girl. She knew him back in Iceland. Knew what he does. She was a loose end."

"What does he do?"

"Miller and the Russians run a syndicate. Both sides use a joint Miller's got in Iceland as a...as a kind of staging post."

"For what?"

"Pseudoephedrine. Big quantities. Like, industrial. Pseudoephedrine is—"

"I know what it is. Why me?"

For the first time since Thurston came into the room, Hall shows something other than pain and panic on his face. He smiles, or tries to.

"You weren't supposed to survive. So when you did, Miller moved quick to make sure you were the perfect patsy. Foreigner. A drifter. Who gives a shit?"

"I do," says Thurston. He stands and replaces Hall's gag. Hall tenses.

Thurston produces Hall's mobile and shows it to the cop. He types a short message containing Hall's name and rank and the location of number 22 and puts in three numbers—Hall's boss, Hall's wife, and the news desk of a particularly vicious tabloid—attaches the video clips of Hall and presses Send.

"So long," says Thurston and, leaving Hall thrashing impotently on the bed, steps out of the room.

Next stop, Reykjavik.

CHAPTER 15

AS MICHAEL FLANAGAN, CODY Thurston has no problem getting into Iceland, although he is mildly surprised not to see any of Nate Miller's people on the plane or at Keflavík Airport.

Leaving Hall alive was a deliberate ploy. Thurston assumes the cop would inform Miller of the encounter. From the absence of a tail, either that hadn't happened or Miller's people were better at surveillance than Thurston gave them credit for.

On the whole, he is coming to the conclusion Hall might have kept quiet, at least as far as Nate Miller is concerned. Perhaps he'd overestimated Hall's ties to the American. It's disappointing: flushing out surveillance was the only thing stopping Thurston killing Hall. Now it looks like he'll have to track Miller the hard way.

At Keflavík Airport, Thurston picks up a specialist, winter-equipped Land Cruiser he'd rented online the night before using the Flanagan credit card. If the drive into Reykjavik is anything to go by he's going to need it. The exposed highway heading west into the city runs along a peninsula bounded by the Atlantic on both sides. Today is darker and colder than a bailiff's heart and blowing a gale.

Or, in Icelandic terms, a stiff breeze.

Thurston battles the ice and wind into Reykjavik, stopping at a sporting goods store on the outskirts of the city to plug some holes in his gear. It's when he's coming out of the store off Reykjanesbraut Road that he picks up the tail: a black Mercedes four-wheel-drive parked outside a closed office block on the opposite side of the parking lot. A thin cough of white exhaust betrays the idling engine, the car angled so Thurston's vehicle is visible in the rearview mirror. It could be coincidence but Thurston assumes that's not the case.

Thurston is impressed Miller's guys have remained undetected for so long but it's a timely reminder for him to up his game. He gets into the Land Cruiser and pulls back onto the main road keeping the Merc in his peripheral vision.

In the city, Thurston puts the Land Cruiser into an underground parking lot and heads on foot to his accommodation, an apartment near the city center. He picks up the keys from a lockbox and lets himself into the block. It's a bland one-bedroom flat with a small kitchenette and all the charm of a dentist's waiting room, but Thurston doesn't plan to stay. This apartment is window dressing.

Locking the apartment behind him Thurston exits

through a side door leading to a back alley. Dropping to one knee, he levers a wooden board out from the side of a set of small steps leading from the door. He stows his backpack in the crawl space underneath and replaces the board. He walks into the alley and takes a wide circle through the quiet white streets until he comes back to the underground parking lot where he'd left the Land Cruiser. Five minutes later he's parked unobtrusively in a line of cars watching the black Merc.

CHAPTER 16

THEY MAKE THEIR MOVE around midnight.

Three big guys, bulky in winter coats and boots, step out of the Merc. Their rising breath is caught in the light from a streetlamp as they walk calmly toward the apartment block.

They're earlier than Thurston had figured but he guesses, in Iceland, the hour is late enough. It won't get much quieter if they left it until two or three and it won't get light until eleven. That's one thing about Iceland in winter: they got plenty of night to play with.

When the men reach the apartments, Thurston loses sight of them in the shadows. He sits back and waits for them to realize he's not inside.

Sure enough, less than sixty seconds after breaking in, the three men come back into the deserted street. They don't waste any time talking—the temperature outside must be somewhere around minus twelve. Thurston, sitting in the darkened Land Cruiser with the engine cold, is glad he'd stocked up at the sports store. Even so, it's difficult to resist turning the ignition. The men clamber back into the Merc and there's a pause as, Thurston guesses, they discuss what to do next. His hope is they'll call it a day and head back to wherever Nate Miller might be.

The Merc pulls out and takes a right. Thurston starts the engine and follows.

The Merc heads north out of Reykjavik before swinging right and taking an inland highway east. With the roads almost empty, and snow falling only lightly, Thurston's pursuit is relatively easy. Once out of the city he keeps his headlight use to a minimum, and stays as far back as he dares. He is confident he has not been tagged but there's no point in taking risks. They pass few cars, which makes the tail harder.

Despite the ice and snow the road is a good one. It's been recently cleared and the Land Cruiser feels secure on the surface. Thurston eats an energy bar and sips from a bottle of water as he drives. He has the feeling this will be a long night.

The road curves around the top of a big lake and then meanders across a wide white plain. The snow stops and the sky clears to reveal a low moon strong enough to pick out deep shadows in the surrounding fields. A kilometer or so ahead, Thurston watches the lights of the Merc. They've been driving for ninety minutes when he sees the headlights pull a sharp left. From the rise and fall of the beam Thurston guesses the road they're on now is unpaved. He pulls the darkened Land Cruiser cautiously closer and checks the GPS. As he suspects, the road is little more than a farm track. In the distance Thurston sees lights.

Thurston's not a gambler, but if he was, he'd bet heavy he's found Nate Miller.

CHAPTER 17

MILLER'S PLACE IS SMALLER than Thurston had envisaged: a cluster of low industrial sheds huddled around a central farmhouse about three hundred meters from the Hvítá River, about a kilometer upstream of the thundering Gullfoss Falls. When Thurston gets out of the Land Cruiser the rumble of millions of tons of water tearing through the canyons over to his right sends a low vibration through the ground under his feet. Iceland has that feeling: that the island itself is alive.

Thurston can see why Miller's chosen this place.

It's far enough from Reykjavik to be remote yet is on a good road that, thanks to the proximity of the popular Falls, is seldom closed. Miller can be at the airport inside two hours. The geography means the farmhouse can't be approached easily without being observed. Bigger picture: Iceland's geographical position and low-key policing make it an ideal staging post for bringing pseudoephedrine into Europe from the US and Russia. Lastly, and this is something right at the forefront of Thurston's mind, is the phenomenal amount of guns in the country. For all its low crime rates, Iceland has six times more weapons per head than Britain. Nate Miller is going to be armed to the teeth.

Thurston gets back into the Land Cruiser and drives slowly back toward the parking lot for the Falls. He puts the car hard up against a maintenance shed in a thicket of shadow. In the back of the car Thurston strips down and hurries into a nine-millimeter-thick drysuit made of neoprene rubber. Over this he dresses in the rest of the high-grade cold-weather gear he'd picked up in Reykjavik.

He locks the Land Cruiser and sets out for Nate Miller.

CHAPTER 18

SOFI'S VOICE COMES BACK to him as he moves across the moonlit snowfield toward the river.

Miller is bad news.

It reminds him to stay alert.

At the river he turns upstream, keeping as close to the surging water for as long as he can. Four hundred meters from the farm he spots a fold in the contours of the land that passes close to the farm and uses it to conceal his approach. Thurston hunches low, thankful the snow has, once more, begun to fall.

He checks his watch. Three a.m. He's been on the move since early morning but bats the fatigue away as a distraction he can't afford.

The fold takes Thurston to within fifty meters of the nearest structure. There are no fences around the property, which he reads as a sign of Miller's confidence.

Or, perhaps, his arrogance.

There's no craft now in getting closer so Thurston simply walks quietly across the snow, banking the late hour and remote location means most inside will be asleep.

He reaches the corner of the steel shed without incident and hears a noise coming from somewhere inside. The dull throb of music echoes from somewhere in the farmhouse. Thurston turns the corner of the shed and finds his way to the door. Inside are four rows of large, spotless, stainless steel silos. The air reeks of chemicals.

Thurston quickly inspects the other two sheds and finds the setup replicated in each. He's no expert but he assumes the silos contain part of the ingredients required for the production of pseudoephedrine. An outline of Miller's operation is forming. Import high quantities of the ingredients for pseudoephedrine from Russia to the east and the US to the west. Mix in Iceland and pour into Europe via the UK. The sheer quantities mean it is a product best concealed in plain sight. Guys like Miller, they always have a plausible cover story for their chemicals. The police would need to dig hard to prove criminality at this point in the chain.

It doesn't matter.

Thurston has no plans to bring in the police.

Closer to the main farmhouse the music is louder. Lights dance behind the curtains. A party is in progress. Thurston is about to try and find a better-placed window when a door opens and orange light spills out across the courtyard.

Thurston slips into a patch of deep shadow and watches as the giant he'd last seen unconscious in the alley behind The V emerges, buttoning his jacket as he moves. The guy heads for one of the vehicles parked under a sheltering roof. Thurston had done some research on his new laptop on the plane over here. This associate of Miller's is Axel "The Axe" Anders.

Thurston is tempted to finish this one now. He reaches for the knife strapped to his waist but hesitates.

Miller is the primary target here. If he fails to disable the big man immediately this could all be over before it's started.

The giant drives away and Thurston turns his attention back to the farmhouse. He walks closer to the window, his boots squeaking softly on the packed snow. Thurston finds a crack in the curtains and puts his eye to the glass.

The farmhouse, largely traditional on the outside, has been decorated inside like Vegas. On a low white sofa that curls around a copper-hooded central fireplace, a naked Nate Miller sprawls back while two girls busy themselves on his crotch. Here and there around the open-plan room are more men with more girls. Thurston estimates the girls to be about seventeen or eighteen, and that's if he's being optimistic. A glass table to one side of the sofa is scattered with cigarettes, drug paraphernalia, and two automatic handguns. A girl wearing only a white bra is unconscious underneath the table. To one side is a video camera on a tripod.

An image of a younger Sofi Girsdóttir in this room springs into Thurston's mind. He feels the cold black thing in his heart compress further until it becomes a diamond of undiluted hatred. For what he did to Barb and Sofi, Miller must be removed from the planet, it's that simple. Cops, courts, judges won't do it, so Thurston will.

But the guns on the table remind Thurston tonight is not the night. If this thing is going to go the way Thurston wants he will have to re-evaluate his strategy. It doesn't matter how clever he is, how adept, how cunning; all it takes is one of Miller's numbskulls to get lucky—to find a split second to aim and fire—and Thurston will find himself on the wrong end of a bullet.

It's of no consequence. Now Thurston has Miller's location and—in the form of the girls—renewed fervor for the job in hand. Thurston needs weapons. He retreats from the farmhouse and starts to retrace his steps back to the Land Cruiser.

CHAPTER 19

THE HVÍTÁ RIVER GLOWS blue-white under a scudding black sky.

Thurston takes particular care on this section: a treacherously narrow strip of rock no more than a meter wide bending around a curve in the river about four meters above the torrent. This close to the water the noise is incredible. But there's another sound, too; the deeper primordial bass growl of the Gullfoss Falls a hundred meters ahead roaring like some caged beast.

Gullfoss Falls lie at one of the widest points of the Hvítá. Above it, the canyons force millions of tons of water faster and faster along the rocks until it is vomited over and down a series of huge stone steps some fifty or sixty meters wide to rejoin the river below.

As seasoned as Thurston is, the thought of falling into the Hvítá makes him light-headed. He takes each slippery step carefully, making sure he moves slowly and deliberately.

He rounds a bend and finds himself on a slightly

wider part of the path that cuts into an overhanging ledge of rock.

Blocking his path is Axel "The Axe" Anders, Nate Miller's giant, the man who Thurston had knocked unconscious back in Hackney. Anders is smiling. In his left hand he holds a short-handled Uzi. From his right dangles a wicked-looking axe.

"Evening," shouts Thurston. "How's it going?"

The big guy doesn't reply but a second voice comes from behind Thurston.

"Keep talking, pussy. See how far it gets you with the Axe."

Thurston turns to see Nate Miller backed by three guys. They all have guns and all look extremely comfortable about using them. Thurston curses his arrogance in underestimating Miller. Until they'd appeared he had no idea he was being followed.

"The *Axe*?" says Thurston. "Jeez, how long was the brainstorming session you bunch of geniuses took to come up with that one?"

"Pretty quick," says Miller. "We don't like to waste time." He shakes his head. "Why'd you come out here unarmed? I thought you were better than that. I offered you a *job,* man. Christ Almighty. I'm disappointed."

"My mother often says the same," says Thurston, weighing up his chances of disarming the Axe. "You sound exactly like her. Although she's got a better beard than you."

"Okay," says Miller. He waves the barrel of his auto

toward Thurston. "Take this guy's fucking head off," he says to the Axe.

Thurston slips off his backpack and lets it fall to the ground as Anders approaches. He backs away until he feels his heels hanging over the edge of the trail. Thurston looks over his shoulder at the racing water. He unzips his jacket and lets it fall and Miller laughs.

Thurston's hand reaches around his back into the waistband of his waterproof pants. His fingers close around the handle of his knife. In a smooth movement, he flips the knife over and hurls it at the advancing Anders. The blade glances off the guy's temple, slicing through his knit cap and taking a chunk out of his ear. Anders bellows in pain and comes at Thurston with the blade swinging. Thurston dodges left and right and then his feet find nothing but cold, thin air.

There's a moment of electric realization and then he falls.

In the split second before he hits the water he gulps down a last lungful of oxygen before he is greedily sucked down into the Hvítá's icy depths.

CHAPTER 20

THE COLD ALMOST STOPS Thurston's heart but the thick wet suit he's wearing underneath his clothes keeps him operational.

Just.

The power of the water is astonishing. In zero visibility Thurston feels himself being dragged downward as though in the maw of some giant beast. He slams hard into a rock wall and then another. It's only pure luck he hasn't been smashed into pulp inside the first ten seconds.

He gets drawn into a comparably quieter zone and takes the chance to shrug off the pants that have been acting as an anchor. He strikes for the surface.

In almost the same moment, some accident of the current brings Thurston to the surface. He gets a brief glimpse of the night sky and registers a noise like a jet engine before he is hurled over the first great stone step and down the Gullfoss Falls.

There's nothing he can do except hold his breath and hope.

He wraps his arms around his head as he tumbles down. He hits the bottom and comes to a brief stop. A monstrous weight of cascading water is pressing him flat against the rock. Thurston inches forward, blindly, fighting the force pulling him down. He will likely die anyway but if he stays at the bottom of this eddy he will die sooner. It takes Thurston several agonizing minutes before he feels the river take him again. Once it does, he is moving faster than ever.

Quite suddenly, he tastes fresh air as the falls spit him over another ledge. He spins and sucks in more air. This time when he hits the water he manages to keep his head above the surface. He feels a fractional easing of the speed of the current and kicks as hard as he can for a spar of snow-covered rock jutting out at an angle. As he gets closer he tries to grab hold of something but his fingers won't work properly. The rocks are slick with ice and water.

"C'mon!" grunts Thurston and he kicks again, finding strength from somewhere.

The river flicks Thurston into a tiny eddy nestling in an elbow of rock. He digs his hands into the shale and hauls himself clear of the water, lungs burning and ice already forming on his hair and face.

Thurston permits himself a few brief seconds before he gets to his feet.

Do nothing and die.

The cold is so intense, so all-consuming, Thurston almost laughs. He feels a drowsiness begin to descend and knows this is hypothermia showing its face. He climbs up a short bank and out across an endless white plain disappearing into the darkness. Thurston has no way of knowing how far he's come from the point where he entered the water but he's guessing it's more than two kilometers.

He flashes on the Land Cruiser parked back by the tourist office. Warmth, shelter, life. He turns back along the river and begins running.

It's all he can do.

CHAPTER 21

THURSTON'S BEEN MOVING AS best he can for ten minutes when it dawns on him he's not going to make it back to the Land Cruiser. He's been dragged too far downstream and the cold is slowing him down too much. If he doesn't get to shelter in the next few minutes he will die out here.

He reaches a relatively high point of land and climbs, trying to ignore the stabbing pains shooting down his arms and legs as he slithers on the snow. At the top of the rise, his breath coming hard, Thurston scrapes ice from his eyes and rubs his hands while he turns 360 degrees.

He's looking at a wilderness. A blasted snowscape bounded on one side by distant black mountains. There isn't a single visible light. The pointlessness of his situation, and the inevitability of his death hits him hard. His breath hurts his lungs. His limbs are heavy and sleep tugs at his eyelids. It would be so good to sit down, so easy to rest on the soft snow, to close his eyes and forget all about Miller and Sofi and Barb.

And then he sees it. About two hundred meters away. An electric thrill runs through his nervous system. A chance.

A roof.

It's a farm building of some sort. A cattle shed.

There's no sign of the farm it belongs to and Thurston can't risk trying to find it. It's this stinking hole or nothing.

Dead on his feet, he stumbles the last few meters to the door, lifts the wooden crossbar lock, and pushes himself inside.

A wave of beautiful, stinking animal warmth hits him and Thurston almost faints with relief. He can't see a thing but inside the stock shed the temperature feels positively tropical by comparison with outside. His arrival is greeted with relative calm and a few disgruntled moans, as though Thurston is a late arrival on an already over-crowded commuter train.

Thurston feels his way around, bumping into the animals as he does. One stands on his foot and he pulls it away, trying not to spook the beast. He has no idea what the animals are apart from the fact they don't seem to be cows.

In a corner of the shed Thurston comes across a stack of thick plastic bags scattered on top of a heap of straw bales. Moving as quickly as he is able, and shivering violently, he fills one of them with loose straw. There are only minutes left before he succumbs to the cold, even in here. He stuffs his wet snow boots with straw. If he's going to survive this he'll need to walk out of here. Without the boots he won't stand a chance.

Thurston places his boots on a hay bale and bends to fumble in the straw on the floor of the shed until he finds what he's looking for: a warm heap of fresh dung. He smears it over his skin as thickly as possible, paying particular attention to his feet and hands. When he judges himself well-covered he slides into the straw-stuffed plastic bag. He finds a gap between the hay bales, drops his wet suit under him, and wedges himself in the space above, stuffing handfuls of straw to plug any gaps. He pulls another bale over the top until he is encased. He curls into a fetal position and jams his hands between his thighs.

Agonizingly slowly, stinking to high heaven, he begins to thaw, hoping he hasn't been so exposed his fingers or toes become necrotic.

After a time, unconsciousness comes.

CHAPTER 22

THURSTON IS WOKEN BY a rough, wet tongue energetically licking the top of his head—the only part of him not inside the straw-stuffed plastic bag.

Feeling like death, Thurston groans and lifts his face free of his makeshift sleeping bag. As thin early morning Icelandic light dribbles in through the cracks in the shed wall, Thurston finds himself staring directly into the disdainful hooded eyes of a white-coated llama.

"Fuck me," Thurston croaks. "Llamas."

The llama regards him curiously and then turns away.

Thurston creaks upright and promptly vomits onto the hay bales as his stomach gets rid of the river water forced down his throat the night before. After the vomiting stops he carefully checks his hands and feet. All seem to be intact, if wracked by cramps. He hopes the cramps don't indicate irreversible damage but he doesn't dwell on it: time will tell and there's no benefit in thinking about what might happen.

Thurston unravels his wet suit and spreads it across the straw. As the llamas gather around to inspect, Thurston puts on the wetsuit. It's like climbing into a discarded bag of ice but Thurston hopes his body heat will warm the moisture. Eventually.

Shivering, he fastens the zips and finds his snow boots. The straw has dried them a little but they are still too wet. For the second time since he'd gotten out of the river, Thurston feels the seductive tug of capitulation. Without boots he's finished. He sits down heavily on a bale and tries to force his mind to concentrate, to think.

And then, from somewhere outside, he hears a noise: an engine.

Thurston puts an eye to a crack in the wall.

Coming slowly over the rise ahead is a snowmobile pulling a sled piled with straw bales. It turns in a wide semicircle before pulling up outside the shed.

The farmer's arrival causes excitement among the llamas. Their noise reaches the farmer because he calls out something in Icelandic.

Thurston positions himself behind the door and waits.

After a few seconds the shed door swings open and a heavyset man swaddled in thickly padded winter work gear walks in staggering under the weight of a bale of straw. He takes a few steps before he stops dead and slowly turns to look at Thurston over his left shoulder.

"G'day," says Thurston and raises his hand.

The farmer looks impassively at Thurston as

though finding a shivering, shit-covered Australian in his remote llama shed is an everyday occurrence.

"Am I glad to see you, llama farmer," says Thurston.

As he speaks, the farmer puts down the bale, reaches into his jacket, and comes out with a short-barreled shotgun.

"I haven't got time for this," says Thurston. He takes two quick strides forward and in one smooth motion twists the gun free of the farmer. "If you're going to point a gun at least look like you mean it, brother, okay?"

The farmer nods.

"You speak English?" says Thurston.

"Yes. A little."

"Okay, good. I need clothes, boots, food, and a car. If I don't get those things I'm going to kill you. You understand?"

The farmer understands.

CHAPTER 23

THE FARMER LIVES ALONE, which is a bonus since Thurston doesn't have to deal with the complication of a wife or family. He ties the farmer securely to a radiator and then takes a long, hot bath in the surprisingly clean bathroom. He borrows clothes and raids the farmer's kitchen, cooking a gigantic plate of eggs and washing it down with a gallon of coffee.

Less than an hour after arriving at the farm, with the farmer's confiscated shotgun nestling in a holdall on the passenger seat, Thurston bundles the farmer into the back of his ancient truck, blindfolded and gagged. Thurston could simply leave the farmer and take the truck but that would invite complications. Easier to take him to Reykjavik and let him make his own way back. The farmer's done nothing wrong—other than point a shotgun—but Thurston can't rule out a link with Miller who is, after all, a neighbor.

Before heading back to the city, Thurston checks the Land Cruiser at Gullfoss Falls. As expected, it's gone. He thinks about heading straight back to Miller's place but dismisses it. With Miller assuming he is dead, Thurston knows he temporarily has the upper hand. Better to make preparations in Reykjavik and come back loaded for bear.

Thurston points the truck east and heads to Reykjavik. The journey passes uneventfully although Thurston has to blink himself awake more than once.

Eight blocks from his rented apartment, Thurston parks the truck. He grabs the holdall and steps out of the car. Leaning into the backseat he unties the farmer's hands and walks away. By the time the old guy has his bearings, Thurston is gone.

He makes his way to the apartment and, although he doesn't expect any, checks for surveillance. Once he's satisfied Miller hasn't left anyone, Thurston goes inside.

The place has been tossed but, since Thurston hadn't spent more than five minutes in the place, there's nothing for him to worry about. Thurston retrieves the backpack he'd stowed under the outside steps last night.

By midday he's in another scalding bath at the Centerhotel Arnarhvoll overlooking the harbor. He stays there for almost an hour before wolfing down a room-service steak and sleeping the sleep of the dead.

CHAPTER 24

FOR THREE DAYS THURSTON licks his wounds at the Arnarhvoll. His main concern had been his hands and feet but they seem to have come through without any lasting damage. He's copped a black eye, bruised ribs, and an impressive lineup of contusions from the battering he took in the Falls. As he recovers he spends time mapping out an approach route to Miller's farm and rents a car to replace the Land Cruiser, which he'll report stolen when he's left Iceland. *If* he leaves Iceland.

Thurston's dreams are plagued by images of Sofi Girsdóttir and Barb Connors—Sofi appearing to him wearing the look of pure animal horror when she saw Miller in the bar. With Barb it is her screams; screams that jolt Thurston awake in the small hours. He spends a lot of time in those hours thinking about the two women and of the party girls he'd seen at Miller's place. Those girls—and it's all too easy to see a younger Sofi as one of them—were as disposable to Miller as paper coffee cups. Children—or as close as makes no difference—used as toys. Thurston flashes back to the smug expression on Miller's face at Gullfoss and fixes the image in his mind.

Thurston's escape from Paddington Green has faded from the online press. He has no doubt the case is still very much alive but at least it means his photo isn't still being splashed around the media. Thurston notes that DS Hall is no longer mentioned as leading the investigation although, so far, there's no tabloid exposé of the video he'd shot of Hall at 22 Logandale Lane.

By day three at the Arnarhvoll Thurston's ready to move on Miller again. He picks up the new rental and starts assembling what he needs. The farmer's shotgun turns out to be a piece of crap so Thurston drops it in the bay. In a tourist bar on Tryggvagata he gets a line on somewhere to score dope, which, in turn, takes him to a run-down cafe in the Efra-Breiðholt district to the east, the nearest thing Iceland has to a rough neighborhood. A few steps and a couple of false starts later, he's out by the warehouse talking to a Russian guy who works at a car body shop about guns. The Russian, despite his energetic sales pitch, doesn't have much stock worth shit. But beggars can't be choosers so Thurston takes a semiautomatic Zastava pistol and an Ithaca M37 shotgun from him. He buys all the ammo the guy has along with a lead-weighted police baton.

By Wednesday night Thurston has what he needs.

He pays the hotel bill and leaves Reykjavik at midnight. By two he's at Miller's place out by Gullfoss, amped up and ready. There's only one problem.

The bird has flown.

CHAPTER 25

"WHERE?"

The guy sitting on the kitchen floor shakes his head. Blood from the crack Thurston had given him spatters across the tiles. He's a big man with a beard, in his late twenties with plenty of tats. Thurston has him pegged as a local recruit. From the look of the guy he might have done some boxing once but he's running to fat now. Probably got a rep in Reykjavik but, fuck, we're talking Iceland here. By Thurston's standards this tub of guts is an amateur all the way up. No wonder Miller was looking to recruit back at The V if this represented the standard local issue. Thurston guesses that's why he's been left behind to look after the joint: the gangster equivalent of a janitor.

"Fuck you!" he snarls, and says something else in Icelandic.

Thurston jams the muzzle of the Ithaca hard into the guy's mouth. He hears some teeth break.

"Don't try that 'fuck you' movie shit," Thurston

snarls. "It doesn't work in real life, buddy, and I'm not in a forgiving mood. Where's Miller?" Thurston pulls the muzzle back and places it flush against the guy's right eye socket.

"English, not," says the guy, spitting blood. Thurston pulls the Ithaca back, flicks the gun around, and smashes him backward into a table with the stock of the rifle.

Thurston has no problem doing it: he remembers seeing this guy through the window getting his tiny dick sucked by one of the teens. He'd poured beer over her head and laughed.

"I told you," says Thurston. He steps forward and stands over the guy, the gun aimed straight at his face. "You speak English just fine so don't try that bullshit with me again, understand me?"

The guy looks dazed. He rubs blood from the gash on his temple.

"So, again," says Thurston. "Where's Miller? I know he's gone: no cars left, rooms all empty, closets empty, girls gone, the equipment in the sheds on standby. I'm guessing there's been a big shipment out and Miller's gone back to whatever hole he calls home. This is where you come in and tell me where that is."

The guy looks around the kitchen as if expecting Nate Miller to show up.

"Miller kill you."

Thurston's tempted to blow the guy away simply for wasting his time. He pulls the slide on the Ithaca and lifts the stock to his shoulder.

"Wait! Wait!" Miller's guy flinches and Thurston nods, lowering the Ithaca a fraction.

"Go on."

"He's in America, okay? Okay?"

"Where?"

The guy shakes his head.

"I said, 'Where?'" Thurston pushes the gun in closer.

"Vermont. He has place there. I don't know where—"

Thurston cocks the Ithaca again.

"Not far from the border! I don't know exact! Some French name. Isle de something. All I know is it's on lake. Supposed to be a chemical fertilizer plant. That's all, I swear! I swear!"

"More," says Thurston. "There's more."

"The compound?" says the guy. "The compound is called 'White Nation.'"

"'White Nation'? You have got to be kidding me. Miller's a Nazi?"

The guy on the floor doesn't say anything but Thurston suddenly clicks on a few images: the skin-head Russian at The V, Miller's eagle wrist tat, the cold stare at Lenin.

"That makes things easier," says Thurston. He looks at the guy on the floor. He represents a problem. As if reading Thurston's mind, the guy starts speaking.

"I say nothing!"

Thurston grimaces. He can't afford for Miller to be aware of him this time. The problem is Thurston has standards—standards that separate him from the Millers of this world.

And then the guy on the floor makes the decision for him. Reaching down he pulls out a pistol stowed in an ankle holster. He probably thinks he's being slick but Thurston blows the guy's head off before he's released the safety.

CHAPTER 26

TO SAY NICK TERRAVERDI looks pleased to see Cody Thurston would not be accurate. As Thurston slides into the corner booth Terraverdi looks like someone who's bitten into an éclair filled with dogshit.

"Jesus, you look like crap, Thurston."

"Gee, thanks, Nicky," says Thurston. "Always a pleasure."

"You're welcome."

They're at a joint called Connolly's on South 4th Street over by the Williamsburg Bridge. It's afternoon in New York and gloomy outside with the dull promise of snow in the air.

Terraverdi is a trim, nervy-looking man in his mid-forties wearing a tailored business suit and glasses. He's one of those guys who seldom look at the person they're talking to. His eyes endlessly flick around the diner as his left leg pumps up and down, his restless fingers constantly picking at labels on the ketchup bottles, or flicking microscopic traces of lint off his sleeve. What he does not look like is a seasoned FBI field agent, something he has been for the past ten years.

A waitress comes over and both men order coffee.

"Be right back," she says. The two men watch her go and wait until she's back at the counter before starting to talk.

"How's the meditation going?" says Thurston. "You're looking mellow as ever."

"Very fucking funny." Terraverdi leans forward. "I'll give you fucking mellow. You know I can get in big trouble talking to you? My bureau chief gets wind I'm meeting a wanted felon it won't matter shit how things have been before. I'll be out on my ear, Cody. Or is there another name? I assume you're not in the country on your regular passport?"

"No," says Thurston. "It got burnt, along with everything else."

"In the fire."

"Yeah, what else?"

"The fire you didn't set."

There's a pause while the coffees arrive. As soon as the waitress is out of earshot Thurston leans forward, frowning.

"What the fuck do you think, Nicky? You think I'd be here talking to you if I did this? What did you hear? I went nuts? Suddenly flipped into a killer rapist with a taste for arson?"

"Pretty much," says Terraverdi. He takes a sip of coffee and grimaces. "If it's any help, I don't swallow any of that bullshit."

"I assumed as much, Nicky."

"And your beef is not on US soil so maybe I was kind of overstating how bad it would be for my boss to find out. We haven't had any notification about you. When you contacted me I did some background reading. It's been a while."

"True," says Thurston. "Ten years." Both men fall silent and regard each other thoughtfully. Terraverdi taps a finger absentmindedly against the table. After a few seconds Terraverdi leans back and opens the palms of his hands in a tell-me-more gesture.

"So…"

"So I need to tell my high-ranking FBI buddy maybe he's going to be hearing some things about me. Probably some bad things. Like about me killing a bunch of people up in Vermont."

"And they're all going to be lies."

"No," says Thurston. "They're all going to be true."

That makes Nicky sit up straight.

"Jesus, Cody. What the fuck are—"

"Listen, Nicky, I'm not here looking for your approval. I just want someone official to take a look at things if…if everything doesn't turn out the way I'm hoping. I don't want this to all be for nothing if I get a stray bullet. The guys I'm dealing with are flat-out bad motherfuckers, Nicky. Killers, rapists. Christ, given the age of some of the girls I saw in Iceland, they're practically child molesters. No one's going to spend a split second mourning. And you get to shut down a sizable North American pseudoephedrine supplier."

"Why don't you give me the details and leave it up to us?"

"Because you'd find nothing, Nicky. From what I hear this operation is running pretty tight. Besides, there's weird vibes about the setup and I'm guessing you don't want to be the fed at the tail end of that kind of fuckup? No, thought not. Listen, this is personal, I admit it. But it's also the kind of thing that's best dealt with off the books, you get me? In, out, nice and—"

"I can't hear this, Cody," says Terraverdi.

"Hear me out. You owe me."

There's a moment's silence while both men flash back to *that* night. The night of the firefight in Fallujah. The night Cody Thurston went right back in to the bleeding eye of the storm for Nick Terraverdi, a man he'd never met before, and got both of them out alive.

"Yeah," says Terraverdi, "yeah, I guess I do."

"You gonna let me take care of it?"

Terraverdi nods. "Now tell me what the fuck it is you got yourself into."

Thurston lays it out and, as snow begins to settle on the darkening streets of Brooklyn, Nick Terraverdi listens.

CHAPTER 27

NATE MILLER HASN'T GIVEN the Australian much thought since he'd gone into Gullfoss but he's thinking plenty about him now. Maybe it's the sound of running water, or maybe it's the dope. Or both. Whatever it is, Thurston's face keeps stubbornly swimming back into Miller's view and Miller's not sure he likes it.

He picks up his roach and takes a long drag.

He's laying back in a cedar tub set up on a deck overlooking the lake with Mercy, the hot little Hispanic bitch Donno brought over from Montpelier yesterday. Donno'd bought her off a guy running girls out of some juvie halfway house for wards of the state too old for the kids' home. Real nice piece. Young, too. Not that Miller's asking.

Mercy's about on the edge of unconsciousness. She's got her eyes half-closed and a sappy smile on her face. Cute, though. Miller thinks he might keep this one around a while longer than his usual. Train her up in his ways.

"What you thinking of, daddy?" Mercy drawls in a baby-doll voice. "Anything nice?"

"Shut the fuck up, *perra,*" says Miller. "I hate that 'daddy' shit."

"Jeez. Touch-*ee.*"

Miller looks her way and it's enough to straighten her right out. The girl drops her eyes and shuts her mouth.

"That's right," growls Miller.

He takes another toke and turns back to the lake and his thoughts on Thurston.

He'd done some asking around about the Australian after that dickwad Brit cop, Hall, fucked things up. Heard Thurston had decked two cops and waltzed out of jail smooth as you like. Disappeared into nothing faster than kiss-my-ass and then shows up in fucking Iceland looking like a completely different guy.

That took training. *Skills.*

Of course, Miller had seen it for himself back at the bar in London.

A guy who can put down the Axe is someone worth taking seriously. Which is one reason Miller had had the place torched. Sofi had been thrown in as a bonus. No sense in having one of his castoffs wandering around London shooting off her dumb Icelandic mouth. It had all gone just fine, but this guy didn't accept his fate like he should have.

And showing up at the farm right before they made the big shipment? Had that been a coincidence?

A thought occurs to him: a thought that, despite the

temperature of the tub, sends chills down his spine. Maybe the Australian was some kind of cop? Miller turns that one over. He was "working" in the same joint where Sofi Girsdóttir had been working. Could Thurston have been tracking the Iceland connection? Jesus Christ.

Miller rubs his mouth. *That* was a fucking idea he really hoped was just dope paranoia. If Viktor thought the same...

Miller shakes his head. It's bullshit. It had all worked out. The Russians never knew Thurston had set foot in Iceland and Miller had seen the fucking guy take a dive into the Falls. No one could survive that shit. He relaxes. He's got this thing all boxed off neat and tidy.

Miller smiles as he remembers again the guy's face as he dropped into the river and flicks the roach through the clouds of steam rising from the tub.

"Come here, baby," he says to Mercy. "Let's kiss and make up."

CHAPTER 28

AT FIRST GLANCE, EAST Talbot doesn't look like much of a place.

A second doesn't improve things.

It's a small ex–lumber town lying in a fold of white hills consisting of a small grid of cross streets that straggle up and out into the woods on either side. The main highway leads to I-89 fifteen miles west. Heading east, the road crawls over a ridge of densely forested hills before hitting the New Hampshire border another fifteen miles away. East Talbot's got a bar, a diner, a farm supply store with a sideline in maple syrup products, and a gallery some hopeful hipster had opened five years ago selling tourist shit for tourists who never buy enough. The gas station does a sideline in canoe trips on Lake Carlson, which sits under East Talbot like an oversized teardrop. There's a motel bigger than you might expect in a town that size that dates back to more optimistic times when Lake Carlson brought in large numbers of summer vacationers from New York and Boston.

Thurston's selected East Talbot because it's the last town before Miller's place at Isle de Rousse although, now he's here, he's wondering if he'll stick out so much he might as well paint a target on his back. But Thurston guesses he's got to start somewhere. Besides, from the look of things, East Talbot has been hit by a neutron bomb that's left the buildings but removed all trace of humanity. Since he reached the edge of town he hasn't seen a single sign of life on the slush-lined streets. A thick blanket of gray cloud sits across the town like a pan lid.

At the Top o' the Lake Motel, Thurston's rented Jeep carves black tracks across the entirely empty snow-covered lot. He pulls up next to the lobby and steps out of the car as a few flakes of snow begin to drift down out of the flat sky.

Inside two women are talking animatedly behind the counter. At Thurston's entrance, both look up, startled, as if a bear had walked in. Thurston guesses they aren't exactly overwhelmed by customers. After a moment's pause, the older of the two women smiles.

"How you doing today?" she says. Of middle-age, she's wearing so much polyester Thurston's certain she'll spark a fire if she crosses her legs too quickly. "The storm's about due so you timed this right, hey."

The other woman is around thirty, wearing jeans and a sweatshirt with the motel logo printed above her left breast. She's got her blond hair pulled up under a striped bandanna and is carrying a clipboard. She looks coolly at Thurston but doesn't speak.

"Well, it's snowing," says Thurston.

He knocks his Australian accent back and tries to give the words a New York twist. It won't pass as American but he's hoping up here in Vermont they might not listen too closely. From what he's heard so far, rural Vermonters don't sound much like Americans anyway.

"I'll see you tomorrow, Lou," says the younger woman. "Don't forget to add detergent to Pablo's list, okay? We're all out." She slides the clipboard behind the counter and shrugs into a thick down jacket hanging on the back of the office door. She acknowledges Thurston with a brief flick of her eyes and leaves.

"Bye," says Thurston to the closing lobby door.

"Don't mind Terri. She's kind of, uh…well, she's Terri. Now, where was we?"

"Storm?" says Thurston, handing over a credit card.

"That's right! Big one comin' they say." The woman swipes Thurston's card and slides it back across the counter. "Could be a doozy! But you'll be cozy with us, Mr. Flanagan. I put you in 205, second floor along to the right, Mr. Flanagan. Kind of an upgrade."

"Kind of?" says Thurston.

The woman shrugs. "Between you and me, all the rooms are pretty much the same but 205 is on a corner. So it's a little bit bigger. And with us bein' so quiet you haven't got no neighbors. Y'can make as much noise as you like."

"Oh, okay. Thanks."

"You want me to pick out the sights, hon?" says the

woman as she hands Thurston the keys to his room. "Or you here on business?"

"Real estate."

Lou's eyes light up.

"Buyin' or sellin'? Because this place is on the market, y'know. Get the right owner it could be a gold mine."

"More of a farming type thing," says Thurston. He shoulders his backpack and turns for the door, keen to end any inquiry into his nonexistent real estate story. "But thanks, anyway."

"Okay, enjoy your stay. Oh, and we don't have a restaurant on the premises but there's a discount on meals over at the diner, and on drinks at Frenchie's."

"Frenchie's?"

"The bar on Main? Stay there long enough and you'll meet most folks in East Talbot. I'll be there myself after eight."

Thurston nods and pushes through the door before she goes any further.

He feels Lou's eyes on his back all the way to his room.

CHAPTER 29

LOU WAS RIGHT ABOUT the storm.

Less than an hour after Thurston checks in he watches from his corner window as the edges of the town blur. After a while all he can see through the thickening blizzard is the neon glow from Frenchie's down the street. Thurston puts on his boots, grabs his down jacket and a beanie, and steps out into the motel corridor. Before he leaves he wedges a sliver of matchstick under one of the door hinges; an old trick, almost a reflex.

Outside, the temperature has dropped ten degrees. Thurston trudges across the parking lot and gets a burger at the otherwise deserted diner. When he leaves, the owner, a deadpan old boy with a lined face that puts Thurston in mind of someone who's just drunk a cup of vinegar, begins switching off the lights before the door closes.

Thurston takes a right. As he turns the corner onto Main Street he cops a face full of snow and flashes back to the night three weeks ago on his way to The V down Hackney Road. Heading toward Frenchie's, the memory is a reminder to him to watch his step and to remember why he's here.

He opens the door to a warm blast of air and the sound of country music and conversation. A long bar is lined with customers, many of them watching the bank of six TVs, all showing sports.

"Close the goddamn door, man," someone yells.

Lou hadn't been kidding about everyone in Talbot turning up at Frenchie's.

From what Thurston can see there are more people inside the bar than he'd have believed lived in the town.

Thurston's arrival doesn't cause so much as a ripple. He'd worried the place might stop dead at the sight of a stranger and feels a little foolish when absolutely nothing happens.

There's no space at the packed bar but Thurston finds a spot at a single table in a corner. He orders a beer from the waitress and sits back, glad to be in the warmth of a bar in full flow without any of the responsibilities of working. Thurston takes a pull on his drink and thinks again about Sofi and Barb. It occurs to him that Janie and Lenin and some of the regulars might have heard he was responsible for the fire and the deaths, and hot anger at Miller flares up once more. He hopes Janie and Lenin won't believe what they hear but he's not certain. They—

"You mind?"

Thurston looks up to see a good-looking blond woman standing in front of him. She's indicating the empty chair across from Thurston. It takes a few seconds for him to place her before realizing she's the woman he saw talking to Lou at the motel. With her hair down and a touch of lipstick she looks different. What was her name? Jerry? Toni?

"This ain't a come-on or nothing," she says, "but I'm not about to spend the night standing up. I been doing that all day. No offense."

"Sure. Be my guest," says Thurston. "I was, uh, miles away."

He waves a hand at the chair. The woman takes off her coat and sinks back.

Thurston calls over the waitress.

"Can I get you something to drink?" he says. "This ain't a come-on or nothing."

The woman smiles. "I'll have what he's drinking, Darla," she says to the waitress. Thurston sees a brief flash of something—approval?—pass between the two.

"Same again, for me," he says.

"Terri," says the woman as Darla weaves back toward the bar. She holds out a hand and, when they shake, her grip is firm, her touch still cold from outside.

"Mike," says Thurston. "We met, kind of, at the motel earlier?"

"Are you asking me? Or is that the way you speak? What is your accent?"

"It's a long story," says Thurston as Darla arrives back at the table with the beers. When she's gone, Terri leans forward and props her hand on her chin. "I like long stories," she says.

CHAPTER 30

A GOOD NIGHT.

Thurston had forgotten how they felt.

He and Terri talk and drink some beer and then talk and drink some more. He's thinking about asking her to dance, then sees a cop come in and exchange a look with Terri. He taps a finger to his snow-dusted hat and walks toward the bar.

"Who's that?" says Thurston.

Terri rolls her eyes. "Sheriff Riggs." She takes a sip of beer and runs her fingers through her hair.

"He seems to like you," says Thurston.

"Yeah, well. That's as may be. The feeling ain't mutual. The guy gives me the creeps if you want to know the honest truth of it." Terri sits back and regards Thurston. "Y'know, if I was a gambling woman—which is a great name for a country song, right?—I'd bet you was some sort of cop."

Thurston shrugs.

"Real estate?" says Terri. "I can't see that. But you've got some cop thing."

"I was in the military," says Thurston. He's aware he's stepping out farther than he wants to, like a man inching onto a frozen lake. "Maybe that's it."

"Maybe. You in the military for long?"

"Let's change the subject. Is that okay?" Thurston smiles to let Terri know there's no offense taken. "I did a few years."

"And you don't like talking about it?"

"Something like that."

The conversation seems to signal a shift in the atmosphere between them.

"Listen," says Terri. "I better go. I've got to work in the morning and I don't want to get there in bad shape."

She stands and puts on her coat. Thurston scratches his head.

"Something I said?" he says. He notices Riggs look up from his conversation with the bar owner and smirks. Thurston gets the idea that Riggs is not unhappy Terri's given him the brush-off.

Terri smiles. "Good night, Mike."

When Terri has gone, Thurston can't help but feel disappointed. Not that he'd been *expecting* anything exactly, but things had looked to be going well. He likes Terri and he'd thought she'd liked him.

You're losing your touch, buddy, says a voice in his head. *Like you ever had it,* comes the response.

Thurston waits ten minutes before leaving. He doesn't want to look like he's chasing Terri.

He walks back to the motel through four inches of

snow piled on the sidewalk. The cold sobers him up although, truth be told, he hasn't had much. And he'd gotten some useful information about Isle de Rousse at Frenchie's. About how there was one road in and one road out. About the way "the folks" up there didn't come into town much and when they did they didn't leave a real good impression. Nothing concrete, but Thurston is building a picture of what he's up against.

The Top o' the Lake Motel is mostly dark when Thurston gets back. He lets himself in the lobby door and heads past the empty desk toward 205.

Thurston is at the door, key in hand, when he freezes. He looks down and bends to pick up an object off the thin corridor carpet.

The sliver of match he'd placed in the doorjamb earlier.

Thurston pulls the hunting knife from his belt and places an ear softly against the thin veneer of his room door.

Nothing.

He glances up and down the deserted corridor. The place is like a morgue.

He pads the few steps to room 206 and puts his ear to the door.

Again, he hears nothing. Thurston bends to the lock and, using the knife as a lever, pops it with a soft *snick*. He waits a few seconds but hears nothing from inside.

As Lou had told him, the room is empty. Thurston moves silently to the window and slides it open. A cold wind slices through the opening and Thurston steps out onto the small balcony, trying to force back memories of stepping out onto the balcony at The V. This one is separated from the balcony outside 205 by nothing more than a chest-high piece of blockwork.

Thurston puts one foot on the icy rail and hauls himself up and over the wall and drops onto the neighboring balcony. He presses his back up against the stucco and peeps into 205 through a narrow gap in the curtains.

He sees nothing except darkness.

Feeling a little foolish, and more than a little cold, Thurston's mind replays the number of ways the match fragment may have dropped clear of the door. He slides the blade of his knife into the gap between window and frame and lifts the latch. Growing more confident by the second, he slips into 205.

He's taken one step inside when he senses movement to his left and turns as someone smashes a table lamp across the back of his neck.

CHAPTER 31

MILLER'S PHONE RINGS TWICE and then goes dead.

He puts down the beer he's working on, looks up from the Canadiens' hockey game on TV, and sighs. Even though two rings is what he'd agreed to with the guy on the other end of the call, it still bugs him when he has to do this James Bond secret code shit.

Miller digits a number and waits for the connection.

"It's me," he says, and then listens a while.

"Tell me what Frenchie said about this guy's accent, again," he says. "In detail."

When Miller hangs up he stands for a minute looking at the figures on the ice and then dials another number.

Viktor needs to know about this.

CHAPTER 32

THURSTON GETS HIS FOREARM up quick enough to take some of the sting out of the attack. Even so, the heavy base of the lamp drops him to his knees. Before the next blow lands he manages to twist and scissorkicks the legs from under his attacker. Thurston hears a body land on the carpet. He flips over to straddle his opponent and brings his knife up—

The table lamp blinks on and Thurston finds himself looking down at a naked Terri, her mouth set in an animal snarl.

"What the fuck?" says Thurston.

Terri twists out from under him and grabs a sheet from the bed.

"You always come in through the fucking window?" she snarls. "And what's with the knife?"

"You break into everyone's motel room?" says Thurston. "And you're lucky I didn't have a gun." He rubs the back of his neck. "You pack a wallop."

"Good," says Terri. "I hope it fucking hurts." She groans and rubs her leg. "I think you broke my leg."

Thurston gets to his feet and holds up his palms in a conciliatory way.

"Let's start over, okay?"

"Maybe."

"How did you get in?" says Thurston, and then holds up a hand again. "Wait. You work at the motel. You have keys. Dumb question, right?"

"About as dumb as it gets."

"Okay. Next one. Why are you here?"

Terri raises her eyebrows.

"That's possibly even dumber. Maybe I did hit you too hard."

She steps off the bed and lets the sheet drop.

"Ah," says Thurston.

"Right," says Terri. "Ah."

CHAPTER 33

VIKTOR DELAMENKO DRIVES CAREFULLY out of Southie—no sense in getting pulled over when the trunk of the Range Rover's rattling with enough hardware to invade Canada. It's an easy four-hour pull up to Isle de Rousse, even in the snow. Miller had told them to take it easy, no panic. So long as the job was done in the next twenty-four hours everything would be copacetic.

And Viktor's inclined to drag the thing out a little, make Miller sweat.

The simple fact of Miller bringing in Viktor and his boys in the first place is a little victory in itself. Viktor wouldn't necessarily say it to Nate Miller's face, but sub-contracting this wet work, even to a sub who's a business partner, isn't a good look when his own boys are right there. Miller can justify it all he wants about not shitting in your own backyard, but it's all Delamenko can do to keep the smile off his face.

"They say why?" asks the man in the passenger seat, Dmitri Puli, Viktor's second in command.

Puli's ex–*Spetsgruppa A*—Alpha Group—a Kremlin True Believer who, after one too many blood and shit details in Chechnya, stopped believing and swapped sides. Seeing his old colleagues back in Moscow cleaning up while he had his ass on the line in the North Caucasus tipped him into this line of work. Puli's a thin man who looks like a civil servant.

In the backseat, looking at his phone, is the youngest of the three, Boris Spetzen, a classic Moscow "bull" cleaned up and put into a suit. Delamenko still checks Spetzen's not wearing running shoes every time they go out on a job. Spetzen's there if they need any heavy lifting done but has about as much class as you'd expect from someone who's fended for himself from the age of eight.

Delamenko shrugs. "Miller doesn't want anything traced back to his place. Says this guy might be connected."

"To who?"

"He didn't say. Does it matter?"

Now it's Puli's turn to shrug. "No, I guess not."

Delamenko takes the ramp onto 93 and settles back.

CHAPTER 34

IT'S BEEN A WHILE.

Two months to be exact. With Sofi, one night after they'd both had a few too many shots. It had been Lenin's birthday and a lock-in at The V after hours.

Thurston sinks back into the bed and crooks an arm behind his head. He lets out a long, slow breath. Next to him, Terri does the same, running a hand through her hair.

She gets up and walks toward the bathroom. Thurston watches her. They'd left the broken lamp lying on the floor and it makes Terri's shadow dance across the ceiling. At the door, aware of his gaze, Terri flicks out a hip like a showgirl exiting the stage.

Two months.

Sofi Girsdóttir. Thurston lets the name run through his mind and doesn't like where it takes him.

Terri comes back in the room and slides in bed.

"You gonna tell me?" she says.

"Tell you what?"

"What you're really doing here." Terri props herself up on an elbow and looks Thurston straight in the eye. "Don't get me wrong, I don't blame you for spinning me a line. All the stuff back at Frenchie's about working in a bar and traveling around—"

"All true," says Thurston, cutting across her.

"Yeah, okay, maybe I can buy that. But you being here, in East *Talbot* for Chrissakes. Nobody comes to East Talbot."

"I did."

"Hmm. Kind of my point." Terri rolls onto her back. "Jeez, I wish I smoked at times like this."

There's a silence.

"It's the place out on the lake, isn't it?" says Terri. "Up at Isle de Rousse. Talbot Chemical. That's why you're here."

Thurston doesn't reply and rolls over on his side.

He's not doing the strong silent routine but he doesn't trust himself not to spill it all to Terri. It's been a long time since he talked properly to a woman—to anyone—and the temptation is strong. Terri's one of the good ones, Thurston knows simply by being here next to her. If he told her everything she'd understand. It would be fine. He could leave this thing with Miller, see how it plays out with Terri. Start again.

Instead he says nothing and the silence grows.

After a couple of minutes Terri gets dressed and leaves without another word. As the door closes behind her, Thurston rolls onto his back and looks up at the ceiling.

"Shit."

CHAPTER 35

WHEN THURSTON WAKES, EAST Talbot sits under a blanket of freezing fog. He showers and dresses quickly before heading downstairs. Lou's back on reception and gives him the frost. Thurston wonders if she's pissed because he slept with Terri, or because Terri's spilled about what a sneaky, lying bastard he is.

Outside it's colder than a hockey puck's belly. Thurston hurries across the ghostly parking lot and into the diner for breakfast. He's working on a second pot of coffee when Sheriff Riggs comes in.

There are about a half dozen customers in the joint but Riggs makes a beeline for Thurston's booth.

Shit.

Thurston knows he should play nice but there's something about Riggs that rubs him up the wrong way. He feels like Riggs could be from the same cop tree as Hall back in London.

"You mind?" says Riggs. He looms over Thurston and points his finger at the bench opposite.

Thurston looks up.

"Does it matter?"

Riggs smiles without warmth. "Not really. Cold as all hell outside. I need coffee."

He slides his sizable ass onto the vinyl and scoots along the bench until he's facing Thurston. Riggs looks across to the counter and raises a finger. Vinegar Face behind the counter must speak Riggs's sign language because he gets busy right away.

"Riggs," says the cop. He doesn't offer a hand, which is fine with Thurston because he flat-out doesn't like Riggs. He's seen these guys before.

"Flanagan," says Thurston.

Riggs smiles. "Okay," he says. *"Flanagan."*

Vinegar Face arrives with coffee and a Danish pastry. He gives Riggs a microscopic glance and treats Thurston like he's got leprosy.

Thurston drinks his coffee and waits. Riggs doesn't say anything and Thurston sits there. He knows this bullshit drill backward. Riggs has the look on his face cops have—the kind of look that suggests they know everything about you and don't like it. It wouldn't matter a crap whether Thurston is polite. Riggs wants this conversation to be a warning—Thurston can see it in his eyes. The thing is, Thurston's not the type to respond. He runs a piece of toast around the egg on his plate and eats. He can do silence.

Riggs raises his eyebrows. "You've talked to cops before, right?"

"I've met 'em."

"You got the look."

Thurston drains his coffee cup and reaches into his pocket. He pulls out a ten and puts it on the table. One thing about being way out in the middle of nowhere: it's cheap.

Thurston slides across the bench seat. As he makes to get up Riggs leans forward and puts a hand on Thurston's arm. Thurston looks down at Riggs's pudgy hands.

"No offense, sweetheart," says Thurston, "but I don't swing that way."

"You were talking to Terri last night," says Riggs.

Thurston shrugs his arm free of Riggs's grip. Thurston stands and puts on his jacket.

"I said—" begins Riggs.

"I heard," says Thurston. "I just didn't reply."

"You need t—"

Thurston walks away from the table as Riggs is talking. He exits the diner and walks down the steps onto the lot. Behind him Riggs clatters through the doors and slips on the snow. Thurston watches the cop pirouette, his arms windmilling through the air before he lands heavily, flat on his ass. Riggs scrabbles to his feet with some difficulty, shoots a look of pure loathing at Thurston, and slithers toward his patrol car.

As Thurston walks away he glances up and sees Vinegar Face laughing so much he's wiping tears from his eyes.

CHAPTER 36

THURSTON DRIVES TO MONTPELIER through the fog along more or less deserted interstate. Every now and again the back of a big semi looms up out of the murk, the taillights blurring as Thurston passes. Outside Barre he sees the flash of emergency vehicles and a tow truck winching a car onto a flatbed. Before he gets to Montpelier he sees two more crashes. It's a day to stay put but there aren't any stores of the kind Thurston wants nearer Talbot.

After an hour and a half he reaches his destination unscathed. At a hardware store he buys a cordless Grex nail gun operating off nothing more than a couple of triple-A batteries. He throws in a box of two-inch nails and an Estwing double-headed axe with a rubberized grip. He could have picked up guns in New York, or maybe even nearer to Talbot, but too risky. Based on what he'd seen at Gullfoss, Thurston reckons on picking up more conventional weapons when he picks off the perimeter guys at Miller's compound.

At an electronics store Thurston buys a Nikon with a decent zoom lens and a weatherproof casing. He stocks up on winter gear at a sporting goods place next door and shells out almost a grand for a TenPoint Shadow Ultra-Lite crossbow and five boxes of aluminum bolts. A lightweight snowproof backpack, a pair of Sightmark Ghost Hunter night vision binoculars, and a lightweight pair of Zeiss regular binoculars tops it off. The Mozambique money is coming in damn useful.

Heading back from Montpelier, Thurston takes the long way around and winds toward Isle de Rousse from the east. On this side of the ridge, the road hasn't been cleared as well as it has on the western side, so Thurston's glad of the Jeep's winter rig. Coming this way means he won't be seen heading out of East Talbot in the direction of Isle de Rousse.

Two miles from Miller's compound, Thurston pulls the Jeep onto a fire trail and bumps along through deep snow for fifty yards before parking under a low branch. He puts on his winter gear and stows the Nikon and crossbow in the backpack. Today is strictly recon but Thurston's not going to take any chances.

CHAPTER 37

THE RUSSIANS GET TO Talbot around three and head up to Isle de Rousse as darkness creeps in. The fog hasn't lifted all day.

Delamenko turns off the highway down an unmarked road that cuts back down toward the eastern edge of Lake Carlson. About half a mile in, Delamenko slows as he approaches a gatehouse with a red-and-white striped boom gate across the road. As the Range Rover's tires crunch across the snow, two men wearing jeans, sheepskin jackets, and Stetsons step out of the gatehouse, both carrying semiautomatic rifles. Puli, who hasn't been here before, reaches into his jacket.

"Easy, brother," says Delamenko, putting out a hand. "Relax."

"They might as well advertise 'we supply drugs,'" replies Puli. "Jesus, what's the point of a cover story if they don't make an effort? At least *look* like a fucking chemical feed place. Put a sign up, wear a security guard uniform."

"I know," says Delamenko. "I've talked with Miller about this before. He says he has the territory taken care of." The big Russian shrugs. "Americans. You know what they're like."

"Hey," says Spetzen, leaning forward and pointing at the approaching men. "Cowboys!"

Delamenko stops the car and lowers the window. One of the men peers inside. Spetzen holds up his hands in mock terror. "Don't shoot," he says with a heavy Russian accent and smiles.

"Wait here," says the cowboy, without giving any indication he's heard Spetzen. The second cowboy walks back to the gatehouse and Delamenko watches him make a phone call.

"Miller said this would be taken care of," says Delamenko. "None of this gate bullshit."

"Yeah, well," says the cowboy, "shit happens, I guess. This ain't Moscow, Putin."

Puli mutters something and Delamenko raises a finger to quiet him. There's a pause during which the only sound comes from the idling car engine. Then the boom raises and the cowboy waves them inside with the muzzle of his rifle.

"Yesh'te der'mo derevenschina," says a smiling Delamenko to the cowboy as he drives through the gate.

Eat shit, redneck.

CHAPTER 38

THIS PLACE IS IN a different league from Miller's joint at Gullfoss.

That's the first thing Thurston registers. By the time he's made his first pass around the perimeter, he's reached the conclusion that this place has been built with two simple aims: to produce lots of drugs and to be easy to defend.

A twelve-foot-tall, heavy-duty electrified fence topped with razorwire sits in a U shape around the compound, with twenty yards of clear ground between it and the forest. Thurston, keeping to the trees, spots CCTV cameras every hundred yards. In the "gap" at the top of the "U" is the lake. Thurston can't get an angle on that yet but he imagines they have double or triple spotters in place there, especially in winter when the lake freezes. Inside the perimeter fence Thurston observes two dog patrols. There's only one road in and one road out. In addition to the two guards at the gatehouse there are two more positioned to the north and two to the south where the fence meets Lake Carlson.

If Talbot Chemical Feed is a genuine company it is taking its security extremely seriously.

Thurston waits for darkness.

CHAPTER 39

DELAMENKO, PULI, AND SPETZEN drive past the three massive chemical storage sheds glowing pale orange under the halogens, the fog forming softly glowing globes around the floodlights. They pass the long low bunkhouse that, Delamenko knows, houses the main staff on site. He has no idea how many men are there at any time but he guesses around fifty. Maybe more. At this time of year he figures Miller will have less crew on the ground. Even white supremacists don't like the cold.

"Christ Almighty," mutters Puli. His mood has been darkening since arriving in East Talbot. "I don't understand," he says, turning to Delamenko, "why we couldn't come in, do the job, and get the fuck back to Boston. Back to civilization."

"Miller has some special instructions. Another job. Extra."

"Miller, Miller, Miller," says Puli.

"He's the boss," says Delamenko.

Puli says nothing.

"Don't let the cowboy shit fool you, Dmitri. Miller didn't get there being a Boy Scout. He is dangerous. And that's *me* telling you, understand?"

"Okay, Viktor. I get it," says Puli.

"Let's get on with it," says Delamenko. "Get back to Southie. I hate the country."

CHAPTER 40

THURSTON ALMOST STUMBLES ACROSS the dead deer as he's looking for a suitable entry point. The carcass is hardly visible, covered by a crust of snow. A youngish female, her broken hind leg caught in a cleft between two logs.

He skirts around and then stops. He retraces his steps to the dead animal.

Grunting with the effort, Thurston hauls the deer free and, as best he can, drapes the body across his shoulders. He looks across at the fence and sees he is, as far as he can tell, outside the scope of the CCTV cameras. It's dark now anyway.

Thurston walks across the open ground toward the fence. About a yard from the fence he lifts the creature clear of his shoulders like a weight lifter and throws it onto the fence, leaping backward as he does.

He's rewarded by a spectacular flash and the smell of burning flesh. As Thurston had suspected, the fence packs a punch. This is not something designed to give a mild shock.

Thurston darts back into the trees and waits.

He doesn't have to wait too long. Less than twenty minutes has passed before he hears the buzz of a quad bike and sees the beams from its headlight bouncing across the snow on his side of the perimeter. As the bike draws closer, Thurston sees a single rider. He slides a bolt into the crossbow and takes off the safety.

The rider, a hunting rifle slung across his back, halts next to the dead deer, steps off his bike, and turns off the engine.

"Shit," Thurston hears him say.

He bends and pulls the animal clear of the fence. As Thurston had hoped, the fence has been shorted by the contact because the quad bike rider has no hesitation in touching the animal. The rider drags the deer back a few more yards. He wipes his hands on the snow and lifts a flashlight from the quad bike. The guy sweeps the area without any sense of urgency. If he's noticed anything weird about the deer it isn't showing. Thurston guesses he's going through the motions. After a few seconds he climbs back on the quad bike and heads back the way he came.

Thurston shoulders the crossbow, breaks from the trees, and reaches the fence in less than ten seconds. He pulls a small pair of wire cutters from his pocket and grabs hold of the fence.

CHAPTER 41

A QUIETER NIGHT AT FRENCHIE'S.

Terri's at the bar with a beer, half watching a hockey game on the TV in front of her. Ellie, a friend, sits to her left and has been talking nonstop for about the last hour—which is why Terri's watching the game. The fact that Terri hasn't said much more than "Is that right?" or "Uh-huh," or "I know," in that time hasn't stopped Ellie's flow. Terri's regretting calling Ellie up but Terri's not a woman who likes to drink alone. Especially when she aims to get loaded. She signals to Flynn behind the bar for another.

Terri's thinking about the Australian—if that's what he was. *Michael.* Somehow she knows that's not his real name. He'd been nice. Terri flashes on a couple of images from the previous night and a smile creeps onto her lips; a smile that gets wiped when she catches sight of the off-duty Riggs on the other side of the bar.

"What?" says Ellie, for once paying attention to Terri. "What's so funny?"

"Nothing," says Terri. "I was thinking about something."

Ellie doesn't ask a follow-up question and while she's prattling away about some new guy up in Barre, Terri thinks about the look on Michael's face when the light came on after she'd hit him with the lamp and a chill runs down her spine. While her adrenaline had been spiking off the charts, he had looked about as calm as a man taking an evening stroll.

She doesn't know much, but she's willing to bet Michael Flanagan is not here shopping for real estate.

CHAPTER 42

NO FLASH. NO BANG. No electricity.

Thurston breathes a sigh of relief and cuts through half a dozen strands. He pulls the fence apart and steps through, making sure there's plenty of room to step back once the power's been restored. The last thing he wants is to be stuck inside the perimeter once the recon mission's done.

Thurston crosses toward the line of trees and is swallowed up in the shadows. A couple of small animals skitter out of the way as he descends the hill toward the floodlights glowing through the fog.

An hour later and Thurston's got a pretty clear idea of where everything sits inside the compound. He's had a couple of ticklish moments when the dog patrol has passed by but had ridden his luck. He shoots a bunch of images on the Nikon and decides he's done enough for one night.

By midnight he's back in the Jeep and heading around Lake Carlson on his way back to East Talbot.

CHAPTER 43

"THERE," SAYS SPETZEN.

He points across the intersection as the door to Frenchie's opens and two women walk out, one of them laughing and holding on tight to the other. Both of them look a little unsteady on their feet.

"Which one?" says Puli.

Delamenko catches a flash of blond hair under the taller woman's knit cap. "The taller one. Miller said she had really blond hair."

"We gonna do both?" says Spetzen.

Delamenko shakes his head. "Not unless we have to."

He motions to Spetzen, who climbs out of the back and heads after the two women; Delamenko puts the Range Rover into gear and pulls out of the side street. He passes the two women and carries on about a quarter mile. Spetzen's going to update them by phone.

"This is bullshit," says Puli. "This bitch isn't our concern, Viktor."

"We been through this." Delamenko doesn't move

his eyes from the rearview mirror. He wishes Puli would stop whining. It's done. Get the fuck on with it.

As if reading his mind, Puli falls silent. The two men wait.

About two minutes later, Delamenko's phone vibrates. He reads the screen and turns to Puli. "It's on. Blondie's on her own."

He pulls the Range Rover around in a circle and heads down Main. Puli spots the woman turning into a side street with Spetzen closing in. Delamenko accelerates toward the curb as Spetzen grabs the woman from behind, his big hand over her mouth. Puli steps out and Spetzen shoves the woman into the backseat. He gets in, deflecting a kick and knocking her out cold with one punch. Puli gets back into the passenger seat and Delamenko pulls away.

No one sees a thing.

CHAPTER 44

SOFI GIRSDÓTTIR COMES TO him again in his sleep. This time she looks distracted. She tries to say something to Thurston but he's not listening. Frustrated, Sofi begins pulling at his sleeve. In the background he hears Barb Connors screaming but now it's at a distance.

"Come on, Cody," says Sofi. "Come on!"

From far in the distance comes a click and Thurston knows what it is. He's heard the sound before, many times, and it's never a good moment.

The muffled slide being ratcheted back on an automatic weapon.

He opens his eyes.

CHAPTER 45

DELAMENKO LEADS THE WAY, Puli behind him with Spetzen carrying Terri over his shoulder, bringing up the rear. Using the unconscious woman's keys for the motel, the three Russians go in via the fire doors at the back and head up the stairs toward 205.

Puli's got a 9mm SIG Sauer automatic fitted with a fat Piston suppressor. Delamenko has a Remington semiautomatic shotgun, its muzzle also blunted by a squat suppressor.

The three men move in complete silence, Puli's bitching subsumed by the requirements of what's happening. All three men have service histories, Puli's the longest and bloodiest. They know how to do this.

In the corridor leading to 205, Delamenko pauses. From what he's been told by Miller, the guy they're here to kill has some military skills. Delamenko's pretty sure Miller hasn't been completely honest about how good those skills are. Delamenko had seen for himself the guy do a pretty good job on the Axe back in London so he's taking no chances. And, although it'd kill him to admit it, Puli was right about the girl being bullshit. Miller's "added extra"—killing her and the Australian and letting Riggs tie up a neat bundle— might be one of those things that sounds like a brilliant idea but is less easy to do in practice. It's a detail they could do without. If Miller wanted them to come in and do a pro job on this Thurston guy that's fine. If he wants to get rid of the chick who shopped Thurston to him then why not shoot her and put her in the fucking woods? Christ, there's an industrial furnace out at White Nation. Why not put both of them in there?

Delamenko shakes his head impatiently. No sense in asking questions now. Get into the room, kill the Australian, kill the woman, and get back to Southie before daybreak.

At the door, Delamenko listens. He can't hear a thing. He puts the key in the lock and silently opens the door.

Still nothing.

Delamenko racks the slide on the Remington and steps into 205.

CHAPTER 46

A FULLY DRESSED THURSTON rolls out of bed, grabs the knife on the bedside table, and comes up in an attack posture.

The room's empty.

Thurston remains completely still. He hadn't imagined the ratchet noise. That hadn't been part of the dream. He listens intently, sure now his instincts to spend the night across the corridor in the empty 207 had been correct.

Thurston hears some soft rustling coming from the corridor and his mind fills in the blanks—three guys, moving quietly.

He pads across to the dresser and picks up the nail gun before crossing toward the door. Thurston looks through the spyhole. Standing outside is a big man carrying an unconscious Terri over his shoulder.

Thurston pads quickly back to the dresser and picks up the crossbow. He loads a bolt into it, and silently turns the handle on the door. The big guy swivels toward 207 and Thurston puts the bolt straight through his eye.

Before he's hit the carpet, Thurston moves into 205 as one unloads three quick rounds into an empty bed. Thurston sees the other bringing up his SIG Sauer and drills a two-inch nail into his groin. The man howls and drops as the first swings the Remington toward Thurston. As the Remington starts *whumping* Thurston presses the trigger on the nail gun and fires blindly. He hears the first grunt as a spray of two-inch nails rip into his chest and Thurston turns his attention back toward the screaming second man. He puts the nail gun against the top of the guy's head and squeezes. He falls forward, his face slamming into the floor.

The first guy, bleeding heavily, the Remington lying at his feet, staggers toward the window and slides back the door to the balcony.

Behind him, Thurston hears noises as the few guests at the motel begin to stir. He runs forward and kicks the man straight over the edge of the balcony rail.

Back in the room, Thurston drops the nail gun and scoops up the Remington and the second guy's SIG Sauer before moving into the corridor. A woman in a bathrobe peers out at him through a crack in her door.

"Call the police!" says Thurston. She disappears. Somebody else appears at the end of the corridor.

"Get back!" shouts Thurston and the guy vanishes.

Thurston looks down and turns Terri over. She's taken a shot to the side of the face—one of the strays from the Remington.

"Shit," says Thurston and lowers her to the carpet.

He runs into 207, collects what little he has, and goes back into 205. He closes the door and moves to the balcony. There's no sign of the man who fell, but a thick trail of blood leads across the parking lot. Thurston jumps and hits the snow hard. Without looking back he follows the blood trail around a corner.

The man is slumped on his back in the snow. He has his hand to his throat and is trying hard to stop the blood. He makes small gurgling sounds and his eyes are wide.

Thurston takes a step forward and puts a single round into the wounded man's head, not sure if he's doing it through kindness or hate. The body sinks back into a snowdrift.

The Jeep is only five meters away.

Thurston stows the guns and crossbow in the passenger footwell and opens the driver's door. He pauses on the threshold before stepping back and returning to the dead man. Taking care not to step in the blood, Thurston drags the dead man toward the Jeep and bundles him up and over the tailgate.

He's going to send Miller a reply.

CHAPTER 47

MILLER'S PHONE VIBRATES AROUND five in the morning.

He's awake already, wired from too much coke, looking at his laptop. Mercy's asleep, her bruised back turned to Miller. He'd been rough with her earlier, maybe got carried away, but she seems fine now. They're resilient at that age, Miller has found. He glances at the screen expecting to see Viktor's number.

Instead, it's Riggs.

"Okay," says Miller when he answers.

"I don't know what was supposed to happen down here, Nate, but it sure don't look like it worked out." Riggs is whispering and Miller can hear talking in the background. "Wait a minute."

Miller hears Riggs's muffled voice talking to someone else and then he's back.

"We got three dead. Two I think you might know. Foreigners."

"Easy," says Miller, reminding Riggs to be careful. No names.

"Yeah, okay," says Riggs. "The woman? Y'know? Terri? She got half her face blown off. They think it was accidental, like."

"They?"

"Well here's the thing of it. There's state cops here. Someone at the motel is an off-duty cop. Up here banging his girlfriend. Y'know, somewheres nice and quiet." Riggs pauses. "Anyway, this guy, Slater, works Robbery/Homicide out of Boston Southside and recognized one of the, uh, foreigners. Called his boss and next thing you know we're knee deep in city badges."

"Isn't this your town?"

"I tried that," says Riggs, "and they said all the right things and so forth—don't wanna step on your toes, jurisdiction, blah blah blah, but bottom line? They ain't shiftin'. They're gonna be doing some digging so I hope the trail don't follow back to—"

"Shut the fuck up," barks Miller. "There's nothing traceable. Quit panicking and let them take it back to Boston. A few days and they'll be chasing…the visitor. And if that doesn't happen we got some pull down there as insurance."

"Listen," says Riggs after a pause. "There's more. We have one big guy with a crossbow bolt through his eye."

"Okay," says Miller, thinking *crossbow?*

"And a smaller dude dead in the bedroom."

Riggs pauses. "He'd been shot with a nail gun. Once in the balls and then in the top of his head."

"Christ Almighty," says Miller.

"And the last guy? The other guy from Boston?" says Riggs. "Looks like our 'visitor' took him. We got a blood trail leading across the parking lot and a wit who says she saw a body getting bundled into the back of a car. Said it sort of looked like he was, and I'm quoting here, like he was 'taking a trophy.'"

"A trophy? What the fuck?"

"All I'm doing is passing it along." Riggs pauses. "I don't think this guy is going to be leaving town. I know you guys are, y'know, *capable* and all but I'd still be careful up there. I think he's coming for you. I think you pissed him off."

Miller hangs up and looks at his reflection staring back at him from the black window.

A *trophy?*

CHAPTER 48

THERE'S A STORM COMING—a bigger one.

Miller can see it in the sky and feel it in his gut. A kind of steel creeps into the already freezing air. The fog lifts slowly to reveal ugly slabs of black cloud crawling across the ridge from the west, like a sheet being drawn over a body in the morgue.

He gets his main guys together in the kitchen at the main house—the Axe, Donno, Carver, and Tannhauser—and brings them up to speed on Delamenko's clusterfuck in Talbot.

"Fuckin' Russians," says the Axe. "We shouldn'ta brung them in, Nate."

"Noted, genius," says Miller. He holds his hands up. "I admit it, I fucked up. Should've kept this in-house, like. So we won't say no more about it, okay? Here's what's going to happen. If this guy comes near this place I want him killed. Nothing fancy, just shoot the motherfucker. I underestimated him. That's not going to happen again. Donno, roust a few of your crew up outta their La-Z-Boys, okay? Get 'em out here now. Same with you, Carver, Tann. All hands on deck. We—"

The kitchen door opens and one of Tannhauser's crew comes in. Seeing Miller's face, he holds up his hands in apology.

"Sorry, Mr. Miller, but, but…"

Tannhauser slams a palm on the table. "Spit it out, Frankie, fer Chrissakes!"

Frankie points to the door. "You got to see this."

"What are we looking at?" says Miller.

He is standing in the middle of a group of men gathered around a pine tree that has a tarpaulin wrapped around its base.

One of his crew unties a couple of ropes and pulls the tarp free.

Miller coughs and takes a step back. He spits into the snow. "Holy fuck."

Viktor Delamenko has been crucified. There's no other word for it. His back lies against the trunk of a giant pine, each hand nailed to a branch on either side. He is naked and a trail of red spots can be clearly seen arcing across his chest. Here and there the light glints on a nail head standing clear of his flesh. He's been shot once in the head through his eye.

"Jesus Christ," whispers someone behind Miller and he whips around to see if it's a joke but the guy realizes what he's said and holds up a hand.

"How long's he been here?" says Miller.

They are at the junction off the highway that leads to the compound.

Tannhauser's guy Frankie, the one who'd brought the news, steps forward.

"Micky saw him about thirty minutes ago on his way in." Tannhauser's guy breaks off to point to a guy in his crew. "Micky figured he'd best cover him up—case anyone spotted him, like."

"Yeah, good," says Miller. He turns away from Delamenko. "Get him down. Get rid of him somewhere far away. He's never been here."

Tannhauser nods. Micky steps forward with a claw hammer and starts digging the nails out of Delamenko's hands. Miller watches for a few seconds, his expression unreadable. Then he walks toward his truck. He's at the door when he hears a shout. He turns to see Tannhauser looking closely at something on the trunk of the pine.

"Hey, Nate," says Tannhauser. "Check this out."

Miller steps over Delamenko's body and sees the word "CHENOO" has been carved into the wood. Blood from Delamenko's wounds has seeped into the grooves.

"Chenoo. What the fuck does that mean?"

Tannhauser shrugs. He turns to the group. "Anyone?"

One of Carver's boys gets out his phone.

"You fuckin' googling this?" says Miller.

The guy looks at Miller and hesitates. "Uh, yeah."

"Good idea," growls Miller. "How come none of the rest of you dumb shits thoughta that?"

He's not expecting an answer and none comes.

"It's, uh, Indian," says the guy looking at his phone. "Like Red Indian. Native American."

"What's it mean?" says Miller.

The guy looks up. "Says here the Chenoo is a human whose heart's been turned into ice. Chenoos are cannibals from the north. Once someone's become, uh, a Chenoo, the only escape is death."

"Fuckin' crock," says Miller. He points into the forest. "Carver, get our four best hunters ready and bazookaed up. Huntin' season is officially open. First man to bag this fuckin' 'Chenoo' gets a fifty grand finder's fee. I want this bastard gutted and hung up to rot out here."

Miller walks back to his truck with Anders. They get in and spin around toward the compound. As soon as he's out of sight of the men, Miller punches the dash hard five or six times. When he's done, he stops, breathing heavily. He glances in his rearview and slams on the brakes, and turns in his seat to look over his shoulder at a single word traced into the ice on the rear window of the truck.

Chenoo.

CHAPTER 49

SLITHERING BACK INTO HIS position in the snow-covered trees across the highway, Thurston picks up his binoculars to see the guy in front of Delamenko looking at his phone. Thurston knows the dude is looking up the word "Chenoo," exactly like Thurston had done earlier.

Thurston knows zip about Native American myths but wanted something spooky sounding to unsettle Miller's crew. Writing the word on Miller's truck had been showy—and risky—but Thurston doesn't care. It was worth it just to think about Miller's face.

Thurston could have taken Nate Miller out with the Remington he'd picked up in the motel—shit, at this distance he'd fancy his chances of hitting him with the crossbow. But after seeing Terri lying dead in the corridor Thurston's coming at this thing with a new intensity. He's already in the frame for the murders of Sofi and Barb back in London so he's pretty sure he's going to be targeted for the deaths at the Top o' the Lake Motel last night. All of which means Cody Thurston is no longer content to kill Nate Miller.

Thurston's going to bring it all down.

CHAPTER 50

THE FOUR GUYS CARVER sends into the forest are hard-core hunters. Like Thurston, they are ex-service and all, bar one, are Northeasterners born and bred. They know every inch of these woods.

That afternoon, Thurston contents himself with observing. He establishes three vantage points dotted around a sloping ridge. Each of these vantage points is placed high in the branches of a tree and Thurston lays a trail to bring the hunters to him. Nothing too obvious. A broken branch here, some footprints in soft snow there.

It works.

To a point.

After an hour the first of the hunters comes into view. He's moving cautiously on a diagonal across the ridge. If Thurston hadn't been extremely vigilant he'd never have spotted him.

Thurston slides the crossbow into position and tracks the hunter's cautious path waiting for the moment. He sees a patch of open ground between two trees. *There.*

Thurston waits.

As the hunter gets to the open ground he stops, just as Thurston expects. The guy knows this section might leave him temporarily exposed. What he *should* do is work his way back down the ridge and then edge back up through the tree cover some eighty yards away.

He doesn't.

Thurston's finger tightens on the crossbow trigger and he gets ready to put a bolt in the guy's head the second he appears in the open.

Any second now…

Thurston stops.

From everything he's seen, these guys are good. Perhaps as good as Thurston.

So why is this dude exposing his position? Why is he taking the risk?

Suddenly Thurston realizes what's happening. This guy is bait. They are waiting for Thurston to reveal *his* position. The hunter becomes the hunted.

Smart move, thinks Thurston.

He leans back against the trunk of the tree and waits.

Snow is falling heavily now, drifting down from the steel sky in fat flakes. Inside the forest, the snow-padded silence becomes tangible, the forest a white cathedral. Any noise here will sound like a thunder-clap.

So Thurston waits some more.

The temperature keeps falling and he's glad of the extra precautions he'd taken with his clothing. He's guessing the hunters, though well-equipped, won't have prepared as thoroughly as he has. They are local. They know there are warm beds and food no more than an hour from here on foot. They won't be willing to wait it out as long.

Thurston's betting his life on it.

CHAPTER 51

IT TAKES ALMOST FORTY MINUTES.

And then Thurston hears the soft crack of a twig underfoot coming from his left, and much closer than he'd imagined. He swivels his eyes and catches a trace of white vapor rising from a low snow bank about thirty yards behind his position.

These guys have been closing in. He'd been right to wait. A shot when he'd seen the first hunter would have resulted in him being trapped. All they'd have to do would be to wait it out or shoot him straight out of the tree.

Carefully Thurston takes his cell phone from his pocket and presses a single digit he'd programmed earlier.

Some hundred meters to his south comes the incongruous muffled sound of a ringtone: Delamenko's cell placed in the crook of a tree and wrapped inside a knit cap.

Immediately all four hunters move toward the

sound. They move more quickly than is advisable, keen to track the ringtone before it gives out. As they edge away from his position, Thurston silently drops to the forest floor.

CHAPTER 52

"SON OF A BITCH."

Kane, the first of the hunters to get to the phone, holds it up as Palmer and Schmidt arrive.

Palmer grabs Kane's sleeve and pulls him low to the ground.

"Jesus, man," he hisses. "Why the fuck you think the phone's there? You want to get us killed?"

Kane's experienced enough to know he's fucked up. A pro, he doesn't get into an argument with Palmer. The guy's right. Thurston's drawn them out. They're exposed. The three of them crawl to the bole of a big pine with two protruding protective branches. From here there is only one firing line. Unless Thurston's dead ahead, this will work as protection.

"Where's O'Hara?" says Palmer.

CHAPTER 53

DANNY O'HARA'S AN ARIZONA BOY.

He cops plenty of flak on that, mainly about how he can't handle the cold up here. Guys handing him sun lotion, that kind of shit.

But O'Hara was raised in northern Arizona, up in Williams where it gets plenty cold in winter. And he's more cautious than the locals. You don't get to survive six tours of duty in some of the most fucked-up places on the planet without learning a thing or two. The others on this hunt are pros but they've let themselves get caught up in the chase. As soon as the phone rang they were off like dogs catching the scent. O'Hara, too, at first before he'd stopped and thought some.

This was a trap. This Thurston guy? From what O'Hara had seen, he's solid. Dangerous.

When the phone stops ringing, O'Hara wonders if the others are already dead. He listens intently, straining, but Danny O'Hara hears nothing, not even the sound of Cody Thurston reaching around and cutting his throat in one swift, silent movement.

CHAPTER 54

PALMER SWITCHES TO NIGHT vision goggles as darkness closes in. It turns the snow-covered forest a ghostly, milky green. Fifty yards to Palmer's left, Kane does likewise. Fifty back, Schmidt is bringing up point, the three hunters making an open-faced triangle. They move slowly, deliberately. The phone thing has rattled them, exposed them, but that's forgotten now.

The key for the hunters is to use their local knowledge against Thurston. With the storm worsening there are only so many places Thurston can go. A steep ravine lies to the east. In these conditions it is impassable. To the west is a scrabble of mud and weeds: a flatland area that runs about two miles from the fire trail to Lake Carlson. Even in winter it is not possible to cross.

The phone may have been a plan to draw out the hunters but—from the information they have—Thurston has made an error, trapping himself in a relatively narrow corridor leading back toward White

Nation and Lake Carlson. This formation is a net in which to catch Thurston.

After ten minutes, Palmer passes a fallen pine that could make a likely spot for Thurston to mount an attack. He approaches cautiously and sees O'Hara sprawled facedown in the snow, the blood spray from his cut throat showing almost black in the night vision goggles. In the second or two it takes for Palmer to register O'Hara, Thurston pulls back the white waterproof under which he'd been waiting and puts a crossbow bolt into the back of Palmer's head. The hunter slumps forward and lands arched across the fallen pine.

Thurston doesn't wait. Sliding his night vision goggles onto his forehead he turns and, moving quickly, crosses a stand of trees to emerge close to Kane on the other side of the hunter's "triangle." Kane sees Thurston and raises his rifle.

Thurston flicks on his Maglite flashlight, blinding Kane as he gets off a round. Thurston hears the bullet smack into the tree less than six inches to his left.

Kane rips off his goggles but still has no vision. He fires blindly and wildly as Thurston sprints forward and stabs Kane in the chest. Kane grunts and falls but isn't dead. He shouts something and Thurston hits the ground while Schmidt sets up a hail of shots that cut Kane almost in two. Blood spurts across the snow as Thurston burrows deep into a drift banked against the base of a big pine. Although not hit, he screams convincingly and pulls on his night vision goggles.

Schmidt approaches, on full alert. Screened by a

tree, he scans the scene. Thurston knows this last guy won't be able to tell if either of the bodies sprawled in the snow are his fellow hunters. Hidden in the drift, Thurston bides his time and then, as Schmidt moves forward fractionally, blows his face off with one round from the Remington.

Thurston emerges from the snow drift and gets to work.

CHAPTER 55

MORNING CRAWLS AROUND IN the shape of a flat blue-gray light seeping into Isle de Rousse.

At the Talbot Chemical Feed gatehouse, the double-duty security detail has been on full alert all night. The four men have heard the gunfire coming from the forest, but Miller's given them instructions to stay put unless advised otherwise.

At five before seven there's enough light for Bridges, the oldest man on duty, to peer through the gatehouse window and see a Jeep parked at the edge of the road where it comes out of the forest.

"Call Miller," says Bridges. "Tell him we got sump'n down at the gate."

Bridges picks up his assault rifle and puts on his hat. He motions to another guard, Foley. "Come with me."

The wind has picked up and, as Bridges and Foley exit the gatehouse, a blast of icy air threatens to rip the door off its hinges.

"Let's go," says Bridges. Foley's moving but doesn't

look exactly enthusiastic about the prospect of leaving the gatehouse.

Battling the wind, Bridges and Foley approach the Jeep, their boots squeaking on the new snow. There's something on the hood of the Jeep but with all the snow and wind it's hard to see until they are ten feet away.

"Jesus Christ," says Foley, and pukes.

The windshield of the Jeep has "Chenoo" scrawled across it in blood. Lashed to the hood like four hunting trophies are the naked bodies of Kane, Schmidt, Palmer, and O'Hara. All of them have had their hearts cut out.

CHAPTER 56

THURSTON'S NO MACHINE.

Exhausted, freezing, and hungry, he crawls inside the refuge he'd prepared the previous day inside the dry "cave" formed by three fallen trees. A thick layer of smaller branches forms a roof fixed in place now by a carpet of snow. Thurston has sealed every draft with more packed snow and put a double-layered thermal mat on the floor. He takes off his blood-spattered outer layers and puts on a clean, dry knit cap. He takes off his boots and carefully wraps them in a protective plastic sheet. Thurston crawls inside a military-grade cold-weather sleeping bag. Sitting up with his back against one of the walls of his refuge he cracks the foil seal on a self-heating pack of stew and opens a thermos of hot tea. Thurston works his way through both before lying down, closing his eyes, and falling almost instantly into a bottomless sleep filled with demons.

CHAPTER 57

ANY ICE STORM IS bad news.

The one whipping down from Canada and slamming into northern Vermont that morning is a flat-out, stone-cold bitch.

The gently drifting snow turns to super-cooled rain and freezes on impact. Within minutes, every available surface is covered with a rapidly thickening layer of hard-glaze ice as the wind picks up. Power lines bow under the weight, roads become impassable, water pipes freeze solid, vehicles not under cover become glued fast to the ground, their locking systems iced and fuel lines as brittle as an old man's arteries.

By midday, East Talbot is effectively cut off from the rest of the world.

At Isle de Rousse, news about the four dead hunters with the missing hearts spreads through the compound like a virus. With the road now an ice rink, eight men take off on foot within an hour of the news breaking and Miller suspects a few more of the weaker-minded ones are thinking about it. The girls at the compound also hear the rumors but Miller doesn't give a shit if they run. Let the dumb sluts freeze out there. Not one of them would last ten minutes. He's already had to punish Mercy for talking back to him.

No, what's done is done. The hunters on the hood of the Jeep, and all the "Chenoo" bullshit tells Miller one thing: the Australian's declared war. Spooking the men at the compound is smart and a tiny part of Miller grudgingly congratulates his enemy. *First create fear.* Isn't that what some Chink warlord said? But Miller doesn't want any more defections, so he gets the Jeep and the bodies towed out to the old quarry and burned to ash. He has no thoughts on the dead men: just like Viktor and his boys, they fucked up and paid the price.

With the Jeep and hunters out of the way, Miller concentrates on making the compound an impenetrable fortress. He divides the crews up between Donno and Carver, and lets them sort out rotational patrols, lines of fire, and the like. If Thurston's going to come to him then let's see what he's got. Even with the defections, Miller's got better than thirty hard-core guys left with an arsenal that'd make a general's mouth water. They have abundant generator power, a ton of supplies, more drugs than a Colombian cartel, plenty of women...all while that Australian bastard's out there freezing his nuts off.

Hell, this might even be fun.

CHAPTER 58

THURSTON CAREFULLY OPENS ONE eye and then the other.

It's more difficult than it sounds—mainly because his eyelids have iced up while he's been sleeping. Although the temperature inside the thermal sleeping bag is pretty good, inside the forest shelter it has to be said things are a little on the fresh side.

Thurston wriggles a hand up and rubs ice crystals from his eyes. He checks the illuminated dial of his watch: almost three in the afternoon. Without looking outside Thurston knows something is different. The forest is creaking.

Thurston wriggles to the entrance to his shelter and digs a hole in the protective packed ice. Thurston pushes his head through and sees a changed landscape. Every branch of every tree groans under the weight of glaze ice, the lowest limbs connected to the snowbound forest floor by thick icicles. Thurston realizes he's slept through the arrival of an ice storm.

He replaces the snow in the entrance and frees his

arms. He prepares more food and, leaning back against one of the fallen trees, considers his next move. He eyes his backpack and makes a mental list of his armory. It doesn't fill him with optimism. Thurston's good but he's not Superman. Even if the little show he put on with the Jeep worked, Thurston doesn't think many of the men at the compound will have been spooked enough to leave. He's hopelessly outgunned and, even if they don't try and find him, he won't last too long out here. All Miller has to do is wait it out.

Which means Thurston's got to even up the odds. He thinks back to previous situations and comes up with one word.

Lasqa.

CHAPTER 59

EVERY MAN'S GOT A breaking point.

For Cody Thurston it came on June 16, 2007, in Lasqa, Orūzgān Province, southern Afghanistan. Along with neighboring Helmand and Kandahar, Orūzgān stands right at the beating black heart of the Taliban.

Bandit country.

Thurston's unit is there under Dutch command as part of the International Security Assistance Force during the battle for Lasqa, a town of some five thousand war-weary souls. The Taliban, seeing Lasqa as a key tactical access point, have taken control of the town in brutal fashion, commandeering civilian homes and farms and exacting brutal vengeance on anyone who resists. The police commander of Tander Station is forced to watch his wife's hands being cut off before he is beheaded. Civilians are given weapons and told by the Taliban: fight with us or be executed.

Thurston's team is instructed to establish a checkpoint a kilometer from town and not to engage. Radio chatter soon tells the Australians that the Dutch and Afghani troops inside the town are in a dogfight.

"This is fucked," says Dobbs, Thurston's unit's comms officer. Dobbs is exchanging intel with an interpreter with the Dutch forward force. "They want us in. It's a bloodbath and we're out here checking license plates."

Thurston says nothing. What is there to say? Dobbs is right: this is another fucked situation in a fucked-up place.

Later, the unit hears the Taliban have begun using a school as an ammo dump with the kids still inside so the Dutch and the Afghanis can't call in air strikes. In the school, the Taliban behead children who do attempt an escape as a lesson to those remaining. On his break, back in the Hummer, Thurston listens to the children's screams for longer than he can stand.

He checks his ammunition and leaves the Hummer, heading for the small rise that doubles as a field latrine before he cuts back north toward the town. As he sees things, something needs to be done. A career soldier to his fingertips, Thurston simply cannot sit back and wait as children get slaughtered. Every step he takes toward the school is a step away from his life as a soldier. There'll be no way back after this even if he survives. But, since that's the least likely option tonight, Thurston doesn't give it much thought.

Thurston knows the Taliban fighters didn't walk to the school. They will have arrived in vehicles and it is these vehicles he intends to find.

After ten minutes, Thurston comes across a marketplace some three hundred yards from the school where eight Toyota pickup trucks are hidden under cover of the dilapidated stalls. Thurston notes only two guards, one on either side, and he kills both by slitting their throats. He opens the gas tanks of all the vehicles and sets them on fire.

Thurston runs back to the school and waits. Less than a minute has gone by before ten or so men exit. Thurston finds a side window and slips inside. In the main hallway are four Taliban fighters at the windows of the school with two or three more standing at the entrance to a back room. Eighty or so children sit in a tight knot in the center, some of them sobbing. On the fringes of the hall are the discarded bodies of eight or nine executed children. Blood spatters the walls.

Thurston opens fire and kills every man standing in a spray of gunfire lasting less than five seconds.

He shouts and points at the door and the children run without speaking. As they disperse into the night to find whatever safety they can, Thurston takes a grenade and lobs it into a back room stacked with ammunition cases and weapons.

He runs.

Fifteen minutes later he's back at the checkpoint and his military career is over.

CHAPTER 60

DONNO—JAY DONOFRIO, ONE of Miller's two remaining lieutenants—is in a room in a small office block tacked onto the rear of the main house. This office is the security hub at the compound and is where the CCTV monitors are housed. Half of Donofrio's crew of twelve are actively patrolling the inner perimeter while the others rest. Donofrio is fighting a losing battle with the ice to maintain the security cameras. The storm has already knocked out more than a third and others are falling by the minute. Donofrio watches the screens go blank.

"Shit." He picks up his radio and updates Carver. Carver's in control of the area around the three sheds containing the fermentation tanks that combine the dextrose and benzaldehyde into pseudoephedrine.

"If he comes in to you I can't give you a heads-up," says Donofrio. "We're blind down here."

"If he's coming in through this shit, I'm a China-man," says Carver. "This storm's kicking up a coupla notches out here."

Carver pockets his radio and turns the corner of Shed 1 into the teeth of the wind.

"Jesus H. Christ," he mutters as ice rattles into his face. He tightens his goggles and the hood of his parka. Up ahead he sees two of his crew on the facing corner. Carver looks out at the icebound forest beyond the fermentation sheds and wonders if the Australian can possibly be still alive.

CHAPTER 61

THURSTON, WEARING LAYER UPON layer of high-quality thermal protection, huddles in the lee of a big pine and watches the guy near the closest shed put the radio back in his pocket. Despite what Carver is thinking, Thurston is doing just fine. He wouldn't like to bet how long he'd last if this becomes a drawn-out battle but Thurston has no intention of letting that happen.

Thurston notes Carver looking thoughtfully at a fence post that houses a security camera. The camera itself is covered in glaze ice and Thurston is betting most, if not all, surveillance cameras protecting the compound are out of action.

Thurston steps out of his cover and walks toward the fence. Wearing white, in near whiteout conditions, he is a ghost.

A heavily armed and well-trained ghost.

By the time he's reached the fence, Thurston is less than twenty yards from the corner of the shed. He's watched Carver's patrols enough to know two men are

441

working each section, the first man some ten yards in front of the other.

Which means that the corner of the shed is an opportunity. Thurston puts a bolt into the crossbow and readies the second.

He waits, forcing himself to concentrate. When the first guy comes around he'll only get a few seconds.

After a couple of minutes, the first sentry comes into view. Thurston lets him come around the corner and puts a bolt into his chest. The guy slumps to the snow. Thurston pulls back the bow-string and slots in the second bolt. As he's coming up, the second sentry comes into view, sees the body on the snow, and begins to lift his weapon.

Thurston shoots him in the head with the second bolt. The entire exchange has taken place in complete silence.

Thurston runs back to the forest and pries a fallen log out of the snow. He hauls it back to the fence and throws it against the wire. As he suspected, the fence is no longer electrified. With the power at the compound now on a generator there's not enough juice in the system to run what they need and keep the fence on. Thurston pulls out a pair of wire cutters and cuts a gap in the fence. He pushes through and runs to the corner of Shed 1. From here he can see Sheds 2 and 3 looking like blurred paper cutouts through the ice storm. The ice is now coming in almost horizontally. Thurston battles his way across the open space to Shed 2. When the sentries come around he kills them both—

the first with the crossbow, the second with his hunting knife. At Shed 3 he repeats the process.

According to his calculations there's still one guy remaining: the guy with the radio. Thurston has him pegged as the boss of this crew but there's no way of telling where he is now. Thurston can't wait. He finds a door leading into Shed 3 and slides it back on its track.

Inside, Thurston pushes back his goggles and takes a breath. At first he thinks there is someone moving inside the vast space but realizes it is the storm lashing the tin walls.

Six gleaming steel vats stand in a row down the center of the shed. A low electric hum sits under the sound of the wind.

Thurston takes off his backpack from which he removes three aerosols of hairspray and a small tin of lighter fluid. He places an aerosol under three of the vats and opens the valves. An acrid stench begins to fill the shed. Thurston squirts the lighter fluid around the base of the aerosols. He flicks a lighter and moves down the shed setting a flame to the lighter fluid.

Thurston exits the shed and runs straight into Carver.

CHAPTER 62

"WE GOT A RUNNER," says Anders.

Miller gets up off his chair and joins Anders at the window overlooking the lake.

One of the compound girls, wearing jeans and a parka, is slipping and sliding across the frozen lake moving away from the house.

"That dumb bitch ain't gonna make it," says Miller.

"You want me to fetch her back?"

Miller shakes his head. "Fuck her."

He and Anders watch the girl get swallowed by the whiteness. It's a three-mile hike across to Talbot on a good day. In this storm, dressed like she is, the girl will be dead before the hour.

"We shouldn't be sitting back and waiting," says Anders. The big man lumbers across to the bar and pours a bourbon. Miller taps out a line of coke on the marble and hoovers it up greedily. He's been getting increasingly wired with each passing hour of inactivity.

"I don't like it any more than you, Axe," says Miller. "But we—"

Miller stops speaking midsentence as a gunshot sounds from somewhere outside. Miller looks toward Anders and then three explosions come in quick succession sending a shock wave rippling across the compound.

"I guess he's here," growls Anders. He smiles and reaches for his gun. "Rock and roll!"

"You dumb shit," snarls Miller. "That bastard's blown the sheds!"

CHAPTER 63

FOR A BIG GUY, Carver moves quick. Almost too quick.

The muzzle of his assault rifle cuts upward toward Thurston in a vicious arc that would have broken Thurston's jaw if he hadn't managed to step inside Carver's blow and drive the heel of his hand hard into the man's nose.

Blood flashes through the air and Carver howls like a bastard. Thurston snaps the rifle out of the man's hands but it spills from his hands and skitters across the ice out of reach.

Thurston takes a step back to give himself room and reaches for his knife. As his fingers close around the handle, Carver recovers his senses enough to come roaring back at Thurston like a grizzly with its tail on fire. Carver traps Thurston's hand inside his parka and wraps a meaty forearm around the Australian's throat. Thurston takes a step back that fractionally unbalances Carver. Using his attacker's weight against him, Thurston dips a shoulder and in one fluid twist, flips Carver over.

As Carver tumbles through the icy air, a trailing boot catches Thurston a glancing blow on the side of his head. Both Carver and Thurston slam to the ice. For a second or so the two men lie still.

Carver's the first one to move.

He rolls over and scrambles for his weapon. His gloved fingers close around the trigger as he sits up to bring the weapon to bear on the still dazed Thurston.

Behind the two men, Shed 3 explodes.

Carver, his body forming a barrier between Thurston and the worst of the explosion, is sliced clean in two by a twisted sheet of flaming metal. Thurston feels a flash of searing heat before everything turns black.

CHAPTER 64

AFTER FINDING THE SIX dead from Carver's crew and seeing Shed 3 going up in flames, three of Donofrio's crew have had enough. They take off in one of the compound Hummers. With the road to East Talbot impassable, they head across the lake.

Donofrio is making his way across to the two remaining sheds when he sees the taillights fading into the storm just as Miller and Anders emerge from the main house heading toward what's left of Shed 3. Donofrio stops in his tracks.

He's loyal to Miller—he's got a slice of the action and, truth be told, it's been pretty sweet so far—but this situation is way beyond messed up. Miller's been holed up in the house snorting coke for what seems like days. He's acting like he's running an army but the fact is his army is now down to less than six. As tight as Miller might be with the local cops, something on this scale will be investigated once the ice storm stops. Unless Miller gets very lucky, there'll be feds crawling all over Isle de Rousse before the weekend.

It's time to call it.

Donofrio gets out his radio and brings his three remaining guys in.

Let Miller and Anders duke it out with whoever this guy is. The Australian might not be this supernatural Chenoo deal but Donofrio knows one thing: he ain't normal.

CHAPTER 65

NICK TERRAVERDI MAKES IT to East Talbot around five. If he hadn't already been in Hanover he wouldn't have attempted the journey. As it was he'd skidded off the road more times than he cared to think about.

Still, he had to come. If this is what he knows it is—that little adventure Cody Thurston had told him about back in New York—then he needs to be there to stop this from turning into another fucking Waco.

In the entrance to the police station Terraverdi finds Bernie Slater, the Robbery / Homicide guy who'd called Boston about the three dead bodies at the Top o' the Lake Motel. A friend at Boston who knew the Russians' link to organized crime had called the FBI. Since Delamenko and his boys crossed several state lines this was a fed case. Terraverdi had pulled a couple of favors to be the one assigned.

"So what's the situation?" says Terraverdi after the preliminaries.

Slater's a thirty-year vet. He moves slow but

Terraverdi wouldn't like to be on the wrong side of him. Like most state cops he's not given to warmth when it comes to the FBI but Terraverdi's seen worse.

"I was in the motel," says Slater. "With a friend." He looks at Terraverdi, who says nothing. "Okay, well, like I say, I was there with a friend. Then this shit happened and I come out to see three bodies. Two in the corridor and one in the bedroom. The woman had been shot—something automatic, large caliber. The first guy had a fuckin' crossbow bolt through his fuckin' head…"

"Jesus," says Terraverdi.

"That ain't the kicker. The second guy? The one in 205? He's taken one in the balls and one in the noggin from a nail gun."

"A nail gun?"

Slater nods. "Uh-huh." He glances toward the station office where Riggs is sitting at a desk. "The asswipe there, Riggs: he's the local sheriff. He told me these guys must have been passing through. Can you believe that shit? Three connected Russians from Southie take a fuckin' winter break up here and wind up dead."

"Three?"

"Oh," says Slater, "I forgot that part. There's a witness who saw a third guy get whacked in the parking lot. From my experience? I'm saying he's Viktor Delamenko. Anyway, this Delamenko was already wounded—I'm guessing nail gun—and jumped outta the bedroom window. Our wit says another guy put one in Viktor's head and took him away in the back of a Jeep. You ever heard anything like that?"

He's about to reply to Slater when a muffled boom echoes across Lake Carlson.

"Christ Almighty!" says Slater. "What was that?"

Terraverdi sighs.

Thurston, you motherfucker.

CHAPTER 66

THURSTON OPENS HIS EYES and sees nothing except white.

He blinks a few times, raises his head, and slowly the world reassembles. Light and sound and smell rush in.

Behind him, Shed 3 burns, the flames ripped diagonally away from where he is lying in the snow—a few degrees different and he'd have been toast.

Thurston pushes what remains of Carver off him and staggers upright. Thurston's goggles are gone and parts of his weatherproof parka look like someone took a cheese grater to them, but there doesn't appear to be any major physical damage: a cut to his head and a ringing in one ear. Right now, Thurston's more concerned about his weapons.

The Remington is screwed. The same goes for the crossbow, which lies in a tangled mess about three yards away. Thurston finds Carver's weapon but it too is hopelessly damaged.

Thurston starts moving toward the main house as fire takes hold of Shed 2. Once that went it's only a matter of time before Shed 1 completes the set. Thurston keeps to what cover he can find and makes his way down to the lake shore.

The house looks deserted as Thurston approaches from the lake. Coming up under the extended deck he forces a side window and slips inside. Thurston moves through the house room by room, becoming increasingly confident the place is deserted. It looks like the tactic he'd used back in Afghanistan has worked, driving out the enemy from their stronghold. If it hadn't been for running slap into Carver he'd have been picking off Miller and Anders right now. Thurston takes a large knife from the kitchen and puts it in his pocket: it's not much but it'll have to do.

In the basement, Thurston comes across a metal door that looks like somewhere Miller might keep weapons. Thurston slowly turns the lock and pushes the door open.

It's not an armory. It's a dungeon.

The walls are painted black with a low red vinyl couch running along one side of the room. Various sadomasochistic items are dotted here and there on the bare concrete floor. A large-screen TV sits on one wall.

Huddled on the red couch are three teenage girls dressed in skimpy clothes. They look terrified and Thurston can't blame them. He is an apparition from Hell. Blood from the cut on his head has run down to form a grisly red mask over one side of his face.

His blood- and smoke-scarred parka hangs in tattered strips down his back.

Thurston approaches the girls and bends low. They scrabble back away from him like startled birds as he approaches.

"I'm not here to hurt you," he whispers, holding his hands up. "But you have to listen to me if you want to get out of here alive, okay?"

There's no response but Thurston carries on. "Are there any more of you in the house?"

They look at each other and then the youngest of them nods.

"Mercy's somewhere upstairs," she says.

"Mercy?"

"She's his favorite," says another girl.

"Miller's?"

"Uh-huh. Yeah. But she done something wrong. Spoke back to him or sump'n, I dunno. Nate don't like anyone speakin' back to him. He's got her up in punishment."

Miller frowns. "Punishment?"

The girl raises her eyes to the ceiling. "In the storeroom."

Thurston stands. "I'm going to get Mercy, okay? You stay here until I come back. I'm going to get you out of here."

As he leaves the dungeon Thurston looks back. None of the girls look like they believe him.

CHAPTER 67

THE PSEUDOEPHEDRINE IN THE three sheds would be worth something north of two hundred million dollars once it's channeled into Europe via Reykjavik. With Shed 3 gone already, Miller's looking at being wiped out if the others follow.

Which they do.

Miller and Anders are less than fifty yards from Shed 2 when it blows. The shock wave knocks them flat on their asses and, before they can get to their feet, Shed 1 erupts, sending a second monstrous fireball up into the steely sky. The air fills with the stench of burning chemicals as glowing embers are whipped away on the wind, mingling with the snow and ice.

Miller staggers to his feet and, peering through the storm, contemplates the ruins of his empire. Next to him, Anders, brushing splinters of metal from his sleeve, remains silent.

Miller's head sinks to his chest and remains there for a while. When it comes up again his eyes glow with a dull red hate.

"Get everyone together," he says, the words rumbling like thunder. "I'm going to skin this motherfucker."

"There ain't no one, Nate." Anders brushes splinters of metal from his sleeve and turns his face away from the wind. "They've gone, man. Every last one of 'em."

Miller turns to face the giant. "And you? You thinking of lightin' out too like all the other pussies? Because, if you are, then be my guest."

Anders's face clouds. He steps closer to Miller and jabs a finger in his boss's chest. "I'm still here, aren't I?" he growls. "And don't forget, *Nate,* I was in for ten percent of the product we just watched go up in smoke. You ain't the only one who's suffering here."

Miller holds up a placatory hand. "Yeah, okay, I know." He turns away from Anders and stalks back toward the main house. "Let's go kill that fuckin' Australian."

CHAPTER 68

THURSTON PAUSES ON THE second-floor landing.

At first, all he can hear is the muffled rattle of ice hitting the walls of the property. The sound rises and falls with the wind.

But then Thurston picks up another noise he can't quite identify. He moves toward a door at the end of a corridor and the sound crystallizes into something human. The sound of crying.

Thurston opens the door cautiously.

The room is some kind of storage space, one wall lined with metal shelving stacked high with cardboard boxes, cleaning products, and household items. It's cold.

Chained to a radiator against one wall is a young girl wearing nothing but a bra and the padlocked dog collar connecting one end of her chain to the radiator. Bruises stand out angrily on her pale skin and one of her eyes is caked in dried blood. She shivers uncontrollably, both knees drawn high, arms wrapped tightly around her shins.

At the sight of Thurston, she shrinks back against the radiator. Thurston takes off his tattered parka and wraps it round her.

"What's your name?" he says.

The girl tries to speak but her teeth are chattering so much that Thurston has to lean in close.

"M-M-M-Mer-Mercy," she stammers.

"I'll try and get you out of here, Mercy," says Thurston. He turns his attention to the collar but the thing is solid.

"You know where the key is?" he asks. Mercy shakes her head. She points a trembling finger at the door.

"Miller's got it?"

She nods, her eyes widening at the name.

"Does he have weapons in the house?" says Thurston.

Before the girl can say anything, from downstairs comes the sound of a door opening and closing. Mercy flashes a look of pure terror in Thurston's direction.

Someone's in the house.

He signals for Mercy to stay quiet and moves toward the door.

Mercy has a strange look on her face that Thurston can't figure out. Then, too late, he realizes what she's doing: making a calculation about her survival chances. A calculation coming down heavily on the side of Nate Miller.

"Here!" she screams. "Up here! He's here!"

Thurston can't blame her. She's a child. Besides,

with things as they are, Miller might *be* the kid's best option. Unarmed and trapped upstairs, his own chances don't look too good right now.

Leaving Mercy screaming, Thurston moves into the corridor and sprints toward the stairs. Looking over the landing rail he sees Miller coming up, holding a shotgun.

Thurston jerks his head back in the nick of time.

A blast from Miller's gun punches a hole in the ceiling, the round passing so close to Thurston's face he can feel the heat. Thurston runs past the storage room to the window and slides the sash up. He's looking out at a high sloping roof extending out over the deck. Behind him he hears Miller clattering up the stairs.

Thurston launches himself through the window as another shotgun blast shatters the glass. He hits the roof and rolls out of control toward the guttering. Thurston tries to grip something but the glaze ice makes it an impossibility and he skids out into space.

For a split second Thurston hangs in the air and then slams, back first, onto the padded cover of the hot tub six yards below.

It saves his life.

The cover splits and Thurston feels the air pushed out of his lungs as he drops into the water. He pushes up and scrambles over the side as Miller gets a bead on him from the upper window. A blast splinters the edge of the hot tub and Thurston slithers across the iced-up deck, his breath rasping as he desperately tries to get oxygen back into his lungs.

"He's on the deck!" yells Miller, and Thurston glimpses Anders at the fold-back doors.

Anders is holding a US Special Ops M4A1 assault rifle. It's a big gun but looks like a toy in the giant's hands. Slung under the barrel is an M203 40mm grenade launcher.

Thurston jumps off the deck as Anders fires the grenade.

Behind Thurston the hot tub and deck railing disappear and Thurston feels a sharp pain in his thigh. As he slides helplessly down toward the lake he sees a huge shard of fiberglass embedded in his leg.

After sliding fifty or sixty yards, Thurston hits the lake and skids three yards more before coming to a halt, the blood from his leg wound tracing a smear across the ice.

He staggers to his feet and begins moving as quickly as he can. Anders reaches the edge of the deck and starts firing. Thurston zigzags as the bullets tear into the thick ice. Now Thurston hears a second blast and realizes that Miller has joined Anders at the deck edge. At this range, Thurston knows he's a difficult target and he pushes forward, ignoring the pain. Every yard is a yard closer to safety.

The shooting stops and Thurston glances back to see Miller and Anders clambering down toward the lake. With eight inches of plastic buried in Thurston's leg, he knows they're going to gain on him once they get onto the lake.

He needs an edge.

CHAPTER 69

"WE GET HIM ALIVE," says Miller. "I want this bastard to suffer."

He and Anders are tracking Thurston across the lake. It's not difficult. Thurston's wound is leaving a trail anyone could follow.

"He's heading north," says Anders. "Maybe he's planning on getting into the woods."

"He ain't gonna make it that far," says Miller and points. About a hundred yards ahead, Thurston lies on the ice.

"Go get him," says Miller. "Drag him back to the house. Have us a party."

"My pleasure," says Anders. He shoulders his rifle and unhooks the axe from the pouch on his belt. "He might be missing an arm or two."

"Fine with me, man," says Miller. He takes out a cigarette and bends away from the wind. "Just bring him back still breathing. We owe this cocksucker."

Anders walks toward Thurston, the axe swinging easy at his side.

He's going to enjoy this.

CHAPTER 70

AS ANDERS APPROACHES, THURSTON forces himself to remain still. For this to work the guy has to be close.

Thurston's using an old spec ops "fishing" tactic with himself as bait. He hasn't picked this part of the lake by chance. Less than fifty yards to Thurston's right lies the marshy estuary area that forms one of the northern boundaries to the compound.

The lake ice here is thinner. Much thinner. Thurston has edged as close as he dares to where the thick ice gives way to the thinner skein put in place by the ice storm. Lying on his back, Thurston hears it creaking below him like the deck of an old wooden ship.

Anders is about twenty yards from Thurston when he hears the first crack. He turns and sees a slice of black water opening behind him like a devil's smile. Miller, some thirty yards farther back, sees it, too, and begins to back away.

Anders stops, unsure of what to do. He slowly takes his assault rifle off his back and takes aim at Thurston.

The ice shifts and Anders almost falls. With his arms windmilling as he tries to regain balance, the M4A1 slips from his fingers and disappears into the water. Thurston twists and swivels around to face Anders. As the ice disintegrates, Anders sprints hard toward the Australian, his axe raised high.

Thurston gets ready.

He's gambled on Anders's greater weight being enough to break the ice and drop him into the lake.

It isn't working: Anders is closing in fast.

Behind him, black water cracks open at a frightening rate but Anders is still closing in. Thurston gets to his feet and picks up the knife. With the storm whipping across the lake, Thurston balances the blade and waits. He doesn't want this to become a hand-to-hand fight.

When Anders is less than three yards away, Thurston takes his shot. Bending on one knee he throws the knife and hits Anders high in the chest.

And does precisely nothing.

Anders brings down the axe in a vicious swing that, if it connected, would have taken Thurston's arm off. Instead, the blade slices through fabric, grazing Thurston's flesh on the way through. Thurston steps in close and grabs the handle of the knife sticking out of Anders's chest. The man screams but before Thurston can stab him, the ice below their feet shatters into a thousand pieces and both men plunge into the dark water.

The water is impossibly, ridiculously cold: a cold so

profound and bone-numbingly shocking in intensity that, for a few seconds, Thurston finds it difficult to think.

Anders, gripping Thurston's arms tightly, wears an expression of grim satisfaction as the two men sink. There's nothing Thurston can do—no way of getting out of Anders's death hold…and Anders knows it. He has the muscle to keep Thurston underwater. All he has to do is wait and let this Australian motherfucker sink to the bottom.

From Axel Anders's point of view, there's only one problem, and it's a big one: not only is Cody Thurston a Special Forces–trained free diver, and the most stubborn individual in the northern hemisphere, under all this padding he's wearing a nine-millimeter-thick wet suit.

The bald fact is that he can wait this out longer than Anders ever can.

Almost thirty seconds elapses before it dawns on Anders that the passive Thurston seems more comfortable than someone should be in his situation. The realization hits the giant like a punch in the face. His eyes widen and Thurston sees the first stream of panicked air bubbles escape the big man's nostrils. In an instant, instinct takes over. Anders releases Thurston and scrambles wildly toward the surface.

Thurston has other ideas.

He reaches out and grabs hold of Anders's ankle, preventing him from swimming. He doesn't need to stop Anders from moving, just from moving quickly.

Now in full-blown panic, Anders thrashes wildly, arms flailing, vital oxygen bubbling from his lungs, his brain unable to compute what is happening. Gradually his movements slow and then, as the last scrap of oxygen leaves his body, Anders's brain shuts down and his body relaxes as he dies.

Thurston releases him, kicks for the surface, and hits the solid ice lying on top of Lake Carlson like a coffin lid.

Shit.

They must have drifted farther than Thurston had thought. He desperately punches the ice but it's no use. Fighting his own rising panic, Thurston wastes precious seconds trying to find the hole in the ice, but comes up short. This isn't like Pakistan when he could stay down nine minutes. In this water, after wrestling with Anders and with eight inches of hot tub plastic jammed in his leg, Thurston's lucky if he has thirty seconds left.

And then he remembers the knife sticking out of Anders's chest.

He pushes down hard, the cold sucking feeling from his fingers. He doesn't have much time left. *Tick tock.*

With his heart rate slowing to cryogenic levels and his adrenaline screaming off the charts, Thurston finds Anders and the knife. As the last of his breath dribbles from his lungs, Thurston hauls the blade free and powers up toward the surface driving the blade as hard as he can into the underside of the ice.

CHAPTER 71

IF ANYTHING, THE STORM'S getting worse.

Miller retreats farther onto solid ice away from the gaping black mouth that had swallowed Anders and the Australian. The open water slices across the lake and curves around Miller, preventing him from going in a direct line back to the house.

He's in no real danger—the ice out here is strong enough to take a truck—but it's going to be a long, cold walk back, especially if the threatened whiteout materializes.

Miller keeps the spot where the two men disappeared in view but so much time has passed he's sure now both men are dead. Still, he waits longer. There've been too many surprises with this Australian fuck.

Eventually, Miller shoulders his weapon and, hunching his shoulders into the teeth of the icy wind, begins the walk back to what's left of his compound through the thickening white spindrift.

He has taken only two paces when he hears an odd crunching sound coming from behind him.

Miller turns to see a knife splinter upward through the ice.

"What the fuck…?" mutters Miller. He swings his gun back around and squints through the snow.

The arm vanishes and then comes back up again, this time followed by another arm and Thurston's head. Miller starts moving toward him as Thurston hauls himself up and out onto the thicker ice. Shivering violently, he crawls to safety and staggers to his feet just as Miller closes in.

CHAPTER 72

"YOU'RE ONE HARD SON of a bitch to kill, Crocodile Dundee," says Miller, pointing the ugly snout of his rifle directly at Thurston's head. "I'll give you that. Now drop the knife, chief, and kick it this way."

Thurston looks at Miller.

"Don't," says Miller. "I know you're thinking about throwing the knife but I have to say you got no—"

Before Miller can react, Thurston throws the knife but it slips from his trembling fingers and skitters harmlessly to Miller's feet.

Miller laughs. "Fuckin' awesome! Some primo James fuckin' Bond shit right there!" He raises the rifle sight to his eye and takes five or six steps forward. "I was planning to get you somewheres quiet and go to work on you for a day or two...y'know, get some 'closure' on this giant clusterfuck. But, shit, it's just getting too goddamn cold so I reckon I'll just blow your cocksuckin' Australian brains out right here."

"Y-you t-t-talk t-too much," Thurston manages to say.

"Oh, r-r-really?" says Miller, and pulls the trigger.

Nothing happens.

He pulls again…and nothing.

Both men realize at the same instant what has happened: the plunging temperatures out here on Lake Carlson have frozen the mechanism on Miller's rifle.

Thurston starts running at Miller as the American throws his rifle to one side and bends to pick up the knife. Miller comes up with it in his right hand and backs off warily as Thurston approaches, the two men moving in slow circles around one another. The spindrift has now developed into the threatened whiteout and Miller and Thurston are the only moving elements in an icy universe. The lake shore vanishes as north, west, south, and east become indistinguishable.

"*Star T-Trek,*" says Thurston.

"What?" says Miller.

"*Star Trek.* There's al-w-ways a-a scene where K-Kirk battles some fuckugly a-alien, y'know? I'm Kirk, b-by th-the way."

Miller charges, the knife slashing viciously through the air but this isn't Miller's game. Thurston dances out of his way and smashes an elbow hard into the side of Miller's head as he passes. The American grunts but keeps slashing with the blade. An image of Mercy chained to the radiator flashes into Thurston's mind and he feels a fresh wave of anger surge through his frozen body. He steps in and breaks Miller's right arm with a pile-driving heel stamp. Miller screams and drops the knife as Thurston whips around with a second kick that pops the American's kneecap.

Miller drops to the ice, his right arm hanging at a sickening angle. Thurston hits him hard in the ribs before driving a short jab into Miller's face, which puts him on his back. Thurston takes the knife and stands above the beaten man, breathing heavily.

Miller groans and tries to stand but can't. The effort puts pressure on his broken limbs and he screams again. He pukes and lies back on the ice looking up at Thurston through teeth ringed with blood.

"You broke my fuckin' arm, man," Miller spits. "Why'd you break my fuckin' arm?"

"L-Lasqa," says Thurston.

"What? What the fuck is Lasqa?"

"A place in Afghanistan, M-Miller. Had a lot of little k-kids there, kids not much younger than the g-girls you got up in that N-Nazi sewer of yours. Let's call the arm p-payback for Lasqa, and the knee for all the shit you d-did to the girls."

Thurston steps closer and stands on Miller's nuts. As Miller writhes, Thurston bends close. "That's for Sofi," he hisses. Thurston steps away and in a quick twisting motion breaks Miller's left arm. Miller howls.

"And th-that's for Barb Connors, you piece of shit."

Thurston stands over Miller and waits for him to stop sobbing.

"What now, smartass?" Miller coughs. "You can kill me but sure as shit you'll freeze to death before you make it back to the fuckin' house, genius. So go ahead, fuckin' do it."

Thurston shakes his head. "You g-got it all back to front, M-Miller. I'm not g-going to kill you."

Miller looks puzzled and Thurston smiles.

"I'm going to rob you."

CHAPTER 73

"MOTHERFUCKER! MOTHER*FUCKER!*"

Miller's agonized screams are muffled by the relentless wind and snow. The blood and snot around his nose begins to freeze solid. His black hair is quickly being covered with a frosting of ice crystals.

Thurston adjusts the zip on the parka he'd taken from Miller and settles Miller's goggles across his eyes.

"This is some grade-A gear you got, Miller," says Thurston. He waggles the fingers of the gloves and looks down at the snow boots. "Toasty."

Miller, shivering helplessly on the ice, is naked except for a pair of boxer shorts.

"I'm only leaving those shitstained drawers on you because I don't want to see your shriveled little pecker, Miller," says Thurston. "That's the kind of shit you can't unsee."

From somewhere out in the whiteness, sirens wail. Thurston bends, his face close to Miller, and drops his voice.

"I guess even out here an explosion that big will have attracted attention. Or maybe one of your loyal little Nazi soldiers blabbed. Or, and this is the option I'm going for, maybe it's my old buddy, Nicky Terraverdi at the FBI, coming to make sure your little pet, Riggs, didn't sweep all this under the carpet? Either way, you are done, Miller. You shouldn't have killed Sofi or Barb."

Miller's mouth opens but no sound emerges.

Thurston holds his eyes on Miller's. The sirens are closer now. Miller's heart tolls like a funeral bell as snow settles on his skin. He listens to the sound of his own last breath, his life dissolving into nothing under the cold flat stare of the Australian.

Thurston waits until he is sure Miller is dead and then, using the rifle as a lever, stands with some difficulty. He'll have to get the splinter in his leg removed when he reaches civilization. There's a medic in Burlington who Thurston can trust. It'll be the last time Cody Thurston calls in an old favor because Cody Thurston will be left out on Lake Carlson, along with Michael Flanagan, both as dead as Nate Miller.

But there'll be other names, and other towns. The world's a big place with plenty of dark corners and an adaptable guy like him can always find work. There'll be somewhere.

Limping, the Australian walks away from the closing sirens toward the welcoming spindrift whipped up by the ice storm. In ten yards, he's nothing more than a gray silhouette, a ghost.

And then, in ten more, he is gone.

**A deadly conspiracy is working against
Detective Lindsay Boxer and soon she could
be the one on trial...**

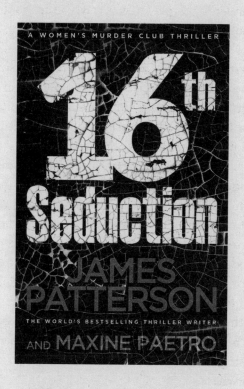

A WOMEN'S MURDER CLUB THRILLER

16th
Seduction

JAMES PATTERSON

THE WORLD'S BESTSELLING THRILLER WRITER

AND MAXINE PAETRO

Read on for an extract.

THAT MUGGY MORNING in July my partner, Rich Conklin, and I were on stakeout in the Tenderloin, one of San Francisco's sketchiest, most crime-ridden neighborhoods. We had parked our 1998 gray Chevy sedan where we had a good view of the six-story apartment building on the corner of Leavenworth and Turk.

It's been said that watching paint dry is high entertainment compared with being on stakeout, but this was the exception to the rule.

We were psyched and determined.

We had just been assigned to a counterterrorism task force reporting back to Warren Jacobi, chief of police, and also Dean Reardon, deputy director of Homeland Security, based in DC.

This task force had been formed to address a local threat

3

by a global terrorist group known as GAR, which had claimed credit for six sequential acts of mass terrorism in the last five days.

They were equal-ethnicity bombers, hitting three holy places—a mosque, a cathedral, and a synagogue—as well as two universities and an airport, killing over nine hundred people of all ages and nationalities in six countries.

As we understood it, GAR (Great Antiestablishment Reset) had sprung from the rubble of Middle Eastern terror groups. Several surviving leaders had swept up young dissidents around the globe, including significant numbers of zealots from Western populations who'd come of age after the digital revolution.

The identities of these killers were undetectable within their home populations, since GAR's far-flung membership hid their activities inside the dark web, an internet underground perfect for gathering without meeting.

Still, they killed real people in real life.

And then they bragged.

After a year of burning, torturing, and blowing up innocent victims, GAR published their mission statement. They planned to infiltrate every country and bring down organized religion and governments and authorities of all types. Without a known supreme commander or national hub to target, blocking this open-source terrorism had been as effective as grasping poison gas in your hand.

Because of GAR's unrelenting murderous activities, San Francisco, like most large cities, was on high alert on that Fourth of July weekend.

Conklin and I had been told very little about our assignment, only that one of the presumed GAR operatives, known to us as J., had recently vaulted to the number one spot on our government's watch list.

Over the last few days J. had been spotted going in and out of the dun-colored tenement on the corner of Turk and Leavenworth, the one with laddered fire escapes on two sides and a lone tree growing out of the pavement beside the front door.

Our instructions were to watch for him. If we saw him, we were to report his activities by radio, even as eyes in the skies were on this intersection from an AFB in Nevada or Arizona or Washington, DC.

It was a watch-only assignment, and when a male figure matching the grainy image we had—of a bearded man, five foot nine, hat shading his face—left the dun-colored apartment building, we took note.

When this character crossed to our side of the street and got into a white refrigerator van parked in front of the T.L. Market and Deli, we phoned it in.

Conklin and I have been partners for so many years and can almost read each other's minds. We exchanged a look and knew that we couldn't just *watch* a suspected terrorist pull out into our streets without doing something about it.

I said, "Following is watching."

Rich said, "Just a second, Lindsay. Okay?"

His conversation with the deputy was short. Rich gave me the thumbs-up and I started up the car. We pulled out two car lengths behind the white van driven by a presumed high-level terrorist known as J.

I EDGED OUR sharklike Chevy along Turk and turned left on Hyde, keeping just far enough behind J.'s van to stay out of his rearview while keeping an eye on him. After following him through a couple of turns, I lost the van at a stoplight on Tenth Street. I had to make a split-second decision whether or not to run the light.

My decision was *Go.*

My hands were sweating on the wheel as I shot through the intersection and was blasted by a cacophony of horns, which called attention to us. I didn't enjoy that at all.

Conklin said, "There he is."

The white van was hemmed in by other vehicles traveling at something close to the speed limit. I kept it in our sights from a good distance behind the pack. And then the van merged into US Route 101 South toward San Jose.

The highway was a good, wide road with enough traffic to ensure that J. would never pick our Chevy out of the flow.

Conklin worked the radio communications, deftly switching channels between chief of police Warren Jacobi and DHS deputy director Dean Reardon, who was three time zones away. Dispatch kept us updated on the movements of other units in our task force that were now part of a staggered caravan weaving between lanes, taking turns at stepping on the gas, then falling back.

We followed J.'s van under the sunny glare on 101 South, and after twelve miles, instead of heading down to San Jose and the Central Coast, he took the lane that funneled traffic to SFO.

Conklin had Jacobi on the line.

"Chief, he's heading toward SFO."

Several voices crackled over the radio, but I kept visual contact with the man in the van that was moving steadily toward San Francisco International Airport.

That van was now the most frightening vehicle imaginable. GAR had sensitized all of us to worst-case scenarios, and a lot of explosives could be packed into a vehicle of that size. A terrorist wouldn't have to get on a plane or even walk into an airline terminal. I could easily imagine J. crashing his vehicle through luggage check-in and ramming the plate-glass windows before setting off a bomb.

Conklin had signed off with Jacobi and now said to me, "Lindsay, SFO security has sent fire trucks and construction vehicles out to obstruct traffic on airport access roads in all directions."

Good.

I stepped on the gas and flipped on the sirens. Behind us, others in our team did the same, and I saw flashing lights getting onto the service road from the north.

Passenger cars pulled onto the shoulder to let us fly by, and within seconds we were passing J.'s van as we entered the International Departures lane.

Signs listing names of airlines appeared overhead. SFO's parking garage rose up on our right. Off-ramps and service roads circled and crossed underneath our roadway, which was now an overpass. The outline of the international terminal grew closer and larger just up ahead.

Rich and I were leading a group of cars heading to the airport when I saw cruisers heading away from the terminal right toward us.

It was a high-speed pincer movement.

J. saw what was happening and had only two choices: keep going or stop. He wrenched his wheel hard to the right and the van skidded across to the far right lane, where there was one last exit to the garage, which a hundred yards farther on had its own exit to South Link Road. The exit was open and unguarded.

I screamed to Conklin, *"Hang on!"*

I passed the white van on my right, gave the Chevy more gas, and turned the wheel hard, blocking the exit. At the last possible moment, as I was bracing for a crash, J. jerked his wheel hard left and pulled around us.

By then the airport roadway was filled with law enforcement cruisers, their lights flashing, sirens blowing.

The van screeched to a halt.

Adrenaline had sent my heart rate into the red zone, and sweat sheeted down my body.

Both my partner and I asked if the other was okay as cop cars lined up behind us and ahead of us, forming an impenetrable vehicular wall.

A security cop with a megaphone addressed J.

"Get out of the vehicle. Hands up. Get out now, buddy. No one wants to hurt you."

Would J. go ballistic?

I pictured the van going up in a fiery explosion forty feet from where I sat in an old sedan. I flashed on the image of my little girl when I saw her this morning, wearing baby-duck yellow, beating her spoon on the table. Would I ever see her again?

Just then the white van's passenger door opened and J. jumped out. A voice amplified through a bullhorn boomed, *"Don't move. Hands in the air."*

J. ignored the warning.

He ran across the four lanes and reached the concrete guardrail. He looked out over the edge. He paused.

There was nothing between him and the road below but forty feet of air.

Shots were fired.

I saw J. jump.

Rich shouted at me, *"Get down!"*

We both ducked below the dash, linked our fingers over the backs of our necks, as an explosion boomed, rocking our car, setting off the car alarm, blinding us with white light.

That sick bastard had detonated his bomb.

JAMES PATTERSON
BOOK**SHOTS**

stories at the speed of life

BOOK**SHOTS** are page-turning stories by James Patterson and other writers that can be read in one sitting.

Each and every one is fast-paced, 100% story-driven; a shot of pure entertainment guaranteed to satisfy.

Under 150 pages
Under £3

Available as new, compact paperbacks, ebooks and audio, everywhere books are sold.

For more details, visit: **www.bookshots.com**

BOOK**SHOTS**
THE ULTIMATE FORM OF STORYTELLING.
FROM THE ULTIMATE STORYTELLER.

Also by James Patterson

ALEX CROSS NOVELS

Along Came a Spider • Kiss the Girls • Jack and Jill •
Cat and Mouse • Pop Goes the Weasel • Roses are Red •
Violets are Blue • Four Blind Mice • The Big Bad Wolf •
London Bridges • Mary, Mary • Cross • Double Cross •
Cross Country • Alex Cross's Trial (*with Richard DiLallo*) •
I, Alex Cross • Cross Fire • Kill Alex Cross • Merry
Christmas, Alex Cross • Alex Cross, Run • Cross My
Heart • Hope to Die • Cross Justice • Cross the Line

THE WOMEN'S MURDER CLUB SERIES

1st to Die • 2nd Chance (*with Andrew Gross*) • 3rd Degree
(*with Andrew Gross*) • 4th of July (*with Maxine Paetro*) •
The 5th Horseman (*with Maxine Paetro*) • The 6th Target
(*with Maxine Paetro*) • 7th Heaven (*with Maxine Paetro*) •
8th Confession (*with Maxine Paetro*) • 9th Judgement (*with
Maxine Paetro*) • 10th Anniversary (*with Maxine Paetro*) •
11th Hour (*with Maxine Paetro*) • 12th of Never (*with Maxine
Paetro*) • Unlucky 13 (*with Maxine Paetro*) • 14th Deadly Sin
(*with Maxine Paetro*) • 15th Affair (*with Maxine Paetro*) •
16th Seduction (*with Maxine Paetro*)

DETECTIVE MICHAEL BENNETT SERIES

Step on a Crack (*with Michael Ledwidge*) • Run for Your Life
(*with Michael Ledwidge*) • Worst Case (*with Michael Ledwidge*) •
Tick Tock (*with Michael Ledwidge*) • I, Michael Bennett
(*with Michael Ledwidge*) • Gone (*with Michael Ledwidge*) •
Burn (*with Michael Ledwidge*) • Alert (*with Michael Ledwidge*) •
Bullseye (*with Michael Ledwidge*)

PRIVATE NOVELS

Private (*with Maxine Paetro*) • Private London (*with Mark Pearson*) • Private Games (*with Mark Sullivan*) • Private: No. 1 Suspect (*with Maxine Paetro*) • Private Berlin (*with Mark Sullivan*) • Private Down Under (*with Michael White*) • Private L.A. (*with Mark Sullivan*) • Private India (*with Ashwin Sanghi*) • Private Vegas (*with Maxine Paetro*) • Private Sydney (*with Kathryn Fox*) • Private Paris (*with Mark Sullivan*) • The Games (*with Mark Sullivan*) • Private Delhi (*with Ashwin Sanghi*)

NYPD RED SERIES

NYPD Red (*with Marshall Karp*) • NYPD Red 2 (*with Marshall Karp*) • NYPD Red 3 (*with Marshall Karp*) • NYPD Red 4 (*with Marshall Karp*)

DETECTIVE HARRIET BLUE SERIES

Never Never (*with Candice Fox*) • Fifty Fifty (*with Candice Fox*)

STAND-ALONE THRILLERS

The Thomas Berryman Number • Sail (*with Howard Roughan*) • Swimsuit (*with Maxine Paetro*) • Don't Blink (*with Howard Roughan*) • Postcard Killers (*with Liza Marklund*) • Toys (*with Neil McMahon*) • Now You See Her (*with Michael Ledwidge*) • Kill Me If You Can (*with Marshall Karp*) • Guilty Wives (*with David Ellis*) • Zoo (*with Michael Ledwidge*) • Second Honeymoon (*with Howard Roughan*) • Mistress (*with David Ellis*) • Invisible (*with David Ellis*) • Truth or Die (*with Howard Roughan*) • Murder House (*with David Ellis*) • Woman of God (*with Maxine Paetro*) • Hide and Seek • Humans, Bow Down (*with Emily Raymond*) • The Black Book (*with David Ellis*) • Murder Games (*with Howard Roughan*)

NON-FICTION

Torn Apart (*with Hal and Cory Friedman*) • The Murder of King Tut (*with Martin Dugard*)

ROMANCE

Sundays at Tiffany's (*with Gabrielle Charbonnet*) •
The Christmas Wedding (*with Richard DiLallo*) •
First Love (*with Emily Raymond*) •
Two from the Heart (*with Frank Costantini,
Emily Raymond and Brian Sitts*)

OTHER TITLES

Miracle at Augusta (*with Peter de Jonge*)

FAMILY OF PAGE-TURNERS

MIDDLE SCHOOL BOOKS

The Worst Years of My Life (*with Chris Tebbetts*) • Get Me
Out of Here! (*with Chris Tebbetts*) • My Brother Is a Big, Fat
Liar (*with Lisa Papademetriou*) • How I Survived Bullies,
Broccoli, and Snake Hill (*with Chris Tebbetts*) • Ultimate
Showdown (*with Julia Bergen*) • Save Rafe! (*with Chris
Tebbetts*) • Just My Rotten Luck (*with Chris Tebbetts*) •
Dog's Best Friend (*with Chris Tebbetts*) •
Escape to Australia (*with Martin Chatterton*)

I FUNNY SERIES

I Funny (*with Chris Grabenstein*) • I Even Funnier (*with Chris
Grabenstein*) • I Totally Funniest (*with Chris Grabenstein*) •
I Funny TV (*with Chris Grabenstein*) • School of
Laughs (*with Chris Grabenstein*)

TREASURE HUNTERS SERIES

Treasure Hunters (*with Chris Grabenstein*) • Danger Down
the Nile (*with Chris Grabenstein*) • Secret of the Forbidden
City (*with Chris Grabenstein*) • Peril at the Top of the World
(*with Chris Grabenstein*)

HOUSE OF ROBOTS SERIES

House of Robots (*with Chris Grabenstein*) •
Robots Go Wild! (*with Chris Grabenstein*) •
Robot Revolution (*with Chris Grabenstein*)

OTHER ILLUSTRATED NOVELS

Kenny Wright: Superhero (*with Chris Tebbetts*) •
Homeroom Diaries (*with Lisa Papademetriou*) •
Jacky Ha-Ha (*with Chris Grabenstein*) •
Word of Mouse (*with Chris Grabenstein*) •
Pottymouth and Stoopid (*with Chris Grabenstein*)

MAXIMUM RIDE SERIES

The Angel Experiment • School's Out Forever • Saving the
World and Other Extreme Sports • The Final Warning • Max •
Fang • Angel • Nevermore • Forever

CONFESSIONS SERIES

Confessions of a Murder Suspect (*with Maxine Paetro*) •
The Private School Murders (*with Maxine Paetro*) • The Paris
Mysteries (*with Maxine Paetro*) • The Murder of an Angel (*with
Maxine Paetro*)

WITCH & WIZARD SERIES

Witch & Wizard (*with Gabrielle Charbonnet*) • The Gift (*with
Ned Rust*) • The Fire (*with Jill Dembowski*) • The Kiss (*with Jill
Dembowski*) • The Lost (*with Emily Raymond*)

DANIEL X SERIES

The Dangerous Days of Daniel X (*with Michael Ledwidge*) •
Watch the Skies (*with Ned Rust*) • Demons and Druids (*with
Adam Sadler*) • Game Over (*with Ned Rust*) • Armageddon
(*with Chris Grabenstein*) • Lights Out (*with Chris Grabenstein*)

OTHER TITLES

Cradle and All • Crazy House (*with Gabrielle Charbonnet*)

GRAPHIC NOVELS

Daniel X: Alien Hunter (*with Leopoldo Gout*) • Maximum Ride: Manga Vols. 1–9 (*with NaRae Lee*)

For more information about James Patterson's novels, visit www.jamespatterson.co.uk

Or become a fan on Facebook